SCARS

DAN SCOTTOW

www.bloodhoundbooks.com

Print ISBN 978-1-914614-25-5

ALSO BY DAN SCOTTOW

Damaged

~

Girl A

This one is for all my readers. Without you I wouldn't be here writing. Thank you!

1

2008, Location unknown

A bright red light blinks in the pit of darkness before her.

She writhes, trying to escape the cramp which creeps up her leg. Her naked skin slides across the gurney, cold metal pressed against her buttocks.

She glances to her right. The girl at the next table is dead, she is pretty sure. She'd finally succumbed. She can't blame her. She would do the same, too, if she could.

That means somebody new would be arriving soon. He always had at least two on the go. She closes her eyes, wishing she could die and be free from this hell. But her body won't let her. It isn't ready yet. So she has to endure it for a little longer.

Perspiration pools inside the leather mask that has been fastened around her head. Wisps of her blonde hair, sweaty and matted, stick out from beneath it. The thick straps dig into her neck, too tight. Painful. But this is the least of her worries.

Soon, he would be back.

She wriggles her wrists, which have been tethered to the end of the table, above her head. The stiff leather cuffs rub against her skin, knocking fresh scabs from her flesh. Blood trickles down her arm, dripping onto the tabletop. He's watching; she has no doubt. The red light indicating that the camera is on. She doesn't know how long she has been in this dreadful place. She knows four other girls have joined her and departed in the time she has remained.

They're the lucky ones.

Without any natural light in the room, she has no idea how many days and nights have passed. It doesn't matter. Nobody will miss her. She sleeps when her body is exhausted; she wakes when it tells her to. It might have been two weeks, it could be two years, for all she knows.

It seems endless. And she prays, begs for death. But it never comes. She's always been a fighter. But for the first time in her life, she wishes she wasn't.

The familiar rattle of keys somewhere in the distance. The girl holds her breath, eyes darting around the darkness, heart pounding.

He's back.

The heavy door creaks open; the sound of metal against metal as it closes again. His footsteps begin their descent down the steps. Clunk, clunk, clunk. Slow. Purposeful.

His feet hit the concrete at the bottom. His breathing is laboured. She hears a thump as he dumps something onto the floor. Turning her head, she watches as he marches towards the gurney to her right, loosening the bonds from the wrists and ankles of the corpse, pushing it off the edge. It slaps to the ground. The girl holds back a wave of nausea.

He returns to the heap at the base of the stairs, heaving it up over his shoulder, and she sees with horror the form of another victim in his arms. A new plaything.

He slings her on the metal tabletop, securing her limbs, before beginning the ritual.

2

Always the same. He takes a large pair of shears from the workbench on the back wall, the one where he keeps all his... implements. He slices the razor-sharp blades through the fabric of her trouser legs in one swift movement, removing her jeans in seconds. Repeating the actions on her top half, he casts her garments onto the floor. Finally, he snips through her bra and knickers, his body juddering as he does so; he always seems to enjoy this last part the most, as the bare flesh is completely exposed. And there she is.

The next one.

Naked, spreadeagled before him. He assesses his work, nodding briefly. She is unconscious, of course. They always are on arrival. Some substance slipped into their drink while they aren't looking, or away in the lavatory. Later on, when they are alone, and the girl wakes, she will comfort her, lie to her, reassure her that everything will be okay. As she had with all the others.

She remembers how he had looked at her in the bar, from across the room. She'd clocked him as soon as he had walked in. She'd seen him many times before. Always with a different beautiful girl.

She liked him. He excited her. The cut of his suit. The scent of his aftershave as he sauntered past her. She caught his eye, and he had looked away. But he'd noticed her. And she wanted him. She wanted him inside her. She may even do this one for free, she had thought.

Was this her punishment? Perhaps. Her mother had always told her she was going to hell.

Her heart had raced when the barman brought a drink over to her.

'The gentleman at the end of the bar wonders if you'd care to join him?' he'd informed her. She had stood from her stool, smoothing out creases from her black satin dress. As she approached, she noticed his eyes, fixed on the hem of her skirt, skimming her thighs.

He wanted her too.

He'd told her his name was Michael, but that was probably a lie. He was a different breed from her usual clients. He had asked her questions, seemed like he actually gave a shit. *Where was she from? Did she have family? Did she have a day job?* She had thought he was genuinely showing an interest in her life. More fool her. In hindsight, he was merely assessing the suitability of his prey.

When he had suggested they continue the conversation in his suite at the Dorchester, she had agreed, of course. A split-second decision which had ultimately been her downfall. No point dwelling on that now. She'd made her bed, as it were.

He crosses the room to the console on the far wall. She hears a click as he presses play, and the same old song fills her ears. Some fifties ballad which she probably would have quite liked had she heard it under different circumstances. It reminds her of her grandmother, the only person in her life who hadn't let her down. The haunting vocal begins, sending a shiver down the girl's spine.

A lovestruck man declares how the object of his affection will be his forever. He sings that they will be together for eternity.

She is his.

In the right circumstances it would be the epitome of romance. But here, and now, in this setting... it is chilling.

She knew what was coming next.

He crosses back to the foot of her station, turning to face the camera. He begins his sickening striptease, removing his tie first, as he always does, then his shirt, trousers, and finally his tight white briefs. Folding each item into a neat pile on a black leather chair beside him. Sometimes he would just sit there for a while, watching. He isn't hard. Not yet.

That doesn't usually happen until some pain is inflicted.

She screws her eyes shut, trying to block out the melody, trying to take herself to another place. A safe place. She hears his bare feet pad across the floor, and a scrape of metal as he chooses his instrument for today's session. She keeps her eyes closed, choosing not to know when it happens. Knowing it is coming is enough.

She can hear his breathing beside her now. His head is by hers. She feels his tongue slip through the slit in the mask where her mouth is. His warm saliva on her lips as he probes her. She had learned there's no point fighting it. It only seems to make him enjoy it more.

The song on repeat echoes round the room. The lyrics promising that the girl will always be his.

And she fears that this may be true for her too. She wonders if she is special to him. He'd told her he was aroused by her resilience. He couldn't believe she'd outlived the others.

She opens her eyes; he looms beside her. Something cold and sharp presses against her abdomen. She draws in a breath as he traces the blade across her skin, up towards her exposed nipples. Circling her areola. He laughs as her body shivers.

'Good girl,' he whispers.

And then the point breaks her skin, a searing pain shoots through her.

But she will not cry, will not scream. Refuses to give him the satisfaction. She stares into his face defiantly, and he smiles. He pushes the blade in further; she winces, and that is enough. His dick stiffens, standing to attention. He pushes down with the knife, slicing her flesh. A tear runs from the corner of her eye, dripping onto the metal gurney, as he forces her legs apart and slides inside her.

She closes her eyes, trying to focus on the music. *Only* the music.

Please God, she thinks, *please just let me die!*

He thrusts painfully into her, and the cold steel of the blade teases at her throat, breaking the skin. Everything begins to go black. The music still plays, but it now seems far away in the distance. Like she is listening from under water.

As her world fades into darkness, she realises that finally, this is it.

The girl lets out one final, anguished breath.

And she is gone.

2

The West Coast of Scotland, some years later

The ferry pulls into the dock with a heavy clunk. Lucy waits patiently, tapping her foot as the exit ramp lowers, and she is away. She hurries through the drizzle towards a row of taxis. She hands the driver the address. He eyes her curiously, frowning.

'Jump in,' he says, an edge to his voice.

He doesn't get out to take her bag, so she opens the rear, throwing her case onto the back seat. She climbs into the front, closing the door behind her.

'Grim weather,' she says.

'Get used to it,' he mumbles, in a thick west-coast accent.

He pulls away from the dock, away from civilisation. A narrow single-track road winds up an enormous hill, a vast drop on either side, down into dense woodlands. Tall spruces tower above. Pink and white foxgloves break up the greens and browns. Huge ferns littering the sides of the road. Now and then the cab emerges from the trees, and Lucy can see for miles, across treetops. In the distance, across a body of water, an entire

7

mountainside is covered in rhododendrons, making it appear bright purple. Low-lying cloud lingers in the damp air. Lucy's head whips around, not wanting to miss a second of the breathtaking scenery. So different from her familiar city dwelling. She has never seen so many different shades of green.

'It's so beautiful here!' she says.

He grunts something unintelligible. The taxi passes over the crest of the hill, stopping now and then for a sheep or a grouse in their path. The road spirals down steeply before them, back into the forest.

A rabbit darts from the undergrowth, scurrying in front of them. The driver curses, swerving a little on the track.

'How much further?' Lucy asks.

He laughs humourlessly. 'A while yet. Ye've picked a fair remote place to visit.'

Lucy lowers the window, leaning out, inhaling the fresh air. Pine and florals fill her nostrils. She smiles. Rain spatters the inside of the taxi, and the driver tuts. Lucy closes the window, apologising.

'So what brings ye to these parts?' he finally asks after another thirty minutes of silence.

'A job.'

'Oh, aye?'

Lucy nods. Doesn't offer any further information. The driver shrugs, focusing on the road ahead.

Deep beneath the trees, Lucy can no longer tell if it's still raining or not. The forest is so dense, hardly any light filters through. She pulls her mobile from her pocket, checking the signal. A single bar is displayed on the screen. It sporadically disappears, and flashes back. She raises her eyebrows, sighing.

'That'll be no use where you're goin,' the driver informs her.

'Yeah, I got that impression.'

'There's no reception once ye reach the edge of the forest. If you need to let anyone know you're safe, I'd recommend doing it now, while you still can.'

'It's okay,' she mumbles, as she slides the handset back into her jeans pocket.

After what seems like an eternity, the car emerges from the gloom.

'Almost there. Just on the other side of those trees.'

Lucy glances down a hill towards a ridge of large beeches. The only indication of life is a plume of white smoke, rising into the air from behind them. As the taxi pulls around, the loch opens up before them. The cottage sits at the outer edge of the water. Grey slate tiles glisten with rain on the roof. There are chimney stacks at each end of the structure, one of which is the source of the smoke Lucy had seen. A Virginia creeper climbs up the whitewashed stone walls at one side. A huge wisteria decorates the other half, arching over the windows and door, spilling its abundant blooms down the front of the house. To the left of the door, a small log store holds a pile of firewood.

Clumps of crocosmia litter the landscape, their vibrant orange flowers arching into the air from spiky green foliage. Wide wooden frames, painted gloss black, surround the glass. Lucy sees a net curtain fall from a downstairs window.

The setting is astounding. Lucy is unsure if she has ever seen anything so beautiful. So peaceful.

A buzzard hovers in the air, fixed to its spot, watching some unsuspecting prey on the ground below. It swoops down out of sight. The driver hands her a card with his number on it.

'Taxis are hard to come by in these parts. You might need that,' he says, smirking.

She pays him, retrieving her case, and watches as he begins his tedious journey back. Trudging through long, wet grass towards the front door, she knocks loudly with her knuckles.

3

-

The door opens almost immediately. A tall woman in her late sixties stands before Lucy. She has greying blonde hair, which is in a long plait over her shoulder, and dangles down to her waist. A fringe covers most of her forehead. She wears a black housecoat and leans her left hand on a silver-topped ebony walking cane. Lucy's eyes dance fleetingly over the pale tendrils of a large ugly scar which decorates the entire left side of the woman's face, spidering out from the corner of her mouth, up towards a milky-looking eye. The agency had pre-warned her, but nothing could prepare her for the reality. The woman self-consciously fiddles with her braid, tugging it closer to her cheek. She seems to struggle using her right hand, and Lucy notices for the first time that the arm doesn't hang correctly. Another injury, she assumes.

'Yes?' the woman asks, eyeing her suspiciously.

'I'm from the care agency. I'm Lucy.' The woman seems to relax at the words. She holds out her hand.

'Diana Davenport.'

'Pleased to meet you, Mrs Davenport.'

'Well, I suppose you had better come in.' Diana steps aside, and Lucy sees inside the house for the first time. The front door opens to a hallway, tastefully decorated, homely. Wood-panelled walls on each side, painted white. Dark oak floorboards, a long taupe runner on top. Three doors to the left, and one directly to the right, another dead ahead at the end of the corridor. On the right of the hallway sits a wide wooden staircase with thick bannisters. Lucy enters, glancing around, placing her bag on the floor. Diana heads to the right, and Lucy follows. As they pass the stairs Lucy's eyes flick towards a large dark stain on the floorboards at the foot. Diana notices the direction of Lucy's gaze

'The first two doors to the left are my bedroom and bathroom, both off limits, apart from when you are cleaning,' she says, matter-of-factly. Lucy stops.

'So, am I to clean the house as well? I thought I was here to help your husband?'

'You'll be responsible for caring for Richard, along with *all* household duties. Preparing meals, laundry, and cleaning. Will that be a problem? I think the money is adequate for the level of work required.'

'No, that's fine, I don't mind.' And she didn't. The pay was indeed better than anything else Lucy had seen advertised.

'You will have the entirety of the upstairs,' Diana continues. 'The ground floor is mine. You may use the kitchen, of course, but when you're off duty, I'd prefer you to stay upstairs if you're at home.'

As they walk through the doorway Lucy finds herself in a large lounge. There are two small sofas arranged in a L-shape around a coffee table, facing a wood burner against the adjacent wall. A double sash window to the right looks out to the front of the house, beneath which sits an antique chest with leather straps and buckles holding it tightly closed. The floorboards are mostly covered by a huge Persian rug, a dining table and two chairs sit in another corner. On a small side table sits an old-fashioned telephone with an answering machine. A Welsh dresser leans against the far wall, beside a door. Diana turns and limps slowly towards it. Lucy scurries dutifully behind her. She opens the door, leading Lucy into an amply sized country kitchen. A huge Belfast sink sits beneath a window, set into a solid oak square-edged worktop. The window has a spectacular view out to the garden, and the loch beyond. The wooden panelling from the hall continues through the entire ground floor.

'It's not modern, but it has everything you need. The groceries are delivered weekly, weather dependant, and Richard and I eat dinner promptly at seven each evening, so if you could base your timings around that, please.'

Lucy nods.

'I prepare my own breakfast, but you will need to feed Richard. He doesn't eat much in the mornings. And usually just a little soup at lunchtime. He can't really manage anything solid. His meals are liquidised. Freshly prepared, of course.'

Diana motions to a door on the right.

'The utilities and laundry are through there. Everything you require should be in there, but if you find anything is missing, tell me and I'll have it added to the list.'

They leave the kitchen through another door to the left which brings them back out to the hallway.

Directly to the right is a final door.

'And this is Richard's room.'

Diana opens the door, revealing a compact box room, with a view out to the loch. In front of the window sits a man in a wheelchair, his back to them. She steps inside. Lucy follows. She crosses the carpet, spinning the wheelchair towards them. The man's face is heavily scarred, like his wife's. The left side droops. His eyes stare blankly ahead. Lucy can tell he would have been handsome once. He is dressed neatly in a white shirt and cream chinos, his dark hair combed tidily. Clean-shaven. Well cared for. As if Diana had read her mind, she clears her throat, and says, 'I've been looking after him up until now, but it's getting a little too much for me.' She nods towards her cane.

'Hello, Richard,' Lucy says.

'You won't get a response. He can't move. Can't speak. He's... locked in. He needs *total* care. I assume the agency filled you in on everything you need to do for him?'

'Yes,' Lucy replies.

'You'll get the odd muscle spasm, his eyes may flicker, fingers move sometimes, but he's pretty much static,' Diana says coldly.

Lucy crouches down before him, so her head is level with his. She looks him in the eye.

'Hello, Richard. I'm Lucy. I'm here to help.' She smiles. His eyes wobble. Fluid wells in the corner of one, running down onto his cheek. She pulls a packet of tissues from her pocket, dabbing at the moisture. She straightens, turning to Diana.

'You don't mind if I talk to him?'

'Do what you like. You'll be wasting your time.'

'Don't you?'

Diana's chin shoots up, lightning fast, resolute.

'Of course I do. But he's my husband.'

Lucy shifts her weight between her feet, fidgeting.

'He makes noises occasionally,' Diana continues, 'but the doctors don't know if he's trying to communicate, or if it's involuntary. There *is* brain function. Not much, but it's there.'

Diana turns Richard back round to face the window, then leaves the room, and Lucy follows behind.

'So they tell me you are an artist?'

'Yes, I paint,' Diana replies.

'What sort of stuff?'

Diana looks at her, with the expression of someone who has just been asked a ridiculous question.

'Abstract mainly. Figurative.'

Lucy nods.

'My studio is in the outhouse, across the garden. It is absolutely off limits. You need not clean in there. It's private. When I'm working I must not be disturbed.'

'Okay.'

They return to the lounge, and Lucy takes it all in for the first time. Chunky woollen throws drape over the backs of the sofas, which are adorned with striped cushions. Lucy imagines this place to be extremely snug in the winter months, with the fire going. Above the fireplace is a gargantuan canvas. Broad swathes of thickly applied paint stand proud from the surface. Messy brush strokes zigzag from one side to the other. Crimson and black, with flecks of white, and hints of brighter reds and oranges. Lucy takes a few steps back and looks up to take in the painting.

'Is this one of yours?'

'No. That's Richard's.'

'He was an artist too?'

'Yes. Much more successful than me. That's one of the last paintings he did, before... the accident.'

'It's beautiful.'

Diana nods.

'You'll work every day. Richard usually wakes by five, so you'll need to get him out of bed shortly after that. Once he's washed and dressed and fed, the day is yours until lunchtime, and the same between lunch and dinner. I expect you to check in on him, but you don't have to be with him twenty-four-seven. The evening routine is very much open to what works for you. You can put him to bed whenever suits you. After that you can do what you like, so long as you don't disturb me.'

Lucy doesn't reply, simply waits for further information. Diana holds her free hand to her temple, massaging gently, closing her eyes for a moment.

'I'll leave you to explore the top floor on your own. I can't manage the stairs.'

She stands aside, and Lucy gets the impression Diana is bored of her already. She steps out to the hallway and ascends the staircase, carrying her bag with her.

'The bedroom is to the left!' Diana calls from below.

The steps lead up to a large U-shaped landing which wraps around the central staircase. One large room spans most of the left side of the first floor. A bathroom, linen cupboard and a small box room on the right side. She turns, opening a door. The space is wonderful. Double aspect windows look out across the loch to one side, and the woods on the other. The light is immense. Even on this grey day, it's beautiful. She heaves her case onto the bed, crossing to the window. The vista is stunning. She smiles. A small couch and a coffee table are against one wall. A chest of drawers and a large oak wardrobe on another. Apart from that, the room is bare. But Lucy doesn't mind. The view is to die for. She hears movement from below, as Diana hobbles across the wooden floor. Lucy returns to the bed, opening her case, and unpacks her belongings.

4

DIANA

She can hear the girl moving around upstairs, unpacking no doubt. She is attractive, late thirties, shoulder-length wavy brown hair, piercing blue eyes. Quite striking-looking really. Richard would have approved. But when she smiles, it seems fake. It's all an act. It's what she thinks people want to see. Diana was the same when she was younger, until she met Richard. He helped to refine her. Tune her. Make her the woman she is today. Lucy seems pleasant enough. Didn't stare for too long at Diana's face, which is always a good sign. And the girl didn't recoil when she first saw her husband either. She was tender. That's what he needs. She would be a suitable fit. Diana would reserve further judgement until she tasted Lucy's cooking. She hears some grunting coming from the room next door, but she can't face it right now. Her duties as a nursemaid are relieved, thankfully. She loves Richard, of course she does. But she can barely manage to look after herself. And Richard needs a lot of help.

She sighs, hobbling towards her bedroom. A creak on the stairs draws her attention. She turns, Lucy is at the top.

'I was wondering if there is any internet connection here?' she asks.

Diana purses her lips.

'No, I'm afraid not. I don't have anything like that here. There's no mobile reception either, unless you're very lucky. There's a phone, but it's not for idle chat. It's the only point of communication here, so keep it free if you can. My agent likes to call from time to time with information.'

'Okay.' Lucy retreats back up to her room.

She wonders how a youngster will cope being this remote. No connection to the outside world, besides the landline. Lucy is quiet. Diana appreciates that. She needs peace. The constant headaches she has since the accident make it hard for her to cope with noise and chatter. She continues her journey to the bedroom, pushing the door open with her elbow. It swings inwards, and she limps inside, bumping it closed again with her bottom. She has learned to be resourceful. She crosses to her dresser. Pulling out a drawer, she rummages through bottles of pills. Her leg is giving her trouble. It comes and goes, but today it is excruciating. Which did she last take? It was hard to keep track.

She picks up a jar of Vicodin. She has to get these mailed over from the States. But they're good.

A little bit too good.

She leans on the dresser and unscrews the lid, pouring two into her palm. She pops them into her mouth, throwing back her head, and swallows without a drink. Closing her eyes, she yearns for the release they offer her. Closing the drawer, she crosses to her window. The rain pummels the glass, distorting her view outside. She doesn't mind. She didn't move to Scotland for the weather.

Richard groans again from his room.

More footsteps above her. Her house guest is busying herself. Diana wants to ask her to see to Richard. His noise is beginning to irritate her. She opens her door, sticking her head out.

'Lucy!' she calls upstairs.

The girl darts out from her room obligingly, leaning down from the top of the stairs.

'Hello!' she replies cheerfully, almost saluting like a soldier.

'I know you've only just arrived, but would you mind checking on Richard?'

'Not a problem.'

She bounds down and enters Richard's room, closing the door behind her. Diana hears muffled noises as the girl chats away.

She'll soon get bored of that, Diana thinks.

Richard's groaning gets louder. She crosses to the door, pressing her ear against it.

'What's all this noise, hey?' she hears Lucy chirp.

More moaning.

'Shall we look out of the window together. The loch is so beautiful.'

The noise stops, and Diana retreats to her room, perching on the edge of the bed. She glances down at flecks of paint on her nails, picking at them with her thumb. She crosses to the dressing table to retrieve an emery board. She looks briefly at the struts which used to support an oval mirror. She removed it years ago, the sight of her scars first thing every morning too depressing. Lucy's room was the only place in the house with a mirror these days, aside from a small cabinet in the bathroom. She'd learned to ignore that. She had no use for them. She wore what she liked. She never saw anyone, so what did it matter? Unless she counts her agent. Valentina arrives unannounced occasionally. Diana hates visitors at the best of times, but when they turn up without warning, she finds it troublesome. She leans across the bed to her side table, grabbing two plastic pots.

She unscrews the lids, popping two Sertraline into her mouth, followed by a Citalopram. One for anxiety, the other for depression. She forgets which is which. Doesn't care. She takes so many pills these days, she's amazed she doesn't rattle when she moves. She picks up a half-empty glass from her bedside table, swigging a mouthful of water. It's old, dusty. She screws up her face.

As the chemicals work their magic, Diana reclines on top of the feather duvet. Her head sinks into the soft down, her eyes close. The cool cotton feels wonderful against her cheek, and she smiles to herself. She hears Richard's door click shut, and footsteps skipping up the stairs, as she drifts away.

5

LUCY

It's quiet downstairs. She has unpacked and seen to Richard. He seemed agitated. It surprised her that Diana had asked her to start so soon, but she doesn't mind. She's here to work, after all. She had heard some shuffling from below, drawers opening and closing. Footsteps. But now silence.

She sits on the edge of the bed, checks her watch. It's early afternoon. Glancing out the window, she sees the rain has stopped. She grabs a light denim jacket from her wardrobe and heads downstairs, pressing her ear against Diana's door. Slow, steady breathing from inside. Is she snoring?

She creeps down the way to Richard's room, peeping in. His chair is where she left it earlier, beside the bed. His eyes are closed, his head lolls to one side. A trail of saliva runs down his chin from the corner of his mouth.

She wonders if he is cognisant. Closing the door quietly, she returns to the lounge area. The fire has long burned out, and the room is cooler now, a sooty smell lingers in the air. A thin layer of dust covers most surfaces. She wipes at a shelf with one finger, rubbing it on her thumb. This place will definitely keep her busy. She glances at the painting above the mantel.

Something inside her stirs. She has never really understood abstract art, but this is different. Taking a few steps backwards, she bumps into the edge of the sofa and sits. From a distance, the canvas makes more sense. Close up, it appears to be a random mess of colour, but from a few metres back, she can make out the shape of a figure. A female, writhing in flames. It is powerful. Frightening.

Something about the picture makes Lucy uncomfortable. But she feels compelled to look at it anyway. She has to force herself to tear her eyes away. Wrapping her arms around herself, she shivers. The only noise comes from an ancient-looking clock on the mantel.

Tick-tock, tick-tock. Mesmerising. Almost hypnotic.

A swallow darts past outside, singing excitedly, shaking Lucy from her reverie. She stands, approaching the window. The contrast between the disturbing scene depicted in the painting and the surrounding landscape is amazing. She crosses to the front door, opening it and stepping outside. She follows a narrow gravel path round the side of the cottage. A small garden, no more than ten metres or so, slopes down towards the banks of the loch. A small shingle beach separates the garden from the water. The grass is shorter to the side and back of the house, more like a lawn. An old mower leans against the side wall. Rusting. Heavy-looking. Lucy wonders who has mowed the grass.

As she rounds to the back of the cottage, a huge willow sits at one edge of the garden. Its branches hang lazily down, casting dappled reflections onto the ripples of the water below. Two chairs sit either side of a table beneath it, facing outwards, giving a beautiful view of the surrounding outlook. A jetty reaches out into the loch, about twenty metres or so. A small wooden fishing boat bobs about at the end of the pier. Lucy crosses the lawn to the edge of the loch, turning to face the house. A tree-covered slope rises up steeply behind it, into the low lingering clouds. Lucy would call it a mountain, but in reality, it is only a hill. From this angle, she can see how secluded the spot is.

Turning towards the jetty, she steps onto the planks of the structure. It feels sturdy, safe enough. Looks well-maintained. She walks to the end, eyeing swathes of kelp disappearing into the depths beneath the boat. Red paint flakes from the outside. Two oars lay criss-crossed on top of each other inside it. Glancing down into the water, she sees the moody clouds reflected, but as it ripples below her, she notices shapes and movement underneath. The ghostly form of a jellyfish glides past far beneath the inky surface. Crouching, she dips her hand into the water. It is icy cold. A shudder flows through her body. Looking away, she wonders how deep the loch is.

She stands, staring out over to the distant shore. Far on the opposite side, a backdrop of rolling hills and giant trees stretch for miles along the coast, blue-grey hues disappearing into cloud.

Lucy turns, retracing her steps back down to the garden. She treads onto the wet grass, and her foot feels moist. She curses herself for coming out in canvas trainers. She glances to the left and sees a large shed-like structure. This must be Diana's studio. She approaches the door, glancing from side to side nervously. Tattered sheets hang in the windows, blocking Lucy's view inside. She edges round the perimeter of the building; the rear side which faces out to the water. The glass at the back is uncovered. She places her hands against the grubby glass, pressing her face into it, peering through. Canvasses are stacked up against the walls, paint-covered rags litter the floor. Light flows in through immense skylights in the roof, illuminating the space. Blue canvasses, black canvasses, unfinished, discarded. So many paintings. Lucy wonders what they are worth.

She makes her way back to the front of the shack, trying the door. Locked, it doesn't budge.

To her right, between the side wall of the cottage and the studio opposite, is a collection of outbuildings of varying sizes. A large lean-to attached to the end of the house has a wooden door, padlocked. Beyond lies a field of tall ferns. Lucy approaches. They are huge and dense.

You could probably get lost in there, she thinks, shivering.

Returning to the middle of the garden, she stands, inhaling, eyes closed. The abundance of birdsong is beautiful. A sound she is not used to in the city. A drop of rain splashes on her cheek. She glances up, and the heavens open. She sprints back to the house, into the kitchen. Turning to her left, she enters the utility room. Another huge window looks directly out to the lake.

The heavy rain drums against the glass, so she can barely see beyond it. The scene becomes a blur of colour.

An ancient top-loading washing machine sits against one wall. A shelf above it holds various boxes of laundry powder, bleaches, and fabric softeners. Rat poison. Dusty, cobweb-covered cartons.

Her foot knocks against a mousetrap as she edges around the room. A large wooden rack suspended from the roof is draped with bed linen, drying, the space smells clean and fresh. Lucy breathes in.

She imagines there are worse places to have to do housework. Spotting a duster and a can of polish, she picks them up, heading back through to the lounge to begin her chores.

6

DIANA

Diana stirs on the bed. As she comes round from her deep slumber, she curses under her breath. Daytime napping is never good for her. She'll have to take extra Valium tonight to sleep. She reaches to her side, frowning as her hand finds nothing. Sitting up slowly, she glances down to the floor.

Confused, she looks around, spotting her stick over by the window.

'You old fool!' she hisses to herself.

She shakes her head, heaving herself to her feet, wincing. She takes a deep breath, closing her eyes. Her brain swims, and for a sickening moment she thinks she might fall down. Steadying herself on the bedside table, she places her good leg forward, bracing herself against the wall. She edges around the room towards the window, stopping halfway. Breathing out steadily, she calms herself, holding back a wave of nausea. She begins her journey once more, rushing the final few steps in the direction of the cane, regretting it immediately. She catches herself on the dresser before she falls, and lowers herself down onto the stool in front of it. She retrieves her stick from the floor, sitting for a second to regain her composure. She can smell something cooking. It is pleasant enough.

As she exits the room, she hears Lucy humming. She is dusting the mantel, lifting each ornament, giving it a wipe, before doing the same to the shelf below it, placing it back down. Diana nods, approvingly. This girl is good.

'Hi! Did you have a nice nap?' Lucy calls out to her.

Diana feels groggy, the fug from the cocktail of pills lingers. She tries to speak. Her jaw aches, as it often does when she first awakens.

'What time is it?' Diana enquires, aware that her words are slurred a little. Lucy checks her watch.

'Just after six.'

Diana nods again. Glancing outside, she notes it's still raining.

'You managed to find your way around the kitchen?'

Lucy smiles.

'Yes, no problem at all. We're on track for seven.'

Diana hobbles towards the door. She pauses, sniffing the air.

'For future reference, smoking is not permitted in the house. And if you're going to do it in the garden, can you go down the far end?'

Lucy tilts her head slightly to one side.

'That's fine. I don't smoke.'

Diana frowns, narrowing her eyes.

'I can smell it.'

'Oh, can you?' She sniffs. 'I can't smell anything. But it wasn't me, regardless.'

The woman continues her journey to the kitchen.

'Do you need something?' Lucy rushes towards her.

'Water.'

'I'll get it.'

She dashes through the door. *Eager to please*, Diana thinks. She hears clattering, and the tap running. Lucy returns, handing her a glass. Diana drinks it down in one.

'Would you like some more?' Lucy looks at her, eyes wide with concern.

'No thank you, that's fine.'

She makes her way to the sofa, stiff from her nap. Lowering herself down, she lets out a lengthy breath.

'Someone called Valentina rang. She said she'll try again tomorrow.'

Diana frowns. Was she expecting a call? It doesn't matter. She pays her agent enough to wait.

'I'm making a bean cassoulet. I assume you're vegetarian? I couldn't find any meat in the fridge.'

'No, I'm definitely a carnivore. I think we're running low on supplies; we'll get more in the morning with our delivery,' Diana replies. Lucy nods.

She finishes her dusting and heads into the kitchen to dispose of the cloth and tin of polish.

As the door opens, the aroma of the cooking strengthens, and Diana's stomach growls. She realises she has not eaten yet today. Lucy returns, still humming a pretty little tune.

'Does Richard come out of his room at all?' she asks.

'It's up to you. I think he's happy enough at his window. He always loved nature.'

'Is he Scottish?'

'No, not at all. We had never even been before I bought Willow Cottage. I saw it advertised, and it seemed perfect for what I needed. I purchased it without having viewed it.'

'I can see why.' Lucy smiles.

'I take Richard out into the garden sometimes, rain permitting. I'm sure the smells and sounds stimulate him. That's what I tell myself, anyway. Obviously, he's not been out today, but there's supposed to be some good weather on the way later in the week. This place changes so much with the elements. You'll be astounded.'

Lucy continues to busy herself tidying things, stacking papers into neat piles.

'Leave that, come sit with me a while.' Diana pats the cushion beside her. The girl joins her on the sofa.

'Tell me about yourself.'

'What would you like to know?'

'Just a little about your background.'

Lucy clears her throat.

'I grew up in Woking, lived there most of my life. I moved into London more latterly and spent a few years there. My parents are still in Surrey. I don't have any siblings. I was a nurse for the NHS for a while, but I couldn't cope with the lack of resources, and the money wasn't great... so I left and became a private carer.'

'And what made you take a job here, with a couple of old farts out in the middle of nowhere in Scotland?'

Lucy looks down momentarily, a flash of emotion in her eyes.

'I fancied a change. Something different.'

She pauses. Diana senses there's more, but she doesn't push. She simply waits, a sympathetic smile on her lips. Lucy clears her throat nervously, then continues, fidgeting with her fingers.

'I was in a relationship for years. I thought... was sure he was the one. We were supposed to get married. But it didn't end well. I needed to get away, somewhere where I don't know anybody. This place seemed perfect, and the setting sounded idyllic so I thought, why not?'

'Good for you.' Diana nods. 'I often think people are far too tied to places. There's no need. Life can be wherever you decide it should be. You shouldn't let a location hold you back.'

'What about you? Do you and Richard have children?'

Diana smiles, but there is a sadness behind it in her eyes.

'We have... had a daughter. Claire. She's... no longer with us.'

'I'm sorry.'

'It's fine. It's been a long time.'

Lucy shifts in her seat, uncomfortable from her perceived faux pas. Diana is used to people becoming awkward when they learn of Claire.

'Does that boat out on the jetty work?' Lucy asks, attempting to steer the conversation in a different direction.

'Well, it floats, but I'm not sure I'd trust it.' Diana chuckles.

'Do you have a car?'

'No, nothing like that. No need. I don't go anywhere. There's an old bicycle out in the shed. It was here when we arrived. Probably doesn't even work. It's no use to me. You're welcome to fix it up if you know what you're doing.'

'Okay, I might try.'

Lucy stands.

'I should see to the dinner.'

Diana nods.

'Before you go, would you mind fetching me some pills from my room?'

'Of course, what do you need?'

'If you look in the dresser by the window and see if you can find me two Vicodin.'

Lucy raises her eyebrows, biting her lower lip. Diana blushes.

'I know, I know. But they help.'

Lucy crosses to Diana's bedroom, and she hears her rummaging in the drawer. She returns, handing Diana the tablets.

'Thank you.'

'That stuff is highly addictive. That's why it's not legal here.'

Diana doesn't say anything. Simply throws them into her mouth, washing them away with a mouthful of water, closing her eyes as they slip down her throat. Lucy stands for a moment, watching silently, then heads out into the kitchen. Diana reclines onto the sofa, letting out a sigh.

7

S he stirs the stew, inhaling the hearty smell of tomatoes and garlic. She's attempted to make the best of a scarcely stocked larder. Not ideal for her first meal in her new residence, but she's sure Diana will understand.

She thought about the earlier conversation. The woman has had more than her fair share of tragedy in life. But who hasn't?

She crosses to a cupboard by the sink, where she had seen bottles of drink earlier. She assesses the selection.

'Would you like some wine with dinner?' she shouts through to the lounge.

'Why not?' Diana replies.

Lucy uncorks a 2004 vin du pays, setting it on the counter to breathe. She fetches a glass, then takes both out to the table. Diana is reclining, drifting in and out of consciousness.

'Won't be long,' Lucy tells her, and her eyes spring open.

Lucy enters Richard's room. He's awake. Saliva has pooled on his chin, a large wet patch decorates his shirt below.

'Let's get you ready for dinner, shall we?' she says cheerfully.

His eyes wobble in his head rapidly. Lucy undoes his buttons, pulling the garment from him. She tosses it into a laundry basket beside the bed, before fetching a clean one from his wardrobe. She pulls him forwards in his chair, placing the shirt around his flabby body, and sits him back as she fastens it up.

'There. Much more presentable.'

She wheels him out to the living room, positioning him at the end of the table, pulling a seat beside him, before returning to the kitchen to finish the meal. Leaving the pot bubbling on the stove, she ladles a serving into the liquidiser. As she turns the dial on the front of the blender, the blades whir into action, making light work of the beans. The casserole whizzes round the jug, turning to a red-brown mush. She pours it into a bowl, placing Diana's onto a plate, carrying them through to the table. Diana takes her seat at the opposite end. Lucy sits beside Richard, picking up his spoon from the tablecloth. Diana touches the rim of her dish.

'You haven't warmed them?'

'No.'

Diana shakes her head, and Lucy feels dejected.

'I'm sorry. I'll do that from now on. I didn't think.'

She fills the utensil with Richard's gruel, lifting it to his mouth. She pushes the edge to his lips, forcing them open, pouring the liquid in. He swallows. Some spills onto his chin. Lucy picks up a napkin, dabbing at his face, before spooning in another mouthful. Diana has barely eaten three spoonfuls, before pushing her food aside. She raises her glass, taking a large gulp of wine.

'Is it okay? I can make you something else if you don't like it.'

'It's fine. I don't have much of an appetite.'

Lucy can't imagine why Diana would insist on eating at seven and then tell her she's not hungry. Perhaps it's more for Richard's benefit. She's unsurprised that Diana doesn't eat, having seen the various containers of medication in her bedroom. Most of which were clearly obtained without a prescription.

She finishes feeding Richard, watching as Diana pours another large glass.

Lucy clears up the dishes, taking them to the kitchen. She returns to the table, wheeling him back to his room. Diana grabs the bottle, and retrieving a bunch of keys from the hall, heads outside without saying a word. Lucy retreats through to the sink to clean up. As she washes the dishes, she hums.

She glances out of the window and sees Diana stumble through the door of her studio, tripping on the threshold, sloshing wine from the bottle down herself.

Lucy finishes the plates, leaving them to drain on the worktop, and heads back to see to Richard.

He is in his usual spot, staring out across the loch. She stands by his side, watching through the glass. The swallows skim the surface of the water in the evening light. The rain has cleared, and the day is quite pleasant now. The sun hits the foxgloves, making them appear to glow. Lucy crouches beside the wheelchair.

'Hello, Richard,' she says cheerfully.

No reaction. She turns him slightly towards her.

'I'm sorry about dinner. I didn't have much to work with. I promise I'll do better from now on... once we have more supplies.'

She leans closer to his face, waving her hand in front of him.

'Can you hear me?'

Saliva bubbles on his lips.

'I don't care what Diana says, I think you are taking it all in, aren't you?'

Smiling, she turns the chair back to the window, and glances around the room. An electric harness, for lifting him, sits beside the bed. A painting hangs on one wall. Lucy approaches it, leaning in to view the signature. *DD* is scrawled in the bottom right corner; Diana's, she assumes. Blacks and blues swirl together, muddying in parts, clearer towards the centre. Splatters of white adorn the canvas, angrily flicked from the side. An arm, painted in pale blue, protrudes from the thick swathes of colour. Lucy stands back, her eyes darting about the picture. It occurs to her that Diana's painting is similar to Richard's which hangs above the fire. She wonders if Diana has taken inspiration from her husband.

Stolen his ideas, now he is no longer able to produce them himself.

She exits the room, deciding to go for a walk, with a few hours to kill before she needs to put Richard to bed. Grabbing her jacket from the chair where she left it earlier, she slips out through the front door.

8

DIANA

She hears the front door, and hobbles to the window of her studio. Pulling back the grubby makeshift curtain, she sees Lucy emerge round the side of the house, carrying a denim jacket. She looks around before heading off into the woods. Diana returns to her chair in the corner, gulping more of the wine from the bottle. The meal had been largely bland. Had smelled far better than it tasted. Lucy is clearly *not* a cook. Diana would need to remember to leave some of her cookery books out on the worktop in the kitchen. Hopefully the girl would take the hint.

She swigs more wine, and stands, approaching her canvas. Leaning her stick against her easel, she picks up a broad brush. Dipping it into some alizarin crimson, she swings it across the surface, leaving a heavy red swoosh. Arcing it back down, she slices through the previous trail. Jabbing the brush at her palette, she collects various colours. Her fringe falls in front of her face as she works, and she flicks it away. Feeling light-headed, she sways, reaching out to steady herself. She drops the brush on the floor, and retrieves her cane, crossing to a chair. Picking up the near empty wine bottle, she downs the remnants.

The warm liquid trickles down her throat, and she wipes her mouth with the back of her hand.

Eyeing the door, she sighs heavily. It was too far to go for another bottle. She'd have to make do. One was probably enough anyway. Her eyelids droop, chin lolls forward. As it hits her chest, she snaps it back up, blinking. She stares at the canvas, shaking her head. She puts her face in her hands, fanning them out, and massages her temples with her index fingers. Inhaling deeply, she stands, returning to the painting. Picking up a smaller brush, she dips it in black paint, flicking her wrist towards the work. Spots of dark liquid splatter across the picture. She tuts.

'Pile of crap!' she yells, pulling it from the easel. It clatters to the ground, and she kicks it with her good foot.

'For God's sake!' she screams, grabbing a blank canvas from a pile, heaving it up to where the other had been, moments earlier. She crosses to her workbench, picking up a tub of pills. She flicks the lid off, pouring two directly into her mouth, swallowing hard. She doesn't even know what they are, doesn't care. They must be American from the packaging. Her vision is too blurred to read the label.

She returns to her seat. Beginning again, she dips her brush into some magenta, mixing it with some white, a little cyan, swirling it on the palette. She traces her arm in fluid movements around the surface quickly. A splodge here, a swathe there. She mixes more colour, pushing her hair off her face, leaving a violet smear on her cheek. It begins to take shape, and she smiles as she works. It amazes her how some paintings just seem to create themselves, as if someone else was controlling her, while she struggles so much with others. She still looks at some of her portfolio and wonders how on earth she did it.

She hasn't exhibited for years. Not since the accident. She has a handful of loyal fans who snap up anything she creates without question. She jokes with Valentina frequently that she would probably be able to shit on a canvas and sell it for thousands. But she is a perfectionist and will not take money for items she's unhappy with. The studio is stacked high with unfinished pieces that she has given up on halfway through. She would *not* become a sell-out. Doesn't need to. She had sold off the majority of Richard's work, keeping a couple for sentimental value. The rest had made a small fortune.

Humming a familiar tune as she paints, she steps backwards, taking in what she has done. Her eyes dart up and down. Smiling, she knows this will be a good one.

The beginnings of a face stare from the canvas, mouth open in a scream. Eyes fixed outwards, following Diana wherever she moves. She squeezes burnt umber straight from the tube, grabbing a palette knife from her side table. She scrapes the paint around the sides, this way and that. Arm moving freely, uninhibited. She shakes her head, laughing to herself. She jabs her tool into the fleshy colour on the board and draws it across the canvas in broad strokes.

Standing back, she gasps, realising what she has done.

She had not meant to. Had not wanted to. But she has painted Lucy, screaming, eyes wild with fear.

She throws the knife down on the floor, exiting the studio. She locks the door, limping along the path to the house. Lucy is already home.

'Nice walk?' Diana asks.

'Lovely. I just ventured into the woods a little. It's a bit wet. Probably better to leave it for a dry day.'

'There are some wonderful walks around here. I can't manage very far, but I do wander from time to time.'

Lucy is crouching down beside the record player by the wall. Diana smells cigarettes again but doesn't bother saying anything. The girl is obviously lying.

'Quite the collection you have here,' Lucy comments.

Diana crosses to her side.

'They're mostly Richard's. Couldn't bring myself to get rid of them.'

Lucy stands.

'Why would you? You should play them for him. I'm sure he would appreciate it.'

Diana shakes her head. She's tried many things, gleaning no reaction from her husband. But she doesn't say this.

'Perhaps,' is all she replies.

Lucy pulls a record from the unit, sliding it out of its sleeve.

'May I?' she asks, glancing at Diana.

'Go ahead.'

Lucy places it on the deck, and moves the needle above it, lowering the arm. The speakers crackle, and the synthesiser intro of an '80s song that reminds her of her parents fills the room. Diana smiles, closing her eyes briefly. She opens them and sees that Lucy is doing the same, swaying back and forth, a smile on her lips.

'I love this,' she says.

Diana stares at Lucy and her painting flashes into her mind. The likeness is spot on, considering the short amount of time Diana had spent with her. Diana smiles broadly. Lucy's eyes open, and she sees Diana looking at her.

'What?' she asks.

'Nothing,' Diana replies, beaming.

'Are you laughing at me?'

'No. You remind me a little of my daughter, that's all.'

Diana looks away, thinking of Claire. The smile fades from her lips.

'It must have been extremely hard... losing a child,' Lucy says softly, averting her eyes from Diana's.

'The hardest part is the uncertainty. We never had closure,' she replies.

Lucy frowns.

'When Claire was in her late twenties, she walked out of the house and didn't come home. They never found a body, but we laid her to rest many years ago.'

'Diana, I'm so sorry. That's awful.'

She nods.

'A piece of me has never stopped wondering. But then I think, she had a happy life. We were close. She had no reason to run away, let alone break off all contact. So when I rationalise it, I think she must be...' She trails off, glancing out through the window.

The record ends and the room is filled with the hiss and crackle of the vinyl. Lucy lifts the arm, flicking the player off.

'I think I'll get Richard ready for bed if that's okay?' she asks.

'Of course.'

Lucy turns to go.

'I may be in bed myself when you're done. I take a couple of Valium to help me sleep, so I'll be dead to the world. There's no rousing me. This place could collapse around me and I would most likely sleep right through it.'

'Okay. I'll say goodnight then.'

Lucy disappears into Richard's room, and Diana stares after her. She suspects she will enjoy having the girl around. Placing the record into its paper sleeve, she slides it back onto the shelf. Her eyes dance across the spines of the collection. She hasn't played them for years. Can't bring herself to. Her gaze comes to rest somewhere in the middle... she blinks a few times, then looks away.

Some are easier to listen to than others.

She crosses to the kitchen, pulling a Rioja from the cabinet. Grabbing a fresh glass, she retires to her room.

38

9

DIANA

2009, Basingstoke, England

The fireplace crackles, flames dancing ferociously in the hearth. A bead of sweat forms on Richard's brow, trickling down his cheek. He wipes it away. Rain batters the window as he paces the living room, jaw clenched, fists balled. He slams his hand onto the mantelpiece, swearing under his breath.

'Will you calm down?' Diana hisses.

'How can I? How can *you*? She'll not let this drop. She'll ruin us.'

'Richard!'

Something in her tone stops him in his tracks, eyes wide. He looks as if he may cry.

'*You* are the one who will ruin things if you don't get a grip. Sit down and stop fussing.'

He lowers himself down onto the seat of a battered old red leather Chesterfield opposite, and begins to fiddle with his hair, smoothing it down from the parting outwards. She eyes the perfect creases in his suit trousers. So smart, so presentable. Thinking of the first instance she saw him at art college, all those years ago, she smiles. Even in his desperate state, her heart still flutters when she looks at him. *They all wanted him*, she thinks. *But I got him.*

Her phone rings for the third time in the space of a few minutes. His eyes dart to the handset on the coffee table.

'Is it her again?'

She glances at it. Picking it up, she nods, rejecting the call. She slides the mobile into an oversized pocket in her mohair cardigan, wrapping the garment tighter around her as she shivers, despite the heat.

'You're going to have to speak to her eventually,' Richard says indignantly. His comment is met with a withering look.

'I'm not stupid, my dear. I'm deciding what to say. This is... delicate.'

'This is more than delicate, Diana. This is bloody dangerous.'

She purses her lips.

'She is our daughter. We've made it through far worse than this.'

Their eyes meet across the room. The phone begins to vibrate once more.

'Answer it. She'll think something is up if you don't.'

Diana sighs, pulling it from her pocket.

'Darling, hello. Sorry I missed your calls. My hands were covered in paint.'

Her voice is so calm, so sweet, that Richard almost smiles.

'Mum, is *he* there?'

Her eyes train on Richard, who stares back at her like a frightened child.

'Your father? Yes.'

'Right. Do you know if he's going out at all today?'

She furrows her brow.

'I'm sure he has an appointment in town with Valentina this afternoon at around three. Why?'

'I need to speak to you. It's really important. But alone. Okay?'

'I wish you two would put your differences aside. This is terribly difficult for me being stuck in the middle.'

'Mum, I don't know what he's told you–'

'He hasn't told me anything. Simply that you aren't getting on.'

There's a pause.

'Claire, what is going on? Talk to me.'

'There's a photo.'

'A photo?'

'Of Dad... and... oh God, Mum, I'm sorry.'

'Claire, you're not making any sense.'

'I think he's having an affair.'

Diana laughs.

'Oh, darling... why would you say that? That's ridiculous.'

'It's not. But I can't do this over the phone. Can I come and see you?'

'Of course you can, always. You know that.'

'Right,' Claire whispers. Diana can hear her laboured breathing down the line.

'Are you okay?'

Another pause.

'I'll see you at around three,' Claire says as the phone goes dead. Diana frowns, placing it on the table.

'Well?' he says.

'She's coming here later.'

'Oh God.'

'It's fine, Richard. We will talk about this as a family. She's only trying to protect me. It's natural really. I'll make her understand.'

'She'll go berserk when she sees I'm here. It won't end well.'

She crosses to the sofa, sitting beside her husband.

'I'm sorry, Diana, I messed up.'

She pats his face gently, cradling it to her breast.

'Don't you worry. It will all be okay. We'll get it sorted. One way or another.'

'But what if we can't?'

Diana's shoulders sag.

'Claire will understand. We just have to make sure everybody remains calm.'

Stroking his head, she stares through the window into the garden. As the water runs down the pane, branching off in various directions towards the bottom, a blue tit perches on the edge of a bird feeder that hangs from an old birch tree. She watches as a sad smile creeps onto her lips.

'We have a good relationship with our daughter, Richard. Everything will be fine.'

He closes his eyes, and as she listens to the sound of his heavy breathing, she thinks, *it has to be.*

The rain abates a little, sun breaking through a patch of cloud.

'You should leave now if you're going to be home in time to see her.'

He sits up, nodding. He stands, smoothing down his trousers. Clearing his throat, he smiles. The panic has passed. He is back to his measured, cool self. He marches from the room. A few moments later, the front door slams. She listens as the sound of the car engine rumbles through the window, growing quieter as he drives away from the house.

She closes her eyes, letting out a long, slow breath.

10

LUCY

The sunshine didn't last long. Rain batters the roof as the wind howls down the chimneys. It's after ten, but still bright. The thin curtains do little to block out any light. It feels like the middle of the day. She makes her way downstairs, hearing heavy snoring emit from Diana's room. She pops her head in Richard's door. He's on the bed, eyes open. She steps inside the room, approaching slowly, leaning over him.

'You having trouble sleeping too?' she asks. He stares straight ahead, and she waves her hand in front of his face. She pulls the blanket up around his neck and leaves. She enters Diana's bathroom, taking some cleaning spray and a cloth from a vanity unit, wiping soap stains from the porcelain, spraying bleach into the rim of the toilet bowl.

A pot of tablets lays open on the tiled ledge behind the sink, the pills dissolving in a wet patch. She replaces the lid, brushing them into the basin. Rinsing them away, she shakes her head.

Balling up the cloth, she rubs hard at toothpaste smears on the mirrored doors of a cabinet. The filth on the surface of the glass so thick, she can barely see herself. It hasn't been cleaned in a long time... as she wipes, she wonders if Diana prefers it this way. Looking over her shoulder, she pulls the door open, peering inside. Shaving foam, bath salts, the usual array of bathroom products. Dusty cakes of soap in various shapes and scents. Lotions, potions, and scrunched-up tubes of creams.

But it's also littered with various medications.

Tramadol, Valium, co-codamol, ibuprofen, antidepressants, more Vicodin. Anti-anxiety medication. You name it, it is probably on the shelf. Bottles, blister packs, orange prescription tubs from the States. There are loose pills in ziplock bags. No labels. *How does she even know what they are?* Lucy thinks, then realises the woman likely doesn't even care. Lucy has seen addiction before, and this stinks of it. Her eyes widen. There's enough in this house to kill an elephant. She's amazed that Diana is able to function at all. But long-term use usually leads to higher tolerance. Lucy hopes she is never around to witness what would happen should Diana ever run out of pills. That would be some heavy come down. She stands the bottles up, neatening them on the shelf, facing the labels out. She tidies the contents of the cupboard, throwing out empty toothpaste tubes. When the bathroom is clean, she exits, closing the door behind her.

She takes a seat on the settee in the lounge, relaxing into the soft woollen throw draped over the back. It feels luxurious; expensive and smells faintly of perfume. She glances around the cottage, and it occurs to her there are no photos. No family portraits. No shots with Claire as a child. Nothing personal at all. Too painful, Lucy assumes. Better to try to forget. A philosophy she can identify with.

We are all running away from something, she thinks.

She stands, crossing the rug to the other side of the room. A beautiful mahogany cabinet which she hadn't noticed earlier sits in one corner, opposite a sofa. Marquetry flowers and leaves adorn the wood. It looks dated, but in good condition. Well cared for. An antique perhaps? Opening the doors, Lucy is surprised to see it is in fact a television set, old-fashioned, built into the casing. A small screen, no larger than thirty centimetres across, housed behind the exterior. Green-looking glass reflects the room behind her, making it appear distorted in its convex surface. A video recorder sits on a shelf beneath the TV. There is little dust inside. Lucy frowns. *No internet, but she owns a VCR*, she thinks. It's like Diana is living in a time warp. She flicks the power switch, and the screen is filled with static. She presses the controls, flicking through channels, but there is nothing. Only grainy fuzz, and white noise. She turns it off, clicking the doors closed.

Glancing around the room, she crosses to the Welsh dresser. Blue-and-cream willow-patterned plates and cups cover the shelves. Safe in the knowledge that Diana is sound asleep with Prince Valium, she slides one of the drawers open. Piles of papers, held with elastic bands, neatly stacked inside. She pulls a band from a pile, fanning the contents out. Bank statements. Lucy raises an eyebrow, sucking in a sharp breath. No wonder Diana can afford to pay so well.

There are regular payments into the account, large amounts. Lucy assumes from sales of artwork.

Not many withdrawals. A payment to what seems to be a general store every couple of weeks.

Telephone bill monthly, which appears to cover the line rental charge, and not a lot of calls. The usual standing orders for insurance and the like. But little else. No splurges in designer shops. No online purchases, clearly as Diana has no internet. Lucy can't help thinking the woman must live a very sad existence. She shakes her head, placing the pile back, rifling through. More pots of pills, nothing of any interest. She closes the drawer, moving to the next one. More of the same.

Diana is meticulously organised, to the point of OCD. Lucy

has never seen anything like it in her life. At the bottom she finds a dog-eared photo. She pulls it out.

Diana, pre-scars, and Richard, pre-wheelchair stand in a garden. A pretty brunette in her late teens beside them. Richard stares down at her, tall, handsome. She gazes off, away from the camera, smiling. They are the epitome of perfection. All good looks and expensive clothes. Perfect white, straight teeth. Diana watches Richard. She throws back her head mid laugh; he looks like a guilty schoolboy... the punchline of his joke caught eternally on film. In the days when people used to print photos and keep them forever. Before the world became so... disposable. They are all dressed in their finery, as if they have been at a wedding, or some other formal occasion. Diana wears a floral gown and wide-brimmed coral-coloured hat, her blonde hair, glossy and pristine, tumbling down about her shoulders from beneath it. She really was quite beautiful.

Lucy places the photograph back in the bottom of the drawer and closes it, a sad smile on her lips.

She crosses to the window, staring out towards the woods. She wonders how Diana copes, being more or less alone here all the time.

The sun is setting, rain bouncing off the ground. The trees sway angrily in the bellowing wind as the wooden frames rattle within the walls. Lucy shivers. It occurs to her that anybody could stand unseen in the forest, watching the cottage. She scans the horizon for movement but sees nothing. She stands a while regarding the sunset. A sight she rarely gets to see at home. It's stunning. Even with the weather at its worst, the colours are astounding; reflected in ripples on the surface of the loch. She can see why an artist would love it here. The light. The vistas. The hues. It's all so... perfect.

As the last of the sunlight ebbs away, she draws the curtains and flicks off the lights. She knows she shouldn't be downstairs.

Diana made that clear. She retreats to her bedroom, changing into a long-sleeved nightie, folding her clothes neatly onto a chair. Pulling the drapes open, she stands at the window, looking out across the water. The boat bounces at the end of the jetty as the rain ripples on the inky surface. An eerie luminescent glow now fills the landscape, highlighting rocks and trees, which glisten with moisture. The scene is transformed with the changing light. Lucy leaves the curtains open, climbing into bed. She sinks down as the last of the evening birds sing their lullabies. A fox cries, an owl hoots. The daytime creatures retreat, making way for their nocturnal friends. Lucy lies with her eyes wide.

Has she made a mistake, she wonders? She's not used to such solitude. She had thought that being away from everything would help. But sometimes, isolation can be even worse. Alone with your thoughts.

She shakes her head, rolling over. Completely awake as the day drifts away.

11

DIANA

Something has roused her from her slumber. Groggy, she places a hand up to her face. She extends her fingers a few times, trying to dissipate the pins and needles from them. She thought she heard a crack but can't be sure if she was still dreaming. Was there a clattering against the window? Reality or fantasy? Who knows? But now she is awake, in the middle of the night. A thing she detests.

It's when the worst of her thoughts come.

She's aware it must be late, as the room is dark, aside from the slivers of moonlight creeping in through the cracks of the curtains. She sits up in her bed, picking up a pot of sleeping pills from beside her. She tosses two into her mouth, washing them down with the dregs of her glass of water. The sound comes again.

Definite, piercing. A sharp smack against the windowpane. Like a pebble striking it.

Still half asleep, she grapples around for her cane, finding it propped against the nightstand. She swings her legs slowly from under the blanket, feeling the reassuring solidity of floorboards beneath the soles of her feet. Heaving herself, she rests the bulk of her weight onto the top of the stick. She knows she relies on it too much these days. The doctor has told her to try to walk without it at least a few times a day. But she doesn't bother. It's easier this way.

The noise comes again.

She frowns as she limps towards the window. Her limbs often take longer to wake than the rest of her. Fiddling with the hem of the curtain, she pulls it slightly, peering through a tiny gap at the side. Her eyes scan the landscape, though her vision is blurry. As she stares, something strikes the glass, the loud crack filling the room again. Her head whips back instinctively. Placing her hand against the surface, she scans the horizon. Her gaze comes to rest on a stack of stones a few metres away from the house, just outside the treeline. The moonlight glistens on the wet structure. A tower of six or seven stones, descending in size as they get towards the top.

Her heart pounds. She shivers, placing her other hand onto the window, her eyes now darting frantically around.

As she squints into the darkness, she sees a figure. It hovers at the perimeter of the woods before stepping backwards into the trees, disappearing in the black.

Diana stares out in horror. Too afraid to look away but terrified of seeing something again.

Eventually, she allows the curtain to fall, and hobbles back to her bed. Pulling the blanket up around her face, she lays staring at the ceiling. As the pills start to wash over her, she drifts off to sleep, the solitary figure in the woods in the forefront of her mind.

12

LUCY

Lucy has been up a while. She has already bathed and fed Richard. By the time Diana is up and showered, she is in the garden tinkering with the old bicycle. She's rubbed it down with some wire wool she found in the shed, removing a great deal of rust, and lubricated the chain and gears. She's also fixed the punctured wheels. It reminds her of her childhood, when she would do these things with her father.

When Diana finds her, she is on the lawn in the sunshine, pumping the tyres.

'Good morning,' Lucy says cheerfully as Diana approaches.

Diana smiles.

'Did you sleep well?' she asks.

Lucy shrugs.

'When it eventually got dark, yes, I was out like a light. It was a long day for me.'

Diana laughs. 'Yes, I suppose you won't be used to the hours of daylight we have up here?'

'Not at all. It's wonderful.'

'Oh God, tell me about it. As an artist, it's amazing.'

Lucy doubts Diana is awake late enough in the evenings to

appreciate it, but she smiles and nods, regardless. Diana hovers nervously, as if she wants to say something.

'Were you outside last night, in the woods?'

'When?'

'Late. After dark.'

'No.' Lucy frowns.

Diana looks confused.

'Have you had breakfast?' Lucy asks.

Diana shakes her head. 'I'm not hungry.'

'Are you sure? I can make you some toast if you'd like.'

Diana holds up her hand. 'No really, I'm fine. Thank you.'

Lucy glances at her. The woman is eyeing her with an expression she can't quite place... she looks... worried. She watches as Lucy moves the valve of the pump to the front tyre and begins to inflate it.

'How's the bike coming on?'

'I don't think it'll win any races, but it's okay.'

'Good. The weather has brightened for you.'

Lucy glances around, grinning from ear to ear.

'Yes, it really is wonderful. You're right, the scenery changes with the elements.'

They both look up into the sky as a blackbird swoops down from the trees, close to the lawn. The morning sun reflects a greenish glint from his feathers.

'I'm thinking of going out for a wander. Unless you require me to do anything before lunch?'

Diana shakes her head.

'No, that's fine. Mylo will be arriving with supplies shortly. I'll need you to help put them away, but after that you're good to go.'

'Mylo?' Lucy stands, rubbing her hands together as she squints into the sun.

'His mother owns the shop on the other side of the loch.

Brings our groceries by boat each week.' Diana nods towards the jetty. Lucy looks out across the water. The loch seems completely different. Yesterday it had been an ominous mass of dark tempestuous waves, lapping at the shingle shore of the beach. Today, a serene mirror of blue stretches out before her.

'No problem. When will he be coming?'

'Should be arriving any time now.'

Right on cue, a boat chugs around from an outcrop in the water. The hum of the engine grows louder as it nears. Diana limps towards the pier, Lucy follows. The boat pulls up to the end of the jetty, and a slim man in his forties hops ashore, tying the boat to a cleat.

Diana smiles as he approaches. Lucy notices her fiddling with her hair, positioning her plait, stroking it gently with her good arm. The man hurries down the pier in their direction. He glances at Lucy briefly, then looks quickly away towards Diana. Lucy eyes him up and down. He wears a thick navy-blue cable-knit jumper despite the weather. The sleeves are rolled up, revealing brightly coloured tattoos adorning both his forearms, all the way down to his hands. A large orange koi carp decorates one arm, surrounded by Chinese symbols and a rabble of faces, clouds and waves. In the space between his thumb and forefinger on his right hand, is a small red rose, with black thorns swirling around it into the shape of a heart.

'Mylo! Hello. I see you brought the sunshine!' Diana chirps. She is cheerful, warm, like a different person.

'Hey. Yeah, it's been horrendous.' His accent is Scottish, but not thick. A slight lilt, as if he's lived away for some time. He looks at Lucy again, nodding, assessing her with serious eyes.

'Oh, how rude of me.' Diana blushes. 'This is Lucy. From London. She's the help.'

Mylo's dark eyes linger on Diana, and then flick back to Lucy.

'Pleasure to meet you.' He holds out his hand, and she shakes it.

'Likewise.' Lucy beams. He has bushy eyebrows, a thick beard, and his head is surrounded by a full mane of shaggy dark-brown curls. It strikes Lucy that he is devilishly handsome. Rugged. If a little unkempt.

'Did you just arrive?'

'Yesterday.'

'And she's already fixed that old heap of junk.' Diana steps forwards, standing in between them, nodding towards the bicycle on the ground.

'Right,' he replies, standing awkwardly as if he doesn't know what to say.

'I thought I'd go and explore. See what's around,' Lucy chirps.

Diana takes another step closer to Mylo, positioning herself further between him and Lucy. She places her hand on his arm.

'We should get these bags unloaded. We're holding poor Lucy up.'

'Of course,' Mylo replies, heading back to the boat.

'I don't mind, honestly,' Lucy shouts, brushing a strand of hair from her face.

'Oh nonsense,' Diana continues. 'We don't want to keep you.'

She doesn't smile. She glares at Lucy. The warmth she was displaying upon Mylo's arrival has disappeared completely.

He begins to unload the shopping from the deck. Lucy picks up a few of the bags and carries them to the cottage. She spies some large, glossy red apples, sitting in the top of a bag, and her stomach rumbles. Mylo follows behind with some boxes. She steps inside. The kitchen is hot from the intense sunshine. Flies buzz around, escaping through the open door. Mylo brings the groceries in.

'If you'd like a tour out on the water, I'd be happy to oblige,' he says, without looking at her.

'Thanks. That would be fantastic.'

'It can be lonely around here. Diana doesn't care, she loves to be left alone, but some people can find it a little isolated.'

He pauses, staring at a wall.

'I can take you down to the marina if you like. We can get some lunch there. It's really fantastic.'

'That sounds lovely.'

Mylo places his boxes onto the kitchen worktop, then heads back to the boat. Lucy strolls beside him, avoiding Diana's stare as she does. Diana takes a few steps along the jetty.

'Here, let me help, Mylo,' she calls after them.

Lucy turns. 'Oh don't be silly, Diana. It's too much for you with your stick. I wouldn't want you to fall and hurt yourself.'

Diana bows her head, looking away. Lucy catches Mylo's eye. He appears embarrassed.

Lucy unloads two more bags, and he grabs a huge box, carrying it behind her.

'That's your lot,' he says as he drops it on the counter.

'Thanks.' She beams.

'Right.' He reaches over, picking up a pen from the worktop. He takes her hand, lifting it. He scribbles on the back of it.

'There's my number. If you want that boat trip, give me a call.'

She nods and begins to unpack the shopping as he returns to the jetty. A few minutes later she hears the engine start, and it speeds off over the water. A thud causes Lucy to turn. Diana is standing in the doorway, a face of thunder.

'He seems brooding,' Lucy says, grinning.

Diana hobbles forwards, so she is right in front of Lucy. She leans in, so Lucy can smell her stale breath.

'Don't you *ever* embarrass me in that way again. You hear me? You'll remember your place.'

'I'm sorry, I didn't mean–'

'I don't care. I'm your employer, and I'd appreciate it if you heed that. Don't ever speak to me like that again.'

'I apologise. I honestly didn't intend to offend you.'

Diana limps away, leaving Lucy in the kitchen. She unloads the bags, placing all the items away. She fills a plastic bottle with water, then walks into the garden. Diana is sitting at the table out back. Lucy ties her hair into a ponytail, pulling a baseball cap onto her head. 'I'll be off then, Diana. Unless you need anything else.'

'Don't get lost. And watch out for snakes,' she replies coldly, without even looking at her.

Lucy picks up the bicycle, wheeling it towards the line of trees. She hops on and pedals away, with a sense of unease building within her.

13

She's been pedalling for about thirty minutes. The distant sound of cattle echoes in her ears as birds twitter and dance through the air around her. The road had zigzagged up a steep hillside through the dense forest. Eventually she emerges from the trees, high up towards the top of the hill.

A huge pink buddleia in full bloom to her left is teeming with bumblebees. They buzz from flower to flower, busily collecting their bounty. She inhales the scent as she passes, perspiration soaking her back. She stops a while, staring out across the loch, sipping some water from her bottle. The land rolls around her, treetops below. In the distance, a wind farm decorates a hilltop, the colours pale with a hint of blue. Even this seems beautiful. A row of fluorescent-pink fishing buoys bob about below. A few yachts are out, making the most of the sunshine, gliding elegantly through the water. Lucy pedals again, heading towards a gorse-covered hillside, its yellow blooms beginning to die off, but still brightening the vista for now. Dense violet thistles litter the landscape, and she thinks how quintessentially Scottish this place seems.

She smiles as she passes foxgloves and wild heather. Sheep

wander fearless from fields into the road. She swerves to avoid them. They pay her no heed.

Halfway up the hill, her legs burn and ache. She can't take it anymore. She hops off the bike and leans it against a silver birch. Her phone beeps to life, and she smiles. It's a long way to come to get reception. But it's something.

A stream babbles over stones, and she skips across boulders to the other side. As she does, an impossibly blue butterfly, no more than two centimetres across, flutters past her face, dancing about her shoulders. It veers away through some nearby bushes. She didn't even know a thing that colour existed in nature. She chases after it, trying to get a better look, clambering over rock faces, pushing past tall vegetation. She skims a huge fern, running her hands over its fronds. It leaves a residue on her skin. She presses on through the bracken, spotting the butterfly again on a branch, and lurches forwards. Suddenly the ground stops abruptly before her, plummeting down almost vertically to the water below. A sheer face of grey rock falls away from the ledge beneath her feet. Had she been moving faster, she might have miscalculated. She shudders, turning to the right, and pushes up further, where she finds herself at the top of a cliff. Edging further, loose pebbles tumble beneath her, dropping down so far she doesn't hear them splash.

A gnarled ancient oak twists out from the edge, trying to reach towards the light. Someone has attached a rope to a branch which hangs out beyond the precipice. It's knotted around a thick stick at one end, to create a seat. Swinging her leg up, she slides onto it, pushing herself away from the edge with her toes. She swings out and her arms tremble as the ground disappears from beneath her, glancing up to check how secure the knot is. Heart pounding in her chest, she dares herself to look down. *Probably should have checked that first*, she thinks.

It's a thick rope, and feels sturdy, so she relaxes a little, taking in the surroundings as she glides back and forth. The skeletal tips of salmon-farm nets off the shoreline poke out from beneath the loch ominously. The water within them white and frothy, from the poor creatures thrashing about, trying desperately to escape. She watches them sadly for a moment. They're far below her, but she can make out the large fish launching themselves above the surface now and then, colliding against the sides, and falling back into their prison. She glances down, and for a moment she wonders, *what if I were to let go and fall backwards into space?* She imagines herself sliding from the swing as it propels forwards, plummeting down into the icy water below. Sinking into the murky depths, her heavy legs tangling with the reeds at the bottom.

The panic as the water fills her lungs. The resignation as she realises there is no escape.

Would anyone miss her? Would anyone care?

She could end it all so easily. All she has to do is let go of the rope.

She removes one palm from the line, letting it dangle loosely by her side as she swings. Her heart feels as though it might explode from her chest. And then as quickly as the thought entered her mind, it is gone. She lifts her hand up, gripping the rope tightly once more. Digging her heels into the earth, she stops the momentum, and steps back from the brink, returning to her bicycle. She diverges from the road, but before too long the bike can't handle the terrain. She abandons it, leaning it against some rocks jutting threateningly from the ground, continuing her journey on foot. Eventually emerging from the woodland, she glances about, blinking frantically as her eyes adjust to the bright sunshine. Close to the edge of another cliff sits a chocolate-box cottage. It makes her think of the witch's gingerbread house from *Hansel and Gretel*. So small, so cute, it looks almost cartoon-like. She heads toward it. A wild rose rambles up the dry-stone wall around the perimeter of the property, its pale-pink flowers casting their strong perfume through the air. Blackberry bushes grow tall along the path, their blossoms promising an abundance of fruit later in the summer.

Lucy laps it all up, breathing in the sweet, freshly scented air. A pyramid of stones is stacked on the ground. She stops beside it, thinking how clever it is, before continuing towards the property. As she approaches, an elderly lady who has been watching her curiously, stands from a bench in the front garden, waving. She is roughly five feet tall, and rotund, with rosy cheeks. Her face is covered with years of wrinkles and smile lines. A long brown paisley skirt flows in the breeze as she waddles across the lawn. She wears a thin white cotton blouse with short sleeves, and black plimsoles on her feet.

Short pale-grey hair sticks up messily in every direction. She beams broadly, revealing a mouthful of straight but yellowing teeth.

'Hello there!' she calls. 'Beautiful day.' Her voice is like honey. Her accent pure west coast.

'Isn't it?' Lucy replies. She approaches the wall of the garden, and the woman leans forwards.

'Not seen you around here before.'

'No, I arrived yesterday. I'm working at Willow Cottage.'

The lady raises her eyebrows dramatically.

'For the *artist*?' The way she says it, she makes it sound like a dirty word.

'Yes, that's right. I'm Lucy.' She offers her hand.

'Lynda,' she replies, shaking it tenderly. 'Lynda Checkley.'

Lucy reaches up, mopping moisture from her brow.

'You must be roasting.' The old lady eyes her long-sleeved jersey and jeans.

'I wasn't sure if it might rain. Didn't want to get caught out,' she replies.

'Would you like a drink?'

Lucy swings her backpack off her shoulder.

'I've got some water somewhere in here...' She fumbles with the buckles of the rucksack.

The woman swats both her hands towards Lucy playfully.

'Oh nonsense, I'll get you something cold from the fridge. Come, sit with me. I don't often have visitors these days.'

Lucy checks her watch, and then ambles through the gate, taking a seat on the bench. Lynda disappears inside, and Lucy leans back, admiring the view. Willow Cottage has a wonderful outlook, but this place, at the top of a hill, almost on the very edge of a cliff... it's breathtaking.

The woman returns with a glass of something cloudy, ice cubes clinking together as she totters towards Lucy. She hands her the beaker, and a strong scent of lemon hits her. She takes a sip, the liquid refreshing on her lips. She presses the glass into her cheek, closing her eyes.

Lynda offers her a cookie. It's still warm.

'Just out of the oven,' she says cheerfully, sitting beside Lucy.

'You've got a wonderful view here,' she says, smiling.

'Yes, I'm incredibly lucky.' The woman surveys the surroundings, nodding to herself with satisfaction.

'So,' she continues, 'you're helping with the husband I take it?'

'Yes.'

Lynda shakes her head.

'Was a terrible thing that happened.'

Lucy assumes she means the accident. She nods, shrugging.

'Anyway, young lady, I can tell you some stories, I'm sure...'

She laughs heartily. It's rasping, infectious. Heartfelt. Lucy can't help but smile.

And the two women begin to chat like old friends.

14

DIANA

Diana sits at her garden table. She shouldn't have snapped at Lucy, she realises that. She feels foolish. Doesn't want to scare the poor girl away on the first day. She sips a glass of cold white wine as she stares out across the water. The loch is flat calm, like a shiny royal-blue mirror. After all these years, it still amazes Diana how changeable the surface is.

She hasn't been into her studio today. Can't bring herself to look at the portrait. Her limbs feel heavy, sore. She probably wouldn't manage to paint anyway. She pulls a pot of pills from her pocket, popping two into her mouth without even looking at the label. It doesn't matter. They all have the same end goal. She closes her eyes, washing the tablets down with her wine. The alcohol dispels the bitter chemical taste from the medicine.

She holds her hand up before her face. It trembles, and she screws her fingers into a fist, shaking her head. She hears Lucy before she sees her, trudging through the grass, wheeling the bicycle beside her. She leans it against the wall of the house.

'Pleasant ride?' Diana calls out.

'Very, but I couldn't get too far on this.' Lucy gestures to her ride. 'The hill is too steep. I abandoned it and walked most of the way.'

She takes a bunch of wild flowers from the basket on the front of the bike. Lifting them to her nose, she inhales deeply. Smiling, she carries them into the kitchen. Diana hears her humming from inside. The girl returns to the doorway.

'I'm going to prepare some soup for Richard now. Would you like some?'

'Not for me, thank you.' She looks at the empty wine bottle on the table.

'Could you be a dear, though, and open another Sauvignon Blanc from the fridge and bring it to me, please?'

'Of course.'

She disappears inside, emerging a few minutes later with the wine. She picks up the empty bottle, returning to the kitchen. Diana hears Lucy rummaging around, clattering pots and pans. She hums the whole time. Diana closes her eyes, letting the melody take her away. She pours herself a large glass, knocking it back. She refills and begins to sip. Before long, she hears sizzling, and the smell of onions cooking drifts outside. Saliva pools in Diana's mouth, and she holds her hand to her lips, leaning forwards in her chair. She doubles over.

Still Lucy hums.

There's a taste on Diana's tongue, like bile, or perhaps it's the chemical residue from the pills. She downs the rest of her glass of wine.

A dizziness washes over her. She tries to stand but falls down into her seat. She glances at the bottle on the table. It's almost empty. Trying to stand again, she steadies herself on her cane. Taking a few paces forward, the nausea radiates through her, her head spins, eyes roll up in their sockets. She blinks, trying to push through it.

'Lucy!' she calls out. In her peripheral vision she sees the girl appear in the doorway. She steps out onto the grass as Diana falls face forward to the ground.

'You're back! You gave me quite a scare there,' Lucy says as Diana's eyes slowly open. She glances about, blinking a few times.

'Keep this pressed to your head.' Lucy passes her a tea towel wrapped around some ice cubes. Diana pushes it against the side of her face.

'What happened?' Her gaze darts round the garden.

'You took a tumble as I was coming out of the kitchen. You called me, and as I stepped outside, I saw you hit the floor.'

Diana is on the grass, with her knees pulled up in front of her.

'Would you like me to call a doctor?'

'No, thank you. I'm okay. I think I just stood up too quickly. It happens from time to time. These pills...'

Lucy's eyes flick to the wine bottle on the garden table, but she doesn't say anything. Diana follows her gaze, then looks away.

'So this has happened before?' Lucy asks, her voice thick with concern.

'Once or twice. Sometimes my brain works before my limbs

do. You would think I'd be used to this by now.' She nods towards her leg.

'Here, let's get you up.' Lucy reaches down, placing her hands under Diana's armpits. Diana braces herself against the ground and pushes.

'Slowly now,' Lucy whispers.

They shuffle to the chair, and Diana slides down onto the slats.

'Lucky you landed on the grass, but I think you still may have quite a shiner. The ice should help. Fingers crossed.'

Diana nods, avoiding Lucy's eyes.

'I'd feel more comfortable if we had a doctor take a look at you. Are you sure I can't call someone?'

'No, honestly. That's not necessary. I'm a tough old bird. I've been through much worse. Besides, it would take him forever to get here.' She smiles.

'But if you ever do need to contact him, there's a diary in the Welsh dresser in the lounge. You'll find any relevant numbers in there.'

Lucy nods.

'I need to check the stove,' she says eventually. She hurries towards the kitchen, glancing over her shoulder as she reaches the door.

Diana sits on the seat, holding the ice pack to her face, shaking her head. Lucy returns to the hob, stirring the soup. It simmers and she breathes in, popping in some fresh herbs, and a palmful of salt.

She turns off the gas, pouring the broth into the jug of the blender, whizzing the mixture to a smooth gloop, adding more water to thin it down, and puts some in a mug, carrying it out to Diana.

'I know you said no, but you should really eat something. It will make you feel better.'

Diana takes it, nodding, and blows on the surface before sipping.

Lucy leaves her, heading back into the house. She slings a tea towel over one shoulder, placing a bowl of soup and a spoon onto a tray, carrying it out of the kitchen to Richard's room.

She knocks on the door before entering. She doesn't know why, but it just seems the right thing to do. She pushes it open, stepping inside.

'Lunchtime!' she calls. Richard is in his usual spot, in front of the window. She wheels the chair round, sliding the free-standing tray table over his lap. She places the soup down and spoons some up to his mouth. The edge of the spoon clatters against his teeth, his jaw locked tight.

'Come on, Richard, open up,' Lucy whispers.

His jaw remains clamped shut. She wiggles the spoon, trying to force it inside, and the brown liquid spills down his chin, dripping onto his clean white shirt.

Lucy sighs. She pulls the tea towel from her shoulder, mopping his face, then attempts to shovel more into his mouth. Again, it drips down his front.

'Not hungry? Okay, not to worry.' She dabs at the mark. An orange stain remains on the fabric. She picks up the tray and exits the room. Richard continues to stare at the wall.

She returns to the kitchen, pouring the bowl of soup down the sink, along with what is left from the pot on the hob, and washes the dishes. Leaving them to drain, she strolls outside to Diana, glad to see some colour has returned to her cheeks.

'You're looking much better.'

Diana nods, handing her the empty mug.

Lucy sits in the empty seat beside her. She stares out over the water, the sun glistening on its ripples.

Two swallows chase each other in circles, skimming the surface of the loch as they chirp playfully. They dart past the end of the jetty and back out towards the middle of the lake. Lucy smiles.

She glances at the wine bottle on the table. Considering what she should say.

'I hope you don't mind me saying, Diana. It's maybe not my place to, but I'm speaking as an ex-nurse now.'

Diana looks at her, narrowing her eyes.

'You're on some pretty heavy meds there,' Lucy continues. 'You might want to take it easy on the alcohol. Next time you fall you may not be so lucky.'

Diana laughs.

'You're right. It's certainly not your place to say. You're here to look after my husband and to clean my house. You can keep your judgements to yourself. I can take care of myself.'

Lucy nods, standing, smoothing down the front of her jersey. She has overstepped the mark, and she knows it. She returns to the kitchen, leaving Diana to watch the birds.

16

S itting on the edge of her bed looking out of the window, she can hear Diana pottering around downstairs. She wants to go down, try to clear the air, but she feels she might only make things worse, so she decides to leave well enough alone. Feeling foolish, she shakes her head, cursing under her breath. Having made the decision to mention Diana's drinking, now she would have to live with it.

If Diana chose to contact the agency because of the incident and ask for a replacement... well, that would be unfortunate. With any luck, it wouldn't come to that.

She crosses to the window, glancing down to the garden table. Diana sits with the dregs of a bottle of wine. Two empties lay discarded on the grass beside her. She has her back to the house, looking out across the loch, sipping from her glass.

The room is hot, stuffy; the air stifling. Lucy pushes the sash up, but it does little to cool her. Hearing the movement, Diana peers over her shoulder up towards Lucy. Straight into her eyes.

Lucy turns away, placing her hand to her face. She chews her thumbnail, shaking her head again.

She decides to go for a walk. Heading out of her room, she

darts down the stairs, stopping at the bottom as she sees the stain. She crouches down, running her palm across the smooth floorboards. Diana stumbles into the hallway from the kitchen, holding a fresh bottle of wine.

She glares. Her eyes flick to the foot of the stairs, and she turns to go.

'What is it?' Lucy asks. 'The stain, I mean.'

Diana stops but doesn't face Lucy.

'No idea. It was there when I purchased the house. There's a man coming next week to sand the boards down, try to get rid of it.'

She hobbles away through the kitchen, out into the garden. Lucy narrows her eyes, lifting the runner which covers the stain. It's large, spilling across the hall floor from the base of the stairs.

Dark. Ominous.

*Why now, Diana? If it's been here all along, why are you choosing to fix it no*w? she thinks.

She stands, dropping the corner of the rug. She pops her head into Richard's room. His eyes are closed, so she doesn't disturb him. She heads out through the kitchen, into the garden, avoiding Diana's stare as she leaves.

17

DIANA

She has drunk way too much. She knows that.

It has always been the same. If someone tells her she shouldn't be doing something, she does it all the more. It used to exasperate her mother.

Diana's face clouds, shaking the memories away.

She stands from her chair. Swaying, she retrieves her stick, leaning her weight on it. She eyes the four empty bottles on the lawn, before downing the dregs of her glass. *Waste not, want not*, she thinks.

She takes a tentative step towards the house. The horizon swirls around her. Lucy has gone for a walk. There's nobody here to help her if she falls again, so she continues slowly. One foot forward, a rest, then the next. It takes her longer than it should to reach the kitchen. The whole time the world spins every which way. She lunges forwards, grasping the door frame, and waits while her head catches up with her body. She steps inside, her legs feel heavy. She smells smoke again, stronger now.

But there's nobody else in the house.

Her vision is double, blurry. Birdsong echoes in her ears, her senses seem heightened. A splash from the loch seems closer than it should.

Where is she?

Who is she?

She's back in the room; can't remember the last occasion she was this drunk. She limps to the sink, just in time to throw up. Putrid stinking vomit splatters the white porcelain, the smell making her gag more. Opening the tap, swallowing down icy water, she rinses her mouth. Suddenly parched, she drinks it down greedily. Leaning on the edge of the worktop, she turns, glancing towards the door to the hall. Her head bobs to the front, then back. She feels like an idiot, getting into this state. At her age, she should know better.

She moves forwards, taking baby steps. With each movement, she fears she may be sick again.

Exiting the kitchen, she opens Richard's door. She sees only blurred shapes. His face a pink mass in a spinning psychedelic tunnel.

'Richard?' she calls. She can hear his laboured breathing.

'Richard... I'm not... I don't feel too well.'

Leaving the door wide open, she heads down the hall to her bedroom. Struggling to breathe, she clutches her chest, screwing her eyes tightly shut. Everything sways. The shapes around her, the window, the dresser... they seem to shrink into pinpoints, then balloon out again to full size, like a bad acid trip.

Feeling her way round the walls of her room, she edges to the bed, collapsing forward onto the mattress. Her leg throbs, even the scar on her face seems sore.

She pulls open her bedside drawer. The entire thing comes free, clattering to the floor. She fumbles around on the ground for pills, grabbing the first bottle her hand falls upon. She can't see the label. Can't even see the pot. It's just a blur of shapes and colours. She flicks off the lid with her thumb, spilling its contents over the duvet. Retrieving a handful of tablets, she throws them into her mouth, swallowing without water. They stick in her throat, the bitter chemical taste rising to her tongue. Burying her face in the pillow, she prays for it all to stop.

The noise. The nausea. The spinning.

It's all too much.

Even in the black, her eyes shut tight, she feels like she is swaying back and forth. The bed is rocking. Will she fall onto the floor? Is the floor even there anymore?

Where.

Is.

She?

All the surrounding sounds seem to swirl into one. The twitter of a starling. The gentle lapping of the waves from the loch on the pebbles of the shoreline. The wind rustling through the trees. A wasp trapped in the window, trying desperately to escape.

All distinctly separate, yet somehow all the same. They grow louder, then dissipate. Over and over.

'Shut up!' Diana screams.

'Shut up! Shut up! SHUT UP!'

She clutches her hands to her ears, and suddenly everything is silent, apart from a high-pitched ringing. She feels like she is falling deep down into a rabbit hole, spiralling down further and further under the ground. She's getting smaller as she tumbles, shrinking, like Alice in Wonderland.

Until she is the size of a flea.

Tiny, insignificant.

Her eyes flick open and she sees a face before her, staring down from above the bed.

As her eyelids slide closed, the vision swirls around in a spiral, and the world seems to stop as a sudden tiredness washes over her, and she drifts away out of consciousness.

18

DIANA

The smell of bacon cooking fills the house, making Diana want to vomit. Her eyelids lift slowly. She squints from the bright morning sunlight that streams in through the open curtains.

She sits up and a throbbing in her head like she has never felt before makes her feel nauseous.

Her mind is foggy. Her entire body aches.

Glancing around the room, everything seems normal. Yet she has an overwhelming feeling that something is wrong.

She reaches to the side of her bed for her stick, but it's not there. She looks about but can't see it. Shuffling to the edge, she is surprised to realise she is in her nightgown. She pulls herself up on the bedside table and supports her weight against the wall. Crouching, she lifts the valance up, staring beneath. The cane isn't there. She stands, frowning, and edges round to the door, holding down waves of sickness as she moves. Her vision is blurry, the light exacerbates the throbbing in her brain. As she opens the bedroom door, the smell of cooking grows stronger. She can hear it sizzling from the kitchen. Lucy is humming a tune, as usual. At first Diana had found it endearing. Now it is beginning to irritate her. The melody is something familiar, but her mind isn't working properly. She can't place it. She shakes her head, calling out.

'Lucy!'

The humming stops. The girl appears at the end of the hallway, a broad smile on her face, cheeks rosy from the heat of the hob, hair tied up in a loose bun.

'Diana, good morning! How are you feeling today?'

'I can't find my cane. Do you know where it is?' she asks in a slur; she suspects she may still be drunk. Lucy cocks her head to one side.

'No, sorry. Did you bring it in last night when you came inside?'

'Yes... I... well, I think I did. I'm sure I must have.'

'Hold on, I'll check.'

Lucy rushes away, leaving Diana supporting herself against the door frame. She clings to the wood with all her strength, knuckles turning white as her fingernails dig into the grain. Her legs feel like jelly, and she thinks today she may need to avoid alcohol. But she has thought that many times before.

After a moment Lucy comes back through from the kitchen holding the cane.

'You left it in the garden,' she says, handing it to her.

Diana frowns, shaking her head slightly.

'I did? But... that's...'

She searches her memory, but the end of the evening is a blur. She leans her weight onto the top of the stick, letting out a deep breath. Was she so drunk that she returned to her bedroom unaided? She didn't see how that was possible. She can manage without it, but this is a long way; her leg has been giving her such trouble lately. It seems unlikely. They do say that drink is a wonderful pain killer, but even so...

Her thigh throbs, and she considers that perhaps this might have been the case after all.

'Would you like some breakfast?'

Diana nods, although in truth she isn't sure if she will be able to keep anything down.

'Go and sit and I'll bring some through to you. Richard is at the table already.'

As she makes her way into the living room, Lucy returns to the kitchen. Diana passes her husband, stroking the top of his shoulder with her fingertips. She takes her usual seat at the end, opposite him. Lucy breezes in, carrying two dishes, placing one in front of Diana. She sits beside Richard and begins trying to spoon the liquidised food into his mouth.

Diana eyes her plate, holding a hand to her mouth. She watches as Lucy attempts to feed her husband. The mixture is spilling down his chin.

'He can be stubborn, but you just need to persevere,' Diana says softly, smiling. Lucy returns the smile from across the table.

'He's had a little. But I don't think he wants any more. He didn't eat much yesterday either. Does he usually have a good appetite?'

Diana shrugs. 'There doesn't seem to be any rhyme or reason to anything he does. I sometimes wonder if it's involuntary... his jaw locking up or something. I struggle to feed him too. The doctor has offered to fit a drip, but... I don't know. I'm not sure I like the idea of that. Not while he's still able to swallow.'

Lucy places the spoon down on the table. Picking up a clean napkin, she tenderly wipes the gruel from Richard's chin. She sees Diana watching her.

'I nursed my grandmother when I was younger. Cancer. It taught me to be patient with people. I believe everyone deserves compassion. Whether they are aware of it or not.' She smiles.

Diana pushes the plate away.

'Thank you for the breakfast. It was lovely... I'm not that hungry. Bit of a hangover.'

Lucy watches her, looking embarrassed.

'I'm sorry for my reaction yesterday when you mentioned my drinking.'

Lucy shakes her head.

'No need. It was wrong of me to comment. I'm the one who should be apologising.'

'No, no. Honestly, you were right to. I can be a little touchy about drink. My mother... she had a problem, and I suppose I've always been super conscious of the amount of alcohol I consume.'

Lucy collects up the plates without commenting.

'It's nice that somebody is looking out for me.'

Diana smiles weakly. She smells smoke again. It's getting stronger each time she comes in the house.

'Do you smell cigarettes?'

'No. I can't smell anything,' Lucy replies, sniffing the air. She takes the dishes through to the kitchen, returning for Richard.

'I was thinking of taking him to sit out in the garden for a while. It's such a beautiful day, it seems a shame for him to be cooped up in that stuffy room. It's stiflingly hot in there this morning.'

Diana hesitates, uncomfortable with the idea.

'If it's a problem, I can just put him in his room. It's only that I thought...'

'Are you going to be here? It's a struggle for me to wheel him back inside if the weather turns.'

Lucy looks out the window at the glorious sunshine and frowns. 'I can make sure he's in before I go anywhere.'

'Okay.' Diana nods, forcing a tight-lipped smile.

She watches as the girl wheels her husband's chair from the

room. She hears her chattering away to him as she takes him outside, giving him a running commentary.

She's glad that Richard is in caring hands. The buzz of a motorboat engine cuts through the silence, and Diana cocks her head. A smile creeps onto her lips. She pushes her chair out from under the table, and stands, hurrying into the garden.

19

She positions his wheelchair at the edge of the garden, facing out across the loch. A group of starlings chase each other above her head as she applies the brake with her foot.

The hum of an engine draws her attention over the water, as the tiny speck of a boat appears on the horizon, heading towards the shore. Lucy strolls to the jetty, hopping onto the planks. She smiles and waves as Mylo approaches. He doesn't wave back; simply nods and looks away. Leaving the motor running, he hops ashore, tying the mooring rope off, before stepping back on to grab something. He returns along the pier carrying a pile of parcels and letters.

'Are you the postman too?' Lucy shouts.

He shrugs.

'I'm basically the general dogsbody. Jack of all trades, master of none.'

Lucy turns to the direction of his gaze and sees Diana hurrying out into the garden; as much as a woman who relies on a walking stick can hurry. He hands Lucy the bundle.

'There's a couple for you there, the rest are for her.'

'Oh, that was so quick! I opted for next-day delivery but never imagined it would actually happen!'

He doesn't reply. They stand in silence as Diana approaches.

'Mylo, good morning!' she calls. 'Isn't this weather beautiful?'

He hops on deck as if he's trying to hurry away before she reaches him.

'Must dash. Got a million and one things to do today. Would you mind casting me off?' He nods towards the rope. Lucy unties the loose knot he has wound around the cleat, tossing him the line.

He reverses the boat away from the pier, manoeuvring it around before heading away from the shore. Diana continues to limp along the jetty, looking dejected.

Lucy stares after the boat, trying to figure Mylo out. On one hand, he was quite forward in giving her his number, but his attitude towards her is indifferent at best, if not a little unfriendly.

'Is he always so matter of fact?' Lucy asks. Diana raises an eyebrow.

'Everyone has their reasons for how they are,' she says, watching the boat. 'His father died while he was living in London. He returned to Scotland to look after his mother and help her run the shop. I think there's a lot of guilt there that he wasn't around when his father passed. It was very sudden… unexpected. He had a stroke.'

As the noise of the engine grows quieter, Lucy sorts through the pile. She hands the bulk of them to Diana, then takes her parcels, heading towards the kitchen door.

'You've been busy, I see.' Diana laughs as Lucy passes her the letters.

'I do love to shop! I took advantage of having a mobile signal yesterday while I was out walking!'

She heads inside to open her packages.

20

DIANA

She sits in the shade of the willow, realising too late that Lucy is approaching. Coughing, she tries to hide the joint she is smoking, swatting the smoke away with her free hand. The smell lingers. As she sees Lucy sniff, she knows she has been caught out. Diana shrugs, offering the spliff to Lucy, with a guilty grin. Lucy shakes her head, smiling, as she fidgets with the long sleeves of a beige chunky-knit jumper.

'Purely medicinal. I promise. It helps with all sorts.'

'It's fine, honestly.'

'I know I shouldn't. But...' She doesn't finish the sentence.

'You don't have to explain yourself to me, really. I'm going to take Richard inside, then I might head out for a walk.'

'Sit with me?'

Lucy crouches down, feeling the grass with the palm of her hand, before sitting cross-legged in front of Diana.

'I've always had a rebellious streak. That's probably why I became an artist rather than a lawyer.'

Lucy smiles.

'I mentioned my mother earlier. Her drinking.'

'Yes.'

'She wasn't a... well woman. She suffered from schizophrenia. Took her own life when I was in my early teens. I went to live with my grandparents after that.'

'I'm sorry.'

Diana shrugs.

'One of those things. My father was never on the scene. I didn't know him. But I think... I've always wanted to show that I'm not like her. Does that make sense?'

Lucy nods.

'I have always worried that she passed something on to me. Some deficiency. That in some way I would be more predisposed to the same issues she had. And I suppose my behaviour... the drinking... this.' She holds up the joint. 'It's all to prove to myself that I'm nothing like her. That I am *fine*.'

'I understand.'

'Do you know much about the accident we were involved in?'

Lucy shakes her head.

'It was a hit and run, in London.'

'That's terrible.'

'We were celebrating our anniversary. It had been such a perfect day.' She pauses for a moment, looking out over the loch. Lucy stares at her face, but she is unaware. She has drifted away, momentarily lost in her memories. She continues.

'We were on our way to dinner in a taxi, and a van ploughed into us. It came out of nowhere. Richard's side of the vehicle took the brunt of the force. I don't remember much about it really. I was in hospital for many weeks. I had to learn to walk again. Every time I asked about Richard, they told me he was alive, but they wouldn't elaborate. I knew it must have been bad, as he was never there visiting me. I wondered why. They didn't allow me to see myself until they were sure I could handle it. And when they let me look in a mirror... They tried to prepare me, of course, but nothing could have. Not for that horror. It was far worse back then, you understand. When the wounds were fresh. You think this looks bad now?' She sucks in air through her teeth, shaking her head. 'When I saw what had happened, I wished I had died. I know it sounds melodramatic, pathetic even. I should have been grateful that I was alive... but I couldn't conceive of a life with a face like this.' She fans her fingers out towards her chin.

'I am so... sorry,' Lucy whispers.

Diana looks at the girl. A tear is welling in the corner of her eye.

'Over the years, I have made my peace with it. I *am* glad I survived... that we both did. We were extremely lucky. But it wasn't easy, and there have been some dark days. Nevertheless, I made it through. Some say I have run away... in a way that's true. But I find it difficult... the way people react to me when they see me. So being here makes life easier for everyone. The thing that I now know, above anything else, is that I am *nothing* like my mother. I am a survivor. She wouldn't have coped with this situation. Not at all. I'm sure of that. But I have.' Diana leans forwards, resting her elbows on her knees, staring across the water.

'So yes, I'll admit I overindulge at times. I may drink too much. I smoke this rubbish. I probably take too many pills. But I know that I am okay. Please don't assume you need to worry about me. I have made it through a lot.'

Lucy wipes her eyes.

'I'm sorry if I've upset you,' Diana says.

'Don't be daft. It's lovely that you feel you can talk to me about this.'

Diana nods.

'It can be very lonely here. It's good to be able to chat.'

Lucy stands, kicking the lock off of Richard's wheelchair.

'I'll pop him in his room, then I'll be off. I'll be back in plenty of time for lunch.'

'No rush. Where are you going to go?'

'I saw a little beach yesterday when I was out on the bike. It's a short walk along the coast. Thought I'd check it out.'

'Lovely. Enjoy yourself.'

She smiles as Lucy wheels her husband into the house.

21

S he throws the empty jiffy bag into the bin in the corner of her bedroom and finishes packing her rucksack, fastening the buckles. She slings it over her shoulder, heading downstairs to fill her flask in the kitchen. Diana is out in her workshop. The smell of cannabis still lingers in the air. Lucy ducks into Richard's room. His chair is facing her, eyes closed, head lolling forwards. She can see his chest rising beneath his crisp white shirt. She closes the door and heads out.

She skims along the perimeter of the forest, heading down a trampled grass path into a small clearing. She stops and gasps. Moss-covered trees twist towards the sky. Dappled sunlight streams in through gaps in the foliage, colouring the entire area the most fantastic shade of emerald green. She stands for a moment, taking it in. Something about the place feels magical, making her smile. It reminds her of a fairy grotto from a child's picture book.

She doesn't want to leave. She strokes her hand across the soft fluffy lichen on a tree trunk. The ground beneath her feet feels like plush carpet. She closes her eyes for a moment, listening to the gentle lapping of the waves on the beach where she is heading, and pushes through the trees out to the rugged coast. Clambering over boulders, she climbs down towards the shoreline. The rocks are slippery in places where the seaweed is still wet. She treads carefully, testing the ground before placing her full weight on the surface.

The baking sun beats down on her. The seat of her jeans is damp with perspiration. She wipes the back of her hand over her forehead, continuing to climb until she reaches the stony beach. Heading down towards it, she takes a towel from her bag, spreading it out across the ground.

As she crouches, she notices a stack of stones to her left, and another, further along towards the water. A third lays half collapsed next to it. She straightens, approaching the structures, kneeling beside them. She picks up a large stone from the tumbled pile. It is smooth, and cool, and as she turns it over in her hand, it shimmers, as if it contains glitter. She strokes it against her cheek, closing her eyes. She inhales deeply. Opening them, she tosses the pebble out into the water, watching as it disappears beneath the surface with a satisfying splosh. She pushes the remaining piles over. The stones clatter noisily to the ground, sending birds fluttering into the sky from the beach, and the trees behind her. Smiling, she returns to her towel, reclining onto it.

22

S till feeling groggy, Diana heads inside. The heat is too much. Besides, she has work to do in her studio. She fills a glass with water in the kitchen, before heading back outside, cutting across the garden to the outhouse. She fumbles for the key in the pocket of her housecoat and unlocks the door.

Stepping in, she swats at some flies with her hand, placing her drink on a sideboard against the rear wall. She leans her cane against it, limping to a stool in front of her canvas. Inhaling, she breathes in the familiar smell of paint thinners. Sitting, she surveys the painting, narrowing her eyes. It might not be what she had intended to create, but there was no denying it was powerful. Picking up her palette, she squeezes a huge mass of black oil paint onto it. Leaning back, she picks up a large, flat brush, squinting at the image before her.

All she has to do is make it less like Lucy. Stabbing her tool into the colour, she works away with fast, angry strokes. A swoosh here. A jab there. Shadows underneath the wide eyes. Softening the cheekbones. Narrowing the jaw. Some cadmium yellow transforms the subject's hazel-brown hair to blonde. She moves quickly, energetically. Sweat trickles down her, soaking into the waistband of her trousers in the small of her back.

As always, when she paints, she loses track of the time. Occasionally she stares out the window of her workshop, over the water to the distant shores. She thinks for a second before returning to her creation. Tossing her brush into a large plastic milk bottle with the top sliced off, filled with white spirit, she regards the image in front of her. The power is still there.

Lucy is no longer present.

Diana nods, satisfied with the morning's effort. Glancing at her watch, she sees that it is almost one thirty. Hours have passed, but she feels like it's only been a short while. Frowning, she stands, swaying slightly as the room swirls around her sickeningly. She steadies herself on the stool, before crossing the studio to retrieve her stick.

When she is sure she won't collapse, she throws open the door. She gasps, gripping the wooden frame with her free hand. Immediately outside her workshop, on the grass, is a tall stack of stones, almost five feet high. She leans out, head whipping from side to side.

A starling twitters, circling above, before darting out across the loch. Diana's vision blurs, her mind swims. She can't make any sense of what she's seeing.

She steps out onto the lawn. Movement in her periphery draws her attention. She turns to face the treeline opposite, as a figure emerges. The sun's flare blinds her, and she holds a hand up to shield her eyes. Her breathing is heavy, sweat seeps from every pore of her body, and for a sickening moment she feels like she might collapse again.

'Why are you doing this?' she shrieks.

As the person steps forwards, she sees it is only Lucy.

'Diana, hi!' she calls across the garden, a broad smile fading quickly from her face.

'Was this you?'

'Sorry?'

'Do you think this is fucking funny?' she screams.

Lucy looks confused, glancing around. She continues to walk towards the studio.

'Why would you do this? Did somebody tell you about this?'

Lucy's confusion turns to discomfort.

'Diana, what's wrong? Has someone upset you?'

Diana lurches forwards, pushing the tower. It tumbles over the lawn, making Lucy jump aside as a boulder rolls past her feet.

'These fucking stones! Was it you?'

Lucy stares at the rocks, shaking her head.

'No, Diana. I've been at the beach. I've only just this minute got back.'

Diana takes a few steps, tripping on a stone. Her stick clatters over the remnants of the tower as she hurtles forwards. Lucy catches her, barely managing to stop the two of them toppling over.

'I don't understand... why... I was... who would do this?'

Lucy steadies her, picking up her cane and handing it back to her.

'Diana, let's get inside. Something has clearly upset you. Why don't we go in, and I'll make you a cup of tea, and you can tell me what's going on. Okay?'

Diana stares wide-eyed at Lucy's face. For a moment, the girl looks terrified, but then her jaw softens.

She places an arm around Diana's shoulders, guiding her across the garden towards the house.

She ushers her inside, turning to stand on the doorstep. She glances out to the woods. Her eyes flick in the direction of the scattered pebbles outside Diana's studio, then back to the treeline. She scans the space, searching for any signs of life. Any movement. Diana watches her intently the entire time.

The leaves rustle in the gentle breeze, and the solitary cry of a lone oystercatcher echoes over the water.

Lucy steps backwards into the house. A knock at the door from the front of the house draws their attention. Diana's eyes dart frantically in the direction of the hallway. She looks... terrified.

'It's okay,' Lucy whispers. 'I'll see who it is. Wait here.'

Approaching the door with trepidation, she pulls it open. Mylo stands on the doorstep. Her shoulders relax as she sees him.

'Oh hi!' she says, raising her brows, unable to hide the surprise from her voice.

He holds something out towards Lucy.

'I missed this out of Diana's pile.'

She glances down at the letter in his hand.

'Right.' She looks over her shoulder. Diana lingers in the kitchen doorway looking afraid.

'When... when did you arrive? Out of interest.'

He narrows his eyes.

'Just now. Why?'

She shakes her head.

'Doesn't matter. I... didn't hear the boat, that's all.'

He motions behind him to a truck.

'I'm not always in the boat. It depends where I'm heading. Not everywhere is accessible from the water. I was on my way somewhere and thought I should drop this in as I was passing. In case it's anything important.' He shrugs.

'Thanks. I'll make sure she gets it.'

He waits in the doorway, as if he wants to say something else, but doesn't. His eyes burn into hers, making her feel uncomfortable. She looks away.

'Right, well I guess I'll be off then,' he mumbles, kicking at the dirt beneath his feet.

'Okay. Cheers.'

She closes the door, leaning her back against it, and listens as the truck pulls away. Frowning, she lets out a long breath. Diana stares at her from the kitchen.

'It was only Mylo, dropping off a letter he missed from your stuff.'

She visibly relaxes, limping away out of view into the kitchen.

Lucy remains at the door for a moment, biting her lip. A strange sense of unease creeps through her. She shakes her head, telling herself she is being ridiculous, and heads down the hall to join Diana.

23

Lucy hands Diana a cup of steaming tea, then sits beside her on the sofa. She seems to have regained some composure; she's no longer shaking, less manic.

'So what the heck was all that about?'

'I'm okay. Sorry if I gave you a fright. I've not been feeling that well today, and I found that stone stack outside the door... it startled me a little. Must have been some kids or something.'

Lucy narrows her eyes.

'Are you sure? We can call the police if you like.'

Diana snorts. 'Don't be so ridiculous. It's nothing. We mustn't waste their time. Honestly, I am absolutely fine.' She takes a sip of the tea, then blows on it to cool it.

'You seemed pretty shaken.'

'I wasn't expecting it. Then I saw you coming out of the woods, and I got a little confused. I apologise, but it's not anything to worry about.'

'If you're sure?'

'Totally.'

Lucy stands.

'Right. I'm going to pop upstairs to freshen up, then I'll be down to sort lunch.'

'Okay, dear.'

She heads out of the lounge, turning briefly back to glance at Diana. She is sitting staring at the wall, blowing on her tea. Lucy bounds up the stairs into her room, slinging her rucksack onto the chair.

She pulls one of the glittering pebbles she found on the beach from her pocket. It slips from her fingers, clattering to the floor, and rolls under the bed. She crouches down, reaching under after it. She swings her arm around, palm flat against the floorboards. Pushing herself down more, she reaches further underneath. Her hand brushes against something jagged.

She moves it backwards and feels something sharp again beneath her fingers. She lies on her side, stretching out. Something small and hard is protruding from between two of the boards. She grabs it between her fingertips and pulls it out. She finds herself looking at a photo-card driving licence.

A pretty blonde in her late twenties stares, beaming out from the surface. *Rose McNulty*, the name says. The address is in Glasgow.

Lucy frowns, tucking the card into her pocket. She heads into the bathroom, splashing some cold water on her face, before spraying some deodorant and tying her hair back into a loose ponytail.

She hurries downstairs to the kitchen. Diana is standing at the window, leaning on the worktop. She stares out towards the loch; doesn't acknowledge Lucy as she enters the room.

Lucy crosses to the fridge, taking some tomatoes and an onion out, and begins to chop them. Diana turns.

'No lunch for me today, thanks.'

'No problem... if you're sure?'

'Yep, far too hot.'

Lucy lifts the chopping board, brushing the vegetables into a pan, and places it on the stove. As it simmers, she faces Diana.

'Do you know a Rose McNulty?'

Diana whirls around, quick as a flash.

'Excuse me?'

Lucy pulls the driver's licence from her pocket, crossing to Diana at the window. She hands it to her.

'I found this under my bed.'

Diana relaxes. She doesn't even seem to look at the card.

'Nope, no idea. Must have been the previous owner.'

She gives it back to Lucy.

'Oh. Okay. Do you think I should hand it in to someone?'

'I wouldn't bother. I've been here for years. They'll have a replacement by now. I'd just throw it away.'

'Right.' Lucy frowns, opening a cupboard beneath the sink. She tosses the photo card into the bin, along with the onion peelings and tomato ends, letting the door shut. She turns to see Diana hobbling out into the hall.

Returning to the stove, she finishes the soup, before liquidising it to a sloppy gruel for Richard. She mixes in a little cream to cool it down, then heads out to his room. As she approaches the window, she sees Diana crossing the garden. Lucy watches her. She walks to the stones outside her studio, pushing a few of them around with her foot. She looks over her shoulder out to the woods, then towards the cottage, shaking her head.

Lucy isn't sure why, but she steps out of view, glancing down at Richard. Some sort of gut instinct telling her to hide. She shakes her head, feeling ridiculous.

She peeks round the edge of the window, in time to see Diana lock the outbuilding, and hobble back to the house.

93

E arly the following week, a man comes to sort the hall flooring. Diana tells Lucy on the Tuesday evening that she can take the next day off, as the guy will be sanding and varnishing the boards, so he'll need her out of the house.

Lucy retrieves a scrap of paper from her room, which she'd copied Mylo's number down onto after he'd scribbled it on the back of her hand. She heads to the antiquated telephone on the small table in the lounge, pushing the dial around, one digit at a time. It rings a few times before he answers.

He seems surprised to hear from her.

Lucy explains that she has found herself to be at an unexpected loose end tomorrow, and if he's free, she would love to take him up on his offer of a boat trip. She hears him rummaging around. Like he's turning pages in a book, possibly checking his diary. Eventually he tells her he's free, and they arrange to meet. He says he'll pick her up at nine. Before Lucy can tell him she's looking forward to it, he hangs up. She shakes her head, staring at the receiver.

The next morning, she throws a few things into a bag and heads down the stairs. The workman is already there, the noise from his sander is deafening, and she's glad she won't be around to hear it all day. She stops briefly at the bottom, and watches as the man rubs at the dark stain on the floorboards, taking the wood back down to its original colour.

She continues through to the kitchen, grabbing a bottle of water from the fridge. As she steps into the garden, Diana is sitting at the table under the willow tree, sipping a steaming cup of black coffee. Her eyes are narrowed, dark circles beneath them. Her hands tremble as she holds the mug to her mouth, blowing on it. Richard is in his wheelchair beside her. Lucy frowns, remembering how Diana had told her she can't manage the chair, but decides not to mention it.

The sky had been overcast when she first woke, but it's beginning to clear now. The day is warm, muggy. *Perfect day to be out on the water*, Lucy thinks.

'Morning!' she chirps as she approaches.

Diana looks at her but doesn't say anything. Lucy is fiddling with the buckles of her rucksack. Diana stares.

'Where are you off to?' Her voice is croaky, dry. She sounds how she looks.

'Mylo is taking me out on his boat for the day. I'm not really sure where.'

Diana blinks a few times, gulping a mouthful of coffee as she considers what to say.

'That's nice,' she says, sounding far from pleased. 'Good that he's moving on.'

Lucy cocks her head.

'Moving on?'

'Yes. I think it's time. He's... struggled.'

'With his father dying?'

Diana stares at her.

'Oh… you don't know?'

'Know what?'

'Well, it's not really my place to say. I'm sure he'll tell you if he wants to. I've probably said too much already.'

Lucy rolls her eyes, exhaling. Diana smiles victoriously behind her coffee cup, teeth glinting like a shark.

The familiar hum of Mylo's boat draws into her ears. As he approaches, Diana looks away, pretending not to have seen him. Lucy steps out onto the pier, catching Mylo's line as he throws it. She ties it to a cleat. He leaves the engine running as he jumps ashore.

He strolls towards her. Today he wears a navy-and-white striped T-shirt, and a pair of ripped jeans, some dirty white canvas Converse on his feet.

'Are you ready?'

'Sure am.'

'Hello, Diana,' he calls across the garden.

She doesn't respond.

He raises his eyebrows at Lucy, who shakes her head.

'Don't ask.'

She stands on the edge of the pier, staring down into the rippling blue water. She's constantly amazed by the different colours the loch appears to be at various times of day and in changing light. The last of the cloud dissipates and the sun batters down on her from a clear cyan sky.

'I'm almost tempted to jump in for a swim,' she says without looking at Mylo.

'I wouldn't.'

'No?'

'This pier is quite long. We're pretty far out. It's deep here. That water will be freezing. Most people would last a few minutes at best. It's the panic when your body hits the cold. Your instant reaction is to gasp. That's the mistake everybody makes, because you usually take in a lungful of loch then as well. That's the beginning of the end...'

He looks at Lucy. She stares, horrified, back towards him. 'I'm sorry! I grew up around here, so this was drummed into me as a kid. Ignore me.'

He climbs aboard, holding out a hand to help her across. She steps on, then leans down to untie the rope, casting them off. As the boat speeds away, Lucy glances over her shoulder. Diana is standing watching them intently.

'How you getting on? Must be nice to have a day off,' he shouts over the noise of the engine.

'Yeah. It's an unexpected surprise.'

'Getting on okay with her?'

Lucy shrugs.

'She's very up and down. I never know where I am with her. One minute I feel like she wants to be my best friend, the next it's like she hates my guts.'

He smirks.

'I think she's more than a little socially awkward. That's what comes from living out here all by yourself for so long. Well... she's not alone... but... you know.' He looks embarrassed. Lucy holds up her hands and smiles.

'It's fine. You don't have to worry about upsetting me. I'm really not that PC.'

She watches as the dark water whizzes by. A gull follows above their heads, but when it realises there is no food, it banks off to one side, landing on the surface gracefully.

'So how come you're not needed today?'

'She's having some work carried out in the house. I think she wanted me out of the way really.'

'About time. She never gets anything done. It's a pure shame. That cottage will collapse around her if she's not careful.' Disdain laces his words.

'I wouldn't get too excited. It's nothing major. She's only having the hall floor sanded to get rid of that stain by the stairs.'

Mylo's eyes dart towards her, then away. His mouth twitches, but he remains quiet. He chews his bottom lip.

'Do you think she's okay? I mean... mentally,' Lucy asks.

'Diana? I think so. I can't say I know her *that* well. We exchange pleasantries when I drop her groceries, and I've done the odd job in the garden for her, mowed the lawn, that sort of thing... but that's about as far as it goes.'

He eases off the throttle, and the noise from the engine quietens. His eyes flick towards her again.

'Why do you ask?'

'It's lots of things. She drinks. A *lot*. And she's on all sorts of medication. Her behaviour is... erratic.'

'In what way? She's eccentric, I think. Typical artist. And let's not forget the impact that solitude can have on a person's mental well-being.'

Lucy sits on the edge of the boat, looking intently into Mylo's eyes.

'I know. But it's more than that. She's downright odd. Like... the other day she threw a complete fit because there was this stone stack in the garden. At first she was apoplectic, but then... she seemed afraid. Terrified, in fact. Come to think of it, it was right before you arrived at the door. You might have noticed her lingering in the kitchen looking odd.'

Mylo seems to be somewhere else briefly. His eyes glaze over, but he doesn't reply.

'It was weird. That's all. Scared me a little if I'm being honest.'

He looks at her.

'A stone stack, you say?'

'Yeah. You know the ones... they're all over the place here.

Where they're piled up, and the stones get smaller towards the top?'

The colour drains from Mylo's face. He looks away.

'I've seen loads of smaller versions, but this one was quite tall. Almost as big as her, and it was right outside the door to her studio. I think that was the issue. Kids playing a joke maybe.'

'Yeah, probably.'

There's something in the tone of his voice... He sounds upset. Lucy decides to drop it. They skim along, bouncing over rippling waves in silence, the hum of the engine, and the occasional bird call the only noise. Lucy watches his face. He is focused, serious.

Although the air is warm, the speed of the boat causes her to shiver, despite her long sleeves. She wraps her arms around her body. He glances towards her.

'There's a jacket in the cabin if you're cold.'

She rifles through clutter on a comfy-looking bench, finding a fleece. She pulls it on over her shirt.

'How far is it?' she calls out.

'Not long now.'

25

They round a small island, and a tremendous glass-and-steel structure emerges from the trees before them. The marina is nothing short of amazing. It looks like something from St Tropez rather than the west coast of Scotland. The sun breaks through the clouds, glinting off the glazing. Colour-changing LEDs illuminate a dark overhang from an angular roof, and expensive-looking yachts line long pontoons that extend out towards the mouth of the basin they have entered. To the left, just outside the main building, a large infinity pool trickles over the edge of a low cliffside. Glamorous girls in revealing bikinis sit sipping cocktails. The entire place is breathtaking, yet it seems to be swallowed up by the scenery... if you weren't watching for it, you'd never know it was there.

As the boat glides through the water, sheer slate rock faces on either side tower above them. Electric-blue agapanthus blooms and lilac buddleias cover the banks where plants are able to grow. Scatterings of heather cling to the rocks, colouring them deep purple. Behind the marina, tall trees and hills hide the entire sight from prying eyes. It blends seamlessly into the landscape, looking like it has been carved directly into the stone.

'Wow,' Lucy whispers. Mylo smiles.

'Something else, huh?'

'It's... amazing.'

Sailors wave as they slow to a stop. An old black Labrador scurries along the pontoon, wagging its tail as Lucy steps from the vehicle. She crouches down to stroke it, and it licks her face excitedly. Mylo cuts the engine and ties off, stepping ashore to join her. The dog limps away.

'You wouldn't expect this to be *here*, would you?'

'It's like something out of a James Bond film, Mylo. I don't think I've ever seen anything like it.'

He smiles again. He's much more handsome when he does. She removes the jacket, tossing it back onboard.

'Come on.'

He trots off down the boardwalk, and she follows behind him. He speaks to various people as they pass. Everyone seems to know him. Mylo is a popular guy.

They climb a ramp at the far end, and head towards the glazed structure. Lucy stops and looks out over the water. It glistens, and as the sunlight hurts her eyes, she thinks she could be absolutely *anywhere* in the world right now.

Mylo carries on walking towards a group of thirty-somethings. Lucy holds back, shy as ever when faced with large groups of strangers.

He greets them, and there is a flourish of hugs and kisses. Three girls, two guys. A curvy brunette in a T-shirt and shorts steps forwards, stroking Mylo's shoulder. A leggy blonde, a little younger than the others, embraces him in a tight hug. He seems happy. An Asian girl waves and smiles.

The guys exchange fist pumps and mock punches.

Mylo says something, and all eyes dart towards Lucy. The blonde, who is facing away from her, turns and stares, then looks back at Mylo. Whatever he is saying, there are no smiles. The Asian girl frowns, her eyes flick towards Lucy, then away.

Mylo turns, beckoning to Lucy. She walks towards the group, fiddling with the sleeves of her blouse.

She holds up her hand, waving nervously. She feels like she is at school; never been good at meeting groups where everyone else knows each other.

'Everyone, this is Lucy.'

A chorus of *hi's* and *hello's* fill the air.

Mylo makes the introductions. Cassie, the leggy blonde. She is the first to step forwards. She's pretty, in a Barbie-doll kind of way. A deep all-over tan suggests she has spent many hours reclining in the sun. She embraces Lucy tightly. One of those *huggy* types. She smells of moisturiser and expensive perfume. Fresh and subtle. Pleasant.

Her tousled, sun-bleached hair has that perfect *I've just been to the beach* wave, that in reality took her an hour to style. A single thin braid is tucked behind her ear. Perfectly manicured nails are painted a fluorescent pink, matching the straps of her bikini, which poke out from beneath an oversized white T-shirt, almost see-through, which hangs loosely off one shoulder.

Lucy imagines she has never worked a day in her life.

The Asian girl who has been hanging back until now, steps forward, introducing herself as Sadiya. She shakes Lucy's hand. Very matter of fact. She is impossibly beautiful, in that natural way that would make some other women uncomfortable. Caramel skin is framed by long, extremely straight black glossy hair. Her eyes are huge, like a Disney princess, lashes thick, curly. Everything about her exudes exotic.

'Lucy, is it?'

She speaks with a very slight accent.

'Hi.'

'Sadiya lived in London for years too,' Mylo offers.

'Whereabouts?' Lucy fidgets.

'Oh all over. Most recently in East. You?'

'Same really. Minus the last bit.'

Molly, the curvy one, waves and says hello. She's plainer than the other two. Lucy wonders if she feels uncomfortable around them or if their friendship transcends that. She has a kind face and seems genuine when she smiles. Her plump skin is pale, almost opaque white.

The guys: Lucas; tall, about six feet of rippling muscle. Handsome, well-dressed and impeccably groomed; probably gay. Red hair sporting far too much gel. Colin; shorter, good-looking, thinning hair, wearing a wedding ring and a cheeky grin. His eyes linger on Lucy's chest for a second too long. They wave, but don't approach. Cautious of this interloper in their group. Another female making them outnumbered.

'To the bar!' Lucas shouts, and they scurry away. Lucy hangs back. Cassie spins round, grabbing her hand.

'Come on! Let's get some shots!'

She skips towards a huge set of sliding doors, dragging Lucy behind her. They spring open as the group approaches. The men, a few steps ahead, line up, surveying an impressive gantry.

'Tequila!' Cassie squeals, holding up seven fingers to the barman.

She winks, and he blushes, as he places a bottle and some shot glasses in front of them, with a plate full of lemon wedges and a saltshaker.

Cassie is the first to grab one. She licks her hand, pouring a little salt onto it, then waits expectantly, watching the others. They follow one by one. Mylo takes his last, leaving them all staring at Lucy.

'I'm really not good with alcohol,' she says pitifully.

'Bull-SHIT! Pick it up now!'

They egg her on, so she reluctantly follows suit.

'One, two, three...' Cassie chants, and they all perform the ritual. Lucy shudders as she sucks her wedge. After two more rounds of slammers, Mylo slinks away to chat to the guys, and Cassie orders a bottle of rosé. She grabs two glasses, dragging Lucy to a small rattan table out on the veranda. The glass wall leading outside has been neatly folded to one end, opening the whole bar up to the decked area. Lucy sits, staring out across the water. White sparkles of sunlight dance around, as her eyes drift towards pale-blue hillsides in the distance.

Some sort of electronic jazz-fusion lift music blares from inside. Handsome men and beautiful women surround them, drinking expensive bottled beer, and goldfish-bowl-sized glasses of gin and tonic.

'It is stunning here. I never knew anything like this existed in Scotland. You wouldn't even realise it was here... it's very well hidden,' Lucy breathes as Cassie pours her a glass of wine.

'Isn't it? That's the idea. It's... exclusive. Very A-list, you know?'

Lucy laughs.

'Really? What are we doing here then?'

'My father owns it,' Cassie says, shrugging nonchalantly. Lucy's eyes bulge a little, as she picks the wine up nervously.

'You'll be fine. You can't come here and not drink! Especially on a day like this.' Cassie glances up to the cloudless sky, grinning.

Sadiya sits at the end of the bar, watching them. Molly is babbling away to her, lots of big hand gestures and laughing, but Lucy gets the distinct impression Sadiya is not listening to her at all. She looks into her eyes. She holds her gaze for a moment longer than is comfortable, before looking away.

'So Mylo seems nice.'

'Oh, he is the sweetest. He can seem aloof, but it's more that he's painfully shy. I met him in London, and we got on like a house on fire.'

Lucy raises an eyebrow.

'No, no. Not like that. Not at *all*. Not my type in the slightest. I like them beefy... More *brawn* than brains. Mylo is definitely the opposite. He and I are just good friends. *Great* friends, in fact.'

Lucy watches him as he messes around with the lads. For the first time since she has met him, his smile seems genuine. He is relaxed... comfortable. It's nice.

'He likes *you*,' she sings, winking.

'Mylo? Shut up. He doesn't even know me.'

She blushes and looks across at him again. He's listening intently to a story Colin is telling. His eyes shift towards the girls, and when he sees Lucy looking back, he glances down at the ground quickly.

'He couldn't stop going on about you last week after he met you. And then when you called him... of course, he's been on cloud nine.'

'I must admit I'm surprised. He hasn't been overly friendly towards me.'

Cassie looks over at her friends, a sad smile creeps onto her face.

'He's a troubled soul. He's not really overly friendly towards anyone these days.'

She bites her lip, staring at her friend.

'He really deserves to be happy.'

Lucy nods.

'He's had a rough couple of years,' Cassie continues, testing the water. She sips her wine, eyeing Lucy over the rim of the glass. She takes a gulp.

'Diana told me that his father had died suddenly, and that's why he moved back here.'

'Yeah. It was terrible. He had a great life in London, but he came home for his mother. He's... loyal like that. He feels so guilty that he wasn't around. He hadn't been back for some time before his dad passed away. He's struggled with that.'

Lucy lets out a slow breath, thinking about how hard it must be for him.

'But it's not only that. I take it he hasn't told you?'

Lucy shifts in her chair, crossing her legs.

'Told me what? Diana hinted at something earlier but wouldn't say anything. I got the impression she was teasing me. Point scoring almost.'

Cassie makes a dramatic show of tutting and rolling her eyes.

'That fucking woman... she takes advantage of him. She has him mowing the lawn and doing all sorts of things around the house for her. I think it's because she fancies him. Dirty old cow.'

Lucy laughs.

'No. Seriously. He hasn't told you about Rose?'

'No. Who is Rose?'

Lucy feels a bead of sweat form on her brow, as her mind flashes back to the driver's licence she found under her bed.

'Rose was... well, she did your job before you.'

Lucy raises both eyebrows as she downs the contents of her glass. Cassie refills it and continues.

'But she was also Mylo's soulmate.'

'Oh right.' Lucy shifts awkwardly in her seat, looking out across the water.

'That's so odd. Diana implied I was the first helper she'd had.'

Cassie frowns.

'Not at all. Rose was with her for a few years.'

'Can I just ask... what was her surname?'

'McNulty. Why?'

Lucy leans forwards in her chair.

'I found her driving licence in my room, but when I asked Diana about it, she said it must have belonged to the previous owner. Told me to throw it away. That is *so* weird! Why would she do that?'

'That woman *is* weird. Full stop. Between you and me, Rose absolutely hated living there. It creeped her out. Hated being out in the sticks, all alone. No wifi, no phone signal. It's like the dark ages!'

There's silence as both girls drink some more wine.

'So what happened?'

'It was terrible. Honestly... I still can't believe it.' Cassie leaves a perfectly timed dramatic pause, watching Lucy like a hawk.

'She died.'

26

Lucy stares at her, eyes agog.

'Yeah, it was so... sad. Tragic.'

She dabs at the corner of her eye to emphasise the point.

'How?'

'She fell down the stairs. Banged her head at the bottom and bled out.'

The stain on the floorboards flashes into Lucy's mind. She thinks of Mylo's face when she was telling him the man was there to sand it away. Her eyes drift towards him, and she bites her bottom lip.

'That's... awful.'

'Oh, it was. Poor Mylo was beside himself. Heartbroken. They were engaged, you see. They had literally just announced it that day. She'd had a few drinks here with us all and then he dropped her home. She had to go back to see to *Richard.*' Disdain creeps into Cassie's voice.

'I know you shouldn't listen to local gossip, but I hear she lay there all night in a pool of her own blood. Diana was too fucked up on drink and pills to wake up and didn't find her until the next morning.'

Cassie's eyes follow Lucy's and they both stare sadly at Mylo for a moment.

'She might have survived... you know, if... if that stupid cow had found her sooner.'

Cassie begins to sob. Lucy reaches across the table, stroking her arm, her eyes on Mylo the entire time.

Now and then, his eyes dart towards her, and he looks away, guiltily. Caught out.

Cassie leans away, wiping tears from her eyes.

'I'm sorry. Please don't tell Mylo I got upset.'

'I think he saw.'

Cassie shakes her head.

'Shit. It's difficult... the circumstances were odd. He was looking for someone to blame... you do, don't you, when something like that happens. But he was adamant that Diana had something to do with it. I mean, I don't particularly like the woman, but that... I don't think so. Rose was pretty wasted that night... it was just a very sad accident.'

'Why would he think that Diana had anything to do with it?'

'Let's just say that Diana and Rose didn't have the best relationship.'

Mylo glances up from his conversation once more, and without warning, breaks away from the group, sauntering over to join them. They go quiet as he approaches.

'Don't let me stop you. What are you ladies gassing about?'

They both shoot each other a nervous glance. Cassie grabs her wine.

'Girl stuff,' she shouts, draining her glass.

Two empty bottles sit on the table. Cassie pouts.

'Shall we swim?'

Mylo looks at Lucy.

'You want to?'

She bites her lip, looking away.

'We don't have to.'

'I didn't bring a bathing suit.'

'I have tons!' Cassie offers.

'I'm not really a swimmer.'

'We can just pose!'

'No, I'm good. You guys go though.'

'Your loss.' Cassie runs off towards the other women.

Mylo sits down in her chair.

'You can go if you want to,' Lucy says. 'I'll go for a walk or something.'

'It's fine. I can live without it.'

Lucy is looking out to the edge of the basin, across the water. She glances at Mylo, opening her mouth as if to speak, but then thinks better of it.

'What?' he says, a worried expression on his face.

'Nothing. It doesn't matter.'

He looks away. A wave of guilt floods over Lucy. She's sure he must know what they've been discussing.

'Shall we head?' he says without looking at her.

'Yeah, maybe. Shouldn't we wait for the others?'

'They'll be fine. Probably be drinking champagne in there for hours now.'

They stand and stroll down the gangway towards the boat.

She doesn't know if she should mention Rose. What *would* she say? She feels she needs to acknowledge it, but it's awkward. She decides to wait and see if he brings it up.

She climbs on board, and he jumps on behind her.

27

DIANA

The smell of varnish fills the house, causing Diana to feel
nauseous, so she sits in the garden. Her leg has been
throbbing today. She's popped so many pills, but the pain is still
making its way through the fug. She's onto her fourth bottle of
wine. She hasn't felt right for a few days now, so she figures she
may as well drink. *Why the hell not?*

She rubs at a small bruise on her arm. Three little red dots
next to it, itch like hell. Something has feasted on her overnight.

Richard is in his chair beside her. The workman instructed
her to keep off the floor until the evening. She checks her watch.
It's not long after three. She glances at her husband,
remembering that she hasn't given him lunch. Lucy told her she
had made some soup up, and it's in the fridge, so she stands,
swaying, heading into the kitchen. It's not until she is out of her
seat that she realises quite how drunk she is.

The smell is stronger indoors. She pulls her sweater up over
her nose, rooting around in the refrigerator. Frowning, she
pushes polythene bags filled with leaves and berries aside,
rummaging in a shelf. She finds the brown slop in a Tupperware
container. As she removes the lid, the stink hits her. She holds

her hand to her mouth, swallowing down bile, and pours the soup into a saucepan. It drips, lumpy and cold, slapping onto the metal, making Diana want to vomit again.

Slamming the pan onto the stove, she lights the gas, and turns the burner up to full. As it begins to warm through, she takes a bottle of vodka from a cupboard. Pouring herself two fingers into a tumbler, she knocks it back, repeating the process. She wobbles over to the door out to the hall, staring at the floorboards. The stain is gone. Not a trace left. She can't see the floor too clearly right now anyway, her vision is a mess. The booze has seen to that.

Wet varnish glistens in the light that streams through from the kitchen. She smiles, returning to the soup. It is bubbling ferociously already. She takes a wooden spoon from a drawer, giving the food a quick stir, before transferring it into a bowl. She carries it in her good hand, out to her husband. As she reaches him, she realises she has forgotten cutlery. She looks over her shoulder towards the house with weary eyes. She can't face the journey again. Every time she moves, it's as if she's floating on water. Bobbing up and down on turbulent waves. Now and then she feels like she is spinning round, as an anchored boat on a chain does, swinging to the direction of the wind. It's a very disconcerting feeling when standing on dry land. Then there is the headache. And the pain in her limbs, her leg in particular. And the constant nauseated state.

She decides to pour it from the bowl. It's not worth struggling back for a spoon. He probably won't even eat it anyway. She blows on the soup, trying to cool it, dipping her fingertip into the middle. It's hot, so she waits a while for the temperature to drop. When she's satisfied that it won't scald him, she raises it up to his mouth. Sticking a finger between his lips, she forces them open. He groans.

She's not sure if she's imagined it at first.

'Open wide, Richard, it's time for lunch. Late today. Your *girl* is out gallivanting with Mylo. Didn't take her long! Not long at all. No.'

His teeth are clamped tight together like a vice. She wriggles her finger against them, trying to worm her way through. She latches on to a small gap, prizing them apart, and tips the bowl. The gloop trickles into his mouth and over his chin. A gurgling noise comes from his throat. Diana frowns, but continues to pour the soup in.

Suddenly his hand flies up, grabbing her wrist.

She tumbles backwards, dropping the food. The contents splash down his front. She lands in a heap at his feet. Dazed, she rolls clumsily over onto her knees, pushing herself up, resting her elbows on his lap.

She stays there for a moment, trying to regain her composure. She takes a few deep breaths. Her heart pounds. She stares up into her husband's face. His eyes are fixed directly ahead, out over the loch. She raises a hand up in front of him, waving it.

Nothing. Not even a flicker.

'Richard?' she whispers.

Silence. Only the sound of his laboured breathing. She glances around. Her stick has rolled away a metre or so. She crawls to retrieve it, pulling herself up on a garden chair. She sits for a while, panting, calming herself. In all the years since the accident, Richard has *never* moved. Never this much anyway. There's been the odd twitch of a finger, or a toe. But nothing as dramatic as this.

A spasm? A reflex? Perhaps the soup was too hot and triggered a reaction? Who knows?

But she didn't like it.

She looks him up and down. The brown gloop is seeping into his clean white shirt.

'Damn,' she hisses.

Standing, she limps back towards the house, making her way through the kitchen, and into Richard's room. She opens his wardrobe. A row of empty hangers dangle on the rail. Everything swirls around her as the vodka takes effect. She can't focus on anything. Her head bobs, her body sways. She flutters her eyelids, trying to see straight.

Cursing, she stumbles out into the hall, edging her way along the perimeter. The floor is tacky, but not too bad. She enters her room. It is hot, sticky. The air is heavy. Flies buzz around the window. She swats them away; can't remember the last time she opened it.

Rummaging in her wardrobe, she pushes her dresses aside. A few of Richard's crumpled shirts still hang at one end. She grabs a pink-and-white candy stripe with a granddad collar, smiling as she thinks of when she last saw him in it. She tends to dress him in white now. It doesn't show the creases so much. She takes the garment and drapes it over her shoulder. Clicking the wardrobe door shut, she turns to go. Something in the corner of her eye makes her stop. She spins towards her bed.

There's an object on her pillow. Small and rectangular. She crosses the room as quickly as possible in her current state. As she reaches the bed, she lets herself collapse into a sitting position before she ends up on the floor. She swivels herself around, picking up the driver's licence that is lying there. Her eyes swim in and out of focus. She can barely read it, but it's definitely Rose's. Her vision remains clear long enough to be certain of that.

The very same item that she saw Lucy toss into the waste bin last night.

She lets out a gasp. Rose's piercing blue eyes stare mockingly back at her. Her smile, broad as ever. Fake. Like her. Everything about her.

'Fuck you, Rose! What do you want from me? Why are you doing this?' Diana shrieks. She drops her face into her hands and begins to sob uncontrollably.

'Leave me alone. Please! Haven't you done enough? I'm sorry, okay? Is that what you want? I am sorry,' she whispers, rocking back and forth.

She stands, wiping her hand across her eyes. Sliding the licence into her pocket, she heads out to her husband in the garden.

28

The boat is skipping across the rippling surface of the loch, quickly, purposefully. Mylo stands at the helm. Now and then, he glances towards Lucy and grins. She smiles back.

She grabs the fleece she wore earlier, draping it over her shoulders.

'Come here,' Mylo beckons. She sidles up to him, and he places an arm around her. She cuddles into the warmth of his body. He smells like aftershave. Manly, fresh, and clean. She inhales deeply through her nostrils with her eyes closed. His scent is fantastic. She slides her arm round his waist, opening her eyes and looking up towards him. His head is fixed forwards, scanning the water.

She tries to imagine what is going through his mind. Is he thinking about Rose? Everything here must remind him of her. Especially coming to Willow Cottage, the place where he ultimately lost her.

He looks down at her briefly. Thick white clouds are forming around them. It seems to have rolled in from nowhere.

'This fog is so weird!' Lucy says.

'It can come and go very quickly here with the changing

temperatures. It's quite a thing to behold if you've never seen it before.'

A cool breeze blows across them, making Lucy shiver. He pulls her in tighter to him.

'Won't be long,' he says. And she can't remember the last time she felt this at ease.

29

DIANA

Richard is right where she left him. She's not sure what else she expected. She's disappointed. Part of her wants him to return. Be with her again. Talk to her. She misses their discussions.

But then she remembers and thinks perhaps it's better this way.

She pulls the shirt from over her shoulder, draping it on the rear of his wheelchair. She unbuttons the one he is wearing, untucking it from the waistband of his chinos, pulling him forwards slightly to slide it from his body. She pushes him back in the chair, exhausted. As she looks down at him, she sees a collection of purple bruises; small, finger-shaped, over his upper arms. Larger welts cover his chest and abdomen. Dark and brooding.

'Richard... what the hell... how has this happened?'

She stares at the marks, and her eyes sting. Moisture trickles down her cheek from her good eye.

She grasps the sides of his head in her hands.

'My darling, I am so sorry!' she slurs.

Pulling him towards her, she sobs into his shoulder. She dresses him, smoothing down the front of his fresh shirt.

'There. All better.'

She wipes the tears from her eyes. Glancing back to the house she swears she sees a figure standing in the kitchen window. Blinking a few times, she screws her lids shut tightly. When she opens them again, she realises it's just a reflection of a tree in the glass. She laughs to herself but decides to remain in the garden for a while longer. As she looks out over the loch, a thick fog is beginning to creep in across the surface of the water.

She's so drunk, the world is a blur by now.

'I think there's a storm coming, Richard,' she says, as they both stare out over the landscape.

30

She stands at her window gazing out, but all she can see is white. Returning to her bed, she lays back, with her arms above her head, staring at the ceiling. She can't remember the last time she was drunk. As the pleasant sensation from the wine washes over her, she feels... happy. Dare she even think it? She'd seen a different side of Mylo today. More human. His odd behaviour around Diana now makes more sense, after Cassie's revelations about his suspicions over Rose's death.

She even understands his coolness when Diana introduced him to her the other day. It must have been a shock. A new girl, in his fiancée's home.

Having changed into a pair of baggy jogging bottoms and a rugby jersey, she is about to settle with a book, when Diana calls her name from downstairs. She leaves her room, heading down to see her.

As she reaches the bottom, she sees that Diana has replaced the runner in the hall. Her gaze drifts to where the stain used to be, the boards now clean.

Diana is in the kitchen, staring out into the fog, swaying at the window.

'This weather is mad, isn't it? I've never seen anything like it,' Lucy says cheerfully as she enters.

Diana turns towards her, does not respond. Simply stares at her.

'I'm going to... ask... you something. I... don't... want any lies.'

Her speech is odd. Slurring, she pauses between words, as if she is struggling to form a sentence. She's drunk.

Extremely drunk.

The corners of her mouth are turned down, eyes stern and piercing, yet they fail to settle on Lucy's face. The lids droop, fluttering from time to time.

Lucy frowns, tilting her head to one side, glancing at the six empty wine bottles standing beside a bin bag.

'I'd like to know how... my... husband has come to be... covered in bruises... whilst in your care.'

'Excuse me?'

'Bruises! Everywhere. He looks like he's been... beaten.' Her voice wobbles towards the end.

'I'm sorry, Diana, I have no idea what you're talking about.'

'My husband, whom *you* have been looking after... *apparently*, is badly bruised. And you know nothing about it? You haven't noticed when you have been changing him?'

Lucy folds her arms across her chest.

'When I dressed him this morning he was fine, I can assure you. Let's have a look...' She turns to head to Richard's room. Diana laughs humourlessly.

'Don't bother. I'm telling you, he is bruised. And these aren't new. Some of them look days old. They're yellowing. You're telling me they just appeared through the course of today?'

Lucy takes a few steps towards Diana.

'Are you accusing me of something, Mrs Davenport?'

Diana backs away, wobbling.

'We can call the police if you think I'm... *guilty* of a crime. Abuse? Or neglect? You can explain to them that *you* have found bruises on your husband's body, while he has been in *your* care. While you have been drinking... a hell of a lot, from the looks of it. Just how many bottles of wine *have* you polished off today? I haven't been here all day. And I will tell them what I have told you. The last time I dressed him he was totally fine.'

Lucy takes another step forward. Diana stumbles as she shrinks away, catching herself on the edge of the worktop. Lucy pulls her mobile from her pocket. As she leans closer, she can smell the alcohol permeating through every pore of the woman.

'Here, you can even use my phone... if you can get any reception.'

She thrusts the device towards Diana's face.

'Well?'

Diana looks away.

'No. Didn't think so.'

Lucy turns to leave, sliding the mobile back into her tracksuit pants. As she walks away, she hears Diana's stick clattering across the tiles behind her. Something hits the back of her head, landing by her feet. She stares at it.

'What's this?' she says wearily.

'You tell me.'

'I don't understand.'

Diana limps towards her.

'Did you leave this?'

Lucy bends, picking up the photo card.

'What do you mean? Did I leave it where?'

'On my bed!'

'No. I threw it in the bin. Like *you* told me to. You saw me.'

'I know. But after that. Did you take it out and put it on my pillow?'

Lucy actually laughs. She can't help herself.

'Of course I didn't. Why would I do that? You're not making any sense.'

'Somebody did.'

'You're drunk and delusional. Accusing me of things you've imagined. I don't deserve to be treated like this. I've done nothing wrong. If there are bruises, you probably did it to him yourself!'

Lucy turns, striding down the hallway to the stairs, tears prickling at her eyes.

'I don't have to stand here and listen to this,' she shouts as she heads up.

She hears Diana hobbling after her.

'Don't you dare walk away from me! We're not done here!' she bellows.

Lucy spins around to face her.

'Yes. Yes we are.'

Diana places a foot on the bottom step.

'Please remember, I *choose* not to go upstairs. It doesn't mean that I *can't*. Don't think for one second that I won't come up there after you if I have to.'

'And what? Push me down them?' she spits. She regrets the words as soon as she's said them, but it's too late.

The colour drains from Diana's face. She sways back and forth.

'Wh... what did you... say?'

For a moment Lucy considers walking away, leaving it. Diana is her employer after all. But the wine, and the tequila, fill her with a false sense of bravado, and she can't let it drop.

'Mylo's friend filled me in on your history. I know everything. And I know who *that* belongs to.'

She tosses the licence at Diana. It hits her forehead and falls to the floor.

'Just leave me alone. I'm going to bed.'

She turns and continues up, leaving Diana standing open-mouthed in the hall.

She slams the bedroom door behind her. Leaning her back against it, she grasps her head in both hands as tears begin to flow down her cheeks. Shaking her head, she crosses the room, cursing under her breath as remorse creeps through her like a forest fire taking hold.

But the damage is very much done, she fears, as she throws herself onto the mattress.

She'll have to deal with the consequences in the morning. When she's sober.

And before long, she passes out.

31

LUCY

The harsh morning light streams in through gaps in the curtains, and Lucy rolls over, fully clothed, on top of her duvet, burying her face deep into the down of the pillow. Her head pounds.

This is why I don't drink, she thinks, cringing, as the previous evening's argument floods into her thoughts. She sees flashes of the showdown. The driving licence. The empty wine bottles.

Diana's glare.

'Oh God,' she whispers, and for a moment thinks she might be sick. If she still has a job this morning, it will be a miracle. She showers quickly, water hot, trying to wash away the dirty feeling she has.

She hates confrontation; avoids it at all costs, usually. The wine and tequila played their part in her behaviour, she knows that. She will have to apologise, explain to Diana that she had too much to drink. And hope for the best. That's all she can do. Surely *she* of all people should understand that.

As she makes her way downstairs, she hears Diana in the kitchen, humming a jaunty melody. She frowns, pausing at the bottom. The smell of fresh coffee fills her nostrils. Continuing into the kitchen, she sees that the room has been tidied and cleaned. The wine bottles cleared away. Sink emptied.

Diana turns to her.

'Good morning.'

Her voice is hoarse. Her usual neat braid is abandoned today, her hair falls loose, unruly, making her look every bit the madwoman. She's wearing the same clothes she had on yesterday. Coloured streaks of paint and food stains smeared down the front. Lucy can't help but sniff at the air. God only knows the last time this woman showered.

'Diana, about last night...'

'Did I see you? Please forgive me if I said anything embarrassing...'

Lucy tilts her head, narrowing her eyes.

'Too much wine. It was such a beautiful day, and I have been working on a new painting. I got carried away. I apologise if I was a little boisterous. Did I sing? Oh God, please, tell me I didn't sing!'

Lucy sits down in an old, high-backed wooden chair, eyeing Diana suspiciously.

'You... don't remember talking to me last night at all?'

'No... I'm ashamed to admit I don't remember anything at all, if I'm entirely honest. I recall the man finishing the floor and telling me to try to keep from walking on it... after that... it's a blank.'

She squints, as if she is trying to piece things together, shaking her head.

Lucy lets out a long breath. Her shoulders relax, and she forces a smile.

'Not to worry. It was nothing important. We've all been there.' She looks away quickly, hoping Diana won't see the guilty look on her face, or the colour in her cheeks.

Diana turns, staring out through the window, fiddling with a thick strand of hair, winding it between her fingers. Lucy stands from the chair, scraping it across the tiles. She watches the woman for a few minutes; she seems completely oblivious.

'I'm going to get Richard up,' she says.

'Okay, dear.'

Lucy walks casually from the kitchen, feeling relieved, yet troubled at the same time. Richard is in his bed, eyes wide open. Pulling back the covers, she uses the hoist to lift him into his chair and wheels him into the bathroom. She unbuttons his pyjamas, tossing them into a pile. Diana was not exaggerating. The bruises are immense. Lucy traces her fingers across one on his shoulder, chewing at the inside of the corner of her mouth. After washing him down thoroughly with a sponge, she crosses to the cabinet. Searching through various empty pill bottles, lotions, and potions, she finds what she was looking for. She knew she had seen it last week when she had been cleaning. She takes the bottle of arnica gel, returning to Richard. She squirts a little into her hands and after rubbing it between her palms, massages it into his skin.

'My grandmother was really into her homeopathy,' she tells him softly. 'This should help. Though from the looks of these, it may be too late.'

Wheeling him back to his bedroom, she fishes around in the wardrobe, but there are no clean shirts, so she dresses him in yesterday's. It still smells fresh. A pair of navy chinos hang on the rail, and she slides them onto his legs, tucking the shirt in neatly. She slips some brown loafers onto his feet, then lifts them onto the footrests of his wheelchair. She takes a comb and a tub of Brylcreem from his dresser, and neatens his hair, slicking it into a side parting.

Wheeling him to his usual spot in front of the window, she positions him staring out to the loch, smiling sadly. She strokes his shoulder as a family of swallows dart around outside, skimming the surface of the water playfully.

Backing away, she hovers in the doorway for a moment, watching. The little finger of his right hand twitches up and down on its armrest. Lucy cocks her head, frowning, and closes the door.

32

DIANA

Staring at a blank canvas, Diana throws her paintbrush down onto the floor of her studio. It clatters across the ground. The new piece is leaning against a wall opposite her. Her eyes drift to it now and then. It stares straight back at her, screaming. She even thinks she can hear it.

A long, anguished drawn-out wail.

The voice is Lucy's. Or maybe it's Claire's. She can't tell anymore. She blinks it away, shaking her head vigorously. The place is silent again.

Each time she attempts to make a mark on the surface of the canvas her hand shakes uncontrollably. The room is swirling around her. Spinning manically, making her want to spew up her guts. She knows she is hungover. She drank far too much yesterday; threw out six empty bottles this morning before Lucy was awake. And the vodka had gone down substantially too. Even for her, that's a lot. She hopes to God Lucy hadn't noticed them.

But this is more than a hangover. Different. Worse.

She can't seem to form clear thoughts. Can't concentrate.

Her mind runs away at tangents mid-thought. Is this what it feels like to be going mad, she wonders?

She closes her eyes, trying not to think of her mother at her worst as she scratches at the bites on her arm. They are driving her insane. A new one has appeared overnight. As her nail rubs over the red blotch, a tiny drop of blood appears on the surface. She wipes it with her hand. Her nails have left angry-looking tracks on her skin.

The creativity is completely gone from her. Each time she tries to paint, she draws a blank. She glances back towards the portrait. Hopefully, Valentina will be able to sell this one for a nice sum.

She picks up the brush from where it landed, stabbing it into her palette, loading it with thick globules of colour. Raising it up, her hand hovers in front of the canvas, as she looks it up and down, wondering where to make the first mark.

She swings her arm over the surface. It glides across, leaving a rough smear of black from the bottom corner to the top, opposite. Instead of a smooth arc, she's practically painted a zigzag.

She curses, slamming the tool down again. Standing, she grabs one edge of the canvas, pulling it from her easel. It clatters to the floor as she hobbles away.

She reaches the door, pausing, hand gripping the knob. Holding her breath, she gently pulls it open, afraid to look outside. There's nothing there. No stack of stones. No ghostly figure.

Relieved, she steps into the garden, crossing to the kitchen. As she enters the cottage, she hears a knock at the front door.

'I'll get it!' Lucy calls from her room. Diana hears her skip down the stairs. She waits in the entrance to the hall as Lucy answers. Diana's view is blocked, but she knows the voice immediately.

Confused, she steps forwards, steadying herself on the wall.

'Val, what on earth are you doing here? Did we have an appointment?' Hearing herself, she is surprised at how slurred her words are. Lucy moves aside, and Valentina Moretti glides inside the cottage.

She sees the bemused expression on Diana's face and sighs.

'I called at the weekend and spoke to your girl here. Told her I was swinging by today to see what you're working on. You've been quiet of late. I was... concerned.'

She looks Diana up and down, grimacing. Diana glances down at herself. Her usually well-groomed hair is loose and wild, flying off in every direction. Her sweater, black as always since the accident, is filthy. She has paint all over her clothes, face and hands.

'You look like shit,' her friend says, deadpan. 'I hope the work is better.'

'Why didn't you tell me Valentina was coming?' Diana hisses at Lucy. The girl appears confused.

'I *did*,' she says defensively.

Diana moves forwards.

'No... no, you didn't. I'm certain. I would remember. You *never* mentioned anything about Val coming.'

Lucy's face crumples, she looks as if she might cry.

'I swear I did. Don't you remember? We were standing in the kitchen, I told you as soon as I hung up the phone, because I knew it was important.'

Diana squints, holding her hand to her temple. She shakes her head. But her eyes flicker as she tries to remember if what Lucy is saying is true.

'Heavens...' she says to nobody in particular. 'Is it Thursday already?' She fiddles with her hair, noticing Valentina shoot Lucy a look.

'Oh well, no bother. I'm here now.' Valentina says matter-of-factly. 'Diana,' she continues, 'why don't you go and take a seat in the lounge? I'll be right there.'

Diana hovers for a moment. Her friend motions towards the doorway, and she obediently goes in. Valentina pushes the door shut behind her, but Diana lingers at the threshold, and holding her breath, leans her ear against the door so she can hear.

'I'm so sorry. I promise you I gave her your message,' Lucy says, her voice wavering on the edge of tears. 'She even wrote it down somewhere. I'll try to find it if you want?'

'It's fine. I'm sure it was simply a misunderstanding.'

Diana hears footsteps, as if they are moving away from the door. She cranes her neck, pulling the door open a crack.

'Is she okay?'

'I don't know. She's been behaving erratically. I'm a bit worried.'

'How so?'

'Forgetful. Not just this. We had an argument last night, nothing major, too much alcohol involved on both sides... but today she has absolutely no recollection of it.'

Diana's cheeks flush as she hears the words. It's been a while since she was so drunk she lost a whole evening. But the revelation there had been an argument sheds some light on the girl's behaviour earlier. Diana thought she had been sheepish. Now it makes sense.

'I can't quite put my finger on it,' Lucy continues, 'but her behaviour has definitely become odder over the last few days. She's been... drinking an awful lot too.'

'Nothing new there.'

Diana hears her friend tapping her stiletto on the hall floorboards.

'Leave it with me. I'll get her sorted. I'm sure a shower and some clean clothes would help.'

She hears Lucy heading up the stairs and moves away from

the door as quickly as she can. She perches herself on the settee just as Valentina enters the lounge. She tries to hide the panic from her face. Tries to keep her voice level. But inside she feels furious about Lucy's words to her friend. Making out like she's mad. Or an alcoholic. Or worse still... both.

'Val, I'm so glad you're here.'

Valentina sits beside her on the couch, crossing her legs.

'What's going on with you?'

'I've... not been feeling well. I can't explain it, but I just don't feel myself.'

'How much did you drink last night?'

'What's that got to do with anything?'

Valentina stands, moving to the window, staring out at her car. She turns to face Diana.

'We are friends, Diana, we have been for a long time. So I'm going to be honest with you. You look like hell. You reek of alcohol, and your clothes are... filthy. This is not the Diana Davenport that I know.' She strides back to the sofa, looking down at her friend.

'You need to pull yourself together. God knows what that poor girl upstairs must think of you.'

Diana shakes her head, giving a small laugh.

'I'm trying... but things feel so odd right now. It's like there's a cloud hanging over me... I can't explain it, but I can't shake it. I'm struggling to sleep... even with my pills. I'm a zombie during the day, I can't eat, I feel nauseous *all* the time.'

'Then speak to your doctor. You don't need me to tell you how important it is that you look after your mental health.'

Diana holds her hands up in surrender.

'I know, I know.'

Valentina sits again.

'And on a professional note, I need you to be producing work. If you don't earn money, I don't earn money. And then we have a problem. The one small blessing is that you are covered in paint, which I suppose means at least that you've actually been painting.'

Diana stands.

'Oh I have. Well, I've done *something* at least. It's only one painting so far, but it's... new. I think you'll like it. I'm quite sure it will sell.'

'Great. Can I see it?'

'It's not finished, but I can show you what I've done.'

She picks up her stick and walks towards the kitchen. Valentina follows behind. They cross to the back, exiting to the garden. Approaching the studio, she notices the door is wide open. She can't remember shutting it earlier, but she is usually so methodical about keeping it locked. She mutters to herself as she approaches. Valentina watches, narrowing her eyes, but says nothing.

As they step inside, Diana appears agitated. She begins to sway.

'No... no! What have you done?' she screams. She drops her stick, limping towards a huge canvas which is sat on her easel. Valentina lingers in the doorway, her eyes drift to the painting.

'Is this supposed to be funny?' she says.

'This wasn't me. I swear to you. Somebody has been in here.'

She steps closer to her easel. Whatever the picture *was* has been obliterated. An empty can of red emulsion lies at the foot of the easel, spilling the remnants of its contents onto the concrete.

The rest is splattered all over the canvas.

Huge scarlet splodges and drips run down the front. Small areas of whatever was underneath show through. An eye? The corner of a mouth. But the vast majority of the canvas is a mass of red.

The paint is still wet, and as it runs to the bottom edge, it drips messily onto the floor.

Like blood.

'Val, someone has done this. Lucy!' she screams, spittle bubbling at the corners of her mouth.

She whirls, barging past her friend. She moves as fast as Valentina has seen her go in a long time, heading towards the house.

'Lucy, get down here!' she shouts as she enters the kitchen.

The sound of footsteps padding down the stairs, and the girl is standing in the doorway.

'Why have you done that to my painting? I told you *never* to go into my studio… let alone… touch my work!'

Valentina steps closer to her friend, placing a hand on her arm. She eyes Lucy, who stands in the entrance, looking afraid.

'I haven't been in your studio. I would never–'

'Liar! Why would you do that?'

Tears well up in the girl's eyes, and as Diana hobbles towards her, she backs away into the hallway.

Valentina grabs her friend's shoulder.

'Diana, please try to calm down. If she says she didn't do it…'

'But she must have! Because… well, can't you see… she simply must have!'

'I promise you, Diana, I haven't set foot in there since I arrived.'

Valentina eases Diana into a chair, moving towards Lucy. She looks her up and down.

'Diana… I don't think it was her. Look at her. There's no paint on her. There's no way she could have done… *that* without getting a spot on herself. Her hands are clean.'

She pulls Lucy's palms in the air. The poor girl is trembling.

'And besides, we were in the lounge the whole time. We would have heard her coming down.'

Diana stares, aghast, at Lucy's palms. She shakes her head.

'I suspected that she might be here… but I never… I couldn't believe it. But… I think she's here. She's trying to get me. She must have done this.'

Valentina crouches beside the chair, taking Diana's shaking hands in her own.

'Who? Who do you think has done this?'

She looks up, eyes wide and wild.

'It's Rose, of course. Who else?'

33

It took a while to calm Diana. She's now in her room having a lie down. Valentina closes the door, stepping into the hall, where Lucy is lingering nervously.

'She's sleeping. I must apologise for that.'

'No, no, it's fine. I'm worried about her, that's all. I'm okay though.'

Valentina looks back towards Diana's bedroom, shaking her head. She leads Lucy into the kitchen.

'I've never seen her like this. She's... terrified.'

Lucy leans against the worktop, running her hands through her hair.

'That's as bad as it's been. She's been a little scatty up until now. This is a whole other level. But if someone has destroyed her painting, then I suppose it's understandable.'

Valentina bites the inside of her cheek. Her eyes linger on Lucy's.

'But did they?'

Lucy cocks her head questioningly.

'I mean... *did* anyone do that? She had red paint on her

137

clothes. I clocked it when I walked in. I remember thinking how odd it was because she usually takes more pride in her appearance.'

'You can't be suggesting she did that herself? Why would she?'

'I don't know. It's... strange. But what other explanation is there?'

Lucy fidgets with the hem of her sweater.

'What she was saying about Rose...'

Valentina sighs.

'Do you know who Rose is?'

'Yes.'

'Then you'll also know she is dead. And as much as I have an open mind about most things, I don't think the ghost of her former nursemaid has broken into her studio and thrown a can of paint over her canvas.'

Valentina stands, arms folded, tapping her foot on the tiled floor.

'No, I think there is probably a much simpler explanation than ghosts and ghouls.'

She glances at an expensive-looking gold watch on her wrist.

'I need to shoot, else I'll miss the ferry. Will you be okay?'

'Of course. I've dealt with far worse. I'll keep an eye on her.'

Valentina pulls a business card from her purse, handing it to Lucy. It's thick, and soft to the touch, with gold foiling embossed on the letters.

'If anything else happens, or you need to talk, call me.'

'Sure.'

She smiles, placing a hand on Lucy's shoulder, giving it a gentle squeeze.

'She's lucky to have you. Most people would have packed their bags and run a mile after that little performance.'

Lucy shakes her head.

'I'm sure she'll feel better after some sleep.'

She shows Valentina out, waving as her red sports car pulls away, crunching over gravel.

Closing the door, she retreats to the kitchen to prepare lunch.

34

DIANA

She wakes in the early evening, head pounding. The cluster of bites on her arm has grown again. She scratches at them manically. There must be something living in her bedroom. She'll need to get Mylo to bring some bug spray.

They're so itchy... she wants to gouge her flesh away with her nails.

Sitting up on the bed, she looks around for her stick. It's nowhere to be seen. She leans over the edge of the bed, but it's not underneath. She tries to stand. Her legs feel like jelly; she can't focus.

Easing herself around the wall, manoeuvring past furniture, she reaches the door. The urge to puke wells up inside her, but she holds it down. Just. The smell of varnish still lingers in the air. She glances at the floor. To be sure. She can't really see clearly, but she can tell the boards are clean. Leaning her weight on the wall, she makes her way to the kitchen.

Her stick lies on the worktop. Shaking her head, she limps towards it, grasping the edges to stop herself from falling, letting out a long breath. As she turns to head back to the living room, she sees a handwritten note on the opposite countertop. She hobbles over, picking it up.

Diana,
I hope you are feeling a little better.
I have seen to Richard. He has had his lunch and dinner. If you are hungry, there is some food plated up in the fridge for you. I didn't want to wake you.
Gone to Mylo's for the evening, I'll be back around eleven to put R. to bed.
Lucy x

She crumples the note, letting it fall to the floor. She's still angry about the conversation she overheard with Val. It feels like a betrayal. And the girl was exaggerating. There's nothing wrong with her.

Opening the fridge, the smell of food assaults her, taking her by surprise. She slams the door shut, only making it to the sink in time, as a stream of bile spews from her. The foul taste sickens her more. Turning on the tap, she rinses the vile, stinking green spatter away, filling her mouth to rid herself of the remnants. She blinks, looking at the clock. She can't make it out. Steps closer.

Nine fifteen.

Food is the last thing on her mind. She needs air. She pushes open the back door, stepping out onto the grass, inhaling deeply. The fresh scent is pleasant enough but does little to alleviate her nauseated state. As she passes her studio, the door now firmly closed, she pictures her ruined canvas.

The red. The drips.

She shakes her head, blinking the vision away, continuing down to the beach. Her feet drag through the shingle, leaving a trail in the stones. She heads towards the water, and sits on the edge of the pier, looking out across the loch.

35

'Thanks again for picking me up. I really needed to get away from that house for a bit,' Lucy says flatly, staring out over the water.

They are sitting at a table outside the back of Mylo's shop. An empty wine bottle between them, and two clean plates. He lives on the adjacent side of the loch to Willow Cottage, further along the shore. She can't quite see the cottage, but she knows it's there. She reflects how funny it seems that when she arrived, she couldn't get over how tranquil it all was, yet now it fills her with dread to think about it. His boat is moored to a short jetty. A small inflatable dinghy with an outboard motor attached bobs up and down beside it. It was this that he had collected her in earlier after she phoned him. It was quicker than the motorboat, he told her, and cheaper to run.

An enormous hydrangea behind them colours the scenery pink and acid blue. The sweet scent of jasmine fills the air. She inhales deeply and feels her heart rate begin to slow. As if simply being away from Diana, and that place, is making her feel better already.

Mylo watches her from across the table.

'No problem. So what happened?'

She pulls at a strand of her hair, twisting it in her fingers.

'Diana... being Diana.'

'Say no more.'

Lucy scratches at her skin on her ankles, through her jeans.

'I think something has been feeding on me,' she says.

'Midges. They're all over the west coast. Annoying little buggers. Have you been sleeping with the window open?'

She nods, raising an eyebrow.

'That'll do it. You don't want to do that round here, not so close to the water.'

'But it's so damned hot some nights. Stifling. I can't sleep otherwise.'

'Get a fan. Or put up with being eaten alive.'

She smirks, not fancying either option, and watches a swallow chasing a butterfly. It darts around, up, down, and back again, before eventually catching the poor creature in its beak and swallowing it whole. She shudders.

'Dinner was delicious, thank you.'

'My pleasure. Are you warm enough?'

'I'm a little cool.'

'Let's head inside.'

They stand, and she follows him up some stone steps into a bijou, but cosy apartment.

To the right, a battered brown leather settee sits facing a large picture window that looks out towards the loch. The view is astounding. A small oval coffee table holds a selection of magazines. The far wall is chock-a-block, floor-to-ceiling shelves, crammed with hundreds of books and family photos.

Mylo with his parents, then more recent ones with only his mother. Lucy tries, but fails to ignore a picture in a frame of he and Rose, laughing, pints of beer in hand, sitting on a beach somewhere sunny. She was exceptionally pretty, with a warm, infectious smile. She can see why he liked her.

He sees her looking at it, and glances away, embarrassed.

'You know about Rose, I take it?'

She nods, and Mylo sighs.

'Cassie mentioned it at the marina when we were chatting. But just so you know... we don't have to talk about it... about Rose, I mean. Not if you don't want to. But likewise, if you *do*, that's cool too.' Lucy tries to sound nonchalant. He nods.

'I don't think I knew what real love was until I met her. She was... amazing. And I miss her every single day. Sometimes, I don't think I'll ever *not* miss her. And those are the hardest times. When I think that I may feel like this for the rest of my life.'

Lucy nods. 'Grief is a funny thing... but it does get better. I promise.' She pauses, remembering what Cassie had said about Mylo's suspicions about Diana.

'Do you honestly think Diana might have been involved?'

He bites his bottom lip, staring out through the window.

'Sometimes. I'd be lying if I said it doesn't cross my mind from time to time. Nobody *really* knows what happened that night. Only her... and she's been quite tight-lipped about it. Conveniently using her drinking and self-medication as an excuse to not have to talk about it.'

'That's common knowledge then?'

'Not really. Rose used to talk about it, but I don't think most people have any idea. I mean... nobody sees her, so how could they?'

Lucy lets her eyes drift past the photo, taking in the rest of the apartment. Two doors on the back wall stand open. She sees through to a messy-looking bedroom on one side, and a compact bathroom directly ahead of her, to the right. A third door on the far wall is closed. A small dining table in front of it holds piles of freshly washed laundry, ironed and neatly folded. The room smells of fabric softener. It's not a tidy home, by any stretch of the imagination, but it is clean, and extremely comfortable, and Lucy instantly feels the troubles of the day begin to fade. He notices her taking in the surroundings.

'I know it's not much, but my mother lives next door, so it's perfect being here, close to her, and above the store. Kills two birds with one stone.'

He shrugs; sounds as if he's apologising.

'It's wonderful. That view!' Lucy breathes, walking towards the window.

'Yeah, it's pretty special, huh?'

And it really is. Even on an overcast evening like tonight, she marvels at it.

'It's as if you've got your own personal work of art, that's constantly changing with the light,' she says dreamily. Mylo gives her an odd look. He seems suddenly distant. Eventually, he slaps his thighs through his jeans.

'More wine?'

'Are you trying to get me drunk?' she replies through a laugh. His cheeks flush as he stands, looking embarrassed.

'You sit down! You made dinner. I'll get it.'

'You're my guest. And I hardly think heating up a packet of shop-bought tortellini warrants *making* dinner.'

'Nonsense. Sit!' she commands.

He perches obediently on the arm of the sofa, drumming his fingers on his knees.

'Okay! Kitchen's through there. Wine is on the side. Have a rummage for cups. You'll find them. It's not that big.'

He points towards the door opposite. She slides her handbag strap over her shoulder, and disappears through, returning a few minutes later with two large, full glasses and the remnants of the bottle, carried expertly like a waitress. Handing one to Mylo. He shifts from the arm of the settee onto the seat. She sits beside him, looking out through the window as she places the bottle by their feet.

'Do you want to tell me what happened?' he says softly.

She bites her lip, shaking her head.

'No. I don't think so.'

He takes a mouthful of the wine, swallowing, before he speaks again.

'I'm used to Diana's nonsense. Believe me.'

'Really. It doesn't matter. Let's just enjoy the evening. I don't want to talk about her.'

Mylo nods, taking another swig as he shuffles along the sofa, closer to Lucy, topping up both their glasses.

She smiles, sipping her drink.

36

Sitting on the shore, watching the waves lap against the beach, things begin to feel a little more normal. As she recalls ranting about Rose to Valentina, she blushes, feeling foolish. She sees Lucy's terrified face as she accused her of destroying her painting.

But *someone* did.

She stands, shaking her head, brushing some loose stones from her bottom. As she turns, she glimpses Richard sitting in his wheelchair in his room, looking out towards the water as usual, and she smiles. Something in the corner of her eye catches her attention. A fleeting movement in an upstairs window.

The house should be empty.

She tilts her head upwards to Lucy's bedroom. The grey evening light reflects in the glass. A darker shape behind it troubles her. A figure? She cranes her neck, trying to change the angle. The glare bounces back in her eyes, but it's definitely there. A woman stands in the window, staring down at her, but quickly steps away out of view.

Frowning, Diana walks towards the house, assuming Lucy is

home earlier than planned. She takes her time to walk back to the cottage, still feeling slightly dizzy. Her limbs are sore from sitting for too long. She crosses the kitchen, entering the hallway, and leans on the bannisters at the bottom of the stairs.

'Lucy?' she calls up to the landing.

No reply. She stands, listening, holding her breath.

'Lucy, are you here?'

Still no answer. She places her foot on a step. A creak from within the lounge draws her attention, head snaps to the side. She steps in. The door at the opposite end of the room through to the kitchen creaks and slowly swings as if someone has just passed through. A cold draft blows through the passage, making Diana shiver.

'Lucy?' she calls again, less confident this time. She crosses the space as quickly as she can, pushing the door. It creaks open in time for her to see a silhouette pass the window outside.

She shudders.

A flash of evening sun had reflected from the girl's hair. It was blonde. *Not* Lucy.

Hand trembling on her stick, she limps across the kitchen. As she steps outside, she sees the figure disappear round the side of the house, between her studio and the lean-to, a white nightie blowing in the cool air.

'Hello? Who's there?'

Still no reply. Although the night is fairly warm, Diana feels icy cold. Tiny goosebumps raise up on her arms. Crossing the lawn, she passes her studio. Nobody there.

Opposite the cottage is a field of tall ferns, much taller than Diana in places. Heavy and overgrown. It's a forest of fronds. A flash of movement within causes her to take a step backwards. The tips of the foliage sway, as something moves through, out of sight.

She edges closer to the perimeter.

'Hello!' she calls, voice wavering.

You're being ridiculous, she tells herself. But that doesn't stop her shaking. She pushes the greenery aside and steps in. Her foot sinks in soft earth, moist from recent torrential rainfall. The air smells musty, the sunlight unable to reach the ground here. Nettles sting her ankles as she passes deeper into the dense foliage. She curses under her breath. In parts, it's clearer, almost like a path. She sticks to that. It's easier with her cane. She moves forwards. A twig cracks to her left. She turns. A wood pigeon flutters into the air, making Diana jump.

The top of a blonde head passes quickly, a few metres away.

'Who's there?' she shouts, pushing deeper and deeper into the mass of greenery.

Another noise, this time from the right, and she turns towards it, undergrowth scratching her face.

She can't tell where she is anymore. Doesn't know which direction the cottage is in. She knows that if she goes too far wrong, she'll fall from a low cliff edge into the loch.

Heart pounding, she spins in all directions. All she can see is a sea of green. The light is beginning to fade. She pushes her way to a small clearing, breathing heavily. She leans her weight on her stick. Perspiration soaks into her clothing, her fringe is stuck to her face.

And then she sees it. A few metres away, in a gap in the ferns. Obscured by the vegetation, but very definite.

A girl, standing with her back to Diana. Blonde hair, long and matted. Tattered white nightie. Dark-red stains on the grubby white fabric.

Despite herself, she shivers. She wants to be strong, but in reality, she is utterly petrified.

'Hello...' she says, voice shaky with terror. She holds her breath, as if that will prevent her from being seen. The figure turns slowly around to face Diana, strands of hair hang limply down, covering the face.

And she knows she must try to run. It's going to hurt, but she feels her life is dependent on it.

She backs away, too afraid to look from the apparition. It doesn't move. Diana spins and begins to rush. She hears movement behind her.

It is following. Twigs crack, leaves tumble.

'Help me!' Diana screams. 'Get away!'

Not sure if she is even heading in the right direction, but unable to look back, she pushes on. She trips, falling into nettles and roots of the undergrowth. She claws her way through, abandoning her stick. Hands raw from the surrounding flora. Finally, she is at the edge of the field, and she pulls herself out to the grass of her garden, rolling over onto her bottom. She slides away, dragging herself backwards.

Her limbs are in agony, but she doesn't care. She keeps crawling until she is close to the house, a few metres back from the ferns. Nobody emerges.

She sits staring, too scared to move for a while. Breathing heavily, watching. Her clothes are soaked through now. Leaves and nettles are tangled in her hair. Her arms and face are raw. Angry red blotches begin to swell up on her skin. Blood trickles from deep gouges all over her.

No figure exits the forest. No ghostly woman.

She still does not go back for her stick. She abandons it, crawling to the cottage, locking the kitchen door firmly behind her, and sobs.

37

Mylo wakes before her. His eyes open, slowly, groggily. Two bottles of wine between them, and they are flat out on the sofa. Lucy's head rests in his lap. She looks so... peaceful. He strokes her hair gently, and her eyelids flutter.

'Oh my God, did we fall asleep?' she asks, voice croaky as she straightens up in her seat. Reaching her arms up above her, she stretches, yawning.

'Yeah. I guess it's been a long day for both of us. I guess two bottles of wine didn't help.'

'What time is it?'

Mylo checks his watch.

'Wow, eleven fifteen. Must have been sleeping longer than I thought.'

'Shit! I told Diana I'd be home by eleven. Damn, damn, damn!'

She jumps up, pulling on her shoes. She rakes her fingers through her tousled locks, straightening out the tangles.

'I need to go, sorry.'

'Relax, I'll take you in the dinghy. You'll be there in less than ten minutes. She won't mind.'

'I'm not so sure. I don't want to cause any further problems.'

They hurry out the front door, and jog down towards the jetty. Hopping into the dingy, Mylo pulls the cord on the outboard. It takes a few yanks, but the engine eventually sputters to life, and they speed off into the darkness.

38

LUCY

The cottage sits in complete darkness when she arrives home, shortly after eleven thirty. Mylo had pelted her over the loch as fast as he could. As the hum of his engine disappears in the distance, she feels suddenly alone. And afraid.

Perhaps Diana is still sleeping? She crosses the garden, moonlight casting eerie shadows over the lawn. A bird shrieks somewhere in the woods. She spins towards the sound, heart pounding. Continuing her journey, she tries the handle of the kitchen door. Locked. Pressing her hands up against the window, she peers through, but can't see any signs of life inside.

Frowning, she heads around the side of the house, searching for her keys in her purse. She unlocks the door, stepping into darkness.

'Who's there?'

A muffled, childlike voice whimpers from the end of the hallway. Lucy flicks a switch to her left, and the ground floor is illuminated.

'Diana? Is that you?'

'Lucy?'

She rushes down the corridor, turning on the kitchen light

as she enters. Diana is huddled in the corner to the back of the room.

'My God! Diana, are you okay? Did you fall?' She glances around for Diana's stick, but she can't see it.

'Oh, Lucy, I'm so glad you're here. I've been so afraid.'

Lucy hurries to her aid, helping her up into a chair.

'What happened?'

Diana's wild eyes dart about the space, lingering on the back door. Her arms and face are covered in scratches and unsightly red blotches. Shreds of greenery are tangled in her messy hair.

'Is she gone?' she whispers sharply.

'Who? Diana, what's going on?'

'Shh!' she hisses, holding a finger to her lips. 'She'll hear you.'

'Who will?'

'Turn off the lights. We can't let her know we're here.'

'Diana, you're scaring me.'

'You should be scared. We all should!'

Something in the woman's eyes tells Lucy she is not joking.

'Where's your stick?'

'I lost it... in the ferns.'

Lucy crosses to the door, turning the key in the lock. Diana scurries, crablike, across the tiled floor, much faster than Lucy would have thought she was capable of. Her hands claw at Lucy's arms.

'Don't go! She's waiting.'

'Diana, I don't know who you *think* is out there, but I can assure you that there's nobody there. It's fine.'

Diana looks confused for a moment. Lucy turns the handle, pushing the door open.

'Don't leave me!' Diana wails. Talon-like nails dig into Lucy's flesh through her jumper.

Lucy gently prises the fingers away from her arm. She bends, grasping Diana's shoulders in both hands.

'Look at me. I am going outside to get your stick. You need it. You can lock the door behind me, and I'll knock when I'm back, okay? I won't be long. Five minutes, max, all right?'

Diana's eyes dart around the kitchen again, then back towards Lucy's face. She nods. Lucy steps out onto the grass. She hears the click of the lock behind her. Shaking her head, she walks in the direction of the field to the right of the studio. She stands at the edge, heart beating fast. *There is nothing to be afraid of*, she tells herself. Taking a few deep breaths to calm herself, and as an owl hoots in the woods, she pushes her way into the dense foliage.

39

S he has no idea how long the girl has been gone. It seems longer than five minutes. Diana remains huddled on the floor. It's eerily silent outside, besides the odd squawk from a woodland bird.

She sees a shadow pass the window. Her heart begins to beat faster as she shrinks down lower, out of view. A loud bang on the door makes her jump. Chest pounding now, she doesn't move. Doesn't dare.

'Diana, it's me, Lucy. Can you let me in?'

She quickly turns the key, backing away and sinking down to the floor, huddled like a terrified child. The door opens and Lucy steps inside, carrying the cane.

'Let me help you up,' she says tenderly, slipping her arms under Diana's pits. She pulls her to her feet, handing her the stick.

'Here.'

She pushes the door closed, locking it, then guides Diana towards a chair.

'We should take a look at those scratches. Some of them are deep.'

She begins to walk away, but Diana clutches at her jumper.

'Stay. I don't want to be alone.'

'I'll be right back. I'm just going to grab some things from the bathroom.'

Diana nods. Lucy hurries away, returning a few moments later with a bundle of supplies from the cabinet. She takes an antiseptic wipe, cleansing the scratches. Diana winces as the cloth skims over her skin.

'I'm sorry. It will sting a little, but we don't want them to get infected,' Lucy whispers, stroking Diana's hands.

Once the wounds are clean, she pours calamine lotion onto a cotton wool ball, wiping the thick pink liquid over the nettle stings. It feels cool, soothing, and Diana closes her eyes for a moment.

'Do you want to tell me what happened?' Lucy asks as she winds a bandage round a particularly deep cut on Diana's left wrist.

'There was someone in the house. A girl. I thought you were back early. But it wasn't you.'

Lucy stops briefly, glancing round the kitchen.

'In here? Are you sure?'

'I followed her into the ferns. She chased me out, and I tripped.'

'Why would you go out in the ferns at night?'

'I had to see. It was her, you know.'

Lucy stares into Diana's eyes.

'Rose?'

'Yes. She was here.'

Lucy crosses the room, fills the kettle and flicks it on.

'Diana, Rose is... dead. You know that, don't you?'

'Of course I know that! I'm not fucking stupid!' she hisses aggressively.

Lucy holds up her hands. As the water boils, she takes a bag of coffee from a cupboard, spooning it into a cafetière. She sees the plate of untouched food still covered in cling film as she returns the coffee to the shelf.

'You should eat. Can I warm this up for you?'

'Not hungry.'

'I know, but you need to. You've had a fright. You're still shaking. Sustenance will help.'

She nods at Diana, smiling. She takes the plate, popping it in the microwave, turning the dial. The light flicks on and the meal begins to spin. After a few minutes it pings, and she places it in front of Diana.

'Eat up. It will give you some strength. I'm going to make sure Richard is all right. I won't be long. Don't worry, I'm only through there.' She points at the adjacent wall. Diana looks terrified, her eyes swoop about the room again, but she nods. She watches as the girl leaves the kitchen.

Pushing limp-looking vegetables about, she tries to fork some into her mouth, holding back the urge to empty her stomach of its contents.

She manages a few mouthfuls of some sort of mashed mess at the side. It's bitter-tasting. Nothing tastes right at the moment. She hears Lucy talking to Richard from the next room. The sound of the girl's voice calms her a little. A few minutes later, she returns.

'He's fine. I've put him to bed. It's late for him.'

Diana doesn't respond. The kettle clicks, and Lucy pours water over the coffee grounds. She waits a while for it to brew, then pushes the plunger. She fills two cups, spooning three sugars into one, handing it to Diana. The women sit in silence for a while, sipping their drinks.

'Diana... I'm not sure what happened tonight, but you know there's no such thing as ghosts, don't you? Tell me you know that.'

Diana stares at her, eyes wide.

'That's what *you* think… but you're wrong. I can prove it. I need to find something, but when I do, I can prove to you that Rose is in this house.'

She's not making sense anymore.

'What do you need to find? I don't understand.'

'You'll see!' She smiles, showing Lucy her teeth. Lucy doesn't know what else to say, so they sit in silence for a few minutes, sipping coffee.

'She's going to kill me, you know,' Diana says suddenly.

Lucy stands, crossing to Diana's chair, squeezing her shoulder reassuringly.

'Nobody is going to kill you. Not while I'm here. I promise.'

'You can't protect me. She can walk through walls.'

Lucy doesn't want to point out the irony that Diana has been hiding behind a locked door all night. It's not the time.

'There are no ghosts.'

Diana's hand darts up to cover Lucy's mouth.

'Stop saying that! You'll make her angry.'

Lucy sighs.

'You must believe me. She *is* here. I can feel her.'

'Why don't I help you to bed?'

Diana nods, and Lucy heaves her out of her chair. She walks with her down the hallway, opening her bedroom door. Turning on the light, she steps in ahead of Diana. The room stinks of stale sweat. Dead flies litter the floor and windowsill.

'Nobody in here. All safe,' Lucy says brightly. Diana hesitates, so Lucy eases her in, watching as she crosses to her bed.

'Goodnight then,' she calls, closing the door.

Diana pulls open her bedside drawer, grabbing a bottle of pills. She swallows a handful, reclining.

The room swirls around her, ghostly images of a blonde girl

in a tattered, bloodstained nightie swim in her mind as she drifts out of consciousness.

At some point in the night, she wakes. The room is in complete darkness. Someone is sitting on the edge of her bed.

'Lucy?' Diana mumbles, confused. Her throat is dry and she struggles to speak. The girl strokes her head.

'There, there. Go back to sleep. Everything will be okay,' she whispers. Her voice sounds... odd.

The girl begins to hum an old tune. It's familiar, but in Diana's fuddled state, she can't quite place it.

As her companion gently caresses her hair, she falls slowly away into slumber.

40

Surprisingly, she slept rather well. That will no doubt have had something to do with the two bottles of wine shared between herself and Mylo. She lay in bed for a short period, thinking about Diana, but as the bizarre events of the evening whirled around her mind, she eventually drifted off to sleep.

She now sits on the grass with a steaming cup of black coffee, staring out over the loch in its morning light. It's not so sunny today, overcast. The air is damp, much cooler.

Richard is washed, dressed, and fed, and is in his chair on the lawn beside her. From what she can tell, he spends his entire life gazing through a window at the water, so she feels he may as well see it closer up, whether he's aware or not. She suspects he might be.

Diana was up late this morning. Her routine is getting later each day. But now she is pulling things out of cupboards inside the house, making lots of noise. Lucy decides to leave her to it. She's not making much sense. Eventually, the woman emerges through the kitchen door. She's made more effort today, her hair is back in her signature long plait, although it's not done as neatly as usual. Strands and loops poke out all the way down. But at least she's trying.

She has clean clothes on too. That is, *different clothes* from the previous two days. She eyes Richard as she approaches.

'You managed to get the chair out okay on your own?'

'Yes, no bother at all,' Lucy replies.

Diana shoots her a weak smile and perches herself on the edge of one of the wooden garden chairs.

'Did you find what you were looking for?' Lucy asks pleasantly.

The woman frowns, confused.

'You were looking for something in the house.'

Diana grins.

'No, but I know it's here somewhere. I'll find it. And then I'll show you. I'll prove it. I'm not mad. I'll prove she's here.'

Lucy sighs, but doesn't say anything. She doesn't want to encourage her delusions.

'Thank you... for last night,' Diana says eventually.

Her speech is still slurred. On closer inspection, her eyes are bloodshot; dark circles beneath them.

Lucy nods, glancing out across the water.

'You must think me utterly insane.'

'I think you had a fright. That's understandable, given... everything.'

Diana gazes across at her husband.

'You're good with him. Much better than... well, you know. I'm sure he likes you.'

Lucy looks at Richard, then towards his wife.

'Have you eaten?'

Diana shakes her head.

'You should. Even if only a slice of toast. You can't function properly without food.'

'I can't manage it. I'm constantly fighting waves of nausea. I can't even smell it without wanting to spew.'

Lucy purses her lips.

'I've got some scopolamine in my room. They're a pretty strong anti-sickness tablet. I can give you some of those if it will help.'

Diana seems to perk up, eyes wide.

'Could you? That would be wonderful.'

'I shouldn't... not really. They're prescription... but you *need* to eat.'

'Please, Lucy, I'd be eternally grateful. I can't bear this feeling.'

'Okay. But you mustn't tell *anyone*. Understand? I'd lose my job.'

Diana nods, as Lucy stands, hurrying inside. She heads up to her room, rummages around in a drawer. Returning to the garden, she sees Diana has slid down onto the seat. She hands her a blister pack of pills.

'Go easy. Maybe start with one, right?'

Diana swiftly grabs the packet, nodding. She pops one from the tray directly into her mouth, swallowing without a drink, and closes her eyes.

'How are you feeling about what happened last night now? Are you any clearer about what went on?'

Diana straightens in her chair.

'I know exactly what went on.' She pauses briefly. 'You may think I'm mad. Or making it up. But I *did* see Rose last night, in your bedroom window, and then again, out amongst the ferns. I assure you.'

Lucy exhales slowly through her nose, sipping her coffee before she speaks.

'I know what you *think* you saw, but–'

'There's no *think* about it. I *did* see!' she hisses, voice full of venom. The change in her demeanour is instant. Lucy decides to drop it. No point arguing with an insane woman.

'Did you have a nice evening with Mylo?' Diana asks, beaming. Her teeth glint between her lips, and just like that, she is all sweetness and light once more.

'It was very pleasant, thank you.' Lucy stands, smoothing out the creases from her jeans with her free hand, and brushes some strands of grass from her bottom. As she turns to go, Diana calls after her.

'Lucy, wait.'

She faces Diana, a forced smile on her mouth.

'That tune you were humming last night... what was it? I recognised it but couldn't place it. It was beautiful.'

Lucy frowns.

'Which tune?'

'When you were in my room, after I woke in the night.'

Lucy shakes her head slowly, narrowing her eyes.

'You were sitting on the edge of my bed and humming to me.'

The colour drains from Lucy's face.

'I wasn't in your room last night.'

41

She's been unsettled since the revelation about the woman in her room the previous evening. Her mind is all over the place right now. She doesn't even know if what she is seeing is real anymore. But the moment she admits *this* is the moment she becomes like her mother.

And that can *not* happen. So for the time being, she must believe that she is not insane. *Do crazy people ever think they are crazy*, she wonders?

Lucy hadn't wanted to leave her. She sat with her a while. Not talking. Simply *being there*. A good girl. After preparing some lunch for the three of them, she wheeled Richard back into the house, then headed out for the afternoon. Although it's overcast, the day is muggy, but she was dressed for cooler weather, as usual. Diana thinks how nice it is to see a woman not feeling the need to expose her flesh all the time.

The food sits untouched on the garden table. She can't bring herself to eat it. Not yet. She pulls the blister pack from her pocket, popping two more pills from it into her mouth. After a few minutes, she picks up the sandwich that Lucy has made, taking a bite. She can't taste anything. May as well be swallowing dirt from the ground. She manages half, then tosses the rest out towards the woods. *Let the foxes enjoy it*. Someone should.

As she glances out at the trees, she can't help feeling they seem closer than usual. *Have they moved?* Everything feels more closed in. Threatening. A large Scots pine looms on the perimeter.

Has that always been there?

A breeze blows through the garden, stirring the leaves on the huge old willow above her head.

She looks up. The sound seems to swirl about her. She feels like she is falling again, but she knows she is sitting. She screws her eyes tightly shut, wishing it would all go away.

Diana, Diana, Diana, Diana, Diana...

The rustling foliage is whispering her name over and over.

She whips her neck around; the sounds are coming from all directions now. A cacophony of murmuring voices. Placing her hands up to her ears, she balls them into fists, but the noise keeps coming. Louder now.

We know, we know, we know, we know, we know...

The volume is rising; the hum becoming a shout, then a scream, all building to a horrendous crescendo.

'SHUT UP!' she hollers, opening her eyes.

And all is calm once more. The breeze has passed, the trees are still. Normality restored.

It's simply a lack of sleep, she tells herself.

She's been waking in the night a lot lately. Taking much longer to drift off in the evenings. Not like her at all. She resigns herself to the fact that she may have to make a trip into town, to use the internet in the library. Search for some stronger tablets. Her body must be building up a resistance to the old ones.

Perhaps Lucy will do it for her, if she asks nicely. The thought of leaving the cottage terrifies her.

The loch, flat, calm, like a millpond, stretches out before her. Sunlight breaks through cloud, glistening on its surface. And in a moment of clarity, so rare these days, Diana smiles. She stands from her chair, heading back inside to continue her search.

42

W hen Lucy returns from her walk, Diana is rummaging about in the trunk beneath the living-room window. She's pulled files and books out. An old baby's blanket lies crumpled in the middle of the floor. Lucy's eyes drift to the letter c neatly embroidered in one corner, then flick away.

'Everything okay?' she asks, raising an eyebrow.

'I know it's in here somewhere. We got it for Claire when she was a child. She used to love it!'

'Love what?'

She is excited, animated. Her movements are quick. She pulls things out, tossing them aside, as Lucy watches, shaking her head.

'Aha!' she cries suddenly, pulling a black box from the bottom of the chest. It appears to be a board game.

'Here, come see.' She beckons to Lucy, who crosses the room, standing above her. She stares at what Diana is holding. One word across the top in chunky capital letters.

OUIJA.

Then smaller, underneath, *Mystifying Oracle*. The brand Parker Brothers, is written at the bottom, below a photograph of two pairs of hands, fingers touching a pointer. Lucy lets out an audible sigh, finding it difficult to hide her irritation.

'You've got to be kidding,' she says through gritted teeth.

Diana passes it to Lucy.

'Here, take this to the table.'

She pulls herself up, lifting her cane.

'Diana, this is ridiculous...'

'No. She's here, I'm telling you!' She places her hand on the game. 'This will prove it. You'll see... I'm not crazy! You'll have to believe me once we've spoken to her.'

She hobbles over, sits on a dining chair, pats the tabletop. Lucy places the box down in front of her, and she opens it up, taking out the contents. Lucy has never seen one before, but she knows what it is. A large sturdy board sits on the table. In the left-hand uppermost edge is a picture of a sun, next to the word *yes*. On the opposite side, *no*, and a moon. Letters from A to M run in an arc through the middle, with a second row beneath it from N to Z. The numbers one to nine, followed by a zero, are in a straight line underneath. At the very bottom, the branding again, and an etching of old-fashioned-looking people playing with the game in each corner, with the word *goodbye* centred between them.

Diana lifts a white plastic teardrop-shaped planchette from the box, placing it beside the board. It has a round clear window towards the point. She is smiling, whispering to herself.

'I'm not doing this, it's stupid,' Lucy says, arms folded.

'Shh... Sit.' Diana motions to the chair opposite.

'No.'

'Are you afraid of it? If we follow the rules, you needn't be.'

'No, Diana, I'm not afraid. It's a load of rubbish. A stupid game from the seventies.'

Diana's head whips towards her, a wicked smile creeps onto her lips.

'If you don't believe, then what harm can it do?'

Lucy lets out a long, slow breath, but sits down. She figures the quickest way to shut Diana up, is by humouring her... for now. Anything to get her to calm down.

'Right. What do I need to do?'

Diana pulls a sheet of yellowing paper from the bottom of the box.

'We simply ask questions. And she will answer.'

Lucy rolls her eyes.

'You have to take it seriously though. If you treat it frivolously, it won't work.'

'Fine.' She glances out of the window.

'It's the middle of the afternoon. Shouldn't we wait until it's dark or something?'

Diana laughs.

'The spirits don't care what time of day it is, my dear. Nor are they bothered by how light it is outside. But there *are* rules.'

She holds the paper up, reading aloud.

'One. Never play alone. Two. Do not allow the board to count down through the numbers...'

Lucy barely manages to stifle a snigger, resulting in a glare from the end of the table.

'Three. Always place a silver item on the board before playing.'

Diana rests the instructions in her lap, reaching her hands up to her throat. She unfastens the clasp of a delicate chain hanging around her neck; a tiny silver crucifix, set with emeralds, sparkles in the light magnificently. She places it carefully in front of her.

She continues to read.

'Four. *Never* mention God.' She stares directly at Lucy. 'Five. Always say goodbye.'

She places the sheet in front of her, pointing to it.

'We must obey these rules. That's how we stay safe.' She pauses, looking at a space beside her. 'You'll need to move down here. You can't reach from there.'

Lucy stands, carrying her chair, and sits next to Diana, who lights a candle in the centre of the table. The flame dances around wildly before settling. She takes the planchette, placing it in the middle of the board.

'So we must both place our fingers on top, but don't apply pressure.'

Diana touches it, waiting for Lucy to reciprocate.

'I can't actually believe we're going to do this,' she says obstinately, but reaches forwards, regardless. Her hand brushes against the other woman's, sending a tingling sensation through her body. She rests her fingers lightly on top of the pointer. The room feels unseasonably cool.

'So what now?'

'Are you ready?' Diana asks solemnly. Lucy nods.

'Then we begin.'

43

Trying not to be irritated by Lucy's lackadaisical attitude, Diana exhales a drawn-out breath. She closes her eyes momentarily, swallowing hard.

'Is there somebody here?' she asks, in a low voice.

Lucy lets out a nasal snigger, shoulders bobbing up and down. Diana shoots her a death stare.

She repeats the question.

The flame of the candle flickers in a breeze, and the two women's eyes meet over the table. In her peripheral vision, she sees something, a spider perhaps, scurry across the carpet. She grimaces, returning her gaze to the table. The planchette wobbles beneath their fingers. Lucy narrows her eyes, giving her companion a sideways glance, smirking. Suddenly the pointer slides across the board, settling above the word *yes*.

'That's not funny!' Lucy cries.

'It wasn't me.'

'Yeah, right.'

'Shh,' Diana hisses.

Clearing her throat, she continues.

'Who are you?'

The plastic begins to skim over various letters, slowly at first, gaining momentum as it goes. Two words are spelled out before it falls still once more.

You know.

She regards the board, considering her next question. Hearing Lucy gasp sharply, she looks at her.

'The candle,' she whispers.

The flame, extinguished, a plume of white smoke spiralling up into the air. A shiver runs through Diana's body. Her eyes dart towards Lucy, who is no longer smirking.

'I don't like this,' the girl breathes.

'Keep your hands on the planchette,' Diana commands, before continuing. 'Tell me,' she says.

Gliding over the alphabet, a single word is produced.

Rose.

'Why are you here?'

Diana.

She frowns.

It begins to move quickly over random letters, at first it doesn't appear to make any sense.

'What is that?' Lucy whispers. Diana shakes her head, shrugging.

'Is it Latin?'

'Could be... *alea iacta est*?'

'What does that mean?' Diana hears panic... or perhaps even fear in Lucy's tone.

'No idea.'

Another quiver, and the pointer lurches towards the numbers.

10, 9, 8...

'I thought the rules said not to let it do that?' Lucy shouts, terror resonating in her voice.

'Quiet!' Diana replies.

7, 6, 5...

'Diana!'

4, 3, 2...

Lucy stands, pushing the planchette. It tumbles from the table, knocking Diana's necklace to the floor.

'No!' she wails.

'This is ridiculous. I'm not doing it!'

'We didn't say goodbye. You've left the board open!'

'I don't care. It's total bullshit. You're moving it. Trying to scare me! It won't work. I'm done.'

'I promise you it wasn't me. I would never–'

'Stop, Diana! I've humoured you, okay, because I felt sorry for you... but I'm not doing it anymore. This isn't funny. This whole situation is...' She laughs, shaking her head, but her eyes look angry as she paces back and forth.

'You've had your fun. I know it was you. Enough is enough,' she says, but Diana thinks a tremor to her voice betrays her.

'I need a glass of water.' She storms out through the door.

Diana lets out a slow, quivering sigh. She bends, picking up the planchette. With trembling hands, she places it back in the centre of the board. She hears a tap running. Her eyes flick down to the sheet of rules on the table.

Never play alone.

Holding her breath, she quickly pushes the lens over the word *goodbye*. As soon as she does, Lucy screams from next door. Something smashes against the wall, shattering. Diana rises, grabbing her cane, and makes her way to the kitchen.

Lucy stands shaking by the sink. Diana follows the direction of her wide-eyed stare. On the floor in one corner, lies a shattered glass, splinters reflecting the light in an iridescent rainbow. She gazes at the girl, mouth open. Tears stream down Lucy's cheeks as she runs towards Diana, embracing her in a tight hug. As Diana gently strokes her back, Lucy whispers three words in her ear.

'She was here.'

44

'You saw her?' she shouts, holding the girl at arm's length. Her voice is brimming with excitement.

'No, I didn't *see* anyone. But it was a feeling.'

Diana furrows her brow.

'The room suddenly became icy cold. I felt something on the back of my neck, like somebody breathing on me. I span around, and the glass flew from my hand. Shattered against the wall.'

She nods towards the remnants on the floor.

'You see! I told you. I knew it! Didn't I tell you?'

Diana turns and paces the floor, shaking her head.

'I don't believe in... ghosts!' Lucy whines.

'You have to believe your own eyes though. You can't deny what has just happened.'

Lucy sits, wiping away tears.

'It doesn't make any sense. There *must* be a rational explanation.'

'We broke the rules. We left the board open. Anything could have slipped through. I closed it... said goodbye, but it may have been too late.'

'Diana...' Lucy's shoulders slump, her head tilts back. 'It's all hocus-pocus. It's not *real*!'

'How do you explain the glass then?'

'I can't.' She looks at her feet, lacing her fingers between themselves. 'But I don't believe in the supernatural.'

'Perhaps it's time to start.'

The girl sits rigidly up in her chair. She turns slowly towards Diana, eyes wide.

'Why did you break my vase?' she asks, voice dull, monotone. She doesn't sound like herself. A shiver runs through Diana.

'Wh... what? What did you say?'

Lucy blinks a few times, looking dazed. She shakes her head.

'I said I don't believe in the supernatural.'

Diana limps to her.

'No, after that. Something about a vase.'

Lucy frowns.

'I didn't say anything else.'

'Yes, you did. You asked me why I broke your vase.'

'My vase? No, Diana, you're mistaken. What are you talking about?'

Diana narrows her eyes, but the girl seems sincere.

'Doesn't matter.'

Lucy looks confused.

'I'm going out to my studio,' the older woman says, crossing to the far wall. She turns briefly, glancing back at Lucy, before exiting, closing the door behind her.

45

DIANA

She sits with the receiver pressed against her ear. Sweat trickles down from her hair, catching on the lip of the telephone. She's dialled the number a few times, but nobody is answering. She dials again, and finally Mylo answers.

'Hello, Mackenzie's.'

Diana breathes heavily down the line... suddenly doesn't know how to broach the subject.

'Hello?'

'Mylo. It's Diana Davenport.'

He sighs.

'Hi, Diana, how are you?' he says impatiently.

'Yes, yes. All fine. I need to ask you something though.'

'Okay, shoot.'

'Do you remember the vase you gave Rose?'

He doesn't respond.

'The fancy one that got broken,' she adds. There's a pause. She knows he must remember. Rose made such a damn fuss about it.

'Yes, what about it?'

'Have you ever mentioned it to Lucy?'

'No. Of course I haven't. Why would I?'

'You're absolutely sure?'

'One hundred per cent. What's this about, Diana?'

'It doesn't matter. Thank you.'

She hangs up, and sits staring at the wall. She wanted to use the Ouija board… was adamant it would prove to Lucy that she wasn't crazy. But now she regrets it. The whole experience has left her terrified. The comment about the vase was the final nail in the coffin. She retreats to her bedroom, pulling the door firmly shut behind her.

It was hot as hell. One of those rare Scottish summer days where there isn't a cloud in the sky. Rose had arrived back from Mylo's one afternoon carrying a delicate crystal vase, tall and slender. Quite beautiful really. Far too nice for someone like her.

She'd been gushing about it, telling Diana how special it was. The following day she picked a bunch of flowers from the garden and the surrounding woodlands, arranging them in the vase. She'd placed it carefully on the kitchen windowsill at the back of the counter.

Diana had stood admiring them for a while, until Rose informed her she was going upstairs to freshen up, as Mylo was coming to collect her soon.

When Diana was sure Rose was upstairs, she leaned across the counter, plucking the vase from the sill. She sniffed the flowers, smiling. Glancing around, she let it slip from her fingers, watching as it seemed to fall in slow motion to the floor, smashing into thousands of tiny shards, spraying water up her legs. A few moments later, Rose came hurrying down the stairs.

'Are you okay? What happened?'

She stopped in the doorway, staring at the floor, mouth

gaping. Her eyes flicked up to Diana, as tears began to well in her eyes.

'You bitch!' she hissed. 'What have you done?'

Diana held her hand to her lips.

'I'm sorry. It was an accident. I don't know how it happened. I tripped and knocked it.'

'Bullshit!' Rose hollered. 'You did it on purpose. I know you did. You can't stand the fact that he loves me. That he gave me something nice. And you broke it out of spite.'

Diana laughed.

'You're being ridiculous. It was an accident. Pure and simple.'

The sound of Mylo's boat drifted into the kitchen. Rose glared at Diana, before grabbing a jacket and storming towards the door.

'Honestly, Rose, you're overreacting,' Diana said calmly.

'Go to hell!' she replied, slamming the door so hard, Diana feared the glass might shatter. She watched as Rose ran towards him, burying her face in his shoulder.

Diana opened the door, lingering on the step so she could hear the conversation.

'Mylo, I hate her! I hate her so much!' she sobbed.

'Hey, what's happened? What's all this about?' he asked as he stroked the back of her head. He leaned in, inhaling deeply. Diana grimaced, looking away. Couldn't bear to see him with her.

'She broke the vase you gave me. Smashed it into smithereens. It's destroyed!'

'What? I'm sure it was an–'

'Don't even say it, Mylo! Don't you dare say it was an accident. You *always* take her side and it isn't fair.'

'Come on, Rose. It's not about taking sides.'

'It is. For once I wish you'd support me, instead of looking at me like I'm making it all up. You don't know her. What she's like.

She's not the helpless innocent cripple she feigns to be when you're around.'

The words stung, but Diana didn't move away. She stood fast, listening intently.

'Right, okay. Tell me. What happened?'

She wiped her eyes, drawing a deep breath.

'I'd picked some flowers from the garden and arranged them in it. I placed them on the windowsill. I should have known better, but I thought I'd *try* and make the cottage seem a bit nicer. I was upstairs getting ready, and I heard a commotion from the kitchen, and when I went down, it was smashed all over the floor.'

She looked at Mylo, and he raised an eyebrow, waiting for her to continue.

'She said it was an accident, she stumbled or something.'

'Well, there you go then. You know she's unsteady on her feet.'

Diana smiled to herself.

'But don't you see? She'd have to have fallen and leaned right *over* the worktop, and even further to the back of the sill. It's not possible! We had *literally* just had a conversation about how special it was to me and why.'

'Okay. Well don't worry about it. We can get you another one.'

'But it won't be *that* one. It was your grandmother's. You can't simply replace it. Besides, you told me you loved me for the first time when you gave it to me. That's what it represents.'

Mylo sighed.

'Rose, you're being silly. It's only a vase.'

'No, Mylo! It's not. It's not even about the vase. It's everything. I can't do this anymore. I'm telling you she is so jealous. She's lusting after you... and I think she *actually* believes she might have a chance with you. She's deluded!'

Mylo frowned, glancing towards the door.

'Shh... she'll hear you.'

'I don't care. You must notice the way she drools over you whenever you're around here.'

'Oh, dear God, not this again, please.'

'It's true. She broke it on purpose because she knew it was important to me. She's a bitter old witch. I hate her, and I hate living here.'

'There's not much we can do about it, though, is there?'

'Can't I come and stay with you? Please?'

'We can talk about it,' he said softly, and a wave of panic washed through Diana.

Mylo guided her to his boat. As Rose busied herself at the stern, he glanced up towards the house.

Diana stood staring at them.

She smiled, waving her fingers flirtatiously at him. He looked away, shaking his head.

Diana remembers the day well. The thought of Rose leaving had terrified her... not because she wanted Rose to stay, but she knew her not being there would mean seeing less of Mylo. And she simply couldn't bear the thought of that. She knew she would have to smooth things over, convince the girl to stay. But fortunately, events over the few weeks that followed the incident would mean that Diana wouldn't have to worry about it anymore.

At the time, she'd taken a great deal of pleasure in seeing how much breaking the vase had hurt Rose and wiped the smug smile from her face. But now, the memory of it terrifies her. There's no way Lucy can have known. Which means one thing. Diana's suspicions are correct.

Rose is back.

And she wants to hurt Diana.

She sits on the edge of her bed, wringing her hands, as she stares vacantly out of the window. Rose's ghost will have to go. Diana had hoped that sanding away the stain from the foot of the stairs would cleanse her house of all traces of that toxic girl and the bitter memories she left behind.

But she can see it will take more. Much more.

And she knows what she must do.

46

DIANA

She hasn't left her room much since the incident with the Ouija board. It's been almost a week. Partly because she's felt so unwell; hasn't had the energy, but mostly through fear. She's terrified. The confirmation that Rose is haunting her has filled her with a new sense of dread... she knows it's crazy hiding herself away, because, after all, a ghost can get at her anywhere it likes... but she simply feels safer in her room. She's heard Lucy pottering around, cleaning, tidying. Seeing to Richard. The girl has knocked on the bedroom door a few times, called through to make sure Diana is all right. Left plates of food outside. Some of it has been eaten, some taken away untouched.

The anti-sickness tablets are helping, but the headaches... they won't ease up. Her limbs are throbbing. Each time she attempts to stand from her bed, she feels like she's on a rollercoaster. She knows she should speak to a doctor, but she's terrified. *What if they commit me*, she thinks.

The sleeping pills don't seem to be working at all anymore. She's waking most nights, at least once, which is unlike her. She used to put her head on the pillow and be out until the following morning. Now she's lucky if she gets a couple of hours. She can't face a trip into town to find new ones.

Opening her door, she waits, listening. The house is silent. She hears footsteps from above. Taking her chance, she hobbles quickly to the bathroom, slipping inside. She hasn't showered for days.

She notices that Lucy has cleaned the mirrored doors of the cabinet. She curses to herself. She should have told her to leave them. She prefers them that way. Glancing up, her eyes linger. Her hair is a mess. She hardly recognises herself; she avoids seeing herself at the best of times. Can't face the monster that returns her gaze.

'Who *are* you?' she whispers.

'I'm you, of course,' her reflection replies, flashing a mouthful of razor-sharp fangs as it grins back at her.

The phone rings, startling her. Panicked, she quickly returns to her room, but she's sure she can hear her reflection cackling from the bathroom. She pushes her door closed just in time. She hears Lucy skipping down the stairs and a muffled conversation ensues. Probably Val checking up on her. Chasing her for work. Her paintbrushes remain untouched since the discovery of the ruined canvas. There's a knock, bare knuckles on wood.

The sound is deafening, it echoes round the room. Diana's head whips about, following it, as it bounces from wall to wall, high up in the corners. She can almost see it.

'Diana, it's me. May I come in?'

'Go away!' she screams, as she limps back towards the bed, sitting on the edge. The door swings open, Lucy is standing in the hallway. She holds a small plate with a sandwich on it, and a glass of milk.

'I said go away! How dare you come in here without my permission. Who do you think you are?'

The girl ignores her, holding up the plate of food.

'I brought you some lunch.'

'Not hungry.'

Lucy walks to the dresser, placing the offering on top.

'I'll leave it here for you in case you change your mind. You should keep your energy levels up.'

Diana purses her lips. The girl stands in the doorway, wringing her hands, as if she wants to say something but is afraid.

'What do you want?' Diana spits.

'That was Mylo on the phone.'

Diana perks up instantly. Her fingers shoot up to her messy plait, fiddling with some loose strands.

'Oh?' She throws the braid over her shoulder, so it falls down her back.

'He was inviting me out tomorrow with him and some of his friends. I wondered if it might be possible to take the day off.'

Diana's face changes. A look of childish wonder is replaced with something else. Something... darker.

'Do what you like,' she hisses mulishly.

'If it's a problem, I won't. I know I'm contracted for seven days, so...'

'Why would it be a problem? Take the day off. Take a week off for all I care. I'm sick of you bothering me. Trying to poison me with your food. Don't think I don't know what you're doing.'

She points a bony finger towards Lucy, who frowns, but ignores the accusation.

'Will you be all right seeing to Richard for the day? I'll get him up and ready in the morning and shouldn't be home too late. If you would be able to give him some lunch? I'll leave some soup in the fridge, it will only need heating up.'

Diana looks slowly up at the girl.

'He *is* my husband. I should think I'm capable of feeding him.'

Lucy rolls her eyes, sighing. She goes to leave but turns to face Diana again.

'Do you speak Latin, Diana?'

'Excuse me?'

'Latin. Have you studied it?'

Diana looks confused for a moment.

'At school, yes. A long time ago, but I can't remember much.'

Lucy looks as if she's mulling this over, nodding slowly. She chews the corner of her mouth.

'The words, from the Ouija board last week. They were Latin. *Alea iacta est*. I did some research online when I got a signal out on my walk a few days ago.'

Diana raises an eyebrow questioningly.

'And?'

'It means *the die is cast*.'

She leaves, closing the door behind her.

Diana sits motionless on the bed. A chill hits her, making her shiver. Something tumbles on her dresser, smashing on the floorboards below. Heaving herself up, fighting the wave of dizziness, she crosses the room excruciatingly slowly. It's as much as she can manage after all the rushing to the bathroom and back.

A picture frame lies shattered on the floor. She kicks it free from the splintered glass. Crouching down to pick it up, she shakes off the last few fragments. It's a photograph from the previous summer. She's in the garden with Richard beside her in his chair. She's kneeling next to him. Rose is behind them, arms draped around both of their shoulders, laughing. She was always *so* wonderful at smiling on cue.

Mylo kneels at the back, gazing lovingly at his girlfriend. He had used a self-timer on his mobile phone; had taken a few attempts to get it right. They'd had a barbecue in the garden. Mylo and Rose did the food.

It was a good day.

It strikes her how much healthier she looked then. She's even wearing make-up.

She smells cigarette smoke once more, so strong she spins around. It's like it's in the room with her.

A strange tickling sensation prickles her skin, as if a spider is scurrying over it. She brushes her hand quickly, eyes shooting downwards. Nothing there.

Glancing about, she places the picture face down on the dresser, kicking the glass underneath. She hears Lucy's footsteps skipping up the stairs, and exits her room, heading to the lounge, pulling her diary from the dresser. She shuffles through the pages until she finds what she's looking for. Picking up the phone, she dials the number, tapping the page lightly with her fingertip as it rings.

A woman's voice answers.

'Hello?'

'Annette, it's Diana Davenport here, at Willow Cottage. I think I need your help...'

The sun is burning hot already. Lucy sits at the end of the jetty, waiting. She tugs the sleeves of her sweater down over her hands, wiping beads of sweat from her forehead. Her jeans are prickly in the heat. Wet patches are beginning to form at the backs of her knees.

Glancing back to the cottage, she sees Diana at the kitchen window, staring out towards her. She's hardly left her room in a week; only comes out when she thinks Lucy isn't around. She made a phone call shortly after the incident with the Ouija board; Lucy has no idea who she called, but it wasn't a long conversation. She's sure she heard her mention a vase. Aside from that, she's been holed up in her bedroom. She's made a few comments about *cleansing the house*, whatever that means, when Lucy has taken her food, or been checking she's alive.

She smiles, hearing the hum before Mylo is visible. He whizzes up on his dinghy, wearing fluorescent-pink swim shorts and a black vest, making her feel entirely overdressed. His eyes linger a second too long on her attire, but he doesn't say anything; he's too polite. He leaves the outboard running as he helps her in. She wobbles, losing her balance and for a sickening moment, thinks she's going to fall over into the water, but he steadies her. He lowers her down, so she's perched on the edge.

'Is she still watching?' she says.

Mylo glances behind her, nodding.

'I suppose I should be happy. It's the first time she's been out of her room in about a week. I'm actually amazed she let me take the day off. Although…'

He raises his eyebrows.

'Doesn't matter,' she says. 'Just go.'

They pull away, leaving Willow Cottage in their wake.

'So where are we off to?'

'It's a surprise.'

'I hate surprises.'

'Rose always hated surprises too,' he says flatly. His eyes flick towards her. He forces a smile, but there's sadness hidden within it.

He takes them further along the loch than Lucy has been. Past his shop and apartment. They ride for close to half an hour, and eventually she sees they are heading in the direction of a yacht, anchored in the shallows near to the shore. An expanse of impossibly white sand behind it runs for miles, totally deserted. Adjacent to the beach, a grassy hill rises high into the sky. Scatterings of wild parsnip and willow weed paint the landscape yellow and pink. Lucy smiles as she takes it all in.

Echoes of music and laughter resonate from the yacht. As they approach, Lucy sees someone stand up on deck. Long tanned legs. Barely-there white crocheted halterneck bikini. She waves frantically.

'Yoo-hoo!' she sings as they draw nearer.

'Hello, Cassie!' Lucy shouts.

The dinghy slows to a stop at the rear of the boat, and Cassie leans overboard, helping Lucy up a metal ladder onto the deck. Mylo cuts the engine, climbing up to join them.

Molly lounges towards the front of the yacht, while the guys sit with their legs dangling over the edge, sipping from bottles of beer. A cheesy pop record bellows out from some Bluetooth speakers.

Molly jumps up, barefoot, walking along the side of the boat to greet them. She wears a one-piece bathing costume, wide navy-and-white stripes. More modest than Cassie, but just as pretty. Lucy hadn't noticed it before, because she was so in awe of the other girls, but Molly really is quite beautiful too. Lucy wonders how Rose would have felt about her fiancé being friends with so many good-looking women.

'This is… spectacular,' Lucy breathes.

The guys wave, but don't get up. Mylo strolls over, and the macho fist-bumping ritual begins.

'I'm so glad you could make it. We weren't entirely sure she would give you the day off. She never let Rose take time off,' Cassie gushes.

Molly looks away, the smile falling briefly from her face.

'I don't know why you'd want to work for her anyway,' Cassie continues. 'She's… oh, I don't know. I can't stand her.'

Molly tuts.

'There's this concept that people whose daddies own luxury yachts struggle to understand, Lucy. It's called *working*, Cassie. Us normal folk have to do it for *money*. Barbaric really.'

'Cow! I work!'

Lucy raises her eyebrows.

'I do!'

'I'm not sure having your nails done counts as a job,' Molly retorts, smiling again. 'Where's Sadiya?'

Cassie rolls her eyes. 'I left her a few messages, but the bitch is ghosting me! Probably for the best. Boats are not her thing. Can't swim.'

She shrugs, offering Lucy a drink, and she notices her fluorescent-pink nail lacquer has been replaced with an equally bright turquoise. Professional job. Perfect. She glances at her own chewed nails, then tries to pull her sweater down over her fingers.

'Actually, I think I'll give it a miss today...'

The girls look at each other but say nothing.

'You must be roasting. Please tell me you brought something else to wear?'

Lucy shakes her head.

'I'm fine though.'

'You can't swim in that. There's tons of bikinis down below. They should fit you. Go and have a root around.'

'Not really much of a swimmer.'

'Oh what-ever!' She saunters to the edge of the boat, and without warning jumps overboard, splashing into the water below. Then a couple of the others do the same. Mylo pulls off his vest, and she sees that although he is slim, he's toned. He has a paunch, and a line of dark hair runs up from beneath the waistband of his trunks, to his belly button.

'Coming in?' he asks.

'I thought you said it was too cold?' A note of panic tinges Lucy's voice.

He looks over the edge.

'We're only anchored in about two metres, if that. It's so shallow it's a little warmer here. Don't get me wrong, it's still bloody freezing, but it's more bearable. They won't be in long.'

Lucy shakes her head.

'Fancy going ashore?'

'Don't let me stop you if you want to swim. I don't mind watching.'

'It's fine. Honestly. Shall we?' He motions towards the beach.

She nods. They descend to the dinghy, rowing the short journey. He secures it to a tree, and they walk along the sand. His fingers brush against hers lightly as they stroll. She smiles but doesn't look at him. They cross to the meadow beyond and climb the hill. By the time they get to the top, Lucy is drenched. She collapses down onto the grass, Mylo plonks himself down next to her. They sit staring out at the view. She can see for miles.

'You're not a swimmer, I take it. That's the second time you dodged it.'

Lucy picks a daisy from beside her, twiddling it between her finger and thumb nervously. She shakes her head. Using her thumbnail, she splits near the end of the stalk, making a slit. Taking another, she does the same again, threading it through the hole to begin a chain.

'It's fine. It's not for everyone. Like I said, it's pretty icy in there.'

'It's not that I don't like it... I...' She lets out a long sigh. 'I had an accident when I was a kid. There was a fire. I've got... scars. I don't really like showing my body. Especially around strangers.'

Mylo reaches up a hand, squeezing her shoulder.

'I'm so sorry. I had no idea.'

'It's cool. I'm a bit... shy about it, I suppose.'

'I understand.'

Cassie screams dramatically as someone dunks her head under the water. Although they are far away, the sound seems closer. Mylo shoots Lucy a sideways glance.

'So what's going on with Diana?'

Lucy rolls her eyes.

'I don't even know where to start. She accused me of *poisoning* her yesterday.'

'What? That's mental. Why would she say that?'

Lucy shrugs.

'She's delusional. I'm probably oversharing here, but... she told me her mother was schizophrenic. Committed suicide. With that in mind her behaviour is... worrying.'

'She called me at the shop the other day. It was so odd. She was asking about this vase that I gave Rose. Asked if I'd ever told you about it. She sounded... wired.'

Lucy finishes the daisy chain she's been making, sliding it onto her wrist. She closes her eyes, pushing her hands out through the grass beside her, letting the blades slide between her fingers.

'She's totally bonkers. She made me do a Ouija board with her last week. I think the stuff with the vase has something to do with that.'

'You're kidding?'

'Nope. She actually believes the cottage is haunted.'

'Haunted? For Christ's sake...'

Lucy looks at Mylo, unsure whether to say anymore.

'She thinks it's Rose.'

She lets that sink in. Watches as the muscles in his jaw tense.

'I'm sorry. I shouldn't have said anything.'

'No, it's all right. It's funny actually... the other day when you were saying about the stone stacks?'

She nods.

'Rose used to make those things. She was *obsessed* with them. She made them all over the place. Really annoyed Diana if she made them in the garden.'

Lucy's eyes widen, as she remembers Mylo turning up at the house shortly after the incident. He continues.

'That's why I went quiet when you were telling me about it. It was... strange. Made me feel a bit creeped out.'

'She says she's seen her.'

'What?'

'In the house. She's adamant.'

Mylo picks a blade of grass, tossing it down the hill in front of him.

'Do you believe her?'

'Of course I don't! She's completely insane.'

He says nothing. Just sits picking grass and throwing it away. Lucy's eyes drift over the landscape, and she smiles.

'It's so beautiful here,' she says, changing the subject. 'The colours are... incredible. It's fascinating how much they've changed even in the short time I've been here. It's like I'm living inside a rainbow.'

Mylo's eyes cloud over. He gives her a peculiar look, his lips part as if he's about to speak, but seems to change his mind.

'What?' she asks.

'You're so much like her, do you know that? Rose, I mean. Not physically. But you've *said* things that she used to say to me. Almost word for word. I've noticed it a few times since I met you. It's... remarkable.'

Lucy shifts her weight between her buttocks, looking away briefly. She takes a chance, leaning towards his face. Their lips touch, and they kiss. But as quickly as it started, it's over. He pushes her from him.

'I'm sorry. I can't.'

She looks to her side, so he doesn't see the hurt in her eyes.

'I thought I could. But I don't think I'm ready. Not yet. I *really* like you, trust me. But all this stuff with Diana, it's made me realise I'm still so raw. It wouldn't be fair on either of us.'

He touches her chin, tilting her head back towards him.

'You understand, don't you?'

She nods. 'I'm sorry,' she whispers.

'You've got nothing to apologise for. You're wonderful. But can we try friends first... see how we get on?'

Cassie comes bounding up the hill. Lucy has never been so pleased to see anyone.

'What are you two lovebirds talking about,' she shouts, plonking herself down beside them.

And the moment is gone.

48

'We were discussing Diana,' Lucy says.

Cassie shakes her head.

'Sorry I dissed her earlier, I know she's your boss.'

'No worries.'

Mylo sits quietly, watching the two girls.

'You deserve a medal for putting up with her though. That cottage is so creepy. I don't like it.'

'Cassie!' Mylo chides.

'I don't. It's so old. My dad says it's been there hundreds of years. And get this. This old woman lived there, like, ages ago. And the people round here thought she was a witch because she was a bit eccentric. So one night they all turned up at the door and dragged her from her bed. Hung her from that willow tree in the garden. Left her there to rot as a warning to other witches.'

Lucy screws up her face.

'That's enough, Cass,' Mylo warns.

'It's fine, honestly,' Lucy replies.

Mylo tilts his head, but she shakes hers gently.

'Anyway, my dad says Diana got the place for an absolute

steal. It was empty for years. Nobody else would touch it. People round here, the proper old locals I mean, not like my family... well, they're a bit superstitious about it. They reckon people have seen the witch's ghost wandering the woods naked, neck broken.'

She jerks her head to the side, sticking her tongue out.

'Oh yeah, sure!' Lucy laughs.

'It's true, I swear! I'd sleep with one eye open if I were you.' She cackles for effect, labouring the point.

'You're such a dick,' Mylo says, standing, brushing grass from his jeans. 'I'm going down to the beach.'

He strolls away, leaving the girls sitting in the meadow. Cassie nudges her elbow into Lucy's.

'So... come on! How's it... developing?'

Lucy smiles.

'It's not.'

'What do you mean?'

'He's not into me... or at least, he's still into Rose, so I think he feels like he's being unfaithful or something.'

The smile drifts from Cassie's lips. She stares down the hill after Mylo, nodding.

'Give him time. I can't even begin to imagine what he's going through. Early days. He's changed a lot since the accident. He used to be a much happier person. These days he's so... moody.'

'When did... *it* happen?'

Cassie chews her lip.

'About eight months ago.'

'Oh God, so soon. No wonder he's still hurting.'

Cassie fingers the daisy chain around Lucy's wrist.

'Pretty,' she says absent-mindedly.

'Tell me about her? Rose, I mean.'

Cassie lets out a slow breath.

'Rose was... amazing. Pure Glasgow. Bolshie as hell, but...

beautiful. Inside and out. Mylo worshipped the ground she walked on. He thought she was totally perfect. And she loved it.'

She smiles sadly.

'How long did she work for Diana?'

'She was there a couple of years. She hated it, you know. She was going to leave. When her and Mylo got engaged, he said she could move in. I was so pleased for them... for her. She *needed* to get out of that house.'

'Why?'

'She changed. Living there. Something about her... I don't know. I'm probably being melodramatic. I tend to do that, if you haven't noticed.'

'No, please, go on.'

'I can't really explain... it's difficult. But the longer she was there, she became... different. It was sad to watch. I hoped that when she moved out, things might go back to how they were... but... you know, we never got the chance to find out. She used to be so chilled... when she first arrived. But towards the end her and Diana would have screaming fights. Diana would rant at her about smoking in the house, and, of course, that would make Rose do it even more, because... well... she hated her, and wanted to piss her off.'

She looks at Lucy intently.

'She also became quite jealous... of Mylo. Got a bit funny when he would talk to me, or Molly. Especially Sadiya, but she *is* stunning. Not sure I'd like my fella talking to her either.'

She laughs, but it seems forced.

'I saw a picture of her in Mylo's flat. I don't think she had *anything* to worry about.'

'That's what I mean though. She was a confident girl... she never felt threatened by anyone else. I admired her for that. When she walked into a room... she owned it. But towards the end... she was paranoid. A bit... psycho.'

They sit in silence for a while, watching Mylo on the beach. He's skimming stones out across the loch. Cassie stands, holding her hand out.

'Come on, I need a drink.'

She pulls Lucy up from the grass, and they head back to the boat.

49

DIANA

She sits facing the house, listening to the gentle lapping of the waves on the beach. She can hear them slapping against the side of the small red fishing boat tied to the end of the jetty. She used to adore watching the swallows and cormorants swooping over the water. On a fine day, she sometimes even spied porpoises, their fins arching out above the surface. But she doesn't dare take her eyes off the cottage. Too afraid. Richard is sitting at his window. She watches for someone behind him, but nobody appears. Her home is deserted.

Her gaze drifts towards the studio, but she can't bring herself to go in. She regrets telling the girl she could have today off, not because she *needs* her, but rather because she doesn't want to be here alone.

She feels a little happier after her conversation on the phone with Annette. But she won't be satisfied until the deed is done.

She raises her hand, fiddling with her braid; hair feels greasy, unpleasant. As her fingers glide over her chest, they suddenly splay, and she gasps.

The crucifix which usually hangs around her neck, the one

which means so much to her... it's not there. She must have forgotten to put it back on after she used it in the seance. Biting her lip, she slowly raises herself from the chair, limping with her cane back towards the cottage. She loiters outside the door, staring through into the empty kitchen. Taking a deep breath, she steps inside. Her heart pounds. *How has it come to this*, she thinks? Afraid to enter her own home.

Richard's laboured breathing is the only sound emitting from the house. Sometimes, depending how he slouches, he gurgles as he draws breath. Small bubbles usually form at the corners of his mouth. She pictures this now as she hears the sickening noise from his room. She grimaces, feeling immediately guilty, hobbling through the kitchen. Recalling that the necklace was knocked onto the floor when Lucy pushed the planchette from the board, she scours the floorboards around the dining table. It isn't there. She checks the rug in case the jewellery has been kicked there. Nothing.

She lowers to her knees, wincing through gritted teeth. Closing her eyes for a second, she breathes in and out, then begins to glide her palms over the floor. She crawls about the entire room but doesn't find the chain. The ground is spotless. Not a speck of dirt anywhere.

A tiny spider scurries across the back of her hand, and she shakes it frantically. Her eyes dart around the room, but she can't see where it landed. She returns her attention to the task at hand, and it occurs to her that she has heard the girl vacuuming most days, while she has been hidden away in her bedroom, afraid to even open the curtains. She heaves herself up, using the corner of the table for support, heading back to the kitchen. She crosses to the utility room. As she enters, she shudders, hunching her shoulders for warmth. Wet laundry hangs drying, the scent of fabric softener filling the space. Inhaling deeply, the aroma fills her nostrils, calming her a little. Spotting the vacuum cleaner in one corner, she hurries towards it, pulling the waste section from the rear, emptying it onto the concrete floor. She lowers herself to her knees again, searching through the crap that has spilled out before her. She brushes it with her hands, thinning it out, but the crucifix is not there. No glistening emeralds. No glint of bright silver in the afternoon sun. A sense of unease begins to wash over her, as she recalls the rules from the game.

Always say goodbye... Lucy had left without completing it, leaving it open.

Never play alone... she had moved the pointer to close the board by herself after the girl left the room.

The silver... knocked from the table. Three of the five rules, broken.

Then there was Lucy's apparent *possession*, straight afterwards. Fleeting as it was, it was none the less terrifying. The girl appears to have no recollection of the words that left her mouth. Diana has wondered more than once if she actually imagined it.

A cold sweat forms on her brow. Her head spins, and she suddenly feels sick.

Standing, she knits her fingers together. She begins to scratch. The backs of her hands, her forearms feel incredibly itchy. The feeling spreads to her shoulders, her ankles. Her face.

She sees something black scurry over her knuckles. A tiny spider dancing across her. She brushes at it, grimacing. They have always repulsed her. Staring down at her limbs, her eyes widen. Her mouth opens, but no sound comes out. She wants to scream, but she is too petrified.

Bugs. Thousands of them, crawling over her flesh.

Their hairy legs scuttle over her, tickling her skin. She scratches, slaps herself, trying to brush them away. She stares in horror as she realises... they are burrowing.

A fleshy lump appears beneath the surface of the back of her hand and moves in an erratic motion towards her wrist. She drops her cane. It clatters on the hard ground.

Falling to the floor, she hears buzzing. It grows louder as she sees hundreds of wasps are flying around the room. The sound continues to grow, and she finally manages to scream.

'Oh my God, HELP! HELP ME!'

She crawls, dragging herself across the concrete, through the muck from the vacuum cleaner. But she doesn't care about that now. Swatting at the insects as they swoop towards her, her heart pounds. She feels them stinging her all over her body. A thousand tiny poisoned pinpricks over her limbs and face. One crawls into her mouth, and she feels it descend inside her throat. She can feel it buzzing about inside her belly.

'GET OFF ME!' she bellows.

She nears the door, but before she reaches it, it swings open; a woman stands staring at her. It's Rose; angry, glaring.

No... not a woman anymore... A huge wasp, the size of a person... it hovers menacingly, then swoops down fast towards her. Diana throws her hands up to shield herself and screams. She screams as loud as she can, screwing her eyes tightly shut.

50

LUCY

Diana writhes around on the floor, wailing. She's swatting at thin air, connecting with the side of Lucy's face from time to time. She claws at Lucy's arms as she tries to stop her, scratching deep gouges in her flesh.

'Mylo, help me! Restrain her!'

Mylo pounces, grabbing Diana's wrists from behind.

'Diana, it's us. It's Lucy and Mylo, do you hear me?'

'GET AWAY FROM ME!' she screams, head jerking from side to side as she watches invisible objects move around the room.

'Diana, please. Calm down.'

Lucy's voice is firm, but level and measured. The thrashing subsides. A look of bewilderment fills Diana's face. Mylo loosens his grip on her. She seems to relax, slumping forwards.

'Let's get her outside.'

They help her to her feet, carrying her out to the garden. She sobs, glancing fearfully at her arms. Brushing at them now and then, as if there is something crawling on them.

'Mylo, inside, in the drawer of the dresser, there's a number for the doctor, in a diary. Can you call, please?' She motions with her head towards the house, and he hurries away.

Lucy grasps the sides of Diana's head with both hands, staring into her unblinking eyes.

'Diana, you're safe. I'm here. Do you understand?'

Her eyes dart from side to side, but settle on Lucy's own. She nods.

'Good. Keep looking at me. Don't worry about anything else.'

Mylo appears back at her side.

'He's on his way.'

Diana's head whips towards him.

'I'm sorry, Mylo. It's my fault. I invited her back.'

He looks, puzzled, at Lucy, who shakes her head. He says nothing, simply smiles at Diana.

'You can go if you need to,' Lucy says.

'You sure? What if she–'

'She won't. She's fine. I've got this. You get home.'

He kicks at the ground, like he doesn't want to go, but eventually heads towards the dinghy.

'Mylo,' she calls after him. He turns to her.

'Thank you.'

He smiles weakly. As he pulls the cord to the outboard, and the engine starts to buzz, he looks over his shoulder.

Lucy helps Diana to her feet, helping her slowly back inside as Mylo's boat hums away.

51

LUCY

'And aside from this, have you had any other... episodes?' the doctor asks, matter-of-factly as he shines a torch into each of Diana's eyes, watching her pupils.

'No,' Diana says, glancing nervously towards Lucy.

'And how have you been feeling in general?'

'Okay. A little nauseous at times, but other than that... fine.'

'Sleeping?'

'Same as usual.'

Lucy narrows her eyes, but the woman shakes her head as the doctor looks away, rifling through his case. Her expression seems to plead. He holds out a bottle of pills.

'Take two of these four times a day, they should help with the anxiety.'

Lucy steps forward.

'She's already on medication for anxiety.'

'I *am* her GP. I realise this. I was about to add, stop taking your Clonazepam. They may interact. Perhaps your body has developed an immunity.'

He hands Diana the tablets. She grabs them like a child accepting candy.

'Honestly, I just dozed off, and was still half asleep, stuck in a bad dream. Nothing to worry about.'

She smiles.

The doctor says goodbye, heading out the front to his car. Lucy follows.

'Doctor,' she calls. He turns to face her.

'I don't think she is well.'

He purses his lips.

'I'm afraid I can't speak to you about a patient.'

He slides his key into the lock, opening the door.

'She wasn't being entirely honest with you there. Despite what she may have told you, this isn't an isolated incident. Her behaviour has been getting increasingly... worrying.'

'In what way?'

'She thinks she is seeing ghosts for a start. She has terrible mood swings. Seems confused a lot of the time, forgetful. Her speech is slurred. She barely manages to dress herself most days. I could go on. And I'm fairly sure that tonight was a full-on psychotic episode. She thought she had *bugs* crawling under her skin, for Christ's sake.'

He pauses, letting out a long breath.

'Hmm, that is worrisome. I tell you what, ask her to come into the surgery to see me tomorrow. If she calls first thing in the morning, I'll make sure I can fit her in. I'll look into it... give her a full check-up, run some bloods, see if there's something going on behind the scenes.'

She nods, and the doctor smiles sympathetically. He pulls a card out of his jacket pocket.

'If you're worried, or anything happens, call me. My mobile is on there.'

He climbs into his car, and Lucy watches his red tail lights fade to pinpoints through the woods. She storms back into the house. Diana is still sitting on the sofa, staring into space.

'What the hell was that?'

The woman gazes at her vacantly.

'Why lie to the doctor? He was here to help. What's the point of him coming *all* the way out here to see you if you're not going to be honest with him?'

Diana exhales, rolling her eyes.

'I'm fine, Lucy... it was an episode. Nothing more, nothing less. I need sleep, that's all.'

'Diana, that was not lack of sleep. That was... terrifying.'

The woman stands, picking up her stick.

'I'm tired. I don't want to discuss this any further. I'm going to bed. Goodnight.'

She limps slowly into the hall, crossing to her room. Lucy hears the door click shut.

52

DIANA

Tossing three pills into her mouth, she undresses, climbing under her blanket, leaning her cane against the bedside table. She flicks off the lamp, throwing the room into darkness. The moon is hidden behind thick cloud tonight. She stares into space, trying not to remember.

But each time she closes her eyes, she hears the buzzing. She sees the bugs crawling on her; *in* her.

She shudders. She doesn't feel her usual wave of euphoria as the sleeping pills kick in. She feels... wired. The sliver of light at the bottom of her door from the hall is extinguished, and she hears Lucy pad slowly up the stairs. A tap runs. More footsteps. She can almost follow the girl's movement across the ceiling with her eyes.

Eventually, she drifts away. Her dreams bring her no peace, though, as she conjures slimy black creatures crawling out of the loch, trying to devour her with razor-sharp teeth.

Something wakes her.

She must have been sleeping for a while, as she is drenched in sweat, fringe plastered to her forehead.

Her arms ache. The pit of her elbow where she has been bitten is itchy and sore. She attempts to reach her hand across to scratch it but realises with horror that she is unable to move. She manages to turn her face slightly from side to side, but the rest of her body is paralysed.

She hears... breathing. Definite, slow and laboured. Coming from somewhere within her room. She tries to call out but can't. She is utterly helpless. Raising her head slightly from her pillow, she looks towards the corner.

A dark mass lingers, upright, beside the dresser.

She can't bring herself to look away. As she grows more accustomed to the light, she is positive there is somebody standing there.

Watching her.

The shape moves, and she screws her eyes shut tight. Doesn't dare open them. Footsteps pad across the room. Her bedroom door creaks. Too afraid to even breathe, she waits. After a few agonising minutes, she musters the courage to look.

The figure is gone. Her door wide open. She is alone once more.

And then the strangest feeling washes over her.

She feels like the bed is swallowing her up, like she's sinking down into the mattress, as if it's made of cotton wool... soft, it envelops her. She felt it before, a week or so ago, but not as extreme. She's falling deep down, but she can see she isn't moving. She hears an owl hoot from the garden. It echoes in her ears. It's the strangest sensation. She can almost picture the sound as it stretches out through a long, endless tunnel ahead of her. Repeating, over and over. Her eyes roll back in her head, and she spins out into oblivion.

53

DIANA

M orning comes, and although she has slept, she doesn't feel rested. Her body aches. But at least she can move.

She sits up, seeing her cane leaning against the dresser beside the door which is now closed. Her eyes dart to the bedside table where she was sure she had left it.

Sighing, she pulls herself out of bed, making the painful journey across the floor for her stick. This is happening far too frequently these days... she's never been so careless with it before.

As she dresses without showering, she pauses, remembering the figure in her room. *No point telling Lucy*, she thinks, *she already believes me to be insane.*

She doesn't even brush her teeth. Heads into the hall. Richard's door is open as she passes. He is sitting with his back to the window, staring out towards her. She smiles as she continues to the kitchen. A pot of fresh coffee sits on the counter. She sees Lucy pass the window, heading around the side of the house. She turns, waving as she sees Diana, who returns the gesture.

She fills a mug, raising it to her mouth. She sniffs. It smells burnt. The pungent aroma assaults her nostrils; her senses seem heightened today. Grimacing, she pours the contents into the sink, heading back out to the hall. But as she passes Richard's room, she stops. The door, which only moments earlier she is sure had been wide open, is now closed. She opens it. Richard still sits in the same position. Nothing untoward. The curtains sway in the breeze from an open window.

Was it open before? She can't remember. Can't picture it.

Doubting herself, she steps inside, scouring the space. It's empty, of course. Crossing to the window, she peers out. She can't see Lucy anymore. She leans through, looking to the sides, but the girl is nowhere to be seen.

She turns, making her way back out to the hall. Taking a few paces towards her bathroom, she pauses briefly. A sound from above. Crying. Soft, but definite. She stands at the foot of the stairs.

'Lucy?' she calls. 'Is something wrong?'

It continues, growing louder, more desperate.

'Lucy!'

No reply. Diana looks around. Tilting her head, she gazes through the kitchen door out towards the loch. She can't see anybody in the garden. Lucy must have come in through the living room and gone upstairs. She calls again. Still no answer. The sobbing continues. Tortured, anguished. The sound almost breaks Diana's heart.

She places a foot on the bottom step. Grasping the bannister, she heaves her weight up, quickly wedging her stick down onto solid ground. A sharp pain radiates up her leg, through her hip. She winces, sucking in air. The crying drones on.

'Lucy, I'm coming up!'

She pulls herself further, grabbing whatever she can, holding tight on to the balustrade. Sweat beads across her forehead. It comes from every pore, trickling down her back.

Her hands are clammy, slippery on the smooth varnished wood. The noise is growing louder. Not just because she is getting closer. It's changing from a sob to a wail. It echoes through the space.

'Lucy?'

Still nothing. She's more than halfway. She wants to puke. Pausing briefly, she can see Lucy's bedroom door now. It's closed. Swallowing down saliva, and a hint of bile, she continues slowly.

In agony, she reaches the top, steadying herself on the posts. She lets out a long breath, her entire body trembles. She sways, takes a tiny step backwards, but catches the bannister with a trembling hand, righting herself. She moves away from the edge, limping towards the door, pressing her ear against it. The girl inside is screaming now.

Manic, desperate wailing.

Diana knocks.

'Lucy, what's wrong?'

She touches the knob. It's slippery in her wet palm.

Pushing the door, it creaks slowly open.

'I'm coming in!' she calls.

Silence.

The room is empty. A pile of clean laundry is folded neatly on the edge of the bed. Bottles of cosmetics arranged tidily on the dressing table. A rucksack hangs over the back of the chair. Diana narrows her eyes, shaking her head. She steps inside, checking behind the door. Nobody.

She shivers, despite the warm day, and returns to the ground floor. It's always easier going down. By the time she reaches the hall she is quite exhausted. She rounds the corner, looking towards the kitchen. Her heart pounds. Richard's door is closed once more.

She hurries towards it, pushing it. It begins to swing, but halfway it stops. Something pushes back hard, and it slams closed, almost knocking Diana over. She grabs the handle, trying to open it again.

The same thing happens. She steps back, staring ahead.

'Lucy?' she shouts through the panels.

The latch clicks and the door begins to creak very slowly inwards.

Diana's fingers tingle. A sense of unease floods over her. Suddenly terrified, she doesn't want to see whatever is on the other side. She grabs the handle, this time pulling it hard closed. Something inside does the opposite. She is screaming now, trying to keep the door shut, but the force inside is yanking. It wobbles, opens a crack, but she manages to keep pulling it shut.

Tears stream down her face. She's dropped her stick and grips with both hands, but her limited strength is waning.

Everything feels suddenly still, but she doesn't dare let go. She falls to her knees, keeps pulling.

'Diana?'

A voice behind her. She whips her head around, staring behind her, eyes bulging.

'Lucy! There's someone in there!'

The girl marches to the door, pushing Diana aside. She shoves the door hard. It swings open, banging against the wardrobe inside.

Richard sits in his wheelchair, staring out towards them. Same as before. Window open.

Nobody else in the room.

They both back away, stepping into the kitchen, gasping as a figure steps in through the back door.

Diana screams.

'What on earth is going on?' Mylo shouts.

'Mylo! What are you doing here?' Lucy sighs, heart thumping.

'I swung by to see if things were okay... after... you know. I heard screaming as I pulled up. Is everything all right?'

Lucy eyes him cautiously, frowning. Diana is watching him too, a curious expression on her face.

'We're fine. Diana had a bit of a scare, that's all.'

Diana scratches at her temple, and Lucy crosses the kitchen. Touching his elbow lightly, she eases Mylo back into the garden.

'What's going on?' he whispers as they step outside.

'How long have you been here?' Lucy spits.

'Not long. I heard Diana screaming as I approached the pier. What's with the animosity? I thought you may need some help.'

She glares at him, shaking her head.

'Thanks for the concern. But we're fine. I don't mean to be rude, but can you go? I need to get her sorted.'

He looks crestfallen but does as she asks. She watches him trudge across the lawn. Starting the engine, he steers the boat away without looking back.

54

'He's gone. Now... what was that all about, Diana?'

'Didn't you hear the wailing? That's what took me upstairs in the first place.' Diana stares at Lucy.

'I didn't hear anything, apart from you screaming.'

'There was crying coming from your room. Believe me, I wouldn't attempt a journey up the stairs for *nothing*! I thought you were hurt. Then when I got in there, it was empty. I came back downstairs, and Richard's door was closed again. I knew something was up because I'd already opened it once.'

Lucy sighs, looking towards the ceiling. She counts silently in her head.

'I think we should call the doctor.'

'No! This was *real*! You must believe me.'

'With all due respect, you thought the bugs were real yesterday.'

Diana's cheeks colour as she glances away.

'I'm not mad.'

'And I'm not suggesting you are. Maybe a little confused, that's all.'

218

'I know what happened. There was somebody in that room trying to get out. I did not imagine it.'

'There's nobody in there. Only Richard.'

Diana pulls a face, swatting at the air with her hand.

'Just because you can't see them, does *not* mean there is nobody there. That's what she *wants* you to think. She wants you to believe I'm mad. Don't you see?'

Lucy doesn't respond. She doesn't want to get into another discussion about ghosts.

'Who was here with you earlier?'

'When?'

'When I waved at you from the garden.'

'Nobody. I was alone.'

'No, there was somebody standing right behind you.'

Diana's face becomes ashen.

'There, you see! I assure you I was here by myself. So how do you explain *that*?'

Lucy runs a hand through her hair, letting out a breath.

'Must have been a reflection or something.'

'Why will you not believe what *all* the evidence is clearly pointing to?'

'Because it's ridiculous, that's why.' She pauses. 'Can you call the doctor, please? He was insistent that you should do it today.'

'Yes, okay. If only I can prove to you that I am quite sane.'

She hobbles through to the living room. Lucy stands in the doorway, arms folded. She watches as Diana picks up the phone, dialling.

'Yes, hello, it's Diana Davenport. I'd like to make an appointment to see Doctor Miller, please.'

She waits, tapping her foot. She gives her name and date of birth.

'That should be fine, I'll make a note of it. Thank you.'

She replaces the receiver, turning to Lucy.

'Nothing available until a week on Friday.'

Lucy narrows her eyes.

'He assured me he would fit you in today.'

'They must be busier than he anticipated. It's usually manic up there. It's the only surgery for miles.'

Lucy tuts, walking away. She heads into the utility room to finish folding laundry. She has already re-hoovered up all the mess that Diana emptied onto the floor yesterday. As she folds a towel, a strange feeling washes over her. She turns, glancing around the space, thinking Diana must have followed her in, but she is alone.

She crosses to the door, poking her head through. Diana isn't in the kitchen either. She frowns. Approaching the window, she slowly runs her eyes along the horizon.

'Get a grip,' she whispers to herself, shaking her head. She returns to the washing, but she can't shake the feeling that she is being watched.

55

The girl seemed to buy the charade on the phone. Of course, Diana had simply dialled a random selection of numbers. She had absolutely no intention of going to visit the doctor.

The events in Richard's room were real.

She accepts that she did not have bugs crawling under her skin. She realises in the light of a new day that it was some sort of hallucination, brought on by her exhausted state, no doubt. But she is sure. Today's events really happened. It felt different. Even now, thinking about it in a calm state... she shudders. Of course, Lucy believes she is bonkers. Won't even entertain the idea that it's not all in Diana's mind. She must have got quite a scare yesterday. It's only natural that she is sceptical. She's looking out for her. Being kind. And poor Mylo... Diana cringes inwardly as she thinks about him witnessing her episode.

She raises her hand to her plait subconsciously. It feels messy, tangled. She heads to the bathroom, pulling the strands loose. She stands staring in the mirror, hardly recognising the apparition that glares back at her with dark-circled eyes. She pulls her hair loose, separating the braid, and taking a brush from the cabinet, she smooths the kinks out, sighing.

Dividing her long mane into three bunches, she begins to plait, pulling tightly. Once satisfied, she ties the elastic band from her wrist around the end, and heads to the kitchen, as Lucy emerges from the utility room carrying a pile of laundry. She places the items onto the worktop and starts to fold them into neat piles. Her eyes dart up towards Diana, who stands in the doorway.

'How long ago did your daughter disappear?' she asks, as she stacks towels on top of each other.

Diana takes a few slow breaths before she answers.

'It's been years now.'

'Do you mind me asking about her?'

'No. I like talking about her.' She smiles, crossing to a chair, and lowering herself down.

Lucy flicks the kettle on.

'Tea?' she offers.

'Please.'

Diana stares out to the garden. A group of swifts dart about, landing among the branches of the old eponymous willow tree.

'She was a lovely girl. I know all parents probably say that about their daughters... but Claire truly was.' She doesn't look at Lucy as she talks. Continues to watch the birds through the window.

'She was kind. She was beautiful. And so bright too... she could have achieved anything she wanted to. We saw her as a blessing. Richard and I had tried for so long to have a child. We'd given up, really. But then when we stopped trying... along came Claire.'

She laughs. The sound brings a smile to Lucy's face.

'It must have been difficult... losing her.'

Diana's eyes drift towards the floor.

'I wasn't entirely honest about her disappearance. I find it difficult to talk about. It was all so awful, the days leading up to her going missing. There's a lot of guilt on my part. She'd had an argument with Richard, you see. It was… delicate. She thought her father was having an affair. Had come by a photograph of him with another woman.'

Diana pauses, her eyes drifting away from Lucy momentarily.

'He was. Richard had… many affairs… but how do you explain to your child that you're willing to turn a blind eye to these indiscretions? These betrayals. Those were my choices, but she would never understand them. So we denied it. Unfortunately, there was no convincing her. We saw her the day she disappeared. She came to the house; I'd engineered a meeting between them to try to get the whole mess sorted once and for all. It didn't go as I had planned. She refused to speak to him.'

The kettle boils. Lucy pours two cups, passing one to Diana.

'They both became angry… it was quite heated. Richard was never the best at keeping his head. And Claire was her father's daughter. All I could do was watch as it escalated.' She pauses, her eyes glazing.

'Anyway… she left. It was terrible. And that was the last time we ever saw her.'

'Diana, I am so sorry. I can't even begin to imagine…'

Diana's eyes flick up to Lucy, then away nervously.

'There's more. If I were to say the name Christopher Kernick to you, would you know who I was talking about?'

Lucy looks blankly back at her, but a sudden flash of recognition crosses the girl's face.

'The Butcher?'

Diana nods solemnly.

'I remember it. Women were terrified to leave their homes. It was awful.'

'He killed nine girls in total... that we know of. Mainly prostitutes, or homeless. Drug addicts. People he knew wouldn't be missed... until the bodies turned up. Claire was the exception. I'll never understand why he chose her. She was nothing like the others. But she was his final victim.'

Lucy gasps, as her hand flies towards her mouth.

'They never found her body, but apparently, they didn't need to. The evidence against him was overwhelming. Traces of her blood on his clothing, and more in the boot of his car. They worked together, Claire and Kernick. He was seemingly infatuated with her. He'd asked her out on a few occasions, but she'd declined. She said something about him scared her.'

Diana gives a small, humourless laugh. 'There's a lot to be said for a woman's intuition. She'd told us about him in passing... the guy at work who wouldn't take no for an answer, but we thought it was funny more than anything else. We never imagined that he would...' She pauses, unable to bring herself to say it. A single tear trickles down her cheek from her milky eye.

'The only blessing is she never got to see the horrors that her parents became.' She blows on her tea, sipping it.

'My mother always said don't let the sun go down on an argument and never allow a loved one to leave after words of anger. I used to laugh at her, call her crazy... roll my eyes. But she was right. Hindsight is a wonderful thing. There isn't a day that passes where I don't regret those last moments we spent with our daughter. How much I wish things could have been different. But it's pointless dwelling. What's done is done.'

Lucy continues to fold the laundry, watching Diana.

'I'm so sorry. It must be hard enough to lose a child... but to know she was a victim to that psychopath...' She trails off, glancing through the window.

Diana nods.

'It was horrendous. You can't begin to imagine... but I take solace from knowing they caught him, and that he will spend the rest of his life behind bars.' She pauses, raising her hand to her bare throat.

'That's what I was doing yesterday in the utility room. I was looking for the necklace. It was hers. *He* gave it to her. I know that may sound odd, but it reminds me. It reminds me to never let my guard down, and never underestimate people. You never know what anyone is capable of. It also reminds me of Claire. It's all I have left of her really.'

She gazes out into the garden, watching a butterfly that patters against the windowpane. It dances around a while, before fluttering away towards the water. A smile flashes fleetingly across her lips.

'I wasn't always like this. A recluse, I mean. I used to love company. Had a wonderful circle of friends. A fantastic existence. Richard and I travelled. God, did we travel. We made the most of life. I know you see a sad, crazy old woman who keeps herself hidden away from the world. But I've had more than my fair share of hardships. I find it... easier this way.'

Lucy opens her mouth to say something, probably some nicety, assuring Diana that she is talking nonsense. But Diana has overheard enough gossip on her rare trips into civilisation, to know what people think about her.

'Don't. You don't need to contradict me. I'm not looking for sympathy, or compliments. I'm simply trying to explain to you. Although I still have Richard, it feels as if I lost him in the accident. Sometimes I wish...' She stops herself, shaking her head.

'If Claire were here, things would be easier. That's all. I wouldn't feel so alone.'

Another tear rolls down Diana's cheek, changing its track as it bumps over the rough, spidery tendrils of her scar.

'So many regrets...' she trails off.

Lucy picks up the pile. 'I'll put this in your room for you,' she says, hurrying from the kitchen, leaving Diana staring after her, alone with her thoughts.

56

LUCY

She heads into Diana's room, placing the laundry on the dresser. As she begins to place it away into drawers, she notices a picture lying face down on the top. She lifts it.

Rose, crouching behind Diana and Richard. Smiling her huge, beautiful smile. Diana looks... happy. Lucy almost doesn't recognise her.

The glass in the frame is smashed, splinters remain around the edges.

She frowns, placing it upright on the unit, and continues to put the clothes away. Picking up an empty cup and plate, she turns to see Diana in the hall. She walks into Richard's room, closing the door behind her. Lucy creeps down the corridor, stopping outside. She hears Diana's voice from inside, muffled. It sounds like she's crying. Lucy holds her breath, gently pressing her ear against the wood.

She can only make out intermittent words.

'...Claire... and I just wish... know that we... but I want... Claire... loss... regret it... your fault!'

There's a slapping sound.

227

Lucy steps back. The plate slips from her fingers, shattering onto the floorboards.

Eyes darting from side to side, she takes a sidestep into the kitchen as she hears Diana's stick click-clacking across the floor.

Ducking down, she crouches beside the units as Richard's door opens.

'Lucy?' Diana calls.

There's a crunch as Diana steps forward, her shoe grinding the smashed porcelain into hard wood.

'What the devil... Lucy?'

Her stick beats the ground as Diana heads towards the bottom of the stairs. Lucy crawls behind the island unit, pressing her back against the cabinet doors. Diana returns along the hall.

'Lucy?' she calls, a hint of fear now lacing her voice.

The cane clicks across tiles. There's a noise from above. Glancing up, she sees the stick resting on the worktop, poking slightly proud of the edge over her head.

Diana limps slowly to the wall. Lucy can't tell what she's doing at first, but then hears the sound of the china being swept into a pile. Diana lets the broom clatter to the floor, inches from Lucy. She retrieves her stick and hobbles down the hall to her bedroom, slamming the door.

The girl waits, barely wanting to breathe. When she's sure Diana isn't returning, she stands from her hiding place. She eyes the pile of china, swept messily inside the kitchen, as she enters Richard's room. He sits in his chair, back towards the window. He looks... odd. His shirt is torn. There are drops of blood on his chest, seeping into the fabric.

As she steps nearer, she sees his nose is bleeding, his cheek is red. She unbuttons his shirt, pulling it from his flabby body. The bruises are healing a little better now, looking more yellow. Less angry.

She dabs at his face, wiping the blood away, grabs a thin

mauve cable-knit sweater from the wardrobe and redresses him. Stroking his cheek with her thumb, she leans her face close to his. His eyes wobble from side to side.

'Why was it your fault, Richard? Is there more to the story? Did you say something so terrible to Claire that it drove her into the arms of her killer?' She tilts her head to one side, and straightens, heading back out to the hall, closing the door behind her.

57

I t rained overnight, leaving a musty smell in the air. As Lucy trudges through the woods, avoiding large patches of wet mud, she sniffs, screwing up her face. She left the bike in the outhouse today, thinking it would be easier on foot. Brushing against huge ferns, droplets of water transfer to her jeans, making them damp. She recognises a small footbridge across a stream and knows she is getting close. She pulls her phone from her pocket. One bar appears on her signal. She pushes forwards, past clumps of St John's Wort, its green berries starting to turn red.

Holding her arm out at full length, the bars jump up. The handset begins to ping and buzz as emails and messages flow into her inboxes. Mostly junk. She wouldn't expect anything else.

Smiling, she opens up a web browser, typing *Claire Davenport* into a search engine. A plethora of results fill her screen. She scrolls down, eyes darting back and forth.

The Butcher caught!

**Christopher Kernick charged with murder of artists'
daughter.**
Reign of terror is finally over.

Lucy scans the stories, clicking on each one, drinking in the
details.

It was much as Diana had said. Kernick, a colleague of Claire's
had been infatuated with her. They had been friendly, but Claire
dropped the friendship after he showed some *worrying* behaviour,
according to her mother. He had turned up at her house in the
middle of the night, on more than one occasion. Her room-mate
had to call the police to get rid of him. Although he has always
denied playing any part in Claire's disappearance or death, large
amounts of her blood and hairs were discovered in the boot of his
Mondeo. Police had also found overalls, stained with her blood,
and containing her DNA, hidden at the back of his garage, along
with evidence linking him to the murders of eight other women.

Lucy furrows her brow as she reads this detail. She
remembers what it was like when the killer was at large. The
police had been stumped, because he was so meticulous. Each
body was devoid of anything that could tie anyone to the crimes.

She clicks on a photograph of Christopher. She knows the
face well from when he was caught. He was on the front of every
newspaper at the time. A handsome lad. Rugby player's build.
Nice eyes. Kind smile. Definitely *not* what you would expect. She
zooms in on the grainy picture, shaking her head. He certainly
doesn't look like a cold-blooded serial rapist and killer.

Finding an interview with his sister, Lucy sets herself down
on a large slab of quartz protruding from the moss-covered
ground.

Melanie Kernick claims that her brother had been framed.
She insists emphatically he is a gentle giant who would never

hurt anyone. She also claims he had been over Claire for some time, and that stories of his stalking had been grossly exaggerated. When asked who would frame him, she has no opinions, but contends that her brother had no enemies. *Everyone who meets him adores him.*

But the evidence against him was too great. He's currently serving a life sentence in HMP Manchester, previously *Strangeways.*

She finds another story, from the day Kernick was sentenced. There's a wide angle shot outside the court. Diana and Richard stand with a suited official, looking sad. Crowds mill around. Something in the background catches her eye.

She spreads her fingers across the screen, zooming in. Squinting, she zooms again, and gasps as she focuses on the blurry face. It's small, and not completely in focus, but she knows exactly who it is. He's clean-shaven, younger, of course, but it's unmistakable. Lurking in the background, watching.

Mylo.

She narrows her eyes, tilting her head to one side. Diana is obviously convinced that Kernick is guilty. The whole country was at the time. You can't argue with the evidence after all.

But seeing Mylo lingering in the background at court troubles Lucy immensely.

'Why were you there, Mylo?' she says out loud, tapping her phone screen.

58

The following day, Lucy returns from a walk to find Diana sitting in the garden, drinking a glass of white wine. Her eyes have that vacant, glazed look that Lucy has come to know well. She makes herself a coffee and takes a seat beside her.

'Did you ever meet Christopher Kernick?' Lucy asks nonchalantly, as if she is talking about the weather, or some other trivial subject. The colour drains from the woman's face. She hesitates before responding.

'No,' she says, matter-of-factly, leaving it there.

But Lucy isn't prepared to let it drop that easily.

'I was reading up on the case. I hope you don't mind. Our conversation had me intrigued.'

No reply.

'I see that it was you who initially alerted the police to his... interest in Claire.'

'It was *not* an interest. It was an infatuation!'

'I see. Claire told you this?'

She avoids Lucy's eyes, stares down at her hands, fidgeting.

'Yes,' she responds eventually. Her voice wavers, betraying her statement.

'It must have been terrible for Claire... being stalked like that.'

'That man made her life a misery. He turned up at her house at all hours, refused to leave. She hated going to work because she had to see him. He caused a great deal of anxiety in the last few precious months of her life, and then he ended that life, in what we can only assume was a terrible, and terrifying ordeal for her. And to add insult to injury, he has never had the courtesy to reveal where her body is. Never given us... closure.'

Diana sounds odd, more like she is reciting a learned passage rather than speaking from the heart. Her voice quietens towards the end. Lucy doesn't like dragging up the past in such a clearly painful way. She's never been one for hurting people unnecessarily. But she feels a desire to hear Diana's side.

'Yeah. That was odd, wasn't it?' Lucy asks.

Diana frowns.

'He dumped all the other bodies in woodland. Why was Claire's never found?'

'I don't know. Perhaps he was caught before he had a chance to... dispose of her.'

'You're sure of his guilt?'

Her head whips around.

'Of course I am sure! The evidence... if you've been "reading up on the case", as you say, you'll be aware of what they found.'

'Yes. I'm aware. It struck me as odd, though, that's all.'

'What did?'

'That he would keep the bloodstained overalls in his garage, along with the other evidence, linking him to the other girls. I mean... I'm no expert, but if it were *me*, I'd have destroyed those. Burned them. And to just leave blood in the boot of his car like that? Wouldn't he have at least *tried* to clean it up? I know it would have shown up with that luminol stuff anyway, but he didn't even make any attempt to hide it. Why? It's almost as if he *wanted* to get caught.'

Diana fiddles with her fringe, splaying it out across her forehead, stroking the strands of her braid.

'Perhaps he did. He claims he was besotted with her. Maybe he was so consumed with guilt that he wanted to be found out. Who knows? Maybe he was racked with guilt over the other killings. Perhaps he wanted it all to end, but he wasn't strong enough to stop. The man was not well... mentally. I think he was beyond behaving in a rational way.'

Lucy shrugs.

'His sister was adamant that he wasn't in love with Claire. She said he had moved on... was even involved with someone new.'

'She *would* say that. She'd have said anything if she thought it would get him off.' Diana purses her lips, continuing, 'And the *new girl* he was seeing... one of Claire's friends from work. A very thinly veiled attempt to make her jealous if you ask me.'

'He doesn't *look* like a killer. I remember that from the time. A lot of people were surprised. He wasn't what anyone was expecting.'

'And *what*, pray tell, *does* a killer look like?' The hint of a smile creeps onto Diana's lips.

'I don't mean it like that... I mean... he looked nice.'

Diana shakes her head, letting out a sigh.

'Never judge a book by its cover,' she says, a knowing tone to her voice.

Lucy lingers, wondering how to tackle the next subject. Diana shoots her a look.

'Spit it out then. There's obviously something else you want to say... so say it and stop standing there like a lemon!'

'Can I ask you something?'

'Go ahead.'

'Did you think it was odd that Mylo happened to turn up at the house the other day, right at the moment that something strange had happened?'

Diana frowns, thinking, but doesn't reply.

'It made me think, he turned up before as well, when that stone stack appeared outside your studio.'

'Your point being?'

Lucy shrugs.

'Nothing, I guess. Just that it was... odd.' She pauses. 'When exactly did Mylo live down south?'

'I'm not sure. His father died a couple of years ago, but I don't know how long he was away. He was there quite a few years. I know him from way back when Claire was much younger.'

Lucy pauses, with her mug midway to her mouth.

'Hold on... so you're saying that Mylo and Claire knew each other?'

'Yes. They dated, very briefly. That's how I initially met him, and why it was nice to cross paths with him again up here. It was lovely to see a familiar face. Although, my face wasn't how he remembered it.' A sadness fills her eyes. 'Why all the questions about Mylo?'

'Oh... thinking out loud really. It doesn't matter.'

Lucy leaves it there. She doesn't want to push too far. She retreats, leaving her with her wine.

Now she sits in her room, staring at a screenshot she took of the image of Mylo outside court. It is a small world. She knows that. But some coincidences just seem too unlikely. A close acquaintance of Diana's daughter, and if the picture is anything to go by, still in contact with her around the time of her murder. And now here he is, right where Diana has ended up. Ending up engaged to her lodger, who then dies in a tragic accident.

All too convenient, Lucy thinks.

59

DIANA

For the first time in days, Diana feels relatively normal. Her head is clear, thoughts together, and her speech is not slurred. She feels as if a cloud has lifted from her.

A conversation with Lucy about Christopher Kernick set her on edge. The girl had implied that he might be innocent. Diana did not like that. It's been too long to start dragging *all that* up again.

Best left buried.

She thinks of Claire, and her heart breaks as it always does. She'd lost her temper with Richard a few days ago; struck him. It's the first time she has ever done that. She's not proud. A testament to the fact that she really hasn't been herself for a while.

Today, though, she feels things may be getting better.

Lucy has gone out. Diana doesn't know where; doesn't care. She has the house to herself, and that's all that matters... well, Richard is here. He's *always* here. But she's not sure that counts.

There have been no ghostly goings on for a few days. Willow Cottage feels... safe. She wonders if she should call Annette, tell her not to bother.

She picks up her cane, crosses to the bedroom door, and heads to her bathroom. Turning on the hot tap, she sprinkles a handful of bath salts into the water, watching them dissolve, turning the water a satisfying blue. She walks to Richard's room to check he's okay. He's sleeping in his chair, head slumped forwards. She watches for a second, holding her breath. When she sees his chest rise and fall, she relaxes.

She returns to her bedroom, undressing, folding her clothes into a neat pile at the end of her bed. She takes her fluffy white towelling bathrobe from the back of her door, sliding it over her skin.

She hasn't worn it for ages; had forgotten how luxurious it feels. She unwinds the strands of her plait, ruffling her fingers through it, letting it fall loose around her shoulders. She makes her way to the kitchen, opening a cupboard. Biting her lip, she eyes the rows of wine on the shelf. She really shouldn't. Not when she is beginning to feel well again.

But she wants to.

Just one glass, she tells herself. As she pours the thick ruby liquid, she knows in her heart that won't be the case. She inhales deeply, holding the drink beneath her nostrils. It smells wonderful. Heavenly.

She slides a stopper into the bottle, placing it back on the shelf, returning to the bathroom. Steam is beginning to fill the air, the scent of the salts swirling around. She sips the wine, sitting on the edge of the roll-top tub, testing the water with her free hand; too hot. She twists the cold tap, crossing to the door. She closes it, and, still feeling slightly uneasy about being alone, slides the bolt in place. She feels safer this way.

She removes her dressing gown, hangs it on a brass hook. By the time she reaches the tub, the water temperature is perfect. Turning off the taps, she sits on the smooth edge, swinging her legs round over the side. She winces as she slides herself down into the water, inhaling the aromas. Pulling her knees up towards her chest, she fingers the rough scars on her legs. Shaking her head, she sips her wine, smiling. A few days ago, she had honestly thought she might be losing her mind. Now she feels... calm.

She hums a tune, relaxing down under the surface. Her shoulders turn red as they sink. She watches distorted shapes of birds swoop past the swirling pattern of the frosted glass window opposite her.

The evening sun is still bright, streaming in, hitting the steam. She can hear the gentle lapping of the waves on shingle.

She thinks of Richard, *before*. She pictures his handsome face, his immaculate presentation. Diana had been the envy of her circle. Unlike most of her friends, their sex life had been fulfilling. They found ways to make sure of that. Never let it dwindle. Never let the excitement go. She used to watch him from across a room, and tremble with unadulterated lust. Wanting to take him there and then.

And now... the poor pathetic creature in the next room is all she is left with.

She remembers the first time she saw him... *after* the accident. She'd not long accepted her own appearance. When she visited him in his hospital bed... she wept. She wept for him, of course. It was a tragedy. But she also cried for herself. For what she had lost.

For the longest time, she wondered if this had been a punishment for being so smug. *Pride comes before a fall*, her mother had always said.

Diana knew Richard was a catch. And that other women wanted him.

Not now. Nobody wants him these days.

She loves him, of course she does. But at times... she wishes things could be different. *We got our comeuppance, and we got it good*, she ponders. She blinks away the thought, laying her head back onto the edge of the tub. Her hair hangs over the lip, dangling down to the floor; she can't face the energy and time it takes to wash and dry it.

Closing her eyes, she conjures up Claire as a child. So beautiful, innocent. Always laughing. She was a gift. Diana had taken her as a sign to never give up. Whenever she thought something was impossible, she remembered her amazing daughter.

She thinks of *that* night. When everything changed. She will never forget the way Claire had looked at her, sitting beside Richard on the red leather Chesterfield, holding his hand. Stroking it with her thumb. Jaw clenched tight.

You are mistaken, Diana had scolded. The disappointment was apparent on the girl's face.

Diana will always regret that. Perhaps if she had said something different, taken another tack, things might not have turned out the way they did.

Why must she always dwell on sadness? She frequently does this to herself, whenever she feels good, she finds a way to make herself feel... not good. Punishing herself.

She empties the dregs of the wine, reaching down and placing the glass on the floor beside her. Closing her eyes once more, she tries to return to a happier state of mind. And as she does, she hears it. A giggle. Almost childlike.

Quiet, but definite.

She holds her breath. A patter of footsteps on the stairs, and down the hallway.

Another giggle.

She sits up, gripping the edges of the tub.

'Hello?'

Silence.

'Lucy, are you back?'

She pulls her knees up towards herself again. Something moves past the bathroom. She sees a shadow on the boards beneath the gap at the bottom of the door. The sound is louder this time. Closer.

She stands, water cascading from her body. Steam rises from her skin as she tentatively steps onto the tiled floor, grappling for a towel. Taking her cane, she limps across the room.

The handle rattles.

She takes a deep breath.

'Who's there?' she shouts.

A force collides with the outside of the door. Diana jumps, heart pounds. She takes another step forward. Again, the wood rattles, so hard, so loud, she's sure it might give way. Her eyes dart to the bolt. It's holding fast.

Another thump. Violent. Aggressive. *Angry*.

Stumbling back, she knocks the wine glass, shattering it. Tiny shards scatter across the floor. Diana takes a step backwards as something pounds outside again. The force is immense. She's sure the entire house is shaking. Her foot lowers onto sharp splinters as she steps back further.

Wincing, she raises her foot, letting it hover above the mess. Glancing down, she sees red swirls appearing on the porcelain tiles. The door continues to bang. She's unsure how long the bolt will hold. It's small, not the strongest. Again and again, the noise fills her ears. She sits on the side of the tub, lifting her leg to assess the damage. Pieces of glass litter the sole. She brushes them with her fingertips. A few fall loose, some larger pieces stick fast. They're in deep. Stinging.

Hopping to the cabinet, foot raised in the air, she pauses, a look of horror on her face.

The mirrored doors are covered in a film of steam. Written on the glass, in crude, childish letters, three words.

I am here.

Wiping the message away with her hand, she throws open the door, scrambling around inside. She finds tweezers, and a roll of bandage, and grabs another towel, lowering herself down to sit on the toilet bowl. Tweezing fragments from her flesh, she squirms, as tiny droplets of blood drip to the ground, splattering in a crown pattern on the cream tiles. She shakes her head. The house is silent once more. She takes a hand towel, pressing it to her wounds, lifting it now and then to check if it's still bleeding. The crimson liquid stains the white fluffy cotton, forming messy red splodges on its surface. She drops it, and winds the bandage around her foot a few times, taking it up her ankle, tucking it underneath itself to secure it in place.

Standing, she holds her foot a few millimetres from the floor, resting her toes gently as she crosses the room. Pressing her ear against the door, she holds her breath. No sound resonates in the house. No movement in the hallway. No footsteps, no laughter.

Only eerie silence.

Suddenly, something thrusts against the wood once more. Diana's head whips backwards painfully, so hard she falls to the ground. Her buttocks slam into the tiles, her towel falls loose around her.

She sits there, naked, mouth open wide, quivering, as she stares up at the door handle. She doesn't know how long she waits. Too terrified to leave. As the evening sun lowers in the sky outside, she finally realises she is alone once more. Standing, she presses her ear to the surface again. Satisfied, she slowly slides the bolt as quietly as she can. It makes a clicking sound as it slips out of its casing, and she screws her eyes shut tight, not daring to breathe. After a moment, she opens them, pushing the handle, letting the door swing out.

The hall is empty.

As it should be. No sounds from upstairs. All is calm. As

Diana steps out, she gasps, eyes flick downwards. Her head whips from side to side, unsure where to look.

It can't be possible, yet here it is.

Her gaze passes slowly across the rug and floorboards, taking in the angry-looking splashes of red liquid that once more cover them, spilling out from the foot of the stairs, running down the plug socket mounted outside the living room.

60

DIANA

S he is sitting on the bottom stair when Lucy arrives home. The girl enters through the kitchen, heading down the hall to the stairs. She pauses halfway along, staring at the floor, then towards Diana.

'My God! What happened? Are you okay?' Her eyes drift to Diana's bandaged foot.

She nods.

'It isn't my blood. It's hers.'

Lucy bites her bottom lip.

'Who?'

'Rose's.'

Lucy's shoulders slump as she sighs.

'Let me see,' she says as she steps over the mess on the floor.

'It's not mine. I trod on a broken wine glass. Tiny splinters. It's hardly bleeding at all anymore.'

The girl looks down at the floorboards.

'I was in the bath. I heard noises. And *this*,' she motions with her good arm, 'is what I found.'

Lucy glances into the bathroom, seeing the remnants of the glass shattered across the tiles.

'How much have you had to drink?'

'I had one *small* glass of red, and most of it ended up on the floor anyway. Check the bottle if you don't believe me. It's on the shelf in the cupboard.'

'If that's what you say you had, then I trust you. We should get this cleaned up, or you'll be paying that man to come back and sand them down again. You'll not have any floor left at this rate.'

She enters the kitchen. Diana hears the tap running, cupboards opening and closing. She's checking the bottle. She finally emerges with a mop and bucket which she places outside Richard's bedroom door. She crouches, rolling the bloodstained runner into a compact heap, taking it through to the laundry room. She sloshes the mop onto the floor. It hits the boards with a wet slap.

'I think that rug has had it, I'm afraid,' she says matter-of-factly while she sloshes over the red patches. 'I'll try to get it out. I've put it in the sink to soak overnight. You never know.'

She glances at Diana. The woman stares back at her incredulously.

'Are you just going to act like nothing has happened here? As if this is completely normal?'

The girl stops, leaning her chin on the top of the handle.

'I don't know what you want me to say, Diana.'

'I want you to say that you believe me. That what is happening here, is... her. Trying to terrorise me.'

'I want to, honestly I do. But I don't believe in ghosts. And anyway, why *would* Rose be out to get you?'

Diana's eyes flick away. She ignores the question.

'What about the Ouija board? You saw it with your own eyes.'

Lucy leans the mop against the bannisters, sitting beside Diana on the stairs.

'I've done some research online. Have you heard of the ideomotor effect?'

Diana shakes her head.

'It's what *the game* relies on. It's when someone… unintentionally moves the pointer, without even realising they're doing it.'

'That's not what happened. What about the glass, afterwards, flying from your hand? You said you felt a presence…'

'We were both pretty spooked… maybe I simply dropped it. I'm not sure.'

Diana looks towards the ceiling, exhaling heavily through her nose.

'No.'

'Diana… I know you *want* to believe she is here. But you're an educated woman. Surely you realise that's… impossible.'

She doesn't respond. Lucy stands, continuing to wash the floor. The water wrings from the head, a muddy red colour. It's coming off, but it's going to stain. She takes the bucket to the kitchen, emptying it down the sink, running the tap. Swirls of pink gush down the plughole. She watches, fascinated by the patterns.

Diana is standing when she returns.

'Would you like me to take a look at your foot?' Lucy asks.

She shakes her head.

'Can I help you to bed?'

'No, thank you. I'm fine.'

She crosses the hall, pushing into her room, slamming the door behind herself.

Lucy sighs, shaking her head. Staring down at the dark stains on the floor, a chill creeps across her, causing her to shiver. She eyes the red patches, biting her lip. *Definitely not blood*, she thinks. But as she returns to the kitchen, she can't help avoiding it, as if touching it might be bad.

61

She wipes the last of the red from the plug socket, staring intently at the dark stains that mark the boards once more. She purses her lips. Diana is moving about. Lucy can hear her banging drawers and cupboards. It's good that she's decided to have a bath, at least. Must mean she is feeling a little better.

Eventually the noise from Diana's room stops. Lucy presses her ear to the door. Silence.

Crossing to the lounge, she pulls her purse from her pocket and slips Valentina's business card from the folds of the leather. She flips it over between her fingers a few times, biting her lip. Glancing towards the hall, she lifts the receiver from the telephone, quickly dialling. After a few rings, the call is answered.

'Ciao!' the woman barks down the phone.

'Valentina... I'm so sorry to call you in the evening. It's Lucy here, at Willow Cottage.'

There's a pause, as Valentina is trying to catch up, or maybe she honestly has no idea.

'Richard Davenport's carer,' Lucy elaborates.

'Oh yes, hi.'

Lucy hears a long breath being exhaled; she imagines Valentina is blowing out a huge plume of menthol cigarette smoke.

'Everything okay?' she asks, a hint of trepidation in her voice.

Lucy pauses, wondering how exactly to tackle this. She doesn't want to panic the poor woman.

'Yes, don't worry. There have been some... developments, and you asked me to call.'

'Oh God, what's happened?'

'So... last week, there was... an episode. We had to call the doctor, Mylo and I. She's fine now, she seems much better.'

'What sort of episode?'

'It was quite scary. She fully flipped out, thought there were bugs crawling under her skin. And she's still going on about this *Rose* thing. She's convinced her ghost is here, tormenting her. She made me do a Ouija board with her. I've been out with Mylo tonight, and when I got home... you know the stain at the bottom of the stairs?'

'Uh huh.'

'She had it removed not long ago. When I got back, red paint had been poured over the floor. I think... I mean... I'm pretty sure she's done it herself.'

Silence from the end of the line.

'Maybe you should come and visit her. See what you think? You know her much better than I do. She's seen the doctor, but perhaps she needs a friend?'

'Right,' Lucy hears tapping, 'this isn't good. Has she been painting at all?'

'Not to my knowledge. But I don't know what she does when I'm not here.'

More exhaling. Lucy can almost see the plumes of smoke.

'I'll come tomorrow. It won't be until about five or six; I've got a thing in the morning. But I'll come after.'

'That's great, I appreciate it.'

The woman hangs up without saying goodbye.

Lucy places the receiver down and slips the card away, heading upstairs.

62

The hum of the boat arriving outside draws Lucy's attention to the window. She's seen him a few times since he rejected her; assured him everything is fine, but she can't help thinking things feel awkward. She needs to keep him onside so she can figure out why he was lingering outside the courthouse at Kernick's trial.

It doesn't help that the only way to speak is on the landline, which inevitably Diana usually answers.

It's madness that in this day and age there are places with no signal.

Shaking her head, she steps out into the garden, pulling the door shut behind her.

He's still on the boat, fiddling with something. She suspects he's procrastinating. Eventually he steps ashore, trudging across the lawn towards her.

'Hi!' he shouts.

She nods, aware that her behaviour must seem odd to him; not inviting him inside. But she doesn't want him to come into the cottage, doesn't want to risk him seeing the red at the bottom of the stairs.

He hands her the pile. She glances down at it, shuffling through. Opening the door, she leans inside, placing the letters for Diana onto the worktop, holding her own parcel.

'How's things?' he asks, with what comes across as forced cheerfulness.

She shakes her head.

'Okay, I guess.'

He gazes over her shoulder. She turns to see Diana is approaching behind her from the hallway. The door swings open.

'Mylo, hello, my dear!'

She's beaming. She looks better today. Hair tidily braided down her back as usual. Speech is less slurred. It's a vast improvement.

'Hello, Diana.' He attempts to smile. 'How are you feeling now?'

She averts her eyes, cheeks flush.

'Yes, I'm... better. Thank you.'

Lucy wishes he had not mentioned anything, pretended the weirdness from the other day hadn't happened. They stand, three people in an awkward silence, for a few moments, none of them quite knowing what to do. Afraid to say the wrong thing.

'Anyway, I guess I should be going. Loads of deliveries to do. Diana, I notice there isn't a grocery order in for Willow Cottage this week... do you need anything?'

She looks at Lucy, blinking a few times.

'It's fine, Mylo,' Lucy says. 'We've still got plenty. We'll get one in for next week. I can make do.'

'If you're sure?'

She nods. Mylo turns, heading towards the boat. He spins round, halfway.

'Lucy, are you free after lunch? It's such a nice day, would be a shame to waste it.'

She looks at the older woman, whose jaw clenches.

She hesitates, but Diana's demeanour pisses her off.

'Yes. Yes, I am. What were you thinking?'

'A walk? I'll come back about one, and we can take it from there?'

'Perfect!' she says, and for the first time that day, she smiles a *real* smile. She feels like a weight has been lifted from her shoulders, and her and Mylo are friends again. She has a habit of overthinking things. Convincing herself of one thing, when another thing altogether is actually happening. She wants to trust Mylo; doesn't want to believe he had anything to do with Claire's death, and in order to do that, she has to spend more time with him. Without Diana spying on their every move and word.

Diana shoots daggers at him as he turns away.

Screw her, Lucy thinks, as Mylo leaps onto his boat, the spring suddenly back in his step.

Slightly nervous about being alone with him, she shakes the thought away, hurrying inside to prepare some lunch for Richard before Mylo returns for their *date*.

Diana follows her inside, shooting her an icy glare. Lucy tries to ignore her, but she begins banging cupboard doors obstinately.

'We're just friends, you know,' she says casually, without even glancing at the woman.

She seems surprised.

'Mylo and I. There's nothing going on there. We get on. We enjoy each other's company. He's still very much in love with Rose.'

Diana stares at her, indignantly.

'I never said–'

'No, I know you didn't. But I'm telling you. I don't want anything to put a strain on our working relationship. And I get the feeling you're not happy with me seeing him. So I thought I'd set the record straight.'

She can tell the woman doesn't believe her, her eyes narrow, as she purses her lips.

'It's not that I don't find him attractive. But he's not interested,' Lucy continues.

A flicker of a smile dances over Diana's face; gone in a split second, but Lucy sees it regardless.

That's what you get for trying to be kind, she thinks.

'I'm sorry,' Diana says finally. But Lucy can tell from her tone that she is anything but. She sounds... triumphant.

'It's fine. I didn't come here looking to meet someone. Believe me when I say, a relationship is the *last* thing I need right now. I came here to work. And to forget about men.'

She isn't lying. Her last relationship left her with mental scars that she suspects will never heal. She crosses to the laundry room and emerges with a bottle of bleach. Diana watches as she heads out to the hall, following behind inquisitively.

'What are you doing?'

Lucy kneels, twisting the cap from the container, and pours the viscous liquid all over the floor. She trots back into the kitchen, retrieving the mop, swirling the bleach around the wood.

'There. See if that helps at all. Have you eaten today?'

Diana shakes her head, grimacing.

'I'll make you a sandwich while I'm doing Richard's. It's important that you eat. When did you say your appointment is?'

She looks confused.

'With the doctor? For blood tests. You phoned the other day.'

Her eyes widen.

'Oh, I forget, I've written it down somewhere. In my diary,

probably. I'm feeling much better now anyway. I don't think there's any need to waste his time.' She shrugs.

Lucy raises her eyebrows, breathing out an exasperated sigh. She steps, crablike, over the wet patch, heading back to the kitchen to prepare lunch.

63

LUCY

The kitchen door swings open almost as soon as Mylo cuts the engine. As he steps from the boat, Lucy comes bounding across the lawn, all perfect teeth and smiles.

'Afternoon!' he calls as she approaches.

She plants a huge kiss on his cheek. His face flushes, and he looks away.

'Where are you taking me then?' she asks playfully. She doesn't want to come on too strong, but she needs him to trust her, so that she can try to get him to open up. A little flirting wouldn't hurt.

'Let's walk and see where we end up.'

She nods but doesn't say anything. They head towards the treeline. As they stroll from the cottage, she glances over her shoulder, seeing a shadowy figure looming in the window.

They clamber through the woods without speaking at first, Mylo taking the lead. He's diverged from the path, opting for an off-piste adventure. Lucy follows obligingly, but the trepidation she feels about being alone and isolated with him doesn't dissipate. She tells herself she's being ridiculous.

The air is warm, and the scent of wild flowers lingers. The

foliage and undergrowth are wet from recent rain, the ground soft. Patches of mud squelch underfoot as they trek. He glances behind, waiting for Lucy to catch up. Beads of sweat are forming on her brow. Eventually, he speaks.

'How are things? You know... with... her.'

Lucy sighs, shaking her head.

'I'm not sure. Honestly, I thought she was improving. But it's a case of one step forward and two steps back.'

Mylo nods sympathetically.

'Have there been any further... episodes?'

She hesitates.

'No.'

She pushes past him, speeding up, heading up a mound.

'Come on, I'll race you!' she calls as she dashes away.

He sniffs, pausing for a second, before following her up the hill. There's a small clearing at the crest. Huge lumps of quartz break through the soil, jutting into the air. Lucy climbs onto one. Scaling it quickly, she perches on the top. Mylo joins her, sitting. He sniffs again.

'Are you wearing perfume?' he asks.

She shakes her head, pulling a bottle of water from her bag. She unscrews the top, taking a gulp, before offering it to him. He does the same and hands it back.

'Strange. I got a whiff of it a moment ago... and then again now as I sat beside you.'

She shrugs, chewing her bottom lip.

'I don't wear perfume. Soap maybe?'

He glances out into the trees. Pulling a lump of moss from the rock beneath him, he balls it up in his fist, throwing it out as far as he can.

'Was she okay about you coming out with me?'

'Do we have to talk about her? I am with her all the bloody

time. It would be nice to forget about her for a while... when I'm not having to look after her.'

He looks down at the ground, before flicking his gaze up to her face.

'Are we... all right?' he asks sheepishly.

She stares him in the eye.

'Yes, we're all right, Mylo. I'm a big girl... I've been turned down before.'

His face colours as he fidgets awkwardly beside her. She punches his shoulder.

'It's fine. I totally understand. Don't worry. It's your loss!'

She squeezes his thigh.

'I'm sorry if you thought I was short with you the other day when we were dealing with Diana. It was my nursing history kicking in. I didn't mean to upset you. I was trying to get the situation under control. That was all.'

'No need to be sorry. You were amazing. I was terrified. It was... disturbing.'

She nods.

'I can understand how it would be scary if you've not seen anything like that before. Unfortunately, I've witnessed many psychotic episodes. With the cocktail of drugs she's on, mixed with alcohol... it was only a matter of time before it happened.'

'What did the doctor say?'

'He told her to make an appointment to go in for some blood tests. She pretended that everything was fine, so I had a quiet word as he was leaving. Let him know that she'd been a bit off lately, so he's doing what he can. She said she phoned in... but something tells me she's lying.'

She lets out a slow breath through her nostrils, glancing down at the grass beneath them.

'If she won't do anything to help herself, there's only so

much *you* can do. You were awesome the other night. She owes you a lot.'

Lucy swats at the air dismissively with her hand. They sit a while without speaking. She wants to ask him about the photograph, but she isn't sure how.

'Diana was telling me that you knew her daughter,' she says, without looking at him. Trying to sound breezy, as if it's unimportant.

He stiffens. She glances at him.

'Yes. I knew Claire,' he finally says softly.

'It was a terrible thing that happened to her. So sad. And you were a couple at one point?'

He nods, clearly uncomfortable with the conversation. But Lucy has never been one to shy away from awkward things that need to be said.

'Did you see her before she was killed?'

Mylo shrugs.

'No. I mean... we were barely out of our teens when I knew her. It was years before.'

'Oh... right,' Lucy replies, hoping he picks up on the doubt in her voice.

He turns to her.

'Why do you say it like that?'

'It was just that Diana mentioned you were at Christopher Kernick's trial.'

His eyes widen. A drop of sweat builds on his brow, before trickling down the side of his temple.

'Right. Yes... I was. I... didn't realise she'd seen me actually. I never spoke to her there. I read about Claire in the paper... and I wanted to be there. To see him go down. That man... he was a monster. I had a lot of affection for Claire. She was a wonderful girl. And we did stay in touch after we split up. So... you know... I felt I should be there.'

Lucy nods. It makes sense. If a friend of hers had been murdered, she would probably want to be at the trial.

'Funny though... don't you think?'

Mylo cocks his head, narrowing his eyes questioningly.

'That you ended up back here, and Diana did too, all these years later. And that you ended up with Rose. Small world.'

He clears his throat, wiping his forehead with the palm of his hand.

'Yeah, I suppose. I moved back after my father's death... to help my mother with the shop and stuff. I had no idea Diana was here until the first time I had to deliver her groceries. We were both very surprised to say the least. It was pure coincidence.'

'Hmm...' Lucy says airily.

He goes to speak again, but she holds her finger to her lips. He narrows his eyes questioningly.

'Do you hear that?'

He leans his head to one side.

'Running water!' she says excitedly. 'We must be near a stream. Come on!' She hops down from the top of the rock, landing below him, before dashing off into the trees. He follows obediently, catching up with her a few metres away. She's crouching by a rocky bed. The sound of a stream babbling over pebbles is louder now.

'Look at this!' she calls to him. 'Have you ever seen anything so pretty?'

As he nears, he sees she is knelt beside a clump of spiky green leaves, throwing beautiful pink blooms on tall stems into the air.

'Is it some kind of orchid?' she asks, picking a stem, holding it to her nose and inhaling.

Mylo shakes his head.

'No. It's Himalayan balsam. It *is* lovely, but it's a highly invasive species. Kills off a lot of our native wild plants and flowers.'

Lucy's face crumples, like a child who's been told that Father Christmas isn't real.

'Oh. That's a pity. It looks so lovely.'

'It also contributes to localised flooding. It dies off in the autumn and winter, and the petals and leaves clog up the waterways. Not a great species. We're trying to control it but it's almost impossible.'

Lucy stands up, tucking the blossom into her rucksack.

'I like it. We brought it here, I assume?'

He nods.

'Well there you go. It's our own crime. We're so quick to blame things when it isn't their fault at all.'

'You have an interesting view of the world,' he says through a broad smile.

She wanders away from the stream.

'I try not to judge. Things, people, plants... I think nothing in life is black and white. Good people sometimes do bad things, and vice versa. We're so quick to say *oh that is awful*. But take this flower, for example. Really, the plant isn't doing anything wrong. It's just... living. Humans brought it here because they liked the look of it, no doubt. *We* introduced it to the landscape. It doesn't know it's not supposed to be here. But somehow it ends up being the villain? How is that fair...?' She trails off.

'Yes, you're right.' He pauses, seeing a flash of movement near the riverbed.

'Oh wow, Lucy, look!'

She turns as he crouches down beside the stream.

'What is it?'

He beckons to her.

'A newt... come see.'

She hurries over, kneeling next to him, narrowing her eyes

as she scours the pebbles. Mylo holds a finger to his lips, pointing to a clump of grass at the edge. Her face lights up.

'Oh, I see him! He's so cute. I don't think I've seen a newt since I was a kid.'

'He's a great crested... quite rare!' Mylo says excitedly.

The newt hops into the water, swimming away with the flow. Lucy collapses onto her bottom, pulling her bag from her back.

'Let's eat!' she says, taking two foil-wrapped packages from inside, handing one to Mylo.

'You made a picnic?'

She nods. 'I was making lunch for Richard and Diana, so I made a few extra.'

He takes his sandwich, unwrapping it carefully. He watches her as she does the same, taking a bite from her food. He's set her mind at ease a little, but she watches him for a few moments, mulling over his explanation.

The coincidence is huge... but stranger things have happened. She shrugs.

There are moments when you feel so happy that you worry that your heart might burst. Lucy doesn't get that too often. But she feels it right now. Glancing at Mylo, she notes that the dour demeanour that radiated from him when they first met, has all but disappeared. He smiles, tucking into his food, and she suspects he may be feeling the same way.

64

After they finish eating, they walk for another hour or so. Lucy points out flora and fauna, Mylo explains what it all is. She's impressed with his knowledge. Not her usual type, she has to admit. Not that it matters. Nothing will happen with him. She's sure of that now.

Friendship is better anyway.

They are heading back towards Willow Cottage. There was a brief moment when their fingertips brushed against each other as they walked. She considered holding his hand, but he snatched it away before she had the chance. In hindsight, she's glad that she didn't try. As they break out from the woods, they see Diana sitting in the garden beneath the willow tree, chatting to an older lady.

'Shit,' Mylo hisses under his breath. 'This can't be good.'

'What? Who's that?' Lucy replies.

'Annette,' he spits as he pulls away from her, marching towards the women. Lucy picks up the pace to catch up.

'Who's Annette?' she calls after him, but he doesn't seem to hear.

'Mylo, hello!' Diana calls as he approaches. Lucy notes her speech is slurred again and wonders if she has cracked open a bottle of wine or two while they were out. She arrives by his side.

'Let me introduce you both to Annette. She's–'

'I *know* who she is,' he spits. Lucy shoots him a look.

'Hello.' Lucy holds out her hand.

The woman takes it in both of her own and strokes the skin with her thumbs. Closing her eyes, she tips her head back, smiling. Lucy pulls her hand away, looking once more at Mylo.

'Annette is a psychic,' Diana slurs. Lucy glances at her. Her pupils are dilated. 'She's going to help us get rid of Rose!'

Mylo runs his fingers through his bushy hair as he sighs, looking away towards the trees.

'Diana,' Lucy says, 'I don't think this is appropriate.'

'Oh nonsense! We need *him* here for it to work. They have a connection, you see!'

The older woman steps forward. 'I prefer the word "medium". Young man, you may not like what you hear, you may not believe... but that doesn't stop it from being true.'

He turns towards her, but before he can speak the sound of a car pulling up around the front of the house distracts them all. Four heads turn to the side of the cottage. A car door slams shut, and moments later Valentina emerges into the garden.

'Val!' Diana claps her hands together like an excited child. 'What a lovely surprise!'

Valentina glances at Lucy, who shakes her head.

The woman saunters towards the group. A mustard-yellow pashmina covers her top half. Black flared trousers emerge from beneath it, hugging her thighs tightly. She's curvy and carries it well. It suits her. A pair of ridiculously high stilettos, totally inappropriate for the terrain, sit on her feet. She struggles to walk on the grass in them, wobbling a little.

Her black hair is tied up in a tight bun at the back of her head. Huge Prada sunglasses cover most of the top half of her face. She slides them down her nose as she looks at Annette.

'Who's this?' she barks, her tone clipped.

Diana lurches forwards, embracing her friend.

'You've been drinking,' Valentina says as she sniffs her. 'You can barely talk.'

'I have *not*.' Diana insists. She motions towards the lady beside her. 'This is Annette. She is here to cleanse the house.'

'Excuse me?' Valentina pulls her shades from her face, folding her arms across her chest. Lucy steps in between them.

'I think Diana wants to do a seance or something.'

She pulls a face that only Valentina sees, shaking her head.

'And how much are you charging this emotionally troubled woman for your sham service?'

Annette holds her hand up with sadness in her eyes.

'Charging? Oh no, not at all. I provide my gift for free.'

Valentina raises her eyebrows, looking to the sky.

'Not a seance... a cleansing ceremony, to rid the house of unwanted spirits! It's fantastic you're here, Val. Annette says it's better with more people.'

'Oh no–'

Lucy steps forwards.

'Diana, why don't you take Annette inside, see what she needs. Mylo, go with them and make sure they're okay.'

Mylo frowns but does as he's told. The three of them cross the lawn in the direction of the cottage.

'I think she's having some sort of relapse. You noticed her speech.'

Valentina nods. 'Are we supposed to entertain this ridiculous charade?'

'It might do her some good. If she believes this psychic can get rid of the apparent ghost in the house, perhaps she will move on after this.'

'Won't we be encouraging her delusions though? If we play along.'

Lucy shrugs.

'Maybe. But it could also bring an end to this situation.'

Valentina lets out a long sigh, pulling a cigarette and lighter from her tiny handbag. She lights it, taking a deep drag, holding it inside, before exhaling through her nostrils.

She takes another few quick puffs before dropping it onto the lawn, stubbing it out beneath the toe of her shoe.

'Let's get this over with then.'

She marches away into the house. Lucy follows behind, closing the door as she enters. The group linger in the hall, discussing the stain on the floor. Mylo waits in the kitchen, looking uncomfortable. Lucy feels for him, she truly does. It must be awful to have to see this. To hear it.

'You okay?' she asks quietly as she stands beside him. He shrugs. She places a hand on his back, stroking up and down.

'I can't believe we're going to do this,' he says sadly. 'It doesn't seem right.'

Lucy remains silent. Nothing she could say will help him.

They enter the hall, approaching the women. Diana pushes the door to the living room. It swings open and the group file in. Mylo and Lucy follow behind. Annette unzips a large holdall which is sitting on the floor, pulling out a foldable table with a round top. She splays the legs, clipping the top in place. She pulls a black silk cloth from the bag, making a dramatic show of flapping it out over the structure.

'Mylo, could you get the chairs, please?' Diana requests. He crosses the room, picking up two from the dining area, placing them beside the women. Fetching more from the kitchen, he sets them out in a circle. Lucy grabs a final chair for herself, resting it next to Mylo.

'I'm going to nip up and change quickly. I got a little sweaty on our walk.'

She hurries upstairs as the others take their seats.

65

Lucy bounds down the stairs, freshened up and looking radiant as Mylo sits at the table beside Valentina. Diana is seated opposite him. Annette, next to her. Mylo's reaction upon meeting her was to be expected. There are some around these parts who value her, and some who despise her. Her reputation precedes her. She lives in one of the smaller villages on the other side of the woods. Most folk have heard of her, or at least have heard rumours of what she claims to do. Many locals have used her.

She had heard talk that Annette had approached Mylo not long after Rose's accident, asking if he wanted her to see if Rose had anything to say. Mylo had apparently in his usual non-confrontational manner, politely declined.

Annette lights a thick pillar candle, placing it in the centre of the table, clearing her throat. She looks towards Diana.

'Do you have the item?'

Diana smiles, pulling something from her pocket. She hands it to the woman, who places it near the candle. Rose's driving licence.

Diana's head whips from side to side suddenly; she sniffs the air, like a dog with the scent of a juicy steak.

'Can you smell that?' she hisses.

Heads turn all around the table, as people begin to sniff.

'Perfume. *Rose's* perfume.'

'You smell it, don't you, Mylo? You know it's her.'

His eyes dart to Lucy, but he says nothing.

'It has begun,' Annette says solemnly.

'I would ask you all to place your hands flat on the table, towards the outer edge. Splay them, so that your little fingertips are touching the person's to each side of you.'

Diana's go straight down. She glances around, waiting for everyone else to do the same. Lucy places hers down, and in turn, each participant follows suit, forming a circle around the tabletop.

'Whatever happens, please do not lift your hands from the table. Do not break the circle.'

Valentina smiles, shaking her head. 'Jesus Christ,' she sneers.

'Blasphemy is extremely unbecoming,' the woman scolds.

She closes her eyes, tilting her head backwards, much the same as she had done when she touched Lucy's hand earlier.

'If there is a spirit here, I ask that you go. Leave this house. Leave the living to live. And you, in turn, join the dead. There is nothing here for you any longer.'

Mylo looks around the table warily. Diana can tell he thinks it's all a sham. A waste of everybody's time.

'Rose. You have caused enough trouble here. You must leave this house.'

The candle flame flickers as Annette's lids spring open.

'There is an unhappy spirit in this place,' she whispers, looking to each participant in turn. She stops at Mylo, staring into his eyes.

'She does *not* want to go.'

Mylo's jaw clenches. Everyone is looking at him. Lucy has an expression of sadness on her face. Diana is fascinated. Valentina appears bored.

The table wobbles. Mylo frowns.

It's lifting, the top rocking from side to side. It suddenly lurches up a couple of inches higher. Diana gasps. Lucy stares towards Annette, the beginnings of a smile on her face. Mylo parts his lips but doesn't speak. Diana's heart pounds in her chest. Wide-eyed, she watches with morbid fascination. Even Valentina is paying attention. The air of someone who doesn't want to believe what they are seeing.

'Please keep your hands flat. Do not break the circle!' the medium commands. The table lowers slowly to the ground, setting itself down with a gentle thud. Annette lifts her palms up, looking at Mylo, a curious expression on her face. Mylo stares downwards, unmoving.

'It is over. But she will not leave.'

'What do you mean?' Diana whispers.

'I still sense her here. There is nothing I can do. She will go when she is ready.'

Mylo stands suddenly, pushing his chair back so hard that it topples over. He storms out of the room.

'Mylo, wait!'

Lucy springs up from her seat, rushing after him, leaving the bewildered women staring.

66

S he runs behind him, grabbing his shoulder.

'Are you all right?'

'I'm pissed off. This is all such rubbish. Did you see Diana sitting there, lapping it all up? She's a fucking idiot. She's loving this. It all creates a drama around her. Makes her the centre of attention. That's the only time she seems to be happy.'

Lucy pulls him towards her, holding him in an embrace.

'I'm so sorry you had to see that,' she whispers in his ear.

He pulls away.

'I'm not. It's confirmed what I've thought all along. She's mad.'

Lucy nods.

'You didn't actually believe any of that, did you?'

She bites her lip.

'It was a little creepy,' she says apprehensively.

'It's all bullshit. An act. That's why she insists on bringing her own table. It's rigged. I saw a documentary about it all. She presses on the edge to make it rock, then slips her foot under the leg once it's lifted. Then she raises her foot to raise it. It's balanced by everyone's hands being on top of it, so it lifts easily. It's all smoke and mirrors.'

Lucy sighs and nods once more.

'I suppose that makes sense. Probably why she wants the curtains drawn and one single candle to light the room.'

'Bingo!' he replies.

Valentina emerges from the house, crossing the garden towards them, pulling a cigarette from her purse.

'Give me strength!' she shouts as she approaches.

'You weren't impressed either, I take it?' Lucy asks.

'Of course not. Because I have a brain. I've told that trickster to get the hell out of here. She had better be gone by the time I go back inside.'

She looks at Mylo.

'You all right?'

He nods.

'I didn't realise who you were, I'm sorry. That must have been terrible for you. If I'd known, I never would have let it go ahead. It was insensitive.' She shoots Lucy an icy glare.

'You're right. It's bad,' Valentina snaps, still looking at her. 'She's totally lost it if you want my honest opinion.' She taps her stiletto on the boardwalk, drawing on her cigarette, turning her head to one side to expel the smoke away from her companions.

'I've known her a long time, and I've never seen her this bad. It's... not like her.'

'What should we do?' Lucy asks, exasperated.

'You said she's seen the doctor?'

'Yes, he came out when she had her episode. But she lied to him... didn't tell him anything that had been going on. I had to fill him in before he left. She also claims she's made an appointment for blood tests. But whether that is true is anybody's guess.' She pauses. 'There's... something else...'

Valentina tilts her head questioningly.

'Follow me.'

Lucy pulls a bunch of keys from her pocket and crosses the lawn to Diana's studio. She unlocks the door, stepping inside. Valentina and Mylo follow behind. Lucy points to a bucket, with remnants of red paint in the bottom, and dripping down the sides.

Her companions frown.

'I think that's what she used... on the floor, I mean. In the hall.'

'Ah.' Valentina steps forwards, leaning over. She extends her arm, dipping an immaculately manicured finger into the liquid, rubbing it between her thumb and forefinger.

'Still wet...' she says to nobody in particular. 'I think it's time I had a talk with her. If you two can make yourselves scarce for a while, that would be wonderful.'

Lucy glances at Mylo, and they both nod. Valentina turns towards the house, but stops, looking back towards them.

'The perfume. Was it Rose's?'

Mylo nods.

'I smelled it. I still smell it. *Something* is going on here. But I sure as hell don't believe in ghosts.'

She marches back to the cottage, slamming the door behind her as she enters.

'Want to go for a boat ride?' Mylo asks.

Lucy shrugs.

'She's made it clear she wants us out of the way for a while, so we may as well.'

They climb aboard, and as Mylo starts the engine, manoeuvring the vehicle away from the pontoon, Lucy glances back at the house. Two shadowy figures stand in the kitchen window, watching them as they pull away.

67

'Wasn't she fantastic!' Diana beams. Valentina purses her lips, waiting for her moment. 'Surely you *have* to believe me now?'

The smile fades from her face as she notes her friend's expression.

'You can't mean to say you *still* have doubts? You saw what happened in there. You smelled the perfume–'

Valentina holds up her hand.

'Enough, Diana. Yes, I smelled perfume. That's about all I can say for that circus act we all just witnessed.'

'Annette is the real deal. She has even helped the police with trying to track down missing persons.'

'I'm sure.' She pauses, closing her eyes, letting out a breath. 'We have been friends for a long time, Di. I would *never* want to fall out with you... but I can't stand by and watch you make a fool of yourself. This has got to stop. I don't know what you're hoping to achieve... is it attention? Because let me remind you, it was *you* who thought it was a wonderful idea to move out here, to the middle of nowhere. Away from your support network. I advised you against it then, but you were having none of it. So if you're lonely, then it's nobody else's fault but your own.'

Diana's mouth drops open, eyes wide. She hobbles on her stick towards her friend. Their heads are centimetres apart. Her hot breath, rank and bitter, is in Valentina's face. She turns away, grimacing.

'You think I'm attention seeking? You know me better than that. This... this is real. I'm not mad.'

'You're drunk! You're not working. You're focusing all your time and energy on this ridiculous ghost hunt. It's pathetic! I've *never* seen you like this. I don't understand it.'

Diana leans in closer to her friend, their noses are almost touching.

'I am *not* drunk,' she says firmly.

'You're slurring. You can barely string a sentence together. Come on, be honest at least.'

'I haven't had a drink for days. I had a glass of wine earlier in the week. One glass. The night the bloodstain reappeared–'

Valentina laughs.

'Oh yes. The *bloodstain*.'

Diana leans backwards.

'What do you mean by that?'

'I've seen the bucket of paint. In your studio. Looks suspiciously the same colour as the stuff on the floor to me. Please, Diana, cut the crap.'

Confusion flickers across her face.

'What paint? I haven't been into my studio for days.' She pauses, eyes clouding. 'Or is it weeks?' She's not even sure anymore. She no longer sounds as if she's talking to anyone in particular.

'And why is that?'

'I'm not inspired. I can't paint when I'm not inspired.'

'Oh bullshit! You know how this works. You splash a few

daubs on a few canvasses, call it a new collection, and we make money. You don't need to be inspired. I've told you before, our professional relationship only works, if *you* work. Otherwise, my time is going unpaid!'

Diana stumbles backwards, lowering herself into a chair. She looks at the floor, shaking her head.

'That's not how I work, Val. I have integrity. I can't simply churn out rubbish and expect people to buy it.'

Valentina sighs, pulling another cigarette from her bag. Diana opens her mouth to speak as her friend lights up, to remind her she doesn't like smoking in the house, but Val shoots her a glare, and she thinks better of it. She takes a few drags, inhaling deeply, letting the nicotine calm her. She closes her eyes again, tapping her foot.

'Diana. People are worried about you. That poor girl out there... she is *trying* to help you. But you are scaring the shit out of her now. To be honest, you're scaring me. If you're not careful, she *will* leave. I can see it in her eyes. This isn't what she signed up for. She's here to help Richard. Not babysit a mad, drunk woman. And that will be two home helps you've lost in a year. The agency won't send a third. Not when she goes back there and tells them what has been going on. And then you'll be alone. You'll be the only one here, to bathe him, cook for him, feed him, wipe the shit from his arse. Are you up to that? Because in my opinion, I don't think you're even capable of looking after yourself right now.'

Diana continues to stare at the floor, the wind knocked from her sails.

'This has to stop. You need to get a grip. Stop talking about ghosts, and spirits, and seances... and Ouija boards! You need to grow up and start working. Otherwise this...' Valentina waves her hand between the two of them, 'this is over! Capiche?'

Diana nods. Her friend tosses her cigarette into the sink,

running the tap to extinguish it. She crosses to the hall, turning back to Diana before she leaves.

'Pull yourself together. Go see the doctor, get your meds upped. Whatever. I don't care. But sort yourself out.'

She doesn't wait for a response. She strides through the hallway, exiting through the front door, slamming it behind her.

68

She listens as her friend's sports car speeds away. *Always drives too fast that woman*, she thinks. She supposes it's the fiery Italian in her. Diana reaches up, brushing her fringe out of her eyes. Her hand drifts to her plait, which she caresses with her fingertips.

She's aware that her speech is not right. She doesn't think she's had a drink today. Or has she? Everything seems cloudy. She can no longer be sure. She crosses to the wine cabinet, pulling the doors open. There's an open bottle of red from when she had her bath. The rest lie neatly stacked on the rack.

She opens a drawer, rummaging inside for a pen. She finds an indelible marker and uses it to draw a line on the label. She places the bottle back on the shelf and closes the cupboard, suddenly feeling very alone. Lucy has gone off somewhere with Mylo. Diana smiles as she thinks of him. *Such a sweet boy. Such a shame.* She shakes away the thoughts.

Had it been a mistake calling Annette? In hindsight, she can understand how it might make her look unhinged. Usually so rational, she doesn't entertain stories about ghosts and ghouls. But the events of the past month or so... they have changed her.

She walks to the hall, staring down at the marks on the floor. The bleach removed some of the stain, but it will need to be sanded again; revarnished.

She knows she needs to start painting, but she feels sick whenever she thinks about going into her studio. Can't bring herself to do it. Aside from when she was recovering from the accident, she can't recall a time in her life when she has gone so long without picking up a brush. It's heartbreaking.

Her art has got her through so many hard times. She painted through the loss of Claire. As soon as she was able, she painted to forget the accident; or at least to stop herself thinking about it.

It has been her therapy for as long as she can remember. For many years, it has been all she has had, and now she doesn't even have that.

She has nothing.

She holds her hand up in front of her face. It trembles, shakes manically. Couldn't paint if she wanted to. Her fingers feel weak. She's not sure she could even grip a brush. Valentina was right.

She is *pathetic*.

Opening the fridge, she notices there's still some soup left that the girl cooked for lunch. She has to admit; it was quite tasty. The first meal, the terrible, tasteless casserole, must have been a blip.

That all seems so long ago now. She can't even recall when it was. Days? Weeks? Longer?

She takes the broth, ladling it into a bowl, and throws it into the microwave. Thick brown liquid sloshes over the lip, splashing onto the glass plate. Jabbing her fingers on the buttons, the machine beeps frantically. She presses start, and it begins to spin. She watches, mesmerised as it rotates before her. She sways from side to side. The appliance pings on completion. She pulls the dish from inside, burning herself. She drops it down on the worktop, spilling more. Running her hand beneath the cold tap, she rubs fingers together, wincing.

Grabbing a spoon, she gobbles the soup up. It drips down her chin. She doesn't care. She's suddenly ravenous. She picks it up, licking the last of its contents greedily from the surface, tossing the bowl into the sink. Lucy can clean it up later. It's what she's paid for, after all.

Opening the wine cabinet once more, she pulls the open bottle from the shelf. *Sod it*, she thinks. She doesn't even bother with a glass. Swigs it directly from the bottle as she heads down the hall to her room, leaving the cupboard doors open.

69

S he hopes he isn't going to take her to his house. It doesn't seem right. It's too soon to be in that kind of setting with him, after the rejection. Her jaw is clenched, eyes fixed firmly on the horizon. Her eyes flick to Mylo sporadically. He's watching her as he steers the boat.

In the warm orange glow from the approaching sunset, she can see the sadness written all over his face.

'You know, I don't believe in ghosts. And I don't think for one second that Rose is haunting us. But...' He shifts uncomfortably.

'Go on,' Lucy replies, intrigued with where this conversation is heading.

'I touched on it the other day when we were talking, but I don't think I made myself clear. It's very odd... and I don't know how to explain it... but you have said in the exact words sometimes, many things that Rose said, during some of our most private conversations.'

He pauses, looking away from Lucy briefly.

'Your comment about the view from my window being my own personal work of art, that's constantly changing with the light. This was *exactly* what Rose said the first time she was there. Not just the sentiment. Those precise words.'

Lucy shrugs, and Mylo continues.

'Then again, when you mentioned the colours of the landscape, making you feel like you're living inside a rainbow. Rose's words once more. It scared me if I'm entirely honest.'

'That's understandable, I guess,' she replies, nodding slowly.

'And then all Diana's nonsense about Rose being here, haunting the cottage... briefly, you know, it did make me wonder. But that's just stupid, isn't it?'

'Yes. I think so.' She pauses, considering what to say next.

'It's odd, I'll admit. But I suppose the whole scenario with you and Diana both ending up living here, of all places, proves that weird, spooky coincidences happen. Sometimes you can't explain things. You simply have to accept them.'

They continue in silence for a while. Watching the peach hues in the sky.

'Are you okay?' Mylo asks.

She shrugs.

'I should be the one asking you that.'

'I'm fine. I'm used to Diana's behaviour. I witnessed a lot of it... you know, when Rose lived there. She's an odd character. But I don't think you can blame her. We're not meant to live so isolated. It's not good for a person's mental health. We need company.'

Lucy frowns.

'She seems so intent on pushing everyone away from her though. As soon as I feel like we are making some progress with our relationship, I'll say something that will somehow piss her off, and she says something spiteful in retaliation. Reminding me of my place, or whatever.'

Mylo nods.

'Perhaps she's afraid to let people close to her,' he offers.

Lucy sighs, a long, drawn-out breath, shaking her head.

'Do you still think she had something to do with Rose's death?'

His jaw clenches, shoulders tense.

'Sometimes I wonder. But in reality... I don't think so. I don't know. Is she a killer?'

'Who knows. Maybe it was an accident, but she didn't want to be implicated?'

He pauses, looking her in the eye.

'We'll never know for sure, will we?'

Lucy shakes her head.

'Where are we going?'

'There's a beach around the corner that I think you'll like. You get some terrific views from there. And there's also something I want to show you.'

She doesn't reply. Just nods and returns her gaze out to the water.

He pulls the dinghy right up on the beach, as shallow as he can, before hopping out to drag it onto dry land with Lucy still sitting in it. Once it's clear of the water, she climbs out. Mylo ties the boat to a huge tree trunk that has been washed ashore and returns to her side. She stares out across the loch.

The cloudless sky is a pale shade of lilac, changing to blue, before fading to a peach colour towards the horizon. The trees on the opposite side of the loch are silhouetted in black against the orange sky, with layers of pale olive-green hills fading to grey, rising up behind them. Lucy inhales deeply. A fresh scent lingers. She still can't get used to this. The clean air. The huge skies.

The sheer joy of being somewhere so... wild.

'This is lovely,' she whispers.

She can tell he isn't looking where she is. His face is pointing towards hers. She pretends not to notice.

'Yes. It really is,' he replies, without glancing away.

Eventually, he turns to look out across the water.

'I love this time of year when the light is like this late into the evening. As the colours begin to change. These are my favourite moments. The light is... special. I sometimes wish I had Diana's gift. So I could capture this on a canvas. It brings back so many happy memories of summers with my parents when I was a child.'

Lucy smiles, shaking her head.

'I'm not sure Diana could paint this. Recreate this beauty. Her work isn't beautiful. It's... frightening.'

He nods.

'I know what you mean, actually. Some of them are downright disturbing. I suppose with all she's been through, it's to be expected.' He pauses, looking over his shoulder.

'Come with me. There's something I'd like to show you.'

He turns, crossing the beach towards a row of large pines. Lucy follows close behind. They push through a scattering of trees, across soft ground. It's darker amongst them, with the light fading. But Lucy isn't scared. She feels safe with him now. He leads her into a small clearing. She stares ahead of them.

'What on earth is *that*?' she asks incredulously.

'It's supposed to be Maggie Guthrie.'

She turns her face towards him, narrowing her eyes and cocking her head.

'The witch. The one that Cassie told you the story about... who used to live in Willow Cottage.'

'Ah, right!'

She takes a few steps closer.

A fallen tree trunk, carved to look like a crude body, is supported by rocks and twigs around its base. Parts of it are painted bright colours. Reds, greens and turquoises adorn it. On top, on a flat stump, a large rock has been placed on its side. It is triangular, with the long point facing out to the left. It has been dabbed with two Picasso-esque eyes, both on the same surface. The perspective is all completely wrong. Rows of jagged teeth cover the long point, framed by two snarling lips. It resembles a wolf, or an alligator more than a woman. It's grotesque.

Lucy shivers, but can't bring herself to look away from it.

'It's horrific!' she says finally, turning towards Mylo. He laughs.

'Yeah. Not the nicest thing, is it? But I kind of like it. It's... quirky.'

'I don't. It gives me the creeps.' She wraps her arms around herself. 'Who made it?'

Mylo steps closer to it.

'Nobody knows. It turned up one day. It wasn't here, and then it was. Overnight. No one has taken the credit for it. It's become part of the local folklore. The weirdos reckon Maggie did it herself. I'm more inclined to think it was Diana... the artistry is fantastic.'

Lucy crouches, reaching out her hand, caressing the rough surface of the tree trunk. Paint flakes off as she runs her fingers along it. Dried leaves and twigs cover boulders at the feet. She shivers again, staring up at the face. Mylo crouches beside her.

'What are you thinking?' he asks.

'I'm thinking that I really, *really* hate it.'

He laughs, placing his hand on her shoulder. He turns her head towards him, leaning in closer. She stands, suddenly.

'Let's not,' she says, brushing leaves from her clothes as she straightens up. He looks hurt.

'Mylo, you're clearly very confused. I like you; you know I do. But I'm not sure now is the right time... for either of us. After what happened this afternoon. You're in shock. Understandably, you're feeling vulnerable, maybe even lonely. But I don't think you want this. I don't think you want... me.'

She turns her head away, so he can't see her heart breaking. Her voice wavers as she wipes a tear from the corner of her eye.

'I do. I do want you. I was watching you on the beach, and you're beautiful.'

'Because I remind you of *her*.'

She doesn't mean it to sound spiteful, but that's how it comes out. Mylo's jaw tenses. He opens his mouth, but she doesn't let him speak.

'I'm sorry. I don't mean that negatively. I'm not being obstinate. But you said it yourself. I remind you of Rose. And maybe that's what is driving your actions tonight. But I don't want you to want me because I remind you of your dead fiancée. I want you to want me... because I'm me.'

The pain is written all over Mylo's face, but he says nothing, telling Lucy what she needs to know.

'Let's be friends, like you said. If things are going to develop, they will. To be honest, I'm not sure how long I'll be sticking around anyway. Things aren't going that swimmingly at Diana's.'

He looks panicked.

'I'm not saying I'm leaving, don't worry. But you don't know what's around the corner. The atmosphere is so tense between her and me... I wouldn't be at all surprised if she were to give me my marching orders when I get home tonight.'

He nods. Lucy sits on the grass at the base of the statue, patting the ground beside her. He sits, cosying up to her, and she drapes her arm around his shoulder. They sit in silence for a while, two friends, giving each other the love and support that they both need. No words are required.

Lucy smiles as Mylo rests his head on her shoulder. She thinks he is crying, but she doesn't look. Doesn't want to embarrass him. Eventually, he wipes his eyes.

'How come you're single, Lucy?' he asks, matter-of-factly.

She straightens up, fidgeting with her fingers.

'I wasn't. Not for a long time. I had a very tempestuous relationship with a guy from back home.'

'What happened?'

'Nothing. That was the problem. We simply drifted apart. We were together for years and years, but towards the end, it was like we were two single people, living totally separate lives whilst inhabiting the same space. It was very odd. But I think that's often how it goes with relationships, isn't it? The turning point, or in hindsight what I now see as the turning point... we were out in town one night for a friend's birthday. We both spent the evening working the room, entirely independently. And I didn't even miss him. It had become so utterly normal for us. There was nothing left. And neither of us cared.'

'That's sad.'

'It was, yes. I remember we took a taxi home. We sat in silence for about half the journey until I burst into tears. I was very drunk, of course. A grown woman, drunk in the back of a cab, bawling like a baby. He looked embarrassed... rather than concerned. I told him I was fine. But I wasn't. And he knew it. But rather than comfort me he just pulled his phone out of his pocket and started scrolling through his social media. That's how much he cared. And that's when it suddenly hit me that we were over.'

Mylo's face crumples. Lucy can tell her words are affecting him. He's kind like that. She knows it's a sad story. The end of a relationship is rarely a happy time.

'Didn't he fight for you though?'

'No. But it wasn't as simple as that. I had... I *have* a lot of issues. Things from my past which I struggle with. He also struggled with them, because I wouldn't let him help me through them. I pushed him away. If I was feeling self-conscious about my scars, and he would try to comfort me... I'd get angry and shout at him. I suppose he got to a point where he didn't know what to do or say anymore. Whatever he did was wrong, so he stopped trying.'

'He's an idiot.'

She laughs, but there is no humour in it.

'He is. But it wasn't all him. It takes two to make something work, and somewhere along the way we *both* stopped trying. It didn't end that night, of course. We struggled on, dead in the water for a few more years... the way so many couples do. Too scared to admit what they know is true in their hearts. I wish I could put all the blame on him, but I can't. I'm as guilty as he is. It's too easy to lump it all on to the other person without accepting any responsibility yourself. Part of being an adult is being able to admit stuff like that.'

Mylo reaches across and takes her hand in his, caressing her skin with his thumb.

'It's fine, honestly. For a while I thought it was the end of the world. He was all I'd known for such a long time, I genuinely didn't know how to be *me* without him by my side. That's partly why I came here.'

'Running away?'

'I suppose so, yes. But also... to find myself. Rediscover who I am. And it's helped. It really has. Being here. The beauty. Fresh air. Meeting new people who don't look at me with pity in their eyes. Don't judge me on my failed relationship. I feel like I'm healing.'

Mylo nods.

'Let's go,' she says abruptly. 'I'm sure Valentina has had long enough to say her piece by now.' She stands, heading into the woods. Mylo straightens, brushes dirt from his jeans, before following her into the darkness.

71

Mylo drops her on the pontoon but doesn't stay; doesn't even cut the engine. She understands it must be difficult for him to go in there. Especially after what he was subjected to this afternoon. She watches as he speeds away, around the outcrop.

She's glad they've cleared the air. She likes him. Round here, she needs all the company she can get. She considers what this place is like in the winter. A different experience entirely, no doubt. Fewer hours of daylight. Less warmth. No flowers or colour.

Shivering, she wraps her arms around her body.

The earlier sunshine of the day has disappeared behind thick, ominous-looking clouds which crept in from nowhere while their boat whizzed back across the water. The sky is quite spectacular. A living, ever-changing canvas.

Diana doesn't have a thing on you, she thinks.

The distant hillsides on the opposite shore are nothing more than grey silhouettes in this light. The loch, a glossy black mirror. Midges swarm around her face. She swats them away, but they are relentless.

As a heron swoops down to the adjacent banks, letting out a harsh cry, she smiles. Even in the fading light, the beauty of this place surpasses. *Winter may not be so bad after all*, she thinks. Will she still be here in winter? Who knows?

She watches the bird as it stalks about, looking for food. The size of the creature astounds her. She was lucky to see a sparrow down south. She's constantly amazed by the wildlife here. Mylo can tell her what any plant, any bird is. She hasn't a clue. Didn't use to care. But since she has been living here, her love of nature has evolved. She appreciates it far more. The silence at night, aside from the odd hoot of an owl, or scream of a fox, was hard to get used to at first. But now, she can't imagine sleeping with anything else. The constant drone of traffic outside her window twenty-four-seven, a distant memory these days.

She slips off her shoes, rolling up her jeans. Sitting down on the edge of the boardwalk, she dangles her legs over. A shudder flows through her body as her feet slide beneath the icy surface. It really *is* freezing.

She can't bear it for long. A searing pain radiates through her ankles. She pulls her feet up, hugging her knees close to her chest, staring out across the water. She thinks about the woman, Annette, at the seance. Her face... her voice.

She honestly believed that what she was doing, the things she was saying, were real. Lucy recalls what Annette had said to Mylo.

You may not believe... but that doesn't stop it from being true.

She shakes her head, letting out a little laugh. It's a shame he has had to become involved. He doesn't deserve it. She tried to keep him out of it... keep him away. But *that woman*, she seems to pull everyone into her drama. She's like a magnet, attracting bad things.

A flash of doubt creeps into her mind again, as she thinks

about Mylo and Claire. His appearance at the cottage at the strangest of times; but she shakes it away.

She stands, carrying her shoes. When she reaches the beach, she crouches to pick up a flat stone. Tossing it out over the water, it skips a few times, before sinking into the murky depths. She realises she's procrastinating; doesn't want to go inside. She imagines this must be how Rose had felt... towards the end. Uncomfortable in what was supposed to be her home.

Poor dead Rose.

She tries not to think about the girl, lying at the foot of the stairs, bleeding out, while Diana was in a drunken stupor a few metres away. She may even have heard the commotion and been able to help her immediately, if she hadn't been out of it. Perhaps she did hear, and simply didn't care.

Lucy wonders how long Rose lay there, dying. Wonders if she realised it was the end. She must have, she supposes, shaking her head sadly.

She glances towards the cottage. No lights on inside. She can make out Richard's dark figure, sitting in his window. Watching. Taking it all in. She's sure he is. He's no fool.

Perhaps he doesn't want to be drawn into Diana's games like everybody else. He's got the right idea.

She crosses the lawn. The long grass feels pleasant between her toes.

Entering the house, her shoulders slump. Cupboard doors are open. Chairs are in disarray. She walks to the sink. There's an empty soup bowl, and a wet cigarette butt sitting in it. She shakes her head and begins to tidy the mess. When the kitchen is back in order, she goes to Richard's room, knocking before she goes in, as she always does. Diana thinks she's foolish. But it's common courtesy.

As she enters the room, she glances around. Darkness. Diana hasn't left a light on for her husband.

Shaking her head, she clicks on a bedside lamp, throwing the room into an orange glow.

'Hello, Richard,' she says, turning his chair to face her. 'What did you make of all that drama today? Exciting, huh?'

She stares at his eyes, which flicker a little from side to side. She leans in closer, putting her face close to his.

'Do you think there are ghosts in this house?'

His eyes are watery. She reaches up, wiping them with her thumb. She undresses him, empties his colostomy bag. Does all the things that she has to in order to make him comfortable.

Using the heavy harness, she lifts him onto his bed. Tucks him in. Shows him the compassion that any good nurse should. She kneels down beside him, leans close to his ear.

'I guess it depends if the ghosts are metaphorical or real. We're all haunted by things from our past, aren't we? I know I am.' She glances towards the wall through to Diana's bedroom. 'But some people's ghosts are worse than others.'

Smiling, she kisses him on the cheek, turns out the lamp and leaves the room. His eyes are wide open, staring up as she closes the door.

72

V alentina Moretti is vexed. Something has been bothering her since her visit with Diana, but she can't put her finger on it. Granted, her friend's erratic behaviour had been worrisome, but it was something else.

She draws on a cigarette, inhaling the smoke deeply into her lungs, enjoying it, before letting it stream out through her nostrils. She stubs it in an ashtray, crossing to her filing cabinet, rifling through the drawers, finding Diana's section. The folder is thick, heavy. Ancient.

They have been friends for years. She started as Richard's agent, but quickly struck up a relationship with his wife. Although they had worked together *forever*, they had managed to retain their affection for one another. That didn't mean that Valentina was incapable of telling home truths, or cracking the whip when need be; she'd demonstrated that.

She'd nursed and supported Diana through her darkest of days, following the accident. Seen her at her absolute lowest. Almost at breaking point.

Her behaviour recently is something different. Given her mother's history, Valentina will have to keep an eye open.

She flips through the file. Photographs of various artworks spill out onto her desk.

A newspaper cutting falls to the floor. She bends, picking it up. The headline reads:

Renowned artist and wife hospitalised after taxi hit-and-run smash horror

She fondles the dog-eared, yellowing paper, biting her lip, skimming over words, and stares at the grainy halftone photograph. Twisted scraps of metal spiral off in all directions. Shattered windscreen, driver, lifeless behind the wheel, blurred out, of course. She shudders. The van had hit Richard's side and was mostly a mangled mess. Valentina lights another cigarette, sighing.

It's a marvel *anyone* survived.

She scans the image, tapping her finger on the top of the file. Breathing out a plume of white smoke, this time through her mouth, she stops. Eyes widen.

'My God!' she whispers.

Scrambling around for her mobile, she remains staring at the cutting. Diana's landline rings a few times before her answerphone kicks in.

'You've reached the residence of Diana Davenport, artist. I am unable to take your call right now, so please leave a message after the tone, and I'll endeavour to get back to you at my earliest convenience.' The machine beeps.

'Di... it's Val. I'm coming to see you, right now. I'll be there as soon as I can. I must talk to you immediately.' She draws in deep from the cigarette.

'It's extremely important...'

She reels off a quick explanation before ending the call. Grabbing her coat from the stand, she drapes it loosely over her shoulders. Hurrying out to her pillar-box-red Porsche, she starts the engine, pressing her foot to the floor. The tyres spin as the car pulls away at speed.

73

Something had woken her. A familiar sound… was it the telephone?

She hasn't had such a deep sleep in the afternoon for a while… not since Lucy's arrival. As she sits up, feeling as if she's moving in slow motion, she raises a hand to her face and it appears to leave a trail behind itself, like a sci-fi television effect.

She stares at her fingers, which seem to turn into fleshy corkscrews, spinning up towards the ceiling.

It's daylight. She can see slivers creeping in between the crack of the curtains. Her senses are heightened. She sniffs. The room stinks. Stale sweat, and unwashed clothes. She clasps her hand to her mouth, holding down the urge to empty her guts.

Feeling around for her stick, she's annoyed and surprised to find it's not there, yet again. She's sure she left it beside the bed. Shaking her head, she heaves herself up. As she limps forward, she feels as if she is rocking back and forth, like one of those egg-shaped toys from the seventies. The slogan from the advert runs through her brain. *Weebles wobble, but they don't fall down.* Except there is every possibility that *she* may.

Taking a few slow, deliberate steps forward, she lunges

towards the window, throwing the curtains apart. Daylight streams in, hurting her eyes. Outside looks like a wash of white. No detail. No trees. No loch. Nothing. Only white.

She narrows her eyes, pulling at the bottom of the sash frame. The window opens wide, and she swallows down the fresh air into her lungs. Sidestepping to the door, she pushes it open, moving out into the hall. Turning her head from side to side, something catches her eye. Halfway up the stairs. Resting against the wall. Her cane.

She hobbles to the other side of the passageway, supporting herself on the bannisters. Reaching through the gaps, she attempts to grab at the stick, but it's too high. She shuffles around to the foot of the stairs.

'Lucy!' she shouts. Her voice is hoarse, throat dry and rasping.

'Lucy... are you here?'

Her calls are met with silence. Sighing, she places her left foot on the bottom step. A wave of nausea washes over her. She holds her fingers over her mouth, but it's too late. Stinking yellow bile spews out, splattering over the steps, and down her filthy clothes. She abandons the attempt to walk up the stairs, opting instead to lower herself to her knees, and begins to crawl. She has to stop frequently, fighting back the urge to vomit again, but she finally arrives at her stick. She grabs at it, pulling it close to her body. She sits there for what feels like an age, breathing heavily, trying to regain her composure.

Why is her cane halfway up the stairs? She can't understand.

She would *never* have left it there. Perhaps Lucy was tidying and placed it there absent-mindedly. She will have to speak to her. Remind her she needs it to be accessible at all times. When she is finally ready, she edges her way down. On her buttocks, the way a small child would. Can't bring herself to stand yet. At the bottom she heaves herself up, using the bannisters for support, letting the cane take the bulk of her weight. She glances down the hallway to the kitchen, and emitting a sigh, heads towards the door, to make a cup of coffee. Or maybe a glass of wine. She'll have decided by the time she gets there.

Although she already knows which it is most likely to be.

74

VALENTINA

Having just caught the ferry in time, she now drives quickly through the twisting roads, staring up at the brooding dark clouds gathering above her head.

There's a storm coming, she thinks.

She's aware that she should probably slow down, but too much rides on this. So she speeds. She needs to speak to Diana immediately; must show her what she has found. She tries the cottage again, but it just rings through to the answerphone once more.

'Damn, Diana, where *are* you?' she curses under her breath, tossing her mobile onto the passenger seat.

As she glances back up, she gasps, slamming on the brakes. The car comes squealing to a stop, yards from a group of sheep wandering aimlessly in the middle of the road. She honks. They refuse to move. She presses it again, lowering the window and revving the engine hard.

'Come on, you stupid animals! Levati dai coglioni!' she screams, hitting her palm down on the wheel, letting out an extended blast of the horn. No response from the animals.

Climbing out of the car, she teeters on her stilettos towards them.

'Shoo, shoo!' she shouts, waving her arms in front of her. They scatter as she climbs back into the driver's seat. Pushing her foot down, she accelerates away quickly. The light is fading fast. These roads are hell in the dark. She passes a cliffside that she recognises, where an outcrop of rocks looks like a monkey's head, and she knows she is almost there. Smiling, she rounds a sharp bend.

There's a girl standing in the middle of the road. A flash of long blonde hair. Tattered white nightie.

Valentina is going far too fast. She'll never stop in time. The girl doesn't budge; stands staring straight ahead. As Valentina draws nearer, she squints, swerving suddenly. The speed is too much for her. She loses control and her beautiful pillar-box-red Porsche careers through the barrier, and into the trees.

She holds her arms up in front of her face as the Porsche bumps and tumbles over rocky ground, windshield shattering. Splinters of glass spin all around her.

And then she is flying. Hurtling over the edge of the cliff, high up in the mountaintops.

The car plummets down, down, down, towards the icy water below.

Valentina screams for her life. But there's nobody to hear it. Nobody to save her.

No one will even know.

Only the blonde girl in the road. As the vehicle splashes into the loch hundreds of metres below, the girl smiles, disappearing into the woods.

75

LUCY

She wakes with a start. Something clatters noisily outside. Groggy, she can't place the sound... not entirely sure where she is for a moment. She glances to one side at her digital clock, surprised to see the display is blank. The wind howls as she has never heard it before. Like a roaring animal.

Having fallen asleep with her bedroom window open, the curtains now billow in the torrent that batters in. Horizontal rain flies through the opening, so forceful, it's even reaching her bed, splattering across her face, making her sheets damp. Sitting up, she reaches for the bedside lamp, clicking the switch.

Nothing.

Now and then, a bright flash of lightning illuminates the room, but that is the only source of light. She climbs out of bed, crossing to the wall and tries the light. The power is dead. A rumble of thunder follows closely after the flashes. Lucy can't remember the last time she saw a storm... she's certain she's never witnessed one like this before. Rushing to the window, she stands for a second or two, listening, trying to locate the various sounds from outside.

As the lightning illuminates the landscape, she notices the

dark water of the loch, raging below. The wooden boat at the end of the jetty bobs manically on the surface as waves crash over it, filling it with water. She pulls the window shut, crossing to her dresser to grab a towel, and wipes the rain from her face. Her pyjamas are soaked. She peels them off, tossing them into a laundry basket in the corner of the room. She throws open her closet, pulling out a hoody and a pair of loose tracksuit pants. They're soft and warm, and smell of fabric conditioner.

As she opens the door, the house is in total darkness. Without the stream of white moonlight flooding in through the windows, the only light comes from momentary flashes which cast creepy shadows across the floor.

She crosses to the top of the stairs, as another burst lights up the hall, and sees with horror a figure standing at the foot. She squints into the darkness, but all she can see is black, blinded by the bright lightning.

Heart pounding, she steps backwards, away from the edge. A floorboard creaks under her weight.

'Lucy?'

Diana's voice is shaky, childlike and afraid. Lucy relaxes immediately.

'Diana! Hold on, I'm going to grab my phone for some light!'

She feels her way through the darkness to her bedroom, fetching her mobile from beside the bed. She flicks the torch on, and the beam casts a bright arc through the room. She hurries back to the stairs, shining the light down towards Diana. She stands quivering at the bottom.

'I think the power is out!' she shouts as she descends to the hall. She stands beside the older woman, who leans on her stick, looking exhausted.

'It's the storm. Must have taken out some power lines. There's an emergency generator in the outbuilding opposite my studio, around the side of the cottage.'

Lucy listens to the rain battering the windows and roof, not relishing the idea of having to go outside.

'I've got some wellies in the utility room,' Diana says, eyeing Lucy's bare feet, as if she has read her mind. They hurry to the kitchen, and Lucy shines her phone around, searching for the boots. The beam flashes over something bright yellow. She shines it back, finding what she's searching for in the corner. Crossing the room, she slides her feet into them. They are cold, uncomfortable. She shudders. Back in the kitchen, Diana rummages about in a drawer.

'It's padlocked. You'll need the key... I'm sure it's in here...'

Lucy joins her.

'Aha!' Diana says, pulling three small keys on a wire hoop from the drawer.

'It's one of these, I think!' She holds it aloft, and Lucy snatches it from her fingers, hurrying away. As she unlocks the door, pushing the handle, the wind blows it, almost throwing it wide open. Lucy grabs at the knob, holding it tightly to stop it swinging and smashing the glass panel.

Rain blusters in through the doorway, soaking the tiles around her feet. With one last look back towards Diana, she slides her phone into her pocket and steps outside into the onslaught, closing the door firmly behind her. The wind and rain batter against her face. She holds her hands up, shielding her eyes. It's so powerful, she struggles to walk against it. She pushes through, hair whipping at her cheeks. She pulls her hood up, pushing the tangled mess inside to keep it under control. Within seconds, her clothing is soaked. She shivers as the sodden garments cling to her skin. Glancing around as she moves, she sees the branches of the old willow, flailing manically. The noise from its rustling leaves is deafening on top of the howling wind. She spots that a few of the smaller trees on the perimeter of the woods have come down and lay strewn on the grass like discarded dolls. And still she pushes on.

A slate tile comes loose from the roof, hurtling down before she has time to react, slamming into the ground beside her feet. She shudders... *an inch to the side*, she thinks. She moves a little further away from the wall... just in case.

The banging she heard from her room grows louder as she edges around the side of the house.

As she reaches the lean-to, she sees the source of the clattering. The padlock lies on the ground. The door, splintered and broken at the edge, swings in the storm. The noises collect together like a horrendous symphony. The boat knocking against the jetty. The trees, swaying back and forth, the leaves of the willow, the outhouse door, banging.

So much noise.

Lucy holds her hands to her ears, wishing it would all stop. She steps inside, and instantly things feel calmer, but it doesn't last. The latch is broken, the door swings, crashing against the wall outside.

The outhouse is pitch black; smells musty and damp. Pulling her phone from her pocket, she lights up the space. Her cold, wet hands struggle to grip the handset.

She swings the beam around in an arc. It falls upon rusty buckets, tools, rolls of tarpaulin. A room filled with mouldy old junk. Towards a far wall, she spots the generator, taking a few steps towards it.

As she does, something in the corner of her eye stops her in her tracks. A dash of movement. The clatter of a metal bucket being knocked.

She spins around, shining her phone in the general direction.

The rain pounds on the roof, like the sound of a thousand snare drums. The wind continues to howl.

And Lucy is certain she is not alone. She cranes her head forwards, peering into the darkness, but sees nobody. Too afraid to investigate further, she hurries back to the generator. It sits on a large workbench against a wall. Some handwritten instructions are taped beside it.

Chunky green metal valves and pipes are covered in thick dust. Cobwebs decorate it from top to bottom.

She suspects it has never been used and hopes it will work.

Again, something in her periphery moves, scurries across the hard ground, rattling against the collection of junk on the floor as it does. She spins, just in time to see an old tarp move in one corner.

Heart pounding, she calls out.

'Hello?'

Swinging her phone light from side to side, hand trembling, she quickly scours the room.

'Is somebody there? Diana?'

But in reality, she knows that Diana could never move that fast. She turns back towards the generator, trying to make sense of the instructions. She brushes her hand over the cold metal, wiping dirt away.

The door bangs noisily behind her. Placing her phone on the bench, she grasps a cord between her fingers, and yanks, sharp and hard, as the directions state. Nothing happens. A few sputters, but not much else. She tries again. It purrs a little more this time. Petrol fumes fill her nostrils.

One last try, and the generator rumbles to life. A plume of smoke rises from the top, and a strong fuel smell fills the space. It chugs and sputters on the bench. Satisfied, she rubs her hands together, expelling the dust and grime from them. Picking up her phone, she steps away from the bench, turning back to the door. Again, something bangs to the far side of the space. She turns once more and sees the old roll of tarp now lies on the floor, knocked from where it was standing. A bucket beside it rocks back and forth. Reaching to her side, she grabs a screwdriver. She's not sure it will offer her much protection... but it's a weapon, at least.

Stepping forwards, both hands held out in front of her, one lighting the way, the other to defend against an attacker, she feels stupid. They're in an isolated location. It's the middle of the night.

Who the hell would be here?

Mylo's face flashes into her mind. She shakes it away as quickly as it arrived.

She edges slowly forward. There is definitely movement behind a pile of boxes to her left. She creeps towards it. The hum of the generator fills her ears, but there's something else... A peculiar scraping sound. Below it... panting. Quick, panicked. She holds her breath. Resists the urge to drop the screwdriver and run as fast as she can back to the house.

'There is no danger,' she whispers to herself.

So why does she feel so afraid? Behaving in a much braver fashion than she feels, she takes a deep breath and steps around the pile of boxes.

76

A s the wind howls, she hears a thousand voices screaming her name.

Diana, Diana, Diana...

We're coming, we're coming, we're coming...

Dappled moonlight casts patchy shadows across the floor through the window. They dance manically, creeping up the walls, like skeletal fingers reaching towards her. She steps away, afraid they might actually be able to grip her ankles if they get too close.

Slowly, she crosses the kitchen. Lowering herself into a chair, she groans. She hasn't been awake long. Her body takes time to come back to life. Something clatters against the windowpane. She spins towards the sound, skin prickling with fear.

There's nowhere to hide, the voices sing.

For a second, she thinks she sees a face pressed against the glass, but in the blink of an eye it is gone.

A flash of lightning. A rumble of thunder. She peers into the darkness.

'There's nothing there,' she says firmly to the room, but she's not sure she believes herself. Her head swims, eyes dart around.

The entire house seems to groan under the immense pressure of the storm. Floorboards creak above her. Outside, the rough water of the loch breaks over the jetty, waves crashing onto the shoreline. The little red boat bounces on the surface. She tries to focus on it. It's tiny, insignificant in the distance. But at least she knows it's real.

And the voices continue to scream. With each moan of the wind comes a new phrase.

We know.

We're coming.

You'll pay.

She balls her fists into her ears, but she still hears the terrifying choir singing to her.

'Please,' she whispers. 'Please stop. Leave me alone.' She watches in horror as a shadow creeps across the floor, twisting towards her, resembling some sort of serpent. She raises her feet. To her surprise, the black mass wraps itself around the leg of the chair, spirals it like a jungle vine, creeping up closer to her. She looks about the room; a thousand spiders scour the walls, crawling over the ceiling, dropping down on silky threads above her. She brushes her arms, but there's nothing there, of course.

She splays her hands across her face, pressing tight, shaking her head. Pulling her hair between her fingers, she tugs until she can't bear the pain any longer.

'What do you want from me?' she screams.

The spectre is gone. Simply shadows of branches on the tiles once more.

She lets out a slow, steady breath. The lights flicker on, and Diana feels the tension ease from her shoulders immediately. With the yellow glow comes a feeling of comfort. She regards the kitchen, satisfied that she is alone. No creatures scurry across the ground. None dangle from the ceiling.

All is as it should be. The storm rages on outside, but for now she is safe.

Standing, she smooths down her robe and crosses to the workbench, flicking on the kettle.

77

She stares down, initially confused by what she sees. Having half expected to find a maniac with a chainsaw, or something similar, her brain struggles to catch up.

The poor pathetic creature huddles in a corner, with its back pushed against the outhouse wall, and the cardboard boxes it hides behind. Orange fur soaked in blood, a bushy, white-tipped tail. Ears down, it snarls, baring sharp teeth. One hind leg is splayed on the floor, at an impossible angle. Even with its broken limb, the animal attempts to scurry away. Poor thing must be in agony.

She places a foot in front of it, and it backs itself into the corner once more. Lucy shines the light across the ground. A wet trail of red shows the animal's exact path to where it now rests, quivering with fear.

She'd missed it earlier because she wasn't shining her phone on the floor. But there's a lot of blood.

She suspects that the fox has been hit by a car or run over by a farm vehicle. It is terrified.

She crouches, and it scrambles against the wall, trying to get away, but it is cornered, trapped. Helpless.

'Hello, buddy,' she whispers gently, propping her phone against the wall. 'You look in a bad way, my friend.'

Sadness fills her voice, for she knows the animal stands no chance of survival. It is soaking wet, shivering. She wonders how far it has crawled in search of a safe, sheltered place to die.

Its head is matted with blood, trickling from the corner of its mouth. It whimpers as she reaches towards it. She stops, holding her hands up slowly, palms out. She doesn't want to cause it any further distress.

Reaching down, she strokes it gently on its side. It twists and turns, eventually settling, resigning to its position. She edges closer, its eyes widen.

'Don't be scared... please...' she says soothingly.

But the animal will not calm down. Scooping it up as quickly as she can, she sits on the floor, cradling it in her lap. It struggles, tries to escape, but she holds her hand firmly on its body, keeping it in place. Its petrified eyes stare about the space, searching for a way out. They settle on her face. She wishes with her whole heart that it would understand.

'I'm trying to help you... please don't be afraid.' But the fox can't comprehend. Too scared, too hurt.

Its only instinct is to escape.

She holds its head still so it can't bite her. It whimpers as she takes its leg in her other hand, feeling along the bones. It's shattered; hangs limply across her palm. She shudders.

'There's nothing I can do for you,' she breathes sadly, leaning in closer. She reaches down, cradling it gently, stroking the sides of its face with her thumbs. Her fingers are wet, sticky with blood.

'I'm sorry,' she says quietly, as she twists quickly, and with a sharp crack, snaps the creature's delicate little neck.

78

DIANA

She is sitting cradling a steaming cup of coffee in her hands when Lucy arrives back. The lights have been on for a while, so she can't imagine what's taken the girl so long.

Diana stands as Lucy drips in the doorway, water splashing onto the tiles below her.

'Oh, you poor thing! Quickly, you must get those wet clothes off!'

She hobbles through the hall to the bathroom, grabbing her spare robe from the hook on the back of the door.

When she returns to the kitchen, Lucy is still standing in her sodden garments. Diana frowns.

'Here, let me help you.'

She takes a step towards the girl, reaching her arms to the bottom of her hoody. Lucy shrugs away, a look of sheer panic on her face.

'I'll go to the bathroom and change,' she says moodily, snatching the robe from Diana, before rushing away. Diana crosses to the worktop, pouring Lucy a hot coffee. She pulls a half bottle of whisky from the cupboard, tipping in a shot for extra warmth, and sits, waiting.

When she comes back, her hair is scraped into a ponytail. Diana's robe pulled tightly around her neck, cinched at the waist with its belt. She carries her wet clothes into the utility room. Diana hears them slap into the sink. Lucy strolls into the kitchen, picking up the coffee that Diana poured for her, blowing on it.

'Thank you,' Diana says softly. 'I'm not sure what I would have done if you hadn't been here.'

'No problem.'

Diana looks at her, narrowing her eyes.

'What took you so long?'

Lucy glances at her.

'The generator needed a few attempts to start.'

'No, I mean... the lights were on a while ago. At least five minutes before you came back.'

The girl walks to the sink, putting her coffee down on the counter. She places both hands out to her sides, resting them on the edge of the worktop, staring out through the window.

'I don't think I've ever experienced a storm quite like this,' she says flatly. Lightning flashes, but with the lights on now, it doesn't seem so terrifying anymore. Diana waits patiently but does not repeat her question. Eventually Lucy turns around, leaning against the counter.

'There was a fox.'

She stares directly into Diana's eyes.

'A fox?' Diana cocks her head, awaiting more of an explanation.

'Injured. In the outhouse. Poor thing was terrified. I think it had been hit by a car or something.'

Diana's hand flies up to her mouth as she gasps.

'How terrible!'

Lucy nods.

'I tried to calm it down, but it was petrified.'

'And where is it now?'

'I dealt with it,' Lucy says, sadly.

Diana's mouth hangs open, she doesn't know how to respond.

'I think that's the kindest thing to do in these situations. Don't you?'

'You mean... you killed it?'

Lucy picks up her mug, taking a large gulp.

'It was dying anyway. It would have been far crueller to leave it to suffer for hours.'

Diana places her coffee on the side, lacing her fingers together in her lap. She doesn't look at the girl. Feels suddenly afraid to.

'I suppose.'

'Really... it's not easy to kill something. But it was the only way.'

Lucy's eyes drift towards Richard's bedroom door.

'There are times... I honestly believe there are... when to put something out of its misery is the humblest thing you can do.'

Diana watches her every movement, a slow sickening feeling washing over her.

'If you don't mind, I'll head up to bed. I'm freezing.' Lucy stands, placing her empty mug in the sink.

'No, that's fine. I think I will too. I'll be exhausted tomorrow after a night like this.'

Lucy nods, smiling, before retreating down the hall. Diana listens as her bare feet pad up the stairs.

She watches across the ceiling as the floorboards above her creak. Lucy's bedroom door clicks shut.

Diana sits for a moment, staring into space. She suddenly has an overwhelming urge to check on Richard. She pulls herself up out of her chair, heading to her husband's room. He lies with his eyes closed. Unaware of the drama that has been unfolding around him.

She takes a few steps towards him until she can see his chest rising up and down, and her shoulders relax. She lets out a long breath, scolding herself for being so ridiculous.

Of course she wasn't talking about Richard, she thinks... *She was simply referring to the poor fox.*

She pulls the door closed and returns to her own bedroom.

79

The following morning she wakes early, after a night of little sleep. She's tired. Groggy. Feeling irritable. She had been straight down to get Richard out of bed, without dressing. With him fed, washed and dressed, she retreats to the bathroom to try to make herself feel human.

She showers for longer than usual, letting the hot jets of water pound her body. She scrubs with a loofah until her skin is red raw, trying to wash away the events of the previous night. She tries to hum a happy tune. But the fox flashes into her mind. Eyes wide, filled with terror, as she snapped its neck.

Not understanding that it was for his own good.

She sees the blood on her hands from its wounded body, remembers wiping them down her wet hoody after the deed was done. Opening her eyes, she shakes her head, letting water cascade over her. She still sees the fox. Still sees the blood.

There was nothing else I could do for it, she tells herself, over and over, but it doesn't help.

She turns off the shower, stepping out onto the cold tiles. Wrapping a towel around her wet body, she retreats to her bedroom. She stands in front of the dressing table, letting the towel fall to the floor. The sight of her body, as always, comes as a shock briefly, as her eyes skirt across the scars. After so long living with them, she's still taken aback when she sees them. She fingers a large one on her thigh, stroking it gently. Sometimes, she thinks it still feels sore when she touches it. But she's sure it's just in her head.

Turning away, she grabs the first clothes she lays her hands on, a thick jumper, and her black jeans. Sliding her feet into a pair of boots, she crosses to the window, pulling the curtains wide open. The day is grey. Wind batters the cottage, but nothing of the scale from the previous evening. White horses roll across the surface of the loch, crashing onto the beach at the foot of the garden. The little wooden boat still bobs at the end of the jetty. Gulls hover, eyeing the water below, battling against each gust. Now and then, they dive-bomb, emerging a few moments later with a fish in their bills.

As she brushes her hair, she hears a knocking from downstairs. She pauses, waiting to see if Diana answers. She hears no movement from below, so she rushes down, throwing the door open. She is greeted by an empty doorstep. She leans outside, looking from side to side. Frowning, she turns to the kitchen. As she descends the hallway, she glimpses a blonde figure quickly pass by the window.

She freezes, heart pounding.

A dark shape appears outside the back door, silhouetted against the daylight behind it.

Lucy darts to the counter, sliding a carving knife from the block, and crouches down behind the island unit. The latch clicks, and the door creaks slowly open. Holding her breath, she presses her back against the cupboard doors, weapon clasped to her chest. She hears footsteps and is suddenly aware of a shape in her peripheral vision.

'Lucy... what are you doing?'

Her head whips to the side. Cassie stands, staring down at her, looking bewildered. Eyes red and watery.

Lucy springs up.

'Cassie, thank God!' She slides the knife back into the block. Cassie watches her every movement.

'What are you doing here?'

'I couldn't get hold of the others. I had to see someone... It's awful. I'm devastated.'

Lucy moves towards her.

'What is? What's happened?'

'A body washed up in the storm last night. I found out this morning. It's Sadiya... she's dead.'

She bursts into fits of tears. Lucy steps forwards, embracing her. Her sweet perfume fills Lucy's nostrils.

'No!' she says, incredulously. 'That's awful! How?' She leads Cassie to a chair, lowering her down.

'They think she's been in the water for a while. I wondered why she hadn't been answering the phone, but she can be flaky like that... so you know, I didn't panic too much.'

'My God,' Lucy breathes, crossing to the counter. 'Can I make you a coffee?'

'Do you have anything stronger?'

Lucy checks her watch.

'Cassie, it's not even nine yet.'

'My friend has just died. I think that warrants a drink, don't you?' She fixes Lucy with a stare that seems to defy her to disagree. Lucy pulls the doors open. A bottle of vodka sits on a shelf. She grabs it and a tumbler, pouring two fingerfuls, handing it to Cassie. The girl knocks it back without a thought, handing the glass to Lucy for a refill.

'I can't believe it,' Cassie says, staring into space. She blinks a few times.

'What on earth were you doing on the floor with that knife?'

Lucy shakes her head.

'Doesn't matter.' She hands Cassie the refill. She sips it, screwing up her face, before downing it.

'Go easy, Cassie.'

She shoots Lucy a withering look.

'How did you get here? I assume you drove?'

Cassie nods.

'Then you can't get drunk, can you? Unless you want your friends to lose someone else today.'

Her shoulders sag as she begins to sob once more.

'It's mad. Sadiya was such a beautiful person... she didn't deserve that... I mean, nobody does, but she definitely didn't.'

Lucy drags a chair beside her friend, sliding into it, placing her arm around her shoulder.

'Do they know what happened?'

Cassie shakes her head.

'I think she must have fallen. Apparently, she was fully clothed. She can't swim anyway... terrified of water. That's why I wasn't overly surprised that she didn't get back to me about the boat party the other week. But to think that the whole time... she was...'

'Don't,' Lucy whispers.

Cassie glances around the kitchen.

'Can we go somewhere... I don't like being here... where Rose... you know...'

'Sure. Where do you want to go?'

'Anywhere. I don't care. Anywhere but here.'

Lucy looks towards the back door, aware that she left the fox in the outhouse last night.

'Sure. Why don't you go and freshen up? I need to quickly take care of something first. It's the second on the right down the hall.'

Cassie nods. Standing, she exits the kitchen heading to the bathroom, as Lucy darts outside.

The day is cooler, air feels damp. She glances about, assessing the damage to the trees. A few slates have fallen from the roof and lie shattered around the perimeter of the cottage. Garden furniture has toppled, and the lawn is littered with general detritus. Lucy hurries across the grass to the lean-to, hugging her arms to her body. As she enters, the generator still chugs, which reminds her to check with Mylo how long she needs to leave it running for.

She finds the fox where she left it, wrapped in a canvas sack. Flies already buzz round it. She swats them away, searching the room for a shovel. There's an old metal spade leaning against a wall in the far corner. Grabbing it, she tucks the animal under her arm, heading for the woods. She doesn't venture too far in. Just inside the treeline. Placing the body on the soil, she begins to dig. Once she's sure she has dug deep enough that it won't be disturbed, she lowers the jute package down to the bottom, filling it in on top with mud. As she shovels on the last few piles of dirt, a commotion draws her attention back to Willow Cottage.

Screaming.

Horrific, terrified wailing.

She drops the shovel, running to the kitchen. As she nears, the noise grows louder. Two voices. Diana and Cassie. Shouting at each other.

'Shit!' Lucy curses under her breath as she darts inside.

She can see from the doorway, Diana in the hall flailing her arms, clawing towards the bathroom.

'Get out of my house, Rose! You're dead... you shouldn't be here anymore! Get out! What do you want?'

'Get off me, you crazy fucking bitch!' Cassie screams, voice filled with hatred, as she shoves Diana, who tumbles backwards, colliding with the bannisters opposite, before collapsing in a heap.

Lucy stares at her, weeping on the floor, then to her friend, shaking in the doorway to the bathroom.

'Cassie, are you okay?'

She crouches beside the older woman.

'No! She attacked me. Started calling me Rose!'

Fresh scratches on Cassie's face begin to spot with blood.

'It's Rose... she's here! See! I told you!' Diana bellows.

'No, Diana,' Lucy says calmly, 'this isn't Rose. This is my friend Cassie.'

Diana's eyes widen as they drift towards the bathroom. Her face is a picture of confusion.

'No... I saw her...'

'It's not Rose,' Lucy says softly, gently stroking her shoulder. She looks at her friend, dripping with blood, shocked, afraid.

'Cassie, there are bandages and disinfectant wipes in the cabinet behind you. Grab some and go and wait for me in the kitchen.'

The girl shoots a death stare towards Diana but does as she's told. Lucy helps Diana to her feet, handing her the cane from the floor, and helps her across the hallway to her bedroom.

'I saw the blonde hair... I'm sorry. I... I was sure it was her.'

'Don't you worry about that. Let's get you down on the bed.' She lowers the woman onto the top of her duvet.

'I thought she had come for me... I thought... I don't know anymore... I'm so confused... she was in the bathroom, I opened the door, and she was standing there... she looked like Rose...'

She's rambling, eyes darting about. Lucy strokes her back.

'I'm going to go and see to those scratches on Cassie, and then I'll take her home. You try to rest, okay?'

Diana nods. Lucy exits the room, pulling the door closed

behind her. Cassie is standing, tapping her foot. She holds a wad of gauze to her cheek.

'I should call the police! That lunatic attacked me!'

Lucy holds her finger to her lips.

'I'm so sorry, Cassie... she's not well. She's... I don't know... I think she's having some sort of breakdown.'

Cassie laughs.

'You're not kidding. And what was all that about Rose?'

'Please, keep your voice down, I don't want her going off on one again.'

Lucy leans on the counter beside her friend, letting out a long sigh.

'God, I don't know where to start. In a nutshell, she thinks that Rose is haunting her. And she thought you were Rose?'

Cassie's mouth hangs open. She tilts her head.

'She's confused, Cassie... she's not well.'

Cassie bites her bottom lip, nodding slowly.

'I really wanted to avoid getting you involved in any of this. It's bad enough that poor Mylo had to hear it all...'

'Mylo knows?'

Lucy nods. Cassie straightens up.

'I am going to go and have a word with that bitch! This is nuts.'

Lucy grabs Cassie's arm.

'Don't! Please. I'll deal with it. I promise. Please don't say anything to her. I can't cope with another fight... not right now. I haven't slept... we had... issues last night. I'm exhausted and I really need to forget about all this.'

Her shoulders slump, her eyes glaze.

Cassie pours herself another large vodka, knocking it back swiftly.

'I don't need this right now either. I came here for some support about my friend's death. Can we get out of here?'

'Yeah, come on.'

Cassie tosses the bloody gauze into the sink. She points to her wounded face and neck.

'If this scars, I'll fucking have her!' She heads out to the hall.

'Cassie,' Lucy calls after her as she follows behind.

Cassie turns. Lucy holds out her hand.

'Keys.'

Her friend frowns.

'I'm driving. You've drunk way too much.'

Cassie reaches into her pocket, handing over her keys indignantly.

'You bend it, you mend it!' she says, smirking as she throws open the front door.

As Lucy catches up, she sees Cassie's car. An uber-expensive-looking lime-green sportscar sits outside the house. Cassie struts to the passenger side, climbing in. Lucy stops, staring at the vehicle.

'What on earth is that?' Her eyes glide over the vehicle's sleek lines.

'It's a McLaren Artura,' Cassie replies, as if that explains everything. Lucy immediately regrets insisting she drive. Stepping forward, she opens the driver side door, sliding onto the plush leather seat.

'Do I want to know how much this cost?'

Cassie looks at her.

'Probably not.'

'Okay.'

As she starts the ignition, the engine growls to life. She lets out a long breath through her mouth, gripping the wheel.

'You can do this. It's only a car,' she whispers gently to herself, grasping the wheel with trembling hands.

'Don't let my dad hear you saying that!'

She presses her foot down and pulls away smoothly. As she glances in the rear-view mirror, she sees Diana hobble out through the front door, staring after them.

80

DIANA

She steps inside the cottage, as the sound of the engine purrs away. As she starts to close the door, a glint in the distance draws her attention. She peers at the trees opposite. Something sparkles as it catches the light. She limps towards the forest, unable to look away from the object. On approach, she sees a delicate silver chain dangling from a branch. Tiny emeralds gleam, shooting a spectrum of colours into Diana's eyes. Shuddering, she reaches out, grabbing the crucifix in her fist. She holds it close to her, glancing around.

She edges back towards the front door, afraid to look away from the trees. When she nears the house, she turns, hurrying in as quickly as her leg will allow her, her old injury aching as she increases her speed. Closing the door, it occurs to her that she hates being outside these days. She can't relax until she is inside, with the doors closed.

She stares down at the chain in her palm, before sliding it into the pocket of her cardigan. Shaking her head, she runs her hand up her face, smoothing her hair. She fiddles with her fringe, splaying it across her forehead. Feeling foolish, she thinks of the blonde girl.

She had felt so sure it was Rose. The voices in the storm had told her they were coming. And she thought they were delivering on their promise. Even now, she's not sure if Lucy was lying. Was it Rose that climbed into a car with her and drove away?

They're all in on it, she thinks. *But I'm cleverer than that. They have no idea what I'm capable of.*

She chuckles to herself, turning to the foot of the stairs. She glances up to the landing.

Not today, she thinks. There was a time when she would have attempted it without a second thought.

But these days she feels drained, shaky. Her legs aren't her own. She relies on her stick more than she ever has. She crosses the hallway, entering the kitchen. A half-empty bottle of vodka sits on the worktop. She'll have to remember to dock Lucy's wages for that.

Opening the cupboard, she assesses her options for wine. There's not much left. Nothing open.

She'll need to order some with the next load of shopping. She shrugs, lifting the vodka. Removing the lid, she takes a swig straight from the bottle, wincing as it fills her mouth and burns her throat.

Pushing through the door, she enters the lounge, crossing to the wood burner. Opening it, she places a firelighter and a few pieces of kindling inside, before striking a match, tossing it on top.

The fire crackles to life as she closes the hatch, waiting for the flames to grow. After a few minutes, she takes a large log from a well-stocked pile beside the hearth, throwing it inside. She retreats to the sofa opposite. As she sits, she downs more of the liquor.

A creak from out in the kitchen draws her attention. She stands, crossing the room, and pushes through. A cabinet door swings open in a draft. Had she left it open? She can't even remember being in the kitchen. But glancing at the bottle in her hand, she surmises that she must have been. She pushes the door shut. A noise from the living room. A thud. She rushes back through. Creeping back towards the fire, she sees something lying on the seat where moments earlier she had been sitting. She draws closer, realising it's a long-stemmed red rose. She narrows her eyes, but as she watches, the flower begins to wither. It shrivels, curling, dying, until it is brown and decaying. It turns to dust. She blinks, and it's gone. The seat is empty.

Shaking her head, she sits. Holding the bottle firmly in one hand, clasping it to her chest, she stares at Richard's painting, high on the wall. The colours swirl as she gulps more vodka. Squinting, she thinks the figure within the flames moves. She shakes it away.

But the edges of the composition appear to be melting in the heat from the fire. The paint, thick and wet, bleeds out onto the mantel. As she watches, the molten mass grows until it engulfs the entire chimney breast, as if it is alive, crawling to escape the confines of the canvas.

She cranes her head forwards, fascinated by the horrifying tableau that emerges before her. The liquid trickles down the walls and flows over the floor towards the settee. It bubbles, swallowing anything it comes into contact with. She knows she should attempt to escape, but her body refuses to move.

As the liquid meets the base of the couch, it begins to climb up the furniture; jumps onto Diana's ankles. She watches, petrified, as the paint swirl over her clothes, over her skin. Her entire world is now a mass of colours, bleeding together, muddying. She closes her eyes, shaking her head again.

As she opens them, the room is as it should be. The hues, perhaps a little more vibrant. Raising her hand in front of her face, she notes there is an ethereal glow around the edges of her limbs.

I'm an angel, she thinks.

An angel of death, the painting screams at her in a demonic snarl.

She smells smoke, glances at the fire. The log she had placed has burnt to ash. Orange embers are all that are left. Little heat remains.

How long have I been here, she wonders?

She blinks a few more times, and a new piece of wood burns in the fireplace. She frowns, looking at the pile of logs beside it.

Only two remain.

Her eyelids flutter, and she's in the garden, sitting in the seat beneath the old willow tree. An empty vodka bottle lies on the grass by her feet.

The wind rages around her, leaves rustle. Her hair is loose, trailing about her face, blowing behind her.

What happened to my braid? she thinks.

Shaking her head, she suddenly finds herself standing in the kitchen, a half-empty bottle of wine in her hand, the rich berry flavours of a Châteauneuf-du-Pape, wasted on her entirely in her current state, linger on her tongue.

What.

Is.

Happening?

Dizzy, she lumbers towards the worktop to support herself, dropping the wine as she does so.

It seems to fall in slow motion, before smashing on the tiles below. Ruby-coloured liquid explodes across the floor, and up her legs, drips down the cabinet doors around her like blood.

In the dark puddle by her feet, she sees Rose's reflection, laughing.

She spins; nobody stands behind her, but the sound of the laughter still echoes in her ears.

Where is my stick, she wonders?

Once more, the scene changes in a flash. She now sits in the boat at the end of the jetty. The bottom is filled with water, soaking into her clothes. She shivers, looking around.

How did I get here?

The red paint from the outside of the boat bleeds into the loch, and with horror she realises she is floating on a lake of blood.

She feels as if she is not in control of herself anymore. Someone else is operating her, like a marionette. She glances up, and sees long strings protruding from her flesh, trailing off into the clouds.

Blinking, they are gone.

Darkness seems to swoop in from the horizon, the light shrinking around her as if she holds a lantern in a vast black space. The glow becomes smaller and smaller until it is tiny. Just a pinprick in the dark.

And Diana Davenport screams, holding her head in her hands, as tears well in her eyes.

81

'Next left,' Cassie says breezily, and Lucy dutifully indicates, before taking the turn. Afraid to damage the car, she drives like an old lady, painfully aware that Cassie is smirking at her from the passenger seat.

'Park up anywhere you can find a space,' she instructs.

They climb out and Cassie watches as Lucy seems to relax as soon as she is no longer in control of the vehicle. They head towards a small double-fronted café. Pushing the door, a bell jingles as it swings inwards, and she holds it open as her friend steps inside.

'Wow. Civilisation!' Lucy breathes. 'This is... nice!'

'Sadiya used to love this place,' Cassie responds, sliding a chair out from beneath a table by the window. Lucy smiles sympathetically, looking away towards the counter as they both sit.

'So what's good here?'

Cassie holds her hand up. A waitress totters over to them, smiling as she approaches.

'I'll take a double G and T, please, and...'

She looks at Lucy, who purses her lips, but doesn't reprimand her.

'Coffee, black, please.'

She glances back towards Cassie.

'You'll have to stay at mine tonight if you keep this up.'

'No chance. I'm not setting foot in that place again. Not with that mad bitch there.'

Lucy doesn't respond. The waitress brings their order, and Cassie takes a large gulp from her drink. Lucy sits blowing on her coffee, eyes fixed on her.

'Want to talk about it?' she finally says, sipping her beverage.

'Which?'

Lucy raises an eyebrow questioningly.

'That Sadiya is dead, or that your employer believes my other dead friend is haunting your house?' She pauses without looking away from Lucy's face. 'Because if I'm being honest, I don't really feel like talking about either of those things.'

Lucy sighs.

'Cassie... you have to understand, Diana is not well. I've been witnessing her spiral out of control mentally for a while now. This *ghost* thing... it's all part of that. She's losing her mind. I'm sure of it.'

Cassie empties her gin, holding her hand up. The waitress glances over, and Cassie nods towards her glass.

'It's fucking sick.' Her words are beginning to sound slurred. The waitress brings her drink, and hurries away to another customer who is trying desperately to get her attention. Cassie gulps a large mouthful, screwing up her face as she does.

'Enjoying that?' Lucy smirks.

'Immensely.'

They sit in silence for a few minutes.

'So she's nuts. Unwell. Whatever you want to call it. Nothing new there. Rose always used to say she was insane.'

Lucy's eyes shoot towards Cassie's cheek.

'Does it hurt?'

'It's sore,' she replies, raising her glass. 'But this is helping to numb the pain.' She takes another sip, pressing the cold glass into her face.

'And Mylo knows about this? That Diana thinks Rose is haunting her?'

Lucy nods.

'Diana made us take part in a seance... roped in some old local lady who claims to be psychic.'

'That woman... she loves to be the centre of attention. Even today, when I should be focusing on my friend, I'm here talking about *her*, instead. You know she doesn't need that stick? I'm sure she uses it to get sympathy. She hardly ever used it when Rose lived with her. Only now and then when her leg was giving her trouble. Now she seems to act like she can't stand without it. And she pretends she's unable to get up the stairs... but she can, let me warn you. Don't leave anything lying around in your bedroom that you don't want her to see. Rose used to find things had moved around... thought it was a bit odd. One day she got home earlier than expected, and caught the cow red-handed in there, sitting on her bed, reading her diary! She had to hide it after that.'

'You're kidding?'

Cassie shakes her head, sipping more of her drink.

'I'm so sorry about Sadiya,' Lucy continues. 'She seemed nice. I... didn't really get to talk to her, but... you know...'

Fiddling with a strand of loose hair, Cassie smiles wistfully.

'She wasn't too friendly towards you. She can be a little aloof, but it's because she's shy. It comes across the wrong way sometimes. If you'd had a chance to get to know her, you'd have loved her.'

'I'm sure.'

'The guys... Colin and Lucas... they're not my type of people. They're Mylo's friends, really. But Molly and Sadiya, they're my world. I can't actually believe she's gone.'

'Shouldn't you be with the others?'

'Molly is at work. I haven't told her yet... but gossip travels fast around here. It won't take long for her to find out. I don't want to be the one to have to tell her... to tell anyone. Mylo... he knows everything before most people usually. That's the thing about working in that damn shop. All the old busybodies go in and spin their yarns... embellishing... they thrive on it. They don't have anything else. It's so fucking boring round here...'

'Why do you stay? If that's how you feel?'

Cassie takes another swig of her gin, shrugging.

'I get to live at the marina in a luxury apartment and dine at a five-star restaurant three times a day. I drink as much champagne as I want. I party on my father's yacht with my friends. All in return for helping out with a bit of paperwork now and then, sometimes pouring a few drinks behind the bar. It's a no-brainer.'

Lucy nods slowly. Cassie sighs, downing what's left from her glass, motioning to the waitress for another. She points at Lucy, who holds her hand over the top of her mug, shaking her head.

'I'm sorry things didn't work out with you and Mylo. I was sure you were going to hit it off. He deserves to be happy again.'

'We did kind of hit it off... we're great friends.'

'I know... but... you know what I mean. He needs to find a nice girl and settle down. I thought you were perfect for him.'

Lucy gazes out the window.

'Did you know Diana's daughter was murdered?' Lucy asks, staring at her friend.

Cassie's eyes widen.

'Shut up! No. When?'

Lucy shrugs.

'Don't know exactly, but it was years ago.'

Cassie shakes her head.

'Mylo knew her, apparently.'

'Did he?'

'Yep. Went out with her for a while. He knew Diana too.'

Cassie screws up her face.

'That's weird. He *never* mentioned that.'

'No? Hmm. Anyway... I just thought it was interesting.'

She lets that hang.

'I really wish you two were a couple,' Cassie says, as if she wants to change the subject. Lucy suspects she is too drunk for anything she has just told her to register too much.

'It doesn't matter. Not in the grand scheme of things. That's not why I'm here,' she says.

Cassie tilts her head. Lucy looks back at her.

'I mean, I'm here to work. To look after Diana and her husband... not that I seem to be doing such a great job there either. But I didn't come to meet a boyfriend. It was the last thing on my mind.'

'You deserve to be happy too, Lucy.' Cassie's words are beginning to run into one another.

Lucy's cheeks flush as she glances away.

'Shut up! You're drunk.'

'No. Well... yes... but I mean it. There's something in you... a sadness. I can see it. I'm good at reading people. I saw it in you when we first met. You smile... but I don't think it's real. It's a shame.'

Cassie twirls a strand of her honey-coloured hair between her fingers, placing it between her top lip and her nose, holding it there. The waitress brings her another drink.

'So... you will definitely be staying over tonight,' Lucy says, eyeing the glass.

'No way. You come to mine! We can order room service and get shit-faced.'

'I can't. I have to see to Richard. Plus, I don't think Diana should be left alone overnight right now.'

Cassie tuts, rolling her eyes like a petulant child.

'Eurgh... I *really* can't sleep in that house. Where Rose died. It creeps me out. Not to mention that woman attacked me!'

'You should have thought about that before you got so drunk.'

She sighs, her shoulders slump in resignation as she downs her drink.

'Right,' Lucy says matter-of-factly. 'That's enough. Time to go.'

She stands, crosses to the counter to pay the bill. She helps Cassie up from her chair, draping one of her arms loosely over her shoulder, and they head out to the car.

82

Neither of them want to return to Willow Cottage, not yet at least.

It's nearing lunchtime, so they pull in next to a burger van in a lay-by. Lucy suspects that cheap burgers are not usually on Cassie's menu, but she probably would have eaten anything to avoid heading back to Diana's house. They sit on a rickety wooden bench, atop a cliff behind the truck, staring out over the loch.

'It's mad... I've been here for a while now, and it still seems there's so much of this place to see...'

She flicks her eyes towards Cassie, who looks as if she's struggling with the food. She picks a gherkin out from beneath the bun between the tips of her fingers, tossing it onto the grass. The burger remains in her lap.

'It is stunning. Even on a day like this... the way the sun breaks through the clouds now and then... it gives me hope. Look...' She nods at the horizon.

Lucy follows the direction of her gaze, gasping as she spies a rainbow in the distance.

'Beautiful,' she whispers.

'This place… it's full of lovely things. People like Mylo, who grew up here… they're always so desperate to get away. If his dad hadn't died, he'd still be living in London. He'd never even have met Rose. Who knows… perhaps your paths would have crossed there.'

'Everything happens for a reason,' Lucy says without looking at her friend.

'Do you believe that?'

'I think so. You have to, don't you? Else what's the point?'

Cassie stands from the bench, walking closer to the cliff edge. A metal railing, the only thing between her and the sheer drop on the other side. She leans on it, taking a bite of her burger.

'I don't know. What reason is there for what's happened to my friends? To Rose… or to Sadiya? They were both good people. What *possible* excuse could there be for two such beautiful human beings to be taken from the world so young?'

'I'm not sure… I don't have the answers. Nobody does.'

Cassie turns, leaning her bottom on the railing.

'Sadiya had a kid. Not even a year old. He has to grow up without his mum now. That's… so *sad*.'

Lucy stares out at the rainbow.

'I didn't know she had a child. That's… terrible.' Her voice trembles as a tear wells in the corner of her eye. Cassie cocks her head.

'Are you crying?'

Lucy wipes her eyes.

'It's sad… like you said. No child should have to go through that. It's tragic.'

Cassie crosses back to the bench, tossing what's left of her burger onto the grass, screwing up her face. She sits beside her friend, draping an arm around her shoulder.

'You're a good person, Lucy.'

Lucy shakes her head.

'No, no I'm not.'

'Yeah, you are. I couldn't do what you do... looking after that guy. Doing everything for him. I take my hat off to you.'

Lucy stands, wiping her hands together.

'I don't do it out of the goodness of my heart. I do it for money. Diana pays well. It's a job, that's all. I'm no saint. I'm far from perfect, and I have *many* flaws. I've done horrible things...'

Cassie cocks an eyebrow.

'Like what?'

Lucy shrugs.

'No, go on. Tell me.'

'Last night, I killed a fox.'

Cassie's eyes widen.

'What?'

'It was hurt... I think it had been hit by a car... but it was in the garden and I knew there was no hope for it. So I... killed it.'

Cassie stares at her friend.

'How?'

'I snapped its neck.'

They both sit in silence, staring at the rainbow until it begins to fade. Digesting that fact. Lucy wonders what Cassie is thinking about her. She doesn't know why she told her. Something in the moment compelled her. She couldn't help herself; regretted it immediately. She heads towards the car.

'We should go.'

'Do we have to?'

'I don't want to go back there any more than you do... but it's my job.'

Cassie stands, grabbing her friend.

'Let's not then. Not just yet. We can drive the long way round. I'll show you some of my favourite spots. Come on. What's she going to do? Sack you? I can't see her managing without you very well at the moment.'

Lucy bites her bottom lip.

'Go on, you know you want to! Besides, I'm sad, and you're supposed to be cheering me up!' Cassie pouts, then grins devilishly, ear to ear.

'Okay!'

'Yes!'

Laughing, Cassie throws her arm around her friend as they stroll back to the car.

83

DIANA

She climbs out of the boat, her clothes soaked, clinging to her skin. For a terrifying moment, she thinks she will fall over the side into the water below, but she manages to steady herself in time to land in a heap upon the jetty.

The wind has died down a little, but the afternoon is grey. In the distance, a rainbow decorates the hillside. Its bright spectrum, the only colour in the surrounding scenery. Suddenly the hues bleed into the rest of the landscape, casting glorious technicolour into the sky, the trees, the water. Diana has never felt like this before. The closest thing she can think of is when she and Richard had tried acid together at art college. She remembers how five minutes passed like five hours. The night seemed endless.

She'd hated it so much she vowed never to do it again. But that's similar to how she feels.

Time doesn't seem to be flowing in a straight line, rather, jumping around. She can't focus. Closing her eyes, she takes deep breaths. When she opens them, the colours have gone, the rainbow all that remains. Turning away, she retrieves her stick from where she left it on the beach, propped against the boardwalk. She crosses the lawn towards the kitchen.

The waves tumble onto the shingle, lapping at the grass behind her, like a threatening whisper.

Diana, it seems to call. She spins, staring out at the shoreline. As wave after wave ripples onto the stones, something in the distance bobs above the surface.

At first, she thinks it might be a seal. But it continues to grow taller as it emerges from the water.

Her eyes widen with terror as she realises it's the top of a head. Hair wet and matted.

Blonde.

As the figure walks slowly out of the loch, Diana's mouth falls open. She wants to scream. But she can't.

'Rose!' she gasps.

The girl steps onto the beach, dripping. Kelp tangled in her locks, draped around her arms. Barnacles grow on her ankles.

'Hello, Diana,' she says in a horrendous, gurgling voice as a crab scurries from her lips, crawls across her face, disappearing over her shoulder.

Diana spins towards the house. She attempts to run, and it surprises her that she feels no pain in her leg or hip. Stepping inside the kitchen, she slams the door, locking it immediately. She turns her back to the glass, leaning against it. Heart pounding, she takes deep breaths. She leans to her left, peering around through the window. Holding her breath, she scours the shoreline, searching for Rose.

But the garden is empty.

A trickling sound from nearby draws her gaze away. Water is running out from the utility room. A huge puddle pools on the tiles, growing by the second. Shaking her head, she crosses the floor, pulling on the handle. The door swings open.

Rose stands dripping in the doorway.

'My God!' Diana screams, stepping back.

She slips. Falling backwards.

Down, down, down. Tumbling much longer than she should be. She feels she should have hit something by now, but she is still going. She lands in the puddle.

But instead of a hard floor, she splashes into a pool, sinking beneath its surface. The icy water washes over her skin as reeds tangle around her ankles, pulling her down. She struggles, flailing. Raising her head, she sees shafts of light breaking through the water, far above her.

How is it so deep, she wonders?

Reaching down, she claws at her feet, tearing at the weeds that wrap themselves round her limbs.

And then she is dry. Rolling on her back on the floor. The utility door wide open, but nobody is there.

No water. Only Diana, alone, in the middle of the kitchen.

Her eyes creep about the room, searching for a sign that someone else is there.

But nothing is untoward. Everything is silent. No ghosts. No Rose.

She reaches up, pulling herself to her feet on the edge of the counter, checking her clothes. They're wet from where she sat in the boat, but her hair is dry. Still tumbling loose, free from the constraints of her braid, it falls about her like a lion's mane. A low rumble of wind rages outside. She feels her ankles, half expecting to find seaweed there. Nothing.

Smoothing her hair down the sides of her face, she lets out a breath, and retrieves her stick from the floor by her feet, crossing the room to the hallway. She has the sickening feeling that the house is rocking from side to side as she walks, like a huge cruise ship, caught in a turbulent sea. She steadies herself against the bannisters as she lumbers along the passageway, stumbling towards her bedroom. Lunging across the hall, she almost falls through the doorway. Throwing open the drawers of her dresser, she pulls pots of pills out, but her hands are shaking too much. Each time she removes a lid, the tablets spill out, falling to the floor, slipping between cracks on the boards. She pushes others through the foil of blister packs using her thumb, but they scatter by her feet, instead of into her hand.

She throws the empty packets down, screaming.

Dropping to her knees, she scrambles around, scooping up the pills, shovelling them into her mouth. Doesn't know which are which anymore. Doesn't care. It's no matter. She simply wants to be unconscious. Away from this hideous waking nightmare.

Crawling to her bed, she pulls herself up onto the mattress. Fully clothed and damp, she slides beneath the duvet. The room swirls around her. She screws her eyes tight, but each time she closes them she sees Rose's ghost, emerging from the loch, reaching a bony arm with pale, water-bloated flesh sagging from it towards her. Pointing a skeletal finger at Diana's face.

Her eyes spring open. Anything is better than that.

She stares through the dim room at the wall opposite her bed. The pattern of the paisley wallpaper seems to dance before her, rearranging itself. She squints, blinking a few times. It's definitely moving.

Crawling like a thousand spiders.

It swirls in undulating movements, and before she can make head or tail of what is happening, it has morphed into a face.

Rose's face.

Mouth wide open in a snarl. That dreadful, watery voice screams, and Diana balls her fists into her ears.

84

They put it off as long as they can but eventually, around four in the afternoon, they head for the house. On a brighter day, the light would still be wonderful at this time, but today, with the thick blanket of cloud in the sky, it feels like dusk. Driving through the woods, the gloom is immense. Memories of jumping into the loch from yachts couldn't be further from their minds.

Lucy glances at her friend beside her. The booze is wearing off, and now she's struggling to stay awake. Neither of them speaks for some time.

'Will she be up?' Cassie asks as the car winds down the side of the hill, towards Willow Cottage.

Lucy shrugs.

'Your guess is as good as mine. Depends if she's been drinking.'

'I haven't had any alcohol since before lunch... I think I'd be okay to drive home now, really.'

'Cassie, is two of your friends dying not enough for one year, without adding your own name to the list?'

345

Cassie turns to look out of her window, as Lucy immediately regrets her words.

'I'm sorry... that was insensitive. Of course, if you want to leave, I can't stop you. But I wouldn't feel happy about it.'

Cassie nods.

'I know this morning wasn't great... but believe me, she's never been violent before.'

Her friend opens her mouth to speak but stops, as if she has changed her mind.

'What?' Lucy asks.

'Nothing. It doesn't matter.'

'Tell me?'

She shifts uncomfortably in her seat.

'She hit Rose.'

'Really?'

'They were arguing about something totally ridiculous, like toilet paper or something... and Diana slapped her in the face. Never apologised for it. I think that was the turning point for Rose... that's when she knew she was done there.'

'Why on earth did she stay?'

'Mylo. She was head over heels in love with him. And she didn't want to lose him. She begged him to let her move in at his, but his mother is... old-fashioned about things like that. So she stayed... she put up with all Diana's shit. For Mylo. Sad really.'

Lucy pulls up at the front of the cottage, applying the handbrake. Both girls sit for a moment. She eventually climbs out onto the damp grass. Cassie follows suit, trailing a few paces behind. As they approach, it strikes Lucy as odd that no lights are on inside. Although it's still early, the light is poor, and the house is in shadow. Frowning, she unlocks the front door, stepping into the hall.

It feels cold. That's the first thing that hits her.

Diana's bedroom is wide open. That's the second.

346

She steps forward, peering into the room. Empty.

The place is silent.

'Hello? Diana?' Lucy calls out as Cassie joins her by her side.

Nobody answers. A creak from somewhere within. Lucy looks at her friend, holding her finger to her lips. She tiptoes down the hallway, pausing outside Richard's room, peeking in. No sign of him.

They enter the kitchen. The back door is wide open. Diana's grey hair lies in clumps all over the floor. A pair of shears sits on the worktop. Another creak from behind them.

They spin, but the hall is deserted.

Turning towards the window, they notice Richard in his wheelchair, sitting out on the jetty.

'What the hell is he doing out there?' Cassie whispers.

'Something is not right. Wait here.' Lucy rushes into the garden, across the lawn to the pier.

She crouches in front of Richard. His eyes are wide open. He stares dead ahead, out over the loch.

His colostomy bag is leaking. The stench of faeces fills her nose. She holds a hand over her mouth, trying not to gag.

'What are you doing out here by yourself? Where's Diana?' she breathes into his ear. Standing, she spins the chair, noticing that Cassie now loiters in the garden, hair blowing in the wind as she hugs her arms around herself against it.

'You okay?' Lucy shouts as she approaches.

'Yeah... I felt weird in there.'

'No worries. Can you wait out here with him? I'm going to check inside for Diana.'

Cassie nods. Screwing her face up as the smell of human waste hits her, she leans against the wall as far from him as she can manage. Lucy steps back into the kitchen, flicking on the light as she enters. A creak to her left makes her jump. Heart pounding, she spins to see the living-room door swing shut.

'Diana?'

She steps through to the lounge, in time to see a figure exit on the opposite side of the room. Edging backwards, she sidesteps to the entrance of the hall.

Someone looms by the foot of the stairs.

Lucy shudders. The dark silhouette dashes across the hallway, into Diana's room. Lucy creeps forward, stopping outside.

'Hello?' she says gently, voice trembling.

'Diana?'

Something tumbles, clattering to the floor. She knows it's irrational, but she doesn't want to enter the bedroom.

'I'm coming in...'

As she shifts her weight on her feet, the boards beneath them groan. The sound seems to fill the entire house. The curtains are closed, as they have been for weeks. There's a stench like sweat, and piss, and filthy bed linen. On reflection, Lucy can't remember the last time she washed sheets for Diana. Flies buzz around the space, landing on dirty soup bowls, and saucers with half-eaten sandwiches.

At least she's been eating the food I've prepared... mostly, Lucy thinks. She pushes in a little further.

She can't see Diana by the bed. Glancing about, she realises with a sense of dread that there's only one place someone could be hiding.

Behind the door.

She turns, too late, as something heavy collides with the top of her head.

And the world goes black.

85

LUCY

There's a ringing in her ears. Her head throbs.

Opening her eyes, she slowly reaches a hand up to her face. It's wet, sticky.

Blood.

It takes her a moment to put everything together.

Someone hit her. Hard.

She's lying on the floor in Diana's bedroom, in the dark. She has no idea how long she's been out. She reaches up, feeling around for her injury. She's groggy, disorientated. There's a lump, and a cut, but it doesn't feel too deep. Scalp wounds always bleed a lot. Climbing to her knees, she stays like that for a while, to make sure she won't collapse again. Blood trickles down the side of her face, dripping onto the floorboards. When she's positive she's okay, she stands, crossing to the dresser, throwing open the drawers. She rummages for something soft, finding a black T-shirt, sniffing it. Smells clean. Balling it up, she presses it to the cut. She steadies herself on the top of the unit, waiting for her eyes to adjust to the darkness. The house is still. Silent. Outside, the wind has died down. All is calm. She steps out into the hall, still pressing the garment to her. It's soaking up the blood. She can feel it seeping through to her hand.

Holding her breath, she creeps along the hallway, back jammed against the wall. She enters the kitchen, clicking the door shut as silently as she can. Doesn't want to risk another attack from behind. She glances towards the living room, and dashes across the floor, stepping out into the garden, sealing the exit behind her again. She looks from side to side. Richard is still sitting in his chair, where she left him, but Cassie is nowhere to be seen.

Peering into the distance, she sees something lying on the lawn, past the jetty, close to the treeline.

Diana's cane.

She sprints towards it, crouching to pick it up. There are footprints in the mud on the perimeter of the forest. Freshly broken branches where someone has barged in. She looks around one last time, before pushing into the undergrowth. As she makes her way deeper into the woods, the light fades fast. The ground is soft, the leaves still wet from the storm.

A twig cracks somewhere in the distance.

She stops, breathing slowly, scanning the trees. The gentle lapping of the waves on the shore the only sound. Behind her, something rustles. She spins, craning her neck as she tries to see what is there. Some nearby branches sway back and forth. Holding her breath again, heart pounding, she rotates on the spot.

Still nothing.

She pushes further into the forest. Straying from the path, progress is slow. She has to climb over fallen trunks and sprawling bracken. Thorns from brambles catch on her jeans, tearing at her ankles through her thin socks. As the woodland grows denser, she finds it harder to pass, holding Diana's cane in one hand, the other pressing the T-shirt to her head. She checks the cloth, it's sodden now, sticky. Tossing it aside, it catches on a branch, hanging a few metres from her. Reaching up, she touches her wound; fingers come away covered in blood. She can feel it trickling down her neck.

She'll worry about that later. Tucking the cane under her arm, she ploughs on, as waves of dizziness wash over her.

To her left, some oystercatchers screech, fluttering from their hiding place, up into the treetops. Did something disturb them? Was it simply her presence that alarmed them?

Senses heightened, she pushes some branches aside, creeping further into the forest. Another crack.

Closer now. She spins. A large stag stands a few metres in the distance, eyes wide, frozen to the spot. It stares her down. Ordinarily, she would be in awe of this creature, but this is not the time to marvel at its beauty. It turns and disappears into the bushes, lightning fast. And Lucy is alone once more.

She tries to stay low, ready for an attack.

'Lucy!'

A whisper. But definitely her name.

'Over here...'

She can't tell which direction the voice comes from. Her heart thumps violently in her chest. Arms trembling, she edges forwards, into the darkness. Her foot sinks into some thick mud, squelching beneath her shoe. She looks down, shoulders slumping.

A pale hand shoots out from the bushes, gripping her ankle.

And Lucy screams.

'Shh!' Cassie whispers, pulling her down to the ground.

'My God, Cassie! Are you trying to scare me to death?'

Cassie claps her hand over Lucy's mouth.

'She's got those shears,' she whispers, eyes wide.

Lucy glances at her friend. Her hair has fallen loose and is tangled with leaves and twigs. The left sleeve of her sweater is torn, bloodied. Beneath the gaps in the fabric, Lucy sees a nasty-looking cut.

'What happened?' Lucy mouths silently.

'She's totally lost it... went berserk. She's not making any sense. Charged at me with the scissors, slashed my shoulder.' She nods towards her wound. 'Screaming about Rose, basically babbling nonsense. Shouting about how she came out of the wallpaper to get her... bonkers. I ran into the woods. She followed, but I think she's struggling.'

'I've got her stick. That must be slowing her down a little.'

Cassie's eyes widen, finger springs to her lips. She suddenly crouches lower, pulling Lucy with her.

She points, slowly, over her friend's shoulder. Lucy pivots to see behind her. A few metres away, on the other side of a large bush, stands Diana. Blades dangling by her side. Her hair is shorn roughly, all different lengths, spiky, longer in places. It trails in wisps about her ears. She wears a black housecoat, baggy and shapeless. Her eyes bulge in their sockets, as her head whips from side to side.

'Where are you, Rose?' she calls in a playful tone. 'I know you're here. Somewhere.'

She takes a few tentative steps forwards, before turning her back to the girls.

Lucy barely recognises the lunatic stalking around before them. The transformation is frightening.

'I'll find you.'

She edges away from them.

'Cassie, do you trust me?' Lucy says as quietly as she can. Her friend nods.

'I'll distract her... and I need you to run in the other direction. Go back and call the police. And an ambulance. Tell them exactly what is happening. Then lock yourself in the house and don't come out until they arrive.'

'No! She'll kill you. She's totally crazy.'

'She won't. I'm faster. She's disabled. She'll not get near me. But we *need* help here.'

Cassie's eyes well with tears as she stares at the madwoman.

'As soon as I'm gone, you have to get up and run. As fast as you can. Do you understand?'

'I'm scared.'

'I know. I am too. But I'll lure her away from you.'

Cassie nods again. Without warning, Lucy springs out from her hiding place, dashing forwards. The commotion makes Diana spin towards them. Lucy sprints past her, bounding over tree stumps and holly bushes. She affords herself a glance over her shoulder. Diana is in pursuit. Behind her, Lucy sees Cassie dart away quietly, heading away to the perimeter of the forest.

Lucy runs, or as close to running as she can in the dense woodland, with what she suspects is concussion. She dodges trees, sidesteps tall ferns, and splashes through puddles. She hears Diana, but she's falling further and further behind. The woman isn't steady on her feet on clear ground. Lucy has a distinct advantage, and she knows it.

When she's confident that Diana can no longer see her, she drops to the floor, rolling to a huge Scots pine trunk, and sits with her back against it, holding Diana's cane in both trembling hands.

Her breathing is so heavy, she's positive Diana will hear it.

'I'm coming, Rose!' The woman's voice echoes through the trees. 'You can't get away from me.'

She's getting nearer.

Lucy turns to face the trunk. She leans the cane against it, and places her palms on the bark, peering round the side. She sees a black shape move amongst the bushes. Darting back to her hiding place, she grabs the stick, standing with knees bent. Waiting.

She hears cracks and rustles as Diana grows nearer. She hadn't planned on letting her get this close, but she's still out of breath, not ready to run again yet.

'Come out, come out, wherever you are...' Diana sings.

The sound sends a shiver down to Lucy's core.

'Rose, you fucking bitch! Get out here right now!' Diana screams. Her voice is high-pitched; doesn't sound like herself.

Lucy spies a large rock at her feet, covered in moss, half sunk in deep mud. Crouching, she grapples with one hand, prising the stone out of the puddle. It comes free easily. Straightening, she turns, throwing it as far as she can into the bushes.

'Got you!' Diana hisses.

Lucy hears a succession of cracks and grunts. She leans around, seeing Diana hobbling away in the other direction, faster than she would have thought possible for the woman. Lucy squats, crawling through the dirt. Her clothes are caked in mud. Blood from her head mixes with it on her jumper.

She scurries through prickly vegetation, slicing her hands and knees, but it doesn't matter anymore.

Diana's weapon would slice her more than the thorns.

A sound nearby makes her wheel around.

She's not sure how it's happened, but Diana has come full circle, and now stands a metre or so away, staring down at her. A smile creeps onto her lips.

'There you are, you naughty squirrel!' she says, lunging towards Lucy.

Lucy swings the cane up, holding it in both hands as Diana comes down in her direction, swinging wildly with the razor-sharp blades. Lucy knocks her with the stick, and she falls backwards, landing in a heap on the ground. Lucy springs up, trying to dart away, but a hand clasps around her ankle. She trips, falls down flat on her face. The cane flies into the undergrowth, too far to reach.

She rolls onto her back as Diana crawls over her. She kneels over Lucy, with one arm raised, holding the shears, staring into her eyes. Lucy grabs Diana's wrists, pushing up as hard as she can. Diana is not a strong woman, but the madness within her, and gravity, of course, gives her the advantage.

They struggle. Lucy continues to push, but the tip of the blades is getting ever closer.

She writhes, struggles, thrusting the entire time. Diana cackles like a witch.

'You thought you would beat me, didn't you?' she says, pressing down with all her might.

'But I will *always* beat you, you stupid little girl! Mylo is mine, you hear? He's mine!'

The tip is touching Lucy's chest. She wriggles, but it breaks her skin. She winces as pain shoots through her.

'Please, Diana, it's me... I'm not Rose... I'm Lucy. Remember? Lucy, from Willow Cottage?'

Diana relaxes for a second. Her eyes cloud over, something flashes on her face... for a moment she seems to calm, but it is fleeting.

'You're trying to trick me. You were always tricking me! But I won't fall for it...'

She pushes again, and Lucy screams.

There is a dull thud.

Diana's eyes seem to glaze, and she falls down on top of Lucy, easing her grip on the scissors which tumble into the mud beside them. Lucy peers over Diana's shoulder. Cassie stands glaring down at them, a huge rock held in both hands.

'Cassie! I told you to stay in the house!'

'Yeah, but aren't you glad I didn't?'

She kneels, flipping Diana's body off of Lucy, holding out her hand. Lucy grips her friend's palm, as she pulls her up from the ground. They both stand together in silence, staring down at Diana.

'You shouldn't have come back...' Lucy whispers, shaking her head slowly, wiping mud, and blood from her face. Cassie drapes an arm around her shoulder.

'I'm not losing another friend today.'

'She really thought I was Rose. But when I pleaded with her, there was a flicker. She's not gone completely.'

Lucy kneels down, placing her fingers on Diana's throat.

Cassie watches on.

'Is she...'

'No. There's a pulse.'

'Okay. The police and ambulance are on their way.'

They turn, heading back towards the cottage.

87

The red-and-blue lights of the ambulance flash through the window. They drove it right down the side of the cottage into the garden. It's parked beside the old willow tree, rear doors wide open.

Lucy sits in the kitchen, as a paramedic tends to the gash on her head.

'It's not too serious. I've disinfected it. It won't need stitches. Try to keep the bandage on for a few days and avoid getting it wet if you can.'

Lucy nods. The paramedic turns, heading to join her colleague with Diana in the back of the ambulance. She is strapped to a wheelchair. They've administered a strong sedative, so at least she is calm now. Lucy stands, crossing to the window. Cassie joins her by her side.

'And you say she's been behaving erratically for a while now?' the policeman asks, holding his notepad.

Lucy nods.

'Yes. A month or so. She's been drinking a lot of alcohol, and she's on loads of different medication. She's been having delusions about her house being haunted. Calling me Rose. She attacked Cassie this morning... but I had no idea it would get this serious.'

He scribbles this down on his pad.

'Right. We'll take her to the hospital. Someone will be in touch over the next few days to take a formal statement, if that's okay?'

'Of course.'

'And you're sure you don't need us to find a bed for the husband?'

'No, that's fine. I can look after him until Diana is better. That's what I'm here for.'

He purses his lips, nodding. They walk outside, towards the ambulance.

'She's poisoning me! She wants to kill me.' They hear Diana mumbling nonsense from inside.

'Nobody is going to hurt you, Diana. We're here to help you,' one of the ambulance crew says soothingly, closing the doors. The siren starts as the vehicle pulls away. The police officers climb into their patrol car, following behind it.

Richard is in bed. Lucy saw to him while they waited for help to arrive. She pops her head in the door. His eyes are still open, but she doesn't have the energy to deal with him right now. Cassie joins her inside the house.

'Are you okay?' she says.

Lucy lets out a long sigh.

'I think so.'

Cassie nods.

'What a day, huh?'

'You get home, Cass. It'll do you good to be in your own bed.'

Cassie frowns.

'No way... I'm not leaving you alone tonight.'

'It's fine. Diana is gone. And Richard... he's harmless.'

'Don't you want some company?'

'Honestly... no. I think I'd rather be alone.'

Cassie bites her bottom lip, nodding.

'I'm pretty sure the alcohol is completely out of my system now, anyway. But I really don't feel great leaving you by yourself.'

Lucy places her hand on her friend's shoulder.

'I'll be fine. Go on.'

They walk out the front to Cassie's car. She climbs behind the wheel, waving before she heads off. Lucy stands watching as the car disappears into the woods.

The woods where she very nearly lost her life today. They both did.

She wraps her arms around herself, hugging her body for extra warmth. She wants to shower, but it's too much faff to keep her head wound dry. She walks inside, using Diana's bathroom. Stripping off her filthy clothes, she tosses them into a pile on the floor.

Taking a flannel from the linen cupboard, she runs the tap, waiting for it to get warm, and wipes it over her skin, cleaning away dried blood and crusty mud. The heat feels good on her body. She rolls her shoulders as she glides the cloth over her armpits. Red-brown water trickles down her legs onto the floor.

Once she is clean, she dries herself with a fresh, fluffy white towel, and grabs Diana's gown from the hook on the back of the door, sliding it on.

She saunters down the hallway, entering Richard's room. Crouching beside the bed, she strokes his hair with one hand.

'It's just you and me now, buddy,' she whispers, smiling as his eyes wobble from side to side as usual.

'I know you hear me. And I'm fairly sure you understand.'

She straightens, staring down at his face. The smile fades from her lips.

'Try to sleep tonight, Richard. Tomorrow we'll have a proper talk. Would you like that? I'm sure you're dying to hear what I have to say.'

She crosses to the door, turning for one final look. His eyes remain wide open.

A single tear meanders down the side of his cheek.

She smiles, leaving him alone in darkness.

88

Dr Miller sits behind his desk, tapping away at the keyboard. Now and then he stops, peering over the monitor at her. She looks away, feeling ashamed.

It's the first day in as long as she can remember that her head is clear. She feels like herself. The events that led to her incarceration are a blur to her. She gets the odd flash, cringing as she does, but on the whole, she draws a blank.

'And how are you feeling now, Diana?'

She fixes him with a stare.

'I feel fine. I'd like to go home to Richard.'

'I'm informed that your husband it being well cared for. Your live-in carer is with him at your cottage. No need to worry. The main thing is to get you well again.'

'I *am* well. I'm totally fine.'

'Okay...' He glances at the screen over the rim of his thin, wire-framed glasses, frowning.

'Your substance abuse is something of a concern, Diana.'

She actually laughs, a high-pitched, hyena-like bark.

'I have a prescription for those meds. It's all above board. I suffer with a great deal of pain. I need them to get by. You know that. And the drink... so I like a drink. But who *doesn't*.'

'Diana, there was extraordinarily little by way of prescribed medication in your blood work. Some over the counter stuff, yes, but I'm talking about the recreational drugs.'

She stands up, indignant.

'I do not take recreational drugs...' She pauses. 'A little dope now and then perhaps, but not much.'

'And the ketamine? The salvia? There were also some troubling herbal substances in your blood. An extremely high level of St John's Wort, for example. Need I go on? You're lucky you didn't poison yourself.'

She sits back down in her chair, mouth hangs open, but she doesn't respond.

'Together with the amount of alcohol you've been consuming, along with the fact you've cut the heavy pain meds, sleeping pills and antidepressants etcetera out without doing it gradually... it's no wonder you experienced a psychosis like you did. I'm amazed it didn't happen sooner.'

'You must believe me... I have *never* taken any of those things you say are showing in my blood, and as for the pain meds and sleeping pills... I've been taking them regularly... probably more than I should.'

'The only medication showing in your blood is paracetamol and some aspirin.'

She frowns.

'Diana, I think you're still a little confused. That's understandable. You were in an awfully bad way when they brought you in. We've flushed you out and had you on a drip to administer some fluids into you, but it will take some time to get you right.'

'But I'm telling you, I *am* right. I feel fine. Listen to me... my speech is clear, I can articulate, my thoughts are coherent. Surely you can see that?'

The doctor leans back in his chair, lacing his hands together behind his head.

'You seem much better, yes. But... I'm afraid unless you can admit that you have a substance abuse problem... I won't be able to let you go home. We're looking at a spell in a rehab centre in Glasgow for you. It will take a while to get you back on the straight and narrow.'

'Won't *let* me go home? I don't need your permission!'

'I'm afraid you do, actually. You've been sectioned, and you're under my care now. You won't be able to go home until I'm satisfied that you are no longer a danger to yourself, or others. You *attacked* two girls. With a bladed instrument. You don't need me to tell you how badly wrong that could have gone for everyone concerned.'

Diana frowns, cocking her head.

'It must be the girl,' she suddenly says out loud, interrupting whatever the doctor is saying. He pauses, staring at her.

'What must?'

'Drugging me, of course! I assume she's been mixing it into my food and drinks. It's the only explanation.'

The doctor looks sympathetically at Diana, sighing.

'Can't you see... she must have been doing this since she arrived. Trying to make it look like I'm crazy.'

'And why would she be doing that?'

Diana pauses. She hasn't thought this through.

She chews at the corner of her mouth.

'I don't know. Maybe she wants to steal my house from me.'

She scratches at the inside of her elbow, glancing down at the red dots there. What she had assumed were bites. She gasps.

'She's been injecting me. That's how she was doing it. While I was asleep. There were a few nights I woke and felt there was someone in my room. I wasn't in my right mind then, and I thought it was Rose... but now I'm thinking clearly, I see... it was Lucy. Look!'

She jabs at the red marks with a bony index finger.

'What am I looking at exactly?'

She stands, approaching his desk, extending her arm out, thrusting her elbow towards his face.

'Injection sites. That's what they are. They were always itchy first thing in the morning. She was sneaking into my room at night and drugging me! See?'

The doctor removes his glasses. Closing his eyes, he squeezes the bridge of his nose between his thumb and forefinger. He sighs and meets Diana's eyes.

'Diana, please take a seat.'

She goes to speak, but thinks better of it, returning to her chair. Her mind is racing. She has not been sure of anything for a long time, but she is sure that Lucy is responsible. She doesn't know why, but she knows it's her. And right now, that woman, who drugged her, and made her think she was losing her mind, is alone in her house with Richard.

A wave of panic washes over her. Sweat beads on her brow. She will have to play this one cleverly.

'Okay,' she says, letting out a long breath. 'I admit it. You've got me. I guess there's no point denying it anymore. You've got it there right in front of you. I've... allowed myself to become somewhat of an... addict, I suppose.'

The doctor nods, smiling patronisingly.

'Good. There you go. That wasn't so hard, was it?'

She'll have to play the game if she wants to get home.

She doesn't know why Lucy has been doing this, but she intends to find out.

89

Lynda Checkley twitches her net curtain, watching as Mylo pulls his pickup truck to a stop outside her cottage. Turning off the engine, he sits for a while staring out over the loch.

She opens the front door, and waddles down the garden path towards him, waving. Her jowls wobble as she trots along.

'Good morning, Mylo, my dear!' she calls, her usual smile beaming from her face.

Today, she wears a turquoise kaftan, with a butterfly print. A thick, chunky woollen shawl covers her shoulders. Her hair, as always, is wild and unkempt, but has a sunshine-yellow scarf tied through it, with a bow on top of her head. Cheeks rosy, as always.

'Hello, Mrs Checkley!'

'Oh please, call me Lynda. *Mrs Checkley* makes me sound like an old lady!'

She winks playfully. She glances as a rust-coloured leaf tumbles from a tree, drifting down to join others on the lawn.

'Autumn is on the way,' she says wistfully. 'I'm sure it comes earlier every year.'

Mylo simply nods as he begins to unload the shopping. She joins him by his side, helping with a few of the lighter bags. Once inside, he places the groceries on the worktop of her kitchen, which overlooks the garden.

'Will you stay for a coffee?' she pleads.

He nods.

'Terrible business with the artist... over at Willow Cottage last week,' she says, raising an eyebrow.

He nods again but says nothing. She's testing the water.

She pours two cups, handing one to Mylo, and they cross through to the living room. He sits on a comfy couch, looking out through a large bay window to the front of the house. She perches on a rocking chair in the corner next to him.

'Oh damn it!' she curses. 'I forgot the biscuits.'

'It's fine, honestly. I don't need any.'

'Nonsense,' she says, swatting her hand dismissively in his general direction as she disappears through into the kitchen. She returns a moment later with a plate full of pastel-coloured Party Rings, offering them to Mylo before she sits. He takes one, placing it on the arm of the settee beside him.

'Where were we?' she says, as if she has forgotten what they were discussing. But she knows full well.

'Oh yes! The *artist*.' She doesn't even attempt to hide the disdain from her voice.

'I hear she went quite mad!'

'Apparently so.'

'I'm not surprised. Keeping herself all cooped up in that place... never mixing with folk. It's not healthy. I know I live alone, but I try to get into town as much as I can. I meet friends for lunch. People visit me.' She reaches for a biscuit, hovering her hand over the plate, trying to decide which colour to take. As if it makes any difference.

'I'm surprised the girl is still there. All alone in that house.

After what happened. I'd have been out of there in a shot if it were me.'

'She's a good person. She's continuing to look after Mr Davenport. I imagine he would have had to go into a care home if she hadn't stayed.'

'Not her responsibility.'

Mylo shrugs.

'She seemed like a lovely girl though. You're right there.'

He cocks his head.

'Oh, you've met Lucy?'

'Yes. She came by on her bicycle the week she arrived. Not seen her since, mind.'

'She never mentioned it.'

'Don't suppose having lemonade and gossiping with an old lady was high on her list of exciting things to chat about.'

Lynda leans in, taking another biscuit, crunching it noisily before she continues. She wipes crumbs from the corner of her mouth and slurps her coffee.

'I maybe said too much that day. Probably scared the girl silly with all my stories.'

Mylo shifts in his seat.

'I hope you don't mind that I mentioned about... you know... Rose and that. And what happened. I thought she should be aware. Didn't seem to put her off though.'

Mylo pauses with his cup to his mouth, narrowing his eyes. He places the cup down on the coffee table.

'Mrs Checkley, are you saying you told her about Rose?'

Her cheeks flush.

'Well... yes. I'm sorry, Mylo. Once I get started, I find it hard to stop. You know what I'm like! And she seemed ever so interested.'

'How much did you tell her exactly?'

She pauses, looking ashamed.

'Everything.'

He stands. What he's hearing doesn't make any sense to him. Lucy claimed to know nothing about Rose before she met his friends at the marina. Cassie told him that she had seemed shocked, and unaware when she filled her in on what had happened.

'I need to go,' Mylo says abruptly.

Lynda Checkley hops up from her rocking chair as he hurries to the front door.

'I'm sorry, Mylo! Have I upset you? Please don't leave!'

'It's okay, Mrs Checkley. It's not you. I've just remembered there's something I have to do.'

He rushes towards his truck, climbing behind the wheel. He starts the engine, speeding away down the road without so much as a glance back. Lynda Checkley frowns, standing in the doorway.

'People around here are very odd,' she says to nobody in particular, as she closes the door.

90

Richard slumps forward, naked in his wheelchair. A string of saliva drips from his chin, landing on the flabby flesh below it. There's a little blood mixed in with it, but not much. She doesn't bother to straighten him up.

'Are you missing Diana yet?' Lucy asks. 'I am. She's bat-shit crazy, but it was quite entertaining at times.'

She crosses the lounge. Stopping by the fire, she gazes out through the window.

'The nights are drawing in. Looks cold out there.'

She turns, jostling the poker as it rests with its end in the embers. The tip is glowing orange. She smiles.

The stench from the other side of the room is horrendous. She hasn't washed him for days or changed his stoma. She allows him to wallow in his own stinking filth.

Blood has crusted over some cuts on his body. The burns she inflicted look red and festering. She hopes they hurt as much as they look like they do.

'Are you enjoying this time we're having together, Richard?'

She stares into his eyes, sure that he's taking it all in.

Suffering.

She fingers the handle of the poker playfully, before swiping it up. She strides towards him and without warning presses the poker against his belly.

It sizzles, and a burning smell fills the air, briefly masking the stench of piss and shit.

He wobbles, eyes flicker; she pulls it away. Doesn't want to push too far.

Not yet.

She hears a sound from the kitchen, and grins.

'Oh, good, kettle has boiled,' she says, smiling at him.

She rushes behind his chair, pushing him through the door into the next room. Glancing at the red welt where the poker had rested, she sucks in air though her teeth.

'That's got to hurt,' she taunts.

Positioning him against one wall, she pours herself a coffee. Placing a teaspoon into it, she stirs for a few moments. She sips, leaving the metal spoon in the mug, staring at him the entire time.

'I really wish this were a two-way thing, Richard. I wish we could have a conversation.' She shrugs. 'But I suppose I'll have to make do.'

She watches the man in front of her, searching for any sign of comprehension. His eyes are fixed on her, staring, anguished.

They sit like that for a few minutes. Lucy knows that the build-up will be terrifying for him. Wondering what is coming next.

She lifts the spoon out, crouching in front of the chair, and presses the metal into his cheek, holding it there for a few seconds.

A tear trickles down his face, and Lucy smiles.

Dropping the spoon back into the mug, she gives it another stir, then pushes it onto the soft fleshy part of his throat. She notices the little finger of his left hand spasm.

'I hope you feel this. You can, can't you?'

She tosses the cutlery into the sink and flicks the kettle on again. It doesn't take long.

Grabbing the mug from the counter, she fills it with boiling water, kneeling at Richard's side. She holds it on the arm rest of his wheelchair, lifting his right hand. His wrist is floppy. Flabby hands droop, almost lifelessly. She lowers it towards the brim of the cup. When the tips of his fingers are dangling just shy of the surface of the water, she leans her face directly in front of his.

'I wish you could scream for me, Richard,' she whispers.

She lowers his arm further. Three of his fingers fall into the liquid.

His eyes wobble. Legs tremble. His mouth falls open, but no sound comes out. Saliva bubbles at the corners. She moves the cup away.

His hand is red, angry-looking.

Scalded.

'That looks sore!' she says gleefully.

Standing, she grabs a handful of his hair, pulling his head back as far as it will go, staring down into his eyes. He seems to look straight through her, almost defiantly.

For a moment she doubts herself; wonders if Diana is right, and he is unaware of anything. But she sees the tears streaming down his face, and it reassures her. His mouth gapes, tongue lolling sickeningly inside. She raises the mug, and in a swift movement pours the contents into his lap, watching as he begins to convulse once more.

She stands, moving behind him, grasping the handles of his wheelchair. She leans down so her lips are next to his ear.

'Let's go for a walk, shall we? The loch is beautiful in this light. Wouldn't you like a closer look?'

She smiles, pushing the chair to the door, bumping it down into the garden, heading for the jetty.

91

He drives quickly, cursing the length of the journey. By road it's at least an hour to Willow Cottage, and that's assuming he doesn't get held up by sheep along the way.

The entire time, his mind races.

Why would Lucy claim to not know anything about Rose, when she knew right from the start?

It didn't make any sense. Something feels wrong.

He doesn't know what... can't comprehend. His brain can't make sense of it.

But he has a feeling.

His gut tells him there is something going on. He traverses the winding single-track roads, taking the bends carefully.

Rounding a corner, he sees a herd of cattle being ushered across the road between two fields. There are hundreds of them. The farmer raises his hand apologetically, as Mylo switches off the ignition. He'll be here some time.

As he sits waiting, he runs through every conversation he ever had with Lucy.

She claims to only have learned of Rose when Cassie had told her the story at the marina. But this simply wasn't correct. If what Lynda Checkley had told him was true, it means Lucy has been aware of the situation from not long after she arrived.

Why lie about it?

He can't piece it together, but it troubles him.

If she lied about that, he wonders, *what else was she lying about?*

92

LUCY

S he stares out over the water, watching the tiny ripples on the surface of the loch. The bright colours of summer are long gone. But the place still feels wonderful.

It's a shame she can't stay.

She could have seen herself settling here. Under different circumstances, maybe with Mylo. He's a good man. So damaged, but then who is she to judge? He really deserves better. If she has any guilt over her behaviour, it is for Mylo. But in the grand scheme of things, he is... collateral damage. She didn't want to hurt him, and hopefully he'll forgive her someday. But she doubts it. He'll never understand. Because he'll never be aware of *why* she had to do this.

Diana doesn't even know. If the woman had been a little nicer, she might feel some remorse over her as well. But she wasn't. So Lucy has no qualms about the part she had to play in the plan. She shakes her head.

'I really hope you're aware, *Richard*,' she says bitterly. 'All this would be... such a waste if you weren't.'

She stifles a laugh, suddenly struck by the ridiculousness of it all.

'Imagine... if I'd done *all* of this, and you were completely oblivious to it. That would be... disappointing.'

Turning to one side, she stares at his profile. A tear trickles down his right cheek. He's crying a lot at the moment. She smiles.

'But you're not. Are you, Dicky?' She stands.

'You know.'

She saunters away from his chair, down to the end of the jetty, stepping onto the grass. Crossing to the lean-to at the side of the cottage, where the generator is housed. She pulls the door, stepping inside. She wanders to the workbench at the back, dreamily, as if she has all the time in the world. She supposes she does really. Nobody is coming.

She trails her fingers across dusty tools. They play at the blade of a chisel. She chews the corner of her mouth, but shakes her head, moving her hand along. She traces circles, and her hand comes to rest on some rusty pliers. She shrugs, sliding them into her jeans pocket. She walks to the end of the bench, surveying the items resting there. Her eyes linger on an old bradawl. She reaches down, pressing her index finger against the tip. It's still sharp. Smiling, she picks it up, returning to the garden.

As she descends the pier, she stares at Richard, slumped in his chair. For a moment, she panics, wonders if she's pushed too far. But as his chest heaves, she relaxes.

She stands by his side, looking out over the water. Turning to him, she thinks how comical this seems. A disabled man in a wheelchair, naked, and covered in wounds, at the end of a jetty with his nursemaid. She shakes her head.

Crouching, she traces the tip of the bradawl across his throat, pressing harder in places, pricking his skin. Tiny spots of blood appear seconds later. She draws it down towards his chest, applying more pressure, leaving deep scratches on his flesh. She circles one nipple, pressing the tip against it. Chewing her lip, she pulls it away, moving it across to the other side, repeating the process.

Playing with him.

Taunting.

'How does it feel, Richard? Does this get you off at all? I bet it does.'

She runs the points down towards his belly button, teasing, pushing, probing. Breaking the skin from time to time. Drawing it across his crotch, she rests her hand on his thigh, the bradawl dangling between her fingers.

'I'm not going to lie, Richard. This is going to hurt. And I'm *really* going to enjoy it.'

93

Mylo pulls his mobile phone from his pocket. He's not sure why he bothers, there will be no reception. Never is round here.

What would he even say to her anyway?

Sighing impatiently, he glares at the farmer, who now leans nonchalantly on a gatepost while his cows wander aimlessly on the road ahead.

Winding down the window, he leans out.

'Mate, I'm not being funny, but how long is this going to take?'

The farmer chuckles.

'You think you can do it quicker, lad, then go ahead.'

Mylo shakes his head, slamming his hands on the steering wheel.

94

LUCY

The pliers have left angry-looking, ridged bruises across his flesh, tearing the skin away in places.

Assessing the damage she has inflicted over the past seven days, she almost feels sorry for him.

Almost.

Two gannets swoop down to the water, circling for fish. A gentle breeze blows wisps of her hair in front of her face. She steps behind the chair, placing her hands gently on Richard's shoulders.

Marvelling at the beauty of her surroundings, a pang of sorrow hits her. She takes it all in, knowing that after today she'll have to leave. She'll never be able to return.

She feels she is ready.

It's time.

She remembers reading once that drowning is *supposed* to be a peaceful way to die. She thinks it's nonsense. She can imagine few things more frightening. And of course, it will be quite different for someone who is paralysed, she's sure. Watching helplessly as they sink into the icy depths. Unable to move as they come to rest at the bottom.

She hopes it isn't pleasant. She hopes it's horrific.

Moving her palms onto the handles of the chair, she leans close to his ear.

'Goodbye, Richard,' she whispers, and, kicking the brake off the wheel, she pushes the chair from the edge of the pier.

95

The cattle have finally cleared. Mylo slams his foot on the accelerator, sticking two fingers up at the farmer as he speeds away. He feels immediately guilty. The man is simply doing his job. It's times like this that Mylo misses the bright lights of London.

Glancing at his watch, he curses under his breath. It will be getting dark soon.

As he drives, he thinks of Lucy. He sees her watching him. He often wondered what she was thinking about as she stared at him, not saying a word.

Now he's desperate to know what secrets she holds, but for entirely different reasons.

Rose's face flashes into his mind and he sighs sadly.

Willow Cottage must be cursed, he thinks. It brings nothing but trouble.

He remembers the first day he delivered shopping to Diana. He didn't recognise her immediately... he didn't know about her accident.

He curses that day now, and as he drives towards the cottage for what will hopefully be the last time, a sickening sinking feeling washes over him.

96

S he was unable to move away from the edge of the jetty for a while. The chair had hit the surface with a satisfying splash, and a rush of bubbles had risen to the top as it sank below.

She stands staring now, as the bubbles turn to ripples, half expecting him to bob back up to the surface.

She didn't know how she expected to feel, but it wasn't this. She thought maybe there would be euphoria, maybe satisfaction. But in reality, she feels nothing.

She turns, heading back towards the house. She knows she must act quickly now.

She rushes to the outbuilding, grabbing a canister of lighter fluid, and a box of matches. Heading to the wood store, she picks up a bag of logs, carrying them to the centre of the garden. She empties the bag into a heap, spraying the lighter fluid on top. Striking a match, she tosses it onto the pile, and the pyre goes up with a whoosh. Heat flashes over her face, and she turns, sprinting into the cottage. She bounds up the stairs, falling to her knees in her bedroom. She pushes a floorboard with her fingers, and it tips, lifting at the opposite end. She pulls at it, revealing a space below. She removes other loose boards around the hole, making a larger opening. Reaching her hand in, she presses her body close to the floor, feeling about. She grabs a small rucksack, pulling it out.

Hurrying back down to the garden, she unzips the bag and begins to remove its contents.

A half-smoked pack of cigarettes, with a blue plastic lighter tucked inside.

A stained nightie rolled up around a matted blonde wig.

She'd been impressed with how quickly her internet purchases had arrived, allowing her to execute her plan much sooner than she had expected.

Other items she had brought with her in her luggage, but she has no use for any longer. Glass vials filled with various coloured and clear liquids, and a selection of syringes.

She picks one of the vials up, reading the label.

Ketamine hydrochloride injection USP. She smiles, tossing the items one by one into the flames.

She pulls other glass vials from the bag, holding them to the light. A bright green-liquid half fills one of the bottles. Unscrewing the silver cap, she sniffs. A pungent aroma assaults her nostrils as the salvia tincture wafts up her nose. Grimacing, she thinks it's no wonder Diana thought her cooking was terrible. She pulls lids from small Tupperware containers containing leaves and berries, and dried flowers, emptying them onto the fire, tossing the boxes aside onto the lawn.

Her fingers come to rest on a small notebook. Tiny pink roses decorate the pale-blue cover.

Smiling, she strokes her index finger across two words, handwritten in a neat cursive on the front. When she'd stumbled across it on her first day while unpacking, she couldn't believe her luck. She'd trodden on the loose floorboard purely by chance. It tipped beneath the weight of her foot. When she'd investigated further she'd found the book stashed away in the space below. This had also served as a great hiding place for her own things she didn't want Diana to discover.

Opening it, she begins to flick through the pages, eyes skimming over words. Phrases jump out at her, the same way they had when she first found it under the floorboards. The smile fades from her face.

I told Mylo today that it's like I'm living inside a rainbow. He seemed to like that.

She skims some more.

His view is wondrous... he's got his own personal work of art, that's constantly changing with the light. I need to tell Mylo how lucky he is with that view. Perhaps one day it will be mine too.

She closes Rose's diary, dropping it, and watches as the flames swallow it. The corners curl, as the paper turns black. She thinks of Mylo, and a pang of regret hits her. Involving him was never part of the plan. She had hoped to execute the entire thing without him getting hurt. She was racked with guilt from having to drug him the night she went to his place for dinner. She had stolen his dinghy to slip away unnoticed while he slept, to terrorise Diana in the forest of ferns. When she returned she simply had to lay her head on his shoulder and wait for him to wake up, feigning sleepiness so he would think they had both dozed off. It had been necessary for her plan, but it didn't mean she had liked doing it.

Drugging Diana, swapping her various meds with placebos, aspirin, paracetamol... it was not an easy thing to do, but Lucy was driven by her end goal. She needed Diana out of the way. And her admission that her mother had suffered with schizophrenia had been a nugget of information that she couldn't afford to ignore. Diana's dependency on the drugs she was taking meant that withdrawing these without weening her off them first, pushed her towards a psychosis. The addition of ketamine, administered in varying doses, and other herbal remedies, increased her symptoms, speeding up the entire process.

If Lucy hadn't known better, she herself would have even believed Diana was going insane. She'd had to stop for a bit, after the episode with the bugs... but it had only set her back a few days really. Rushing to her room, she throws a few things into a bag. Just the essentials. Clothes can be replaced. There's very little she actually needs to take. She hurries down to the phone in the lounge, taking the card the taxi driver gave her when she arrived out from her purse. That day seems so long ago now.

Dialling, she turns it over between her thumb and fingers, waiting for someone to pick up. After a few rings, a woman with a gravelly voice answers.

'Aye?' she growls, emitting a series of guttural coughs and wheezes, sounding like she's lived on a diet of cigarettes and whisky for most of her life. Lucy orders a cab, asking her to send it as soon as she can. Now the deed is done, she needs to be gone. She gets to work cleaning; she must erase all the evidence.

When she is satisfied, she returns to the garden to wait, warming herself next to the fire. Standing on the grass, staring at the cottage, she recalls the first time she saw it. So pretty. So peaceful. Starlings twitter as they dart around her head. A blackbird forages for worms a few metres away. All is calm.

It is over, she thinks.

97

The light is almost gone when Mylo finally arrives at Willow Cottage. The front door is locked and there are no lights on inside. Crossing to the living-room window, to the right of the door, he presses his hands against the glass; he peers inside. The lounge is empty.

He heads around the back, frowning as he sees the embers from a fire glowing in the middle of the lawn.

He makes his way to the kitchen door, opens it, and steps inside. Sniffing, he screws up his face as the smell of bleach assaults his nostrils. Covering his mouth and nose with his hand, he makes his way across the kitchen.

'Hello?' he shouts.

There is no reply. The house is silent.

He steps into the hallway, poking his head into Richard's room. It's empty.

'Lucy?' he shouts, panic beginning to creep into his voice.

He edges along the hallway, trying not to look at the dark stain.

Must. Not. Look, he thinks.

But he knows he will.

He places a foot onto the bottom step. Gripping the bannister, he scoots up the stairs; knows the layout like the back of his hand. He's been into this room many times.

Pushing inside, he leaves the door open so he can hear any noise from downstairs.

As he scans the space, he stops at the dressing table. He takes a few steps forward, picking up the item that caught his attention. Sniffing it, he closes his eyes.

He'd know the scent anywhere. It's ingrained in his senses. Perfume. Rose's perfume, to be exact.

He places it down, frowning. Coincidence?

Perhaps. But Lucy had told him in the woods that she didn't wear perfume.

Crossing to the wardrobe, opening the doors, he rifles through a rail filled with sweaters. Pairs of jeans folded on shelves. Nothing sinister. Nothing hidden. The room is sparse. Nowhere else to conceal things.

He runs a hand through his bushy hair, letting out a long breath. Suddenly he feels guilty and foolish. Until now, she hasn't given him any reason to distrust her. And on the word of one of the local gossips, he's searching her bedroom behind her back.

He returns downstairs, entering the living room. It's spotless, gleaming, like the rest of the house.

Darting from room to room, he checks the entire space, but the place is deserted.

Lucy is gone.

Five months later, London

She works her way along the bustling street, making her way back from the postbox, winding between people blocking the path. It's hectic, but it's wonderful. She exhales and her warm breath clouds in front of her face, rising up to the sky.

She wonders briefly if posting the letter to Mylo had been the right thing to do. But then she realises, of course it was. He and Cassie had a right to know what had happened to their friend.

She hadn't meant to kill Sadiya, of course.

The girl had recognised her from London. From another life... a life that Lucy would rather forget entirely. She couldn't recall meeting her, but she has met so many people over the years, mostly at drunken parties. She'd come to confront Lucy at the cottage that night, after they had met at the marina. They'd walked along the jetty in the thick fog, which in hindsight hadn't been the most sensible idea, but she couldn't risk Diana overhearing their conversation. Sadiya had demanded to know why she was lying to Mylo about her identity, insisted she tell him the truth. Lucy had tried to tell her she was mistaken, but she wouldn't back down. There had been a scuffle, and Sadiya slipped, fell from the edge. Lucy had tried to help her, but the mist was so thick, she couldn't see. Could only listen helplessly as the girl thrashed about. And after everything went quiet, she returned to the house feeling terrible, but it was done, and she was too driven to let anything get in the way of her plan. It was a tragic accident which Lucy would regret for the rest of her life.

Shaking her head, she stops for a moment, staring at all the people rushing around, doing their chores. Filing in and out of the busy shops. Spending money. Enjoying life.

It's marvellous to be alive, she thinks.

Continuing along the pavement, she takes a few last drags on her cigarette, before dropping it onto the frosty ground and treading on it, swivelling her foot to extinguish it. She blows out a plume of white smoke as she fumbles in the pocket of her duffle coat, searching for her key. Somebody collides with her from the side, almost knocking her off her feet.

'Sorry!' the woman says without turning, as she walks away down the street.

Lucy stares after her, but she has disappeared among the throng of shoppers. Rubbing a sore patch on her arm, she frowns. She finds the key, sliding it into the lock, and pushes the door open. Pulling off her pink bobble hat, she shakes her head, ruffling her bleached blonde hair, trying to get some life back into it. She was glad to be able to return to something closer to her own colour.

She removes her woollen gloves, jamming them into her coat pocket, and slides the duffle coat from her shoulders, hanging it on a hook at the foot of the stairs, before ascending the steps to the apartment proper. The flat is bijou but has everything she needs. An open-plan lounge with a kitchen in one corner. A single, good-sized bedroom to the right, with plenty of storage. She never has guests, doesn't need more beds. A door to the left leads to a small, but well-equipped bathroom. A bath, being her only prerequisite while searching for this property. It's one of the few pleasures she gets from life. A long, hot soak.

At the far end of the lounge, opposite the kitchen, large windows overlook the street below. This view, along with the faint but constant sound of horse racing coming through the floor from the bookies beneath her, means she rarely feels alone.

And who wants to feel alone?

She smiles to herself, picking up a small green scented candle from the coffee table. She holds it under her nose, inhaling the fresh, sweet aroma of jasmine and ylang-ylang. Closing her eyes, she smiles sadly, thinking how amazing it is; the power of certain smells, to take you back to an exact time, or place... or person. She lights it and places it on a coaster, before returning to the kitchen.

Pulling open the fridge door, she takes out a half-empty bottle of Pinot Grigio. She unscrews the top, grabbing a glass from the draining board, and fills it with the pale liquid. She sips, strolling to the windows. In the street below, people swarm like ants, narrowly avoiding collision everywhere she looks. Rubbing her arm again, she crosses the room, topping up her wine. Blinking a few times, she staggers, steadying herself on the edge of the worktop. She stares at the glass, thinking how strange it is that her vision is becoming double.

The drink slips from her hand, shattering with a loud smash on the bare boards below.

Frowning, she takes a few steps towards the settee, fearing she may pass out. But she makes the move too late.

She blacks out before her head collides with the floor.

390

99

S lowly opening her eyes, she wants to throw up. She sits on the sofa, slumped over. Feeling groggy, she glances about the room; vision blurred. She's aware of somebody moving around at her sideboard near the window.

A dark silhouette in her periphery. Rummaging.

Trying to sit up, she groans as her head pounds. Each movement makes her feel like an ice pick has been plunged into her brain.

'Ah, you're awake?' the voice rings into her ears.

She'd know it anywhere. She stares defiantly ahead.

'Interesting record collection you have there. I might have to take a few of those after I'm finished with you.'

The woman smiles; a wicked, knowing smile.

'I like the new hairdo. Blonde suits you. The brown made you look a little... frumpy.'

'Hello, Diana.'

She stands, holding a pistol up, pointing it towards the sofa. Her hair has now been styled into a neat pixie, dyed jet-black. It takes years off her.

'Hello, Lucy. I'd love to say it's nice to see you... but it's not.'

'The feeling is mutual.' The words slur from her mouth, making her sound drunk. Her head still spins. She attempts to stand, but her legs won't obey her; won't bear any weight. She falls in a crumpled heap on the sofa. Diana pouts.

'I'd take it easy if I were you... that was quite a heavy dose I injected you with.'

'Wh... what have you done to me?'

'It's not nice to be drugged against your will, *is* it?'

'How...' She can't get the words out.

Diana smirks.

'Busy street. Syringe. Collision. Simple.' She shrugs, clearly pleased with herself.

Lucy rubs her arm, remembering the clumsy cow bumping into her at the front door.

'Getting inside wasn't hard either. It really is true what they say about London... nobody gives a damn. I can literally pick a lock standing on a street in broad daylight, and not one person stops me, or even gives me a second glance. Not one!'

The women look at each other. Lucy shuffles forwards in her seat, starting to feel more human.

'Don't!' Diana shouts, raising her weapon.

'A gun? Impressive. I didn't think you had it in you.'

'It was my grandfather's service pistol. And before you consider trying anything, I assure you it is in *full* working order.'

Diana paces the room, picking up ornaments, stroking her fingers across surfaces, as if checking for dust. She's limping, but managing without her stick, which is propped against a wall by the door.

'How did you find me? I'm intrigued.'

She laughs.

'When you have enough money, *anything* is possible.'

Lucy nods, raising an eyebrow.

'You were very clever... I've got to hand it to you. The whole *ghost* thing. Very clever indeed. In hindsight, I've figured out how you did most of it... but I have a few questions. The message... on the bathroom mirror. How did you do that?'

'It was exhausting. Climbing in and out of windows, sneaking about. Tape recordings, remote controls. The message wasn't hard in comparison. I wrote it in Vaseline, then dabbed it off. I knew eventually the mirror would steam up, and you'd see it.'

Diana nods, clearly impressed with her ingenuity.

'One other thing I can't work out. The photograph of Rose on my dresser. How *on earth* did you make it topple?'

Lucy furrows her brow, tilting her head. She looks confused.

'Not that it matters... I was simply intrigued. But if you don't wish to tell me, I'll not lose any sleep over it.'

'What do you want, Diana?'

She turns to face Lucy, incredulous.

'Where is my husband?'

Lucy pauses, waiting for her brain to catch up. The effects of whatever she's been dosed with making her sluggish.

'He's at the bottom of the loch.'

Diana smirks.

'I did wonder. So you killed him?'

Lucy slowly nods again.

'Yes. Yes, I did. About that... I've been studying the news every day since I left Scotland. There's been no mention of what happened. I'm... curious as to why.'

Diana laughs.

'I didn't report it.'

Lucy cocks her head, questioningly.

'I wanted to deal with you myself. And if the police were looking for you, that would have made my job... problematic.'

'Mylo called round a lot looking for you. I told him you'd

handed in your resignation after the incident in the woods, hadn't left a forwarding address. Poor man looked crestfallen.'

Lucy winces at the mention of his name, as Diana perches her bottom on the edge of a wooden chair.

'It was never personal, Diana. I hope you know that,' Lucy says sadly, but sincerely.

Diana doesn't reply. Raises one eyebrow.

'I needed you out of the way, so I could deal with Richard. Your family history made my plan so much easier to execute. I also hoped that with everybody thinking you were crazy and addicted to drugs, any suspicion would be diverted from me... for a little while at least. But Diana... you have to believe me when I tell you... your husband was *not* a good man.'

Diana smiles.

'He was a rapist... and a murderer.'

She *actually* laughs.

Throws back her head and lets out a heartfelt, hysterical cackle.

'I swear to you. He kidnapped me... held me captive... did... unspeakable things to me. And to other girls too. Christopher Kernick was *not* The Butcher. Richard was.'

'Shut up!' Diana spits. 'You stupid, stupid girl.'

Lucy's mouth hangs open. Diana pulls a record from the shelf, flicking on the stereo, she places it onto the deck, lowering the needle. The speakers crackle to life, and the familiar vocal begins.

Lucy stares at the older woman as the melody fills the room.

The fifties ballad with the lovesick singer proclaiming that he and the object of his affection would always be together, and that she belongs to him.

She stiffens in her seat, thinks she might throw up. She hasn't heard the song in a very long time, but the music acts as a trigger. Suddenly, she is back there. Strapped to a gurney, naked, while he watches. Red camera light blinking. She trembles.

'Turn it off...'

'Don't you like it? Ritchie Valens was my favourite. This song, "We Belong Together"... Richard and I used to fuck while we listened to it. I'm surprised *you* have it though... if what I suspect about you is correct. You were one of his girls, weren't you? I wonder which one you were? It's impossible to know with those leather masks he used to put on you. I watch the videos on my old television from time to time. They still excite me. I wonder if I can find you among them.' She smiles wickedly.

Lucy can't bring herself to speak for a moment. Tears well in her eyes as she stares at Diana's smiling face.

'You *knew*?'

'Of course I did! Behind every dangerous man, is an even more dangerous woman. Whose benefit did you *think* the camera was for?'

100

LUCY

A chill runs through her. Until that very moment, she had believed she would be able to talk Diana round. Convince her that her husband had deserved to die, and that she would understand.

She couldn't have been more wrong.

'You were *in* on it? How? How could you let that happen to us... those poor girls? Me?'

'It was *my* idea!' Diana beams, as if she has just won the lottery.

'But I am intrigued to know how you got away. Richard was always so careful about these things. And he never told me one escaped.' She sneers, looking at Lucy as if she is a piece of dirt that has been trailed on a clean carpet.

'Oh, he didn't tell you?' Lucy forces a smile, although it's the last thing she feels like doing. Diana shrugs, waiting.

'I befriended him. He said I was... special. I knew when he hadn't killed me as quickly as the others, he must've had a soft spot for me.'

The smile falls from Diana's face.

'You're lying. Richard would never–'

'Oh, but he *did*, Diana. He cared about me. I think he may have even been in love with me. I died on that gurney. I could feel it coming, and I rejoiced that the suffering would finally be over. And then the bastard revived me. He told me he wasn't ready to let me go. And I can't tell you how I despised him for that. He wouldn't even let me have my peace in death. So I played him...'

Diana glares at Lucy, lips parted in an unspoken question.

'Yes... that's right, Diana. Your husband took the shackles off my wrists. He *trusted me*. He allowed me to walk free around that... place. Men are so easy to manipulate if you learn how. And when I had him exactly where I needed him, as soon as he allowed me to get off that gurney, I took my chance. I ran. And guess what? I'm certain he didn't even try to catch me. He *wanted* me to get away.'

Diana strides to the settee, striking Lucy across the cheek with the back of her hand.

'Shut up!'

Lucy tastes blood in her mouth, but she knows she's hit a nerve. She grins.

'You haven't heard the best part yet...'

'I said shut up! I don't want to hear any more from you!'

Lucy pauses, waiting. Diana hobbles up and down the living room. She stops at the window, staring out to the street below. Lucy edges forwards on the cushion, quietly, slowly. Diana spins, thrusting the gun towards her.

'Get back on that fucking sofa! Now!' Spittle flies from her mouth. 'Put your hands where I can see them! Behind your head!'

Lucy hesitates.

'NOW! Do it! Don't think I won't shoot you right in that pretty little face of yours... because I will! I will blow your fucking brains out! And I'll take great pleasure in doing it!'

Lucy laces her fingers together, resting them on her hair. The record finishes, and static crackles through the speakers, as the needle remains stuck, clicking in the run-out groove.

The women's eyes meet. Lucy can tell she has rattled Diana's cage. Until this point, she has seemed calm, calculated, as if she was executing a meticulous plan. Now she is agitated. Furious, in fact. She stares at Lucy, eyes wide, looking every bit like the madwoman she remembers.

Diana turns suddenly, kicking the record player. Lucy wouldn't have believed she had the strength or dexterity if she hadn't seen it for herself. A horrendous scratching sound emits from the speakers, as the blow sends the hi-fi hurtling, crashing to the ground. The stylus arm breaks off, rattling across the floorboards.

The room is quiet, apart from the hum of traffic from the busy street. Lucy's head, still cloudy from whatever Diana injected her with, pounds.

'I think you'll want to hear this,' Lucy says, gleefully.

'There is *nothing* you have to say that is of any interest to me.'

Lucy fixes her with a stare, a smile plays on her lips.

'I drove the van into your taxi. It was me. Obviously, I hadn't intended on either of you living... but that's why I came to Scotland. To finish the job. It took me a while to track you down, but I got there in the end.'

Diana pauses, raising her hand to the side of her face. She caresses the rough tendrils of her scar with her fingertips as she stares into space.

'Valentina recognised me... she'd been looking at some old newspaper cutting from that night, and saw me, lingering in the crowd. She called the house to warn you... thank heavens you were off your head at the time. I intercepted her voicemail message before you. That could have ruined everything. So... she had to go. I was so close. Couldn't have her spoiling things.'

A sadness fills Diana's face, changing quickly to fury.

'And there's something else. Even better...'

The woman glances at Lucy, but it's as if she's staring through her.

'Claire.'

Diana takes a step towards the sofa.

'What did you say?' she whispers, eyes bulging from their sockets so much that Lucy thinks they might pop.

'I told her about Richard. I slipped the photograph under her door.'

Diana screams, swiping her arm over the top of the sideboard. Lucy's ornaments, television, everything... go flying across the room, smashing into pieces on the floor. Diana howls like an injured animal, spinning towards Lucy.

'You! Do you know what you did? What you caused?' Diana lunges at Lucy, striking her with the butt of the gun. A sharp pain radiates through her head. She closes her eyes as a warm trickle weaves its way down her face, running into her ear, and dripping onto her shoulder.

'He killed her. Richard killed *our* daughter. She wasn't going to let it drop. She had a photo of him with a dead girl. She didn't realise it, of course... but it was only a matter of time until she recognised the face in that picture. She was on the front page of so many newspapers... we *had* to... we had no choice.'

'There's always a choice, Diana. You *chose* to kill those girls. To watch while your husband raped us. Tortured us. You both *chose* to murder your own daughter to protect yourselves. You picked that life. Nobody forced it onto you.'

Diana inhales deeply. She lets out a long, steady breath. Her body shakes, but as she breathes in and out, she regains control.

'I should have killed you as soon as you started flirting with Mylo,' she spits.

Lucy smirks.

'He used to flirt with me terribly, you know, the same way he did with you. Until that bitch Rose showed up... made her slutty eyes at him, and he wasn't interested in me anymore. I knew that she had to go. I hadn't planned on it being quite so... *final*, for her though. If her employment was terminated... then surely their relationship would have to end? But then she came home early that night... caught me in her room again.'

'Are you saying that Rose's death wasn't an accident?'

Diana smiles a triumphant smile.

101

Rose waves as Mylo's boat hums away into the distance. Giddy, she removes her shoes, skipping across the grass. She's drunk too much champagne. But she doesn't care. She can finally leave this shitty job. Cassie has sorted her with some temporary bar work at her father's marina, and after that, she'll find something more long term. The important thing is, she won't have to deal with Diana's craziness anymore.

She crosses to the back door, pushing it open. Stepping inside, she spies a half-empty bottle of red on the side. The house is quiet. Diana is usually in bed by now, so that's not strange. She'll be unconscious, doped up to her eyeballs, out for the count until at least ten the following morning.

She picks up the wine, swigging it straight from the bottle. It tastes expensive. *All* of Diana's wine is expensive. *Stuck up cow*, she thinks.

Smiling, she drains the rest, wiping drips from the corner of her mouth with the back of her hand.

'Oopsie!' she says, giggling, placing the empty bottle down on the bench.

A creak above her head raises her eyes to the ceiling.

She steps out into the hallway. Diana's door is wide open. Frowning, she peeks inside. Empty.

'Diana?' she calls, voice shaky.

She turns, heading up the stairs. When she's about halfway up, Diana comes limping out of her room. Swaying. Drunk, as usual.

'Rose,' she says, flustered. Her cheeks colour. Caught in the act.

'I didn't expect you back so early!'

Her hand drifts to her thick braid, and she strokes it gently, the way she always does when she's feeling guilty. Rose continues to the top of the stairs.

'Evidently,' she spits. 'In my room again, I see. Did you have a good read?'

Diana blinks a few times, tries to avoid Rose's eyes.

'I was... putting some of your laundry away for you.'

Rose laughs.

'That would be funny if it wasn't so ridiculous.'

Diana cocks her head.

'You're lazy, Diana. You don't do a thing. You barely even paint... you sit, and you drink. That's *all* you ever do. You're pathetic!'

Diana takes a few steps towards the stairs.

'Get out of my way. You're drunk. You'll regret this in the morning.'

Rose doesn't budge.

'No, Diana, I won't. Because I'm leaving.'

She raises an eyebrow.

'Yes, you heard me. Mylo and I are engaged!' She thrusts her hand in front of the older woman's face, wiggling the diamond ring back and forth. 'I'm moving in with him... and I don't need this crappy job anymore. So have a good read. Fill your boots. I don't care. Because it's the last time you ever will.'

Diana's mouth opens, but she closes it without speaking.

'And you know what? I'm taking him away from this place. We're going to move away. To Glasgow. Maybe even back to London. Anywhere... as far from you as I can get.'

Panic flashes into Diana's eyes.

'Oh... that hit a nerve, didn't it? Your precious Mylo won't be coming around anymore. Do you actually think he would look twice at an old hag like you?'

'Shut up!' Diana shouts, stepping closer.

'Shall I tell you what he thinks about you? He thinks you're disgusting! Pathetic. He says that scar on your face repulses him. We *laugh* about you, Diana, when we're alone together. We laugh *at* you–'

'Shut up!' Diana screams, 'Shut up, shut up, shut UP!'

She thrusts her arms, jabbing her palms into Rose's shoulders, giving her a heavy shove.

The girl topples, eyes wide, mouth open.

Diana shuffles forward, watching. She stretches her hand out, but it's too late. Rose is beyond her reach. She falls awkwardly, landing with a loud thud as her head connects with wood. She continues tumbling backwards down the full length of the staircase.

Diana swears she hears a crack as Rose's neck snaps.

The descent seems to take forever, but in reality it's over in a second. The blink of an eye.

The girl lies lifeless at the bottom of the stairs, the back of her skull wedged against a plug socket.

Diana's hand flies to her mouth.

'My God!' she whispers, as a dark pool forms around the body, spreading out across the floorboards.

'Rose?' But Diana knows she's dead. Her eyes are wide open. Neck at an odd angle.

She takes a few deep breaths, moving down towards the hall.

She fiddles with her plait, standing on the bottom step. Before the blood spreads too far, she steps over it, trying desperately to avoid any contact, and crosses to her bedroom. She flashes one last glance at Rose, before closing her door.

She grabs a bottle of her strongest sleeping pills from her bedside drawer, throwing three of them into her mouth, washing them down with a glass of dusty water. Resting her cane against the wall, she reclines back onto her pillow.

As the tablets suck her down into the depths of unconsciousness, she smiles.

102

S he sits staring at the woman, lips parted slightly, considering what to say. It's not that surprising. She'd always wondered, and the revelation that Diana was aware of Richard's activities, and even encouraged them, demonstrated that she is capable of anything.

'It pushed him closer to me in the months following her death. He came to the cottage more… I think he found comfort there, knowing it's where she had lived. He would sit in her room crying. It broke my heart to see him like that. I would comfort him as he lay on the sofa, face resting on my breast, while I stroked his hair. It was beautiful. She was gone, and he was mine once more.'

Lucy shakes her head.

'So… you tracked us down, and came to finish the job. Was this not enough?' Diana screams, waving her hand in front of her face, motioning to her scar. 'Was *Claire*, not enough?'

Lucy lets out a breath.

'I may not have died in that room… but part of me did. I can't explain to you… you won't care, anyway. But it destroyed something in me… that experience. I could never really give myself to anyone. Was ashamed of the scars that your husband left on my body. Embarrassed by intimacy... so although I escaped from that place... he may as well have killed me. Because I stopped living anyway. My entire existence became about tracking him down. Fortunately, I knew his hunting ground, and he was a creature of habit. I didn't have to hang around those bars long before I found him. At first, I was worried that he might recognise me... I disguised myself, of course, but still... it was a concern. But he was so arrogant, he didn't even notice me. Walked right past me. And his hubris allowed me to follow him quite easily... to find out where he lived.'

Diana shrugs.

'I'll never forget when I first saw you. So beautiful... it broke my heart. I had never imagined that he would be married, let alone have a family. I was surprised. I wanted to tell you... A few times I almost knocked on your door, when I knew you were there by yourself. But my desire to hurt him, outweighed my instinct to help a stranger. And to think... you were aware all along, anyway. I'd hoped that showing the photo to Claire would get you to leave him... but it didn't work. Now I understand why. I thought you were just stupid and devoted.'

Lucy shifts her weight on the sofa, sliding her hands underneath her thighs. Glancing out the window briefly, she sighs, returning her gaze to Diana.

'So I followed you both. A lot. And that night in London, when you were on your way to wherever you were going... all dressed up... I saw how smug and happy he looked... I had never planned to do it then... but something took over me. Knowing that I would never feel like that again myself. It drove me crazy seeing him smiling. It didn't seem fair. I don't even remember the crash. It's almost as if I wasn't there. I found myself standing in the crowd, staring at the mangled vehicles. Nobody witnessed me get out of the van. They were all too focused on you and Richard. I watched as those ambulances took you both away, and I felt *guilty*. That I had hurt you. Can you imagine? And then picture my horror when I read in the paper that you had both survived.'

Diana fixes her with a cold glare.

'Am I supposed to feel sorry for you?' she says indignantly.

Lucy fidgets in her seat.

The woman takes a few steps towards Lucy. Suddenly remembering the gun in her hand, she raises her arm, pointing it at her adversary.

'You ruined my life. Took *everything* from me–'

'And what about you? What did you take from me?' Lucy screams.

'You were just a cheap whore. Never supposed to leave that room!'

'I was a different person when I met Richard in that bar... or *Michael* as he told me his name was. I was broke, my family had disowned me... I'd resorted to things I'm not proud of to make ends meet. I never *wanted* to be that girl. I was desperate. But I didn't deserve what you and he did to me. Nobody does.'

Diana crouches in front of the settee, weapon levelled at Lucy's chest.

'You should have died there... like the others. I should've known he would screw it up. He was always so good at that. Thinking with what was in his pants instead of his brain. Typical man.'

Lucy slides her fingers down between the cushions beneath her.

'But don't you worry, Lucy... I intend to put that right. Finish what we started all those years ago. You should have killed me when you had the chance.'

Lucy wraps her hand around something hard, hidden under the seat.

'A situation like that changes a person, Diana.'

She smirks unsympathetically.

'Being abducted... held captive. Tortured. It teaches you to never let your guard down. Always be prepared. And I am.'

She swings her arm up, bringing with it the small knife which she keeps concealed in the sofa, plunging the blade into Diana's shoulder. The woman howls in agony, dropping the pistol. Lucy shoves her, and she topples backwards onto the floor. The gun clatters over the ground, disappearing beneath a sideboard.

Lucy springs up. She can't make it to the door, Diana is in her way, clambering to her feet... the window is her only option. She bounds across the room, throwing open one of the large double windows.

'Help me!' she screams.

Bemused faces glance up, unsure what is happening. Some people smile, assuming it's a joke. Others ignore her entirely.

'She's trying to kill me! Call the police! Please!'

The crowds below continue to mill around, drifting in and out of shops. Some are now looking up with worried expressions, but the majority behave as if this is totally normal.

Suddenly, Diana grabs Lucy's hair from behind, wrenching her backwards. She yelps as she is tugged away from the window. Screaming, she spins towards her attacker. The blade still protrudes from Diana's shoulder. Lucy reaches forward, twisting it, and the woman screeches. Blood soaks into her coat. Diana's hand flies up, slapping Lucy across the cheek. She pulls the knife out of her body, hurling it across the room.

Lucy grabs Diana's forearms, knowing that she has the advantage of strength. They struggle, Diana trying to pull her arms free from Lucy's grip, twisting, writhing... but Lucy is stronger. Diana pushes forward, making Lucy stumble back. She feels the edge of the low windowsill behind her thighs.

'Help me!' she screams again.

She hears murmurings from the crowd far below.

'Is she okay?'

'It's a joke!'

Diana's hands find their way to Lucy's throat. She wraps her fingers around it and begins to squeeze. Lucy tries to push back, but as she struggles to breathe, she feels herself begin to lean precariously out through the window.

'Your little friend isn't here to save you this time, is she?' Diana hisses, wincing as the pressure on her leg takes its toll. Lucy shifts, squirms. Her arms wobble now. She's gripping Diana's wrists, but she can't get free from her grip. She tries to turn her head to one side. She knows she has to act. It's now or never. Her strength is beginning to wane.

Allowing her legs to slide down, she ducks, falling to the floor, simultaneously thrusting her knees up as hard as she can muster. Diana, still moving forward with all her power, freefalls. With no counter force against her any longer, she topples through the window with a howl. Lucy hears a dull thud.

'Oh my God!' someone shouts.

'Call an ambulance!' another cries.

A woman screams.

Lucy sits panting, her back against the sill, trying to regain her breath. Her arms feel weak. Head spins. After what seems like an age, she hauls herself up on the edge of the window frame. Leaning out, she looks down to the pavement below. A crowd has gathered round the body, which lies broken on the pavement. A dark crimson puddle spreads out from it. A few of the onlookers glance up, shaking their heads. Others stand with mobile phones to their ears, gesticulating wildly.

Lucy sinks down, rolling onto her back.

Turning her head to the side, she notices something glinting in the corner of her eye.

With the last of her energy, she reaches her arm out, scooping it up from the floor. She closes her eyes, listening as the distant sound of sirens fills the apartment.

103

He waits nervously on a bench. The sun gently warming his back. His hands are clasped in his lap, fingers laced, fidgeting. He had considered bringing a bunch of flowers but didn't know if that was appropriate, so in the end he brought nothing.

He doesn't recognise her immediately, as she approaches through the park, but as she draws nearer, he sees her, and knows her face from the news. She smiles, giving him a little wave and perches herself on the edge of the seat beside him. They both stare ahead. She glances around from time to time, as if she's worried she may have been followed.

'I wasn't sure if you'd turn up,' he says quietly.

'Why?'

'You're on the run, aren't you? After... what you did to Richard. Although they should be thanking you, really.'

'Murder is murder,' she replies matter-of-factly.

'I suppose I should say thank you,' Kernick mutters eventually.

'No need. Honestly. I did this for myself. Your freedom was a serendipitous by-product.'

And it had been. Lucy hadn't intended to try to free Christopher from prison. It had never been on her agenda. She had been honest with Diana when she said that the experience in captivity with Richard had changed her. Not only did it drive her to leave various weapons concealed in locations around her home, for if the worst were ever to happen, it also made her extremely security conscious.

A top-spec home-monitoring system, with cameras covering all angles of her flat, and noise-activated sound recording equipment, meant that Diana's entire conversation had been digitally imprinted, and sent directly to Lucy's phone. Of course, turning this evidence over to the police had also put Lucy on their radar. That was a small price to pay. She'd done so much bad over the last year, she felt it was time to do some good. A penance, if you like.

It's not like she had anything to stick around for anyway.

She slides her hands into her pockets, fiddling with the object that is nestled there. She's been in two minds about whether to give it to him, and now as she sits beside him she still isn't sure.

'Thanks anyway. It doesn't change what happened... to either of us. But at least the truth is out. People know what they did.'

Lucy nods.

'So, Mr Kernick... any great plans?'

He turns to face her, letting out a long sigh. He shrugs.

'The world is a very different place than I remember. Not sure anyone will want to employ me either.'

Lucy raises an eyebrow.

'The compensation should help there. Can't see you would need to work anyway.'

'What else would I do?'

'Make up for lost time? Enjoy it.'

He nods, pursing his lips. She glances at her watch, looking about again. Her eyes linger on a smartly dressed gentleman leaning on a tree on the other side of the park. She stands, thrusting her hands in her pockets.

'I should go. I don't like being out in public places for too long.'

He nods again. She pulls her hand from her jacket, offering it towards him. He thinks she wants to shake, but realises she is holding something. He reaches out. She drops the object into his palm.

'Be seeing you around,' she says.

'Hopefully,' he replies, but she has already walked away. She doesn't hear. She dodges between groups of teenagers and mothers with prams.

Christopher stares down at his hand. A delicate silver crucifix, encrusted with impossibly green emeralds, sparkles in the sunlight. Smiling, he looks back up, wanting to call out to her.

But she is gone.

He slips the jewellery into his pocket. Standing, he turns, heading towards the park gates.

He doesn't know what he will do, or where he'll go.

But it doesn't really matter. He is free.

With a sad smile, he suspects this may be a luxury that Lucy will never be able to appreciate.

THE END

ACKNOWLEDGEMENTS

So here I am at book number three. I can hardly believe it. It's been a difficult year, but writing has kept me busy and focused for the most of it, so I have to thank the readers for giving me something to do!

Also to the usual suspects... you know who you are by now. And to Colin, your help and feedback helps me get things right. Thank you.

To each and every one of you who has bought a copy of my books, I will never stop saying thank you. Haters gonna hate, but it's the lovers that make everything worthwhile. We just need to learn to listen to them more.

I'd also like to thank Ian, my editor, and the rest of the team at Bloodhound, for continuing to believe in me, and giving me a platform to release my work. It really is a lifelong dream come true for me, and there are still times when I see my books, and almost have to pinch myself.

Last but by no means least, I have to give a special mention to a wonderful author, and now good friend, Keri Beevis, who helped me get this story to where it needed to be. Cheers, Beevis!

Until next time... see you soon!

A NOTE FROM THE PUBLISHER

Thank you for reading this book. If you enjoyed it please do consider leaving a review on Amazon to help others find it too.

We hate typos. All of our books have been rigorously edited and proofread, but sometimes mistakes do slip through. If you have spotted a typo, please do let us know and we can get it amended within hours.

info@bloodhoundbooks.com